THE

NUN OF GNADENZELL.

A Romance.

BY ROBERT HUISH, ESQ.

If walls could speak, and tell all they have seen,
How sad a record would the convent's cell
Present to wondering humanity.

The Broken Vow.

LONDON:

PUBLISHED BY EDWARD LLOYD, 12, SALISBURY-SQUARE,
FLEET-STREET.

—

1846.

THE NUN OF GNADENZELL.

A Romance.

BY ROBERT HUISH, ESQ.

See page 4.

CHAPTER I.

The sun rose gloriously behind the majestic Stauffenberg, and gilded the grey tower of the cathedral, and the tops of the houses of the town of Baden. The early chimes called the inhabitants to their matin prayers; and in the streets and the squares before the church all was life, and motion, and bustle, and tumult. The workmen who were employed in the erection of the new castle of the Margrave Christopher, were seen wending their way singly and in groups up the hill to resume their daily labour. The ladies and their servants, the antiquated devotees, and the hypocritical sinner, were seen tripping along with their rosaries and tapers, towards the church, in the hope of returning exonerated from a load of their sin by the absolving power of a presumptuous priest. The remaining part of the people had their eyes partly directed to the spot from which the magistrates were to appear, clad in their official habiliments, and partly towards the bathing-houses which surrounded the church; and the doors were thrown wide open to admit the ingress and egress of the guests.

It was the holy day on which the baths of Baden were to be opened for the present season, with all the customary formality, attended with the priestly blessing, and the solemn proclamation of all the rights, privileges, and immunities which had been granted to the ancient town of Baden, by the emperor and the holy Roman empire, as well as by his serene highness the Margrave of Baden, who, like many other potentates, was very willing to bestow his privileges, provided his own interest would be thereby promoted. On the previous day the noise in the inns had been incessant, arising from the continued arrival of the guests, and in the morning the wooden rattles of the servants attached to the baths awakened the fatigued travellers, who were still sleeping and snoring on their beds of down. They, however, assembled at an early hour in the court-yards of their respective inns; and as the clock struck seven, they all appeared, equipped in the most elegant and fashionable costumes, and ready to walk in procession to the church. And many there were who on that day entered the church, who had carefully abstained from ever entering it before.

The magistrates, in all the pomp and pride of office, had stationed themselves in the square before the church, and greeted the strangers as they passed with all becoming civility and respect; bowing very low to the ermined nobleman, and welcoming the humble citizen with a familiar nod of the head. The vergers of the church conducted the guests into the nave of the holy edifice, where the vicar chorals bawled aloud the customary chant, invoking the blessing of Heaven on the salubrity of the Baden waters, praying for restoration of health to the afflicted, and joy and happiness to the young and healthy. The best places in the church were reserved for the nobility and gentry; for such were the orders of the margrave, who was particularly indulgent to his ancient town of Baden, and who was desirous that the efficacy of the salubrious water should be celebrated in all the four quarters of the world, and who had very patriotically determined to leave his usual residence, on a rocky eminence contiguous to the city, to build a mansion for himself and his illustrious family, from the towers of which he could look down upon the hubbub and the racket, the fooleries and the vices of the visitors to his baths, like an eagle from his mountainous eyrie, on the grovelling emmets of the world beneath.

His endeavours to raise his favourite Baden to a high degree of celebrity had been attended with the most signal success. Princes, lords, barons, and counts, had found out the way to the health-restoring waters. The dignitaries of the church, and the learned professors of the high schools and the universities, and the rich citizens and merchants from the banks of the Danube and the Rhine, had very wisely followed so excellent an example.*

It was said—but it was a libellous saying—that the dignitaries of the church—may Heaven bless their good and righteous souls!—were not instigated to visit the l ths so much on account of the salubrity of the waters, as that their eyes might be feast wi'h the spectacle of the beautiful women who congregated thither, not to purify ther.. with the aqueous ablutions, but to inflame the hearts of the young scions of nobility, who were to be seen fluttering about in every quarter, in all the pride and folly of the senseless coxcomb. It was also said that the baths were the resort of many of those unfortunate women, who have yielded to the laws of nature in defiance of the laws of man, and also by many of that particular class of the female sisterhood who are standing on the verge of an antiquated virginity, but who are inspired with the hope that fortune would, in an auspicious moment, throw in their way some kind and charitable bachelor, who

---

* Some notion may be formed of the conflux of visitors to these celebrated baths by the following official statement of the number of persons who visited Baden from May to October, 1841 :—Princes, 163; natives of Baden, 4,634; Germans, 5,176; Hungarians, 97; English, 3,556; French, 5,650; Russians, 632; Dutch, 476; Belgians, 282; Swiss, 753; Danes, 81; Swedes, 33; Italians, 178; Spaniards, 35; Portuguese, 12; Greeks, 5; Moldavians, 5; Poles, 46; Americans, 262; Asiatics, 6; Africans, 8;—making a sum total of nearly 23,000 visitors.

might have the prudence to prefer the steadiness and sobriety of a matron of fifty to the giddiness and volatility of a girl of twenty.

At the precise period when this important history commences, the town of Baden was thronged with visitors, and in the principal seats of the cathedral shone many a nobleman, with his ermined cloak, with his gewgaws, and his golden chains, and his crosses, and his stars, which rather impertinently proclaimed, that although fortune, in one of her blind and foolish freaks, might have bestowed upon them the exterior decorations of the nobleman and the prince, yet it by no means followed that she had bestowed upon them any of the many properties or virtues of the man.

There were also present many ladies and children, the haughty scions of haughty families, and the former of whom dazzled the envious eyes of the plain and humble ladies of the citizen or the merchant, by the splendour of their garments, and the pomp and pageantry of their motley-coloured retinue. High mass was also performed on this most momentous occasion; and as the surpliced priest whirled about his little besom dipped in the silver font of blessed water, some felt themselves inspired with a most holy feeling, when a drop of the precious liquid was so fortunate as to fall upon them—whilst others, most unbecomingly and unsanctimoniously, presumed to laugh at the holy mummery. Nevertheless, faith is a most blessed thing; and the priest, after having completed the requisite sprinkling, proceeded to read from the pulpit the rules and regulations of the baths, which in the first place confirmed to every guest undisturbed peace and tranquillity within the circuit of the town and the baths.

All insulting words were prohibited, under punishment expressly stipulated—all threats of violence, under expulsion from the baths—the drawing of a weapon, with the loss of the hand—and a blow from a sword with the loss of life. The head of him was to be forfeited who took any indecent liberties with a virtuous woman—who uttered any abusive epithets against the emperor, or the princes of the empire; who unlawfully laid his hand upon the property of a nobleman, or who preached heresy with a blaspheming tongue. The man was sentenced to be deprived of his armorial bearings, and all knightly and corporate honours, who promulgated a calumnious report against any of the visitors at the baths—who was discovered to cheat at play—who was detected in peeping at a modest woman in a bath—who seduced a virtuous girl, or who gave offence, by indecent words or gestures. He was sentenced to leave the baths who showed himself three times drunk at table—who, without some sufficient and proper cause, gave a thrashing to his host, or to any of the attendants upon the baths—who should bring a lady of spurious virtue into his inn or lodging house, or who showed himself openly in the streets with a lady of that description, as if she were a good and reputable woman. In regard to minor offences against good manners, civility, and decorum, they were to be punished by fines and forfeits, according to the extent of the transgression, the proceeds of which became the property of the church, or the poor, although it was well known, that when once they got into the clutches of the former, a very small portion indeed of them fell to the maintenance of the latter.

These regulations, however strict and severe as they appeared, were by the aged listened to with the greatest attention and respect; and in their hearts they determined not to infringe them, for the best of all possible reasons, that nature would not allow them to infringe them, and in regard to the violation of some of them the aged ladies were most clamorous for the immediate infliction of the punishment awarded to them, or otherwise there would be no security for the sanctity of their persons in the bath, nor their exemption from contamination by being thrown into contact with the wicked and impure of their own sex.

On the other hand, however, the young men, the unruly libertines of the place, cast upon them their smile of contempt, and regarded the man as a fool, who thought to impose upon them a strict obedience to such extravagant rules, especially those which immediately concerned the ladies. They knew that the menaces of the law are frequently nothing more than tinkling cymbals, and that a halter is seldom spun, nor the axe of the executioner sharpened for the head of a nobleman; independently of which they were not ignorant that the severity of the punishment is often a guarantee for the exemption from it.

Amongst the many lawless youths was one, who rendered himself particularly conspicuous, and who would have been considered as the picture of health, had it not been for a wound in one of his feet, which he received in the wars under the Duke of Burgundy, and for which he was recommended to try the efficacy of the Baden waters. The host of the inn where he lodged, highly praised his gaiety—his disposition to extravagance—his rashness at dice, and his propensity to the bottle; and he pointed to three or four young noblemen, who were sitting in a drowsy state, and just recovering, but slowly, from the state of intoxication into which they had been thrown in the society of his libertine guest, whom he wished might long remain an ornament of his house, and continue in the same course of dissipation and extravagance.

Whilst the host was thus employed in proclaiming the virtues of his guest to those by whom he was surrounded, the young gentleman himself had entered the church, not with any feelings of devotion or piety, but he was like many others who enter a church, merely because it is fashionable; and who would seldom go at all if it were not to exhibit some new fangled head dress or a gown, with which the ingenuity of the milliner had provided them.

The priest was indeed in the pulpit, but that was an object to which he paid very little attention; but at first he amused himself with the motions of the swallows which were fluttering about the dome of the cathedral; and then he directed his looks to the ladies in their splendid attire, some of whom were kneeling, and some standing; some were ogling him from under their veils, and some looked him unblushingly in the face, not in the least abashed by the bold and libertine look which he gave them in return. His eye, however, wandered from the transparent veils, and the half covered bosoms of the bedizened ladies, to search amongst the less gaudy flowers of the humbler ranks, for a violet which he might ruthlessly crop from its native bed, with secret rapture and delight.

We often look for that at a distance which blossoms for us in our immediate vicinity, and so it was constituted with the gentleman; for the solemnities of the place were now over; the congregation were preparing to leave the church, when, on a sudden, a female rose from her knees, close to the spot where he was standing; and whose form and features made the most powerful impression upon his heart.

A paleness, like that of marble just hewn from its native bed, overspread the countenance of the lovely girl; but there was a brilliancy in her eye, though partly shaded by her luxuriant hair, which imparted an extraordinary animation to her otherwise melancholy countenance. Although apparelled in mean attire, the outward form of the beauteous girl betrayed the most perfect symmetry, full and voluptuous, and far more noble than is generally to be met with in females of a low condition.

The gentleman pressed forward, favoured by the crowd, to look the girl boldly and impertinently in her face, and to touch her tender hand; but he soon relinquished his intrusive design, for the girl raised her head towards him, and viewed him with a look, resolute and repellant. A certain triumphant sense of innocence, a powerful consciousness spoke intelligibly from her serious look, as if it would say, "What do you want with me, sir? and how dare you venture to annoy me with your impertinence?"

The young gentleman felt himself abashed, but swore secretly by all the saints in Heaven, that he would not rest until he had told his love to the coy and prudish girl, for as yet, there was not one throughout all Burgundy, nor in the valleys of his German fatherland, who had not returned his condescending familiarity with a favourable look, if not with something more precious and desirable.

Lost in thought, he mingled amongst his companions, and totally inattentive to their coarse and indecent jokes, he descended the hill, at the foot of which stood the inn in which he had fixed his residence, and before which a band of musicians were pretending to amuse, but in reality were annoying the inmates of the surrounding houses by their obstreperous and discordant noise.

"I wish the vagabonds were at the top of the Blocksberg," said the young gentleman to his servant Lutz, and to the corpulent, bald-headed waiter, who attended at the baths; "if it is the will of Heaven that the wound in my leg should be healed, it will certainly take place without this heathenish hubbub."

"As you please, noble, sir," said the waiter, with a marked degree of incivility; "if, however, it be your wish to take a bath, everything is prepared, and I am ready to wait upon you."

Whilst Lutz was employed in taking off the boots and spurs of his master, the latter looked the waiter full in the face, and said, half surprised, and half joking,—

"To judge by your rudeness, and your uncouth language, you are a countryman of mine?"

"I am a true-born Suabian," said the waiter, in a surly tone.

"I see that you are," said the gentleman, and pointed to the door.

The waiter took the hint, and left the room. Whilst Lutz was undressing his master, he said,—

"Give the fellow a good scolling from me; and tell him to lay aside his rude familiarity when he has anything to do with me. A Suabian, in forty years, ought to have acquired some wisdom, and know how to suit his manners to his company. Give him, however, these two florins, and make my liberality known to him."

Lutz punctually executed the orders of his master; and on leaving the apartment, he met the waiter, and said,—

"Let me advise you, be a little more civil to my master; he is one who rewards civility with the contents of his purse, but rudeness he punishes with a box of the ear. For the present, he will look upon your rudeness as not intended to give offence, and, therefore, sends this money."

The waiter having looked at the money with a sparkling eye, put it into his pocket, and said,—

"I now know the sort of people with whom I have to deal; I will try and be civil to your master, provided he does not jeer me in the presence of other people. But pray who is your master, to warrant him in giving himself such monstrous airs?"

Lutz opened his eyes with astonishment, and with a degree of pomposity exclaimed,— "What! not know who my master is? why he is the young Hurdegen von Sperbeneck. His family mansion is not far from Kerckheim, on the banks of the Leck. He has inherited a noble property, and spends it freely, whether in joke or earnest. There is not a more noble family in all Suabia; he is received into the society of princes and nobles; and, I warrant you, there is many a lady fair who would gladly go to the altar with him."

The sluices of Lutz's volubility were opened, and he was proceeding to enlarge most voluminously on the opulence and respectability of his master, when, to his boundless astonishment, he perceived that the forehead and cheeks of the person whom he was addressing were flushed with an unusual redness, and that some heavy tears came rolling down his cheeks. The waiter had clasped his hands, and stood with his head bent sorrowfully to the ground. Lutz, therefore, desisted from any further detail of the opulence and dignity of his master; for the faithful fellow had a tender heart, and perhaps was not wrong in his judgment, when he drew the conclusion, that where there are tears, there must be grief; and, therefore, it did not become him to touch upon any topic which, if raising up the memory of the past, might open again the wounds of a buried sorrow.

The waiter dried his tears, and hastened to the kitchen, where having obtained a plate of savoury soup, he hastened with it to the apartment in which Hurdegen was sitting. On entering the room, Hurdegen said to him, for he had been previously informed by Lutz of the extraordinary character of the uncouth waiter,—

"What have you lying heavily on your heart, you old curmudgeon? Your eyes are red, as if you had been weeping, and you look as miserable and woe-begone as a monk on Good Friday."

For some time the waiter made no answer, but at last he said,—

"Alas! my countryman, it grieves me much that you are so well off in the world, and that with me it is just the contrary."

"A very wise remark for a Suabian to make," said Hurdegen; "but what have I done, that you should express your regret that my circumstances do not resemble yours? Let me tell you, that such impudence is by no means pleasing to me."

The waiter stepped back a few paces, and said, in an insolent, joking tone,—

"Indeed, if I were not impudent, how should I be a nobleman?"

On Hurdegen looking at him with the greatest astonishment, he continued, with a kind of peevish familiarity,—

"Stare at me as much as you will, friend and countryman. I had my armorial bearings as well as you; the hangman did not break my escutcheon to pieces, but I did it myself, because I have been mighty rich, and am now as very a pauper as any who begs a bit of bread on the highway,—because the beggar boy does not well agree with an emblazoned escutcheon, and because it would be a shame to wear the helmet of a knight on the head, and the besom of a scavenger in the hand. You see before you the wreck of a Suabian nobleman,—a man who once lived honoured and respected; and now what is he?—a wretch, who depends for his daily bread on the charity and caprice of others. The rage for pomp and splendour made me dizzy; there was no desire, no aim, no design, which I thought too much for me. I was stung by the viper of madness, and as a madman I have conducted myself. But I know not how it is that I should thus make known to you the circumstances of my condition; why should they concern you, as a stranger, more than any one else? But you appear to me to have an honest countenance; though in your manners you are somewhat wild and dissolute; you are my countryman, and I hear you have a mansion at Hall, as I had once. You are of an ancient family, and so am I. You are in possession of wealth, and consequently of all the good things of the world; so was I once. You appear to be possessed with the devil of extravagance and libertinism; so was I. Therefore, let my melancholy example be a warning to you, and as you must be well acquainted with the affairs of the inhabitants of Hall, you cannot be ignorant of my history, for I now tell you that I am Gotz von Bachenstein."

Hurdegen rose involuntarily from his seat, and exclaimed,—

"How! what the old Gotz, whose folly and licentiousness are proverbial?—of whom my mother has often spoken to me, as the pattern of the lowest depravity, and whose general mode of life was a scandal to himself and his suffering family?"

"All very true," said Gotz, with an evident emotion of chagrin; "we know what we are, but we know not what we may be. Look to that, young man; persevere in the road on which you are now travelling, and it does not require the prophetic power of a Moses to foretell what your fate will be. Who knows, but yet you may have a besom in your hand, as I have now?"

"I feel myself highly indebted to you for your advice," said Hurdegen, ironically, "but I can scarcely believe what my eyes see, nor what my ears hear. You were once the richest man wherever the Suabian tongue was known,—you were said to measure your gold by shovelfuls, and of you the wondrous tale is told, that you once liberated the town of Hall from the importunate and excessive imposts of its rapacious lord."

Gotz gave a heavy sigh, and thought within himself, "Those were indeed prosperous days!"

Hurdegen, however, continued,—

"Matters, however, soon took a different turn in your house, because your kitchen chimney was smoking from morning to night,—because you led a riotous life with your companions from morning to night; and when you took up your residence at Dettingen, matters then became still worse; your house was a pandemonium, and a congregation of devils dwelt within it. Not one of you scarcely ever saw the blessed light of Heaven, but from your blood-shot eyes as you lay in the recovery from the debauch of the preceding day. One of the choristers of Stutgard was your friend and purveyor; one moment he was praising God with a loud voice, from his place in the cathedral, and the next he was prowling the country for some new victims to your brutal passions. If the hypocrite did not exactly steal your purse, he squandered it away in the livers of pike, in the brains of peacocks, and the tongues of larks. Thus, by degrees, your supposed inexhaustible riches were consumed, and you were obliged to fly your fatherland, and no one could tell where you and your wife and child had taken refuge."

"What a fine story," said Gotz, "have you related of that old debauchee, Gotz of Bachenstein! But in many things you are my very counterpart. You are far more partial to a tournament than to a sermon from the pulpit; a brothel is more agreeable to you than the house of God, and the cursed money is round, and runs, as if it were possessed with the devil, through the world, when once we have set it a going. In the same manner that my riches run through the sieve, so may yours; and verily, from what I now experience, I should be sorry for you."

"My ancient nobleman," exclaimed Hurdegen, in an ironical tone, "have the goodness to attend to your own affairs, and I will attend to mine. The riches which I inherited from my father, added to those which I acquired on the decease of the Duke of Burgundy, are not easily squandered away; and should I follow a career as mad and foolish as yours has been, and if at last—but that can never take place, I will not mention it. See, I am not yet five-and-twenty, and should I have squandered away a portion of my patrimony, a rich bride will soon make up the deficiency. I am a vigorous soldier, I covet not many pleasures, and I have no dread for any calamity that may befal me; let it, however, be so, I will fight my way manfully through it; and I now intreat you to accept of some slight assistance in your present necessities from a countryman, who, with all his faults, can feel for the miserable condition to which you are reduced."

After some consideration, Gotz answered, with a shrug of the shoulders,—

"Well, by the holy cross! I have given away much in my life-time, and therefore I am not now ashamed to accept of a lift from another. Poverty, my young madcap, gives a man a bold front, and an itching comes over my hand when I only hear the sound of money, as I at this time should not be worth a single penny, were it not for my temporary employment here at the baths. It is my opinion, that you would not put off a nobleman like myself with a miserable alms, and your gold will be as well in my pocket as in the chest of an innkeeper, or of a Jew, or a prostitute, or a perjured borrower.

PUBLISHER'S NOTE

pp.7-8 are missing.

the eyes. A cold heart beats beneath a tranquil breast, and love is a power which never rests. The woman is pleasing to thee when she plays with children, and kisses them passionately in thy presence; when she tenderly flatters and fondles over her husband whilst thou art an eye witness, it is all deceit; it is a snare laid to entrap thee. Deceit is the constituent principle of woman. God has made her so, and she cannot alter her nature."

"Oh, thou senseless chatterer!" said Hurdegen, with an ebullition of passion, and appeared to sit uneasily on his chair; "you have been preaching things to me which the very sparrows taught me in my youth. If you cannot impart to me any better information, hold your tongue. I am not disposed to listen to such a tirade against the most beautiful of nature's works. I feel my breast as if it were oppressed with leaden armour, and I want something to dissipate my uneasiness."

On a sudden his faithful Lutz stood behind his chair.

"I would not willingly trespass upon you, sir," he said, "at your dinner, but the messenger who has brought the dismal tidings is anxious to set out on his return. He is the bearer of the intelligence that your farm at Urach is devoured by the flames."

"Hell and fury!" exclaimed Hurdegen, and sprang almost frantic from his chair.

Lutz continued,—

"All the cattle are burnt to death, except an old measly sow, which lay in the hut with the shepherd; and not only your own property, but the mills of the Masters Schwargart are also burnt to the ground, and the messenger is obliged to return immediately to the monastery, to obtain the assistance of the priest, in preparing the victims who have been injured by the flames, and who are at the point of death, for their happy passage to another world."

Hurdegen ran out of the room, and was soon made acquainted, from the mouth of the messenger himself, with the full extent of the calamity. At first he vented his passion in curses and imprecations; he, however, soon so far regained his wonted composure, as to be able to dismiss the messenger with his orders as to the steps that were to be taken to assist the sufferers under the present calamity.

"Am I not the possessor," he said, "of a dozen other farms? The advance of a small sum of money will soon repair all the injury that I have sustained. And is not the morrow the day on which Henry Rubenheim promised me, on his life and soul, to repay me the sum of money which I lent him about a year ago? Away, then, all chagrin and vexation, and let me not be disturbed in my pleasures and amusements. I will, however, not return to the table to be annoyed by that everlasting gabbler, Landsap, who takes a delight in vilifying and calumniating the female sex, and yet he is a very slave to their power and fascination. But I promised to visit the reprobate to-night, and I will keep my promise."

CHAPTER II.

"Love that disturbs
The schemes of wisdom still; that winged with passion,
Blind and impetuous in its fond pursuits,
Leaves the grey-headed reason far behind."

HURDEGEN repaired to his private apartment, and having filled his purse with money, he set forward in pursuance of his promise; but a strange presentiment hung upon his mind that his future fate was in a degree connected with the visit, although, from a general review of his condition and circumstances, he could not divine what possible connection could subsist between him and Gotz of Bachenstein, especially considering the low and impoverished state to which the improvident knight was now reduced. Shaking from him, however, all these gloomy and disheartening feelings, he bent his steps towards the gates of the city, according to the directions which Gotz had given him. and by following the path prescribed to him, he soon saw at a distance the three birch trees, at the foot of which he perceived the miserable hut which Gotz von Bachenstein had exchanged for his baronial castle.

With what strange and inexplicable feelings was his breast oppressed when he entered the miserable room in which he could scarcely stand upright, although he had respectfully taken off his Spanish hat with its waving plumes. Poverty in its most confirmed character was visible in every part of the miserable tenement; the light of day was almost ashamed to break through the dirty squares of horn which served as a window; and thus a disheartening gloom pervaded the whole of the apartment, rendering every object almost imperceptible, and charitably concealing a portion of the wretchedness of the place. As the eye began to be accustomed to the gloom, Hurdegen perceived an old stool, on which an aged woman was sitting, with her hands clasped and resting on her lap, and close to her was a broken three-legged table, behind which Gotz was apparently comfortably seated, and from which, in an unembarrassed manner, he muttered a hearty welcome.

He had not so soon expected the visit of his friend, or, perhaps, he would not have allowed himself to be caught partaking of the sorry meal which was spread before him. Before the old gormandizer stood an earthen dish, filled with lampreys, which the culinary skill of the mistress of the hut had dressed in the most savoury manner, and at his right hand stood a bottle of genuine Hochheimer, the moiety of which had already been consumed by the insatiable toper.

"Well," exclaimed Hurdegen, "I wish you a good appetite for your dainty meal. Though poor in purse, I see you know how to enjoy some of the good things of the world."

"And why not?" said Bachenstein. "What could I do better with the proceeds of your bounty, than provide ourselves with something that was strengthening and refreshing; and would it not have been imputed to me as an act of neglect, if I had not brought a bottle with me, wherewith to drink your health? and if, as I believe, your intentions towards me are friendly, you will not refuse to partake of a glass with me."

"And why not?" said Hurdegen. "The flavour will be as fine to me as if it were drank under a golden dome. It may also be the case that it is tendered to me by the hand of friendship and good-will, which is more than can be said of many a glass that is tendered in the palaces and mansions of the great; but, before I partake of a drop, let me present a glass to the noble Lady of Bachenstein."

The wife of the old knight rose slowly from her seat, and having put her lips to the glass which Hurdegen offered her, she said,—

"I hope, noble sir, that you will not turn our shame and poverty into ridicule."

A blush of shame came over the countenance of Hurdegen, who was now conscious to himself that he had committed an offence against good manners, and that he had inflicted a painful and unnecessary wound upon the feelings of one who had perhaps been reduced from a state of affluence to one of the most abject poverty by no fault nor co-operation of her own; he, therefore, turned to the old woman and said,—

"God forbid that I should pass an unreasonable joke, or be guilty of casting any ridicule upon fallen greatness. Cheer up, my good woman; I come to alleviate your misery, not to aggravate it by an unkind word, or an unfriendly action."

A heavy sigh broke from the breast of the woman, as if she did not place any great confidence in the words of her visitor, and Hurdegen continued,—

"Come, seat yourself by our side. It is my desire that we should be better acquainted; share with us of what we are going to partake, and with which it appears your husband intends to celebrate the little gift I have bestowed upon him."

The woman answered, with a melancholy look,—

"You know not, noble sir, the regulations of our household, or you would not be ignorant that the dainties which our lord and master now and then brings home, in our poverty, are reserved entirely for his own appetite, but that we are never allowed to partake of them. We, however, most willingly submit to it, because we should be satisfied were we not the victims of his continual complaints and ill-humour, with which he torments us night and day, although he must himself be conscious that he is the sole cause of our present shame and misery."

Gotz moved backwards and forwards in his chair, as if the most violent passions were at work with him, but as he perceived that Hurdegen regarded his wife with a look of compassion, he determined to play the hypocrite, and said,—

"Now, Greta, matters are not so bad as you represent them. It is Heaven that punishes us with hunger, for having formerly gormandised so much. I am willing to share my morsel with you, but it is not my fault if you obstinately refuse every joy that I offer you. The married state," he continued, addressing himself to Hurdegen, "is a most miserable condition. My wife was one of the best-tempered and most amiable of women so long as the sun of prosperity shone upon us; but now that we are in the darkness of adversity, she has not only become herself crabbed and morose, but she has affected all the children with her stubborness."

"All the children?" repeated the woman, in a most emphatic manner. "Where are they?"

"I mean our child," said Gotz, in a hasty manner, and casting the look of a fiend upon his offending wife.

"Ah, thou unnatural father!" exclaimed Greta, with her hands uplifted, and tears streaming from her eyes. "Will you then for ever deny your son? Is it not enough that your curse has driven him from his home in misery and wretchedness? Perhaps his bones are bleaching on the highway, or they are mouldering in the vaults of some hospital. I could, most noble sir," addressing herself to Hurdegen, "have borne poverty, distress, and all the accumulated ills to which humanity is subject, without a murmur. I should have looked upon them as the hand of Heaven, and have submitted with resignation to the infliction of the punishment, but my heart broke when I saw my darling son driven from his home into the wide world by an unnatural father, merely because he attempted to protect me against the maltreatment of that barbarian."

"Thou old grumbling wretch!" exclaimed Bachenstein, "I would thou wert with thy son, side by side on the highway, or in the vaults of the hospital. Why annoy my young friend with thy everlasting complaints? And what was the boy after all?—a rude unmanly fellow, who, with the mere down on his chin, assumed the importance of the man, who consequently became insolent and overbearing to his father, and acted so long the champion and defender of his mother, that for the sake of peace I drove him out of the house. And what is it, after all, that such a hubbub should be made about it? The boy does not want talent, and therefore he will not starve. But who knows what may befall us, if you, my countryman, do not come speedily to our assistance?"

Incensed as the heart of Hurdegen was against the cruel and unnatural conduct of the old knight, still, on the other hand, it was deeply affected at the sight of so much misery, and drawing, therefore, his purse from his pocket, he threw it on the table, with that haste as if the following moment the relief would have come too late.

"Take the gold," he said, "from a true Suabian hand. My father has perhaps often partaken of your hospitality,—he has perhaps caroused over your wine, and partaken of the good cheer of your table; therefore, receive back from me what he and other noblemen have received from your hospitality. May it prosper with you, and it shall not be the last gift that I will bestow upon you."

Gotz still played the hypocrite, and appeared to be deeply affected; but tears of unfeigned gratitude rolled down the cheeks of the affected woman, and she said,—

"May the money procure for my weary head a decent pillow on which to breathe my last, and for my poor girl a settlement, however small it may be."

"Where is the girl?" asked Gotz, weighing the heavy purse with delight in his hand. "What has the girl to do so long in the outhouse? Gisela, where art thou? Come hither and thank our generous friend for his bountiful gift."

The mother knocked on the wooden partition of the room, and in a minute afterwards Gisela entered. Hurdegen, however, could scarcely credit his eyes, when on a sudden he saw before him the beautiful girl who had so enraptured him in the church, and to meet with her again in a place where, of all others, he so little expected it, threw him into a state of confusion and embarrassment. The unexpected visit came also so suddenly upon the bashful maiden, that the natural paleness of her countenance was flushed with a roseate hue. Her astonishment, however, gradually subsided, and with an air of coyness and timidity, she said,—

"What are your commands, dear mother?"

"Here is a generous nobleman," said her mother, "who is charitably disposed to turn our sorrows into joy. Perhaps we can now manage to obtain you admission into the convent. If your father will allow us to appropriate a part of the money to defray the expenses of your equipment."

Hurdegen contemplated the girl with feelings yet unknown to him, but in those feelings was mingled a kind of gloom, when he saw a beam of joy sparkling in the eye of Gisela at the mention of a convent, and he beheld her hastening towards her father in an imploring attitude, as if to solicit his sanction to the suggestions of her mother.

Gotz nodded with his head, and in a grumbling tone said,—

"With all my heart—with all my heart! so that there may be peace and quiet in the house. My Gisela has been long wishing to become the resident of a convent, and her mother is most anxious to protect the poor lamb from the snares of the seducer."

"From the seducer!" exclaimed Hurdegen, looking Gisela full in the face, whilst she sat, with downcast eyes, close to her mother on the bench, and then turning to Gotz, he said,—"What do you mean by her seducer?"

"I must inform you, my young friend," said Gotz, "that the young and haughty knight of Harras, who lives for the greater part of the year on his estate at Winderk, has seen our Gisela, and, alas! he is privy to my family extraction, having once in the moment of intoxication betrayed it to him. He has, it is true, given me his word of honour, as a knight, not to divulge the secret; but, instead of courting my daughter in an honourable way, with whom he pretends to be deeply enamoured, he follows here and there, as if he could purchase her favours with a few florins, so that my poor daughter is scarcely able to put her foot out of the house without being subject to his importunities."

Hurdegen gnashed his teeth with rancour and revenge, he clenched his fists involuntarily, and pulled the feathers to pieces which decorated his hat. He felt as if the knight of Harras was trespassing upon his property, and he considered it most unpardonable in him to attempt to obtain possession of a jewel on which he had placed the fondest wishes of his soul.

In the meantime a slight tapping was heard at the window; Margaret, the wife of Gotz threw open the shutter, and said,—

"It is only the widow Irmel, the washerwoman. What can she want with me? She's beckoning me with her finger—I will see on what errand she is bent. I will soon return," and Margaret left the hut.

Margaret had not long left the room, before the hoarse voice of the host of the inn at Baden, in which Gotz was employed, was heard, calling him by name, in a commanding tone, intermingled with some abusive epithet, not very agreeable, even to the ear of a dependent.

"What brings the purse-proud fool here, at this unreasonable hour?" muttered Bachenstein, highly chagrined; "day after day he is plotting some new work for me, with which he vexes and annoys me, because I have the misfortune to owe him a few florins. I am just in a proper mood to repay him rudeness for rudeness, and to knock his teeth down his throat with a crown-piece. Have patience for a moment," said Bachenstein, addressing himself to Hurdegen, "I will soon finish my business with him."

Gotz left the room, and Hurdegen found himself alone with the beautiful Gisela. She employed herself, with her back turned towards Hurdegen, to remove the things which stood on the table. Hurdegen, under the momentary influence of the passion, became emboldened by the opportunity that was afforded him, and, in a tender manner, put his arm round her waist. Gisela repulsed him with the same look of dignified virtue, with which she had abashed his libertine look on the preceding morning, and so powerfully impressive was her conduct on the present occasion, that he faintly articulated,—

"Are charms like yours made to be immured in a convent?"

"I love the convent," answered Gisela, coldly and formally; "and I hate and despise your flattery."

"Why," exclaimed Hurdegen, "should I be hateful to you? or why should you despise any of my actions?"

"And why," said Gisela, "should I be called upon to love one who is a perfect stranger to me, and in whom I have no reason to place my confidence?"

"Your future," said Hurdegen, "may be illumined by the sun of pleasure and happiness; and, were that the case, would not mine be also equally bright?"

"You speak as if you were a bridegroom," said Gisela.

"Would that I were," said Hurdegen.

"Would you pay such compliments and flatteries to your bride?" asked Gisela, "as you now seem disposed to pay to me?"

"Would that you were that bride!" said Hurdegen.

"May Heaven forgive you that falsehood," said Gisela.

"It is an accusation, of which I am undeserving," said Hurdegen.

"A man of rank and fortune," said Gisela, "ought to be ashamed of himself to make a poor girl like myself the object of his sport."

"What shall I do," said Hurdegen, "to prove to you my sincerity?"

A smile of contempt sat upon the countenance of Gisela, and she answered with a most penetrating look,—

"Go hence, and become as poor as I am, then come again and you shall receive my answer."

Hurdegen was astonished at the unexpected answer, and looked confused and embarrassed at the diamond ring which he wore on his finger. Gisela looked at him for a moment, with a kind of scornful compassion, and, turning away from him in derision, she said,—

"You do not appear, sir, to be very well."

Hurdegen was overcome with confusion, and ardently did he rejoice when the parents of Gisela returned and extricated him from his embarrassment. Gotz vented on the host the most unmeasured abuse, and swore with the most vehement oaths that, from that hour, he would leave his service, and, on the other hand, Margaret appeared to be highly delighted, and related, giving her tongue the utmost possible volubility, that another piece of good fortune had befallen them, as the widow Irmel had informed her of a rich and highly respectable lady, who had lately obtained a sight of Gisela, and who wished for nothing more sincerely than to promote the fallen interests of the girl. The lady had her residence in the barony of Ebentein, and the widow Irmel offered her services on the following Sunday to conduct Gisela over the mountains to the residence of the benevolent lady, in order that a formal introduction might take place.

Gotz did not appear to attach much importance to the information, but Gisela rejected the offer in the most positive manner, saying,—

" The old widow is a bad woman, and I have been already warned against her. Besides, I do not stand in need of a benefactress; the convent is the home I long for; and, if you will only equip me in the most common manner, the white sisters of Strasburg will most willingly receive me."

Hurdegen could scarcely contain himself when he heard Gisela express herself in this resolute and determined manner, and he determined to hasten his departure, so that he might not betray the tempest that was raging within him. With the promise that he would speedily return, and accompanied by the most exuberant thanks of Gotz and his wife, Hurdegen left the hut. Gisela did not deign to bestow upon him a single look, and his pulse beat so much the more tumultuously as the enjoyment which is denied us is generally more ardently desired, than the pleasure which is easily obtained. The conduct of Hurdegen now in the hut appeared to him in the most despicable light; he was ashamed of the trifling gift which he had left behind him; he called himself a miser—curmudgeon, who was not ashamed to look upon a musty crust of bread as an invaluable treasure. The possession of Gisela appeared to him not too dear, if purchased with the sacrifice of all his property, and he determined to venture anything for the gratification of his passion, to deprive the convent of a nun, and to snatch away a booty from the decoying seducers. He never put the question to himself as to what his real intentions towards Gisela were, whether he intended to conduct the beautiful girl as his wife to the altar, or by his artifices and pretensions to reduce her to shame and ignominy. The thoughtless libertine trembled at the notion of imposing upon himself the chains of matrimony, but yet he entertained too high a respect for Gisela, to behold her the victim of his unbridled passion, and thereby be the destroyer for ever of her terrestrial happiness. The object to which all his endeavours were directed, was to liberate her from the poverty and wretchedness of her paternal dwelling; to protect her from the base and criminal designs of Harras; to carry his beloved one to some remote corner of the earth, where, in undisturbed retirement, he might protect her, watch over her, pass night and day in the contemplation of her charms, which, like some desert flower, bloomed only for himself; and then having surfeited himself with the sweets of it, to cast it away to those who were willing to pick it up.

Amidst this struggle between vice and virtue—this unequal contest between passion and principle, he bent his steps homewards, and he had nearly reached the town, when, to his mortification, he beheld Landsap approaching him. At no time was the man agreeable to Hurdegen. He could sit with him at table during the hours of their bacchanalian joviality, he could fritter his time away with him at the billiard-table, or with the cards and dice, but he did not like him as a general associate or companion. Harras was one of those men who make a figure at a watering-place, on account of the dashing nature of their character, and who in general entertain so high an opinion of themselves, that they look down with disdain and contempt on all those whom they deem to be their inferiors, and who fancy if they can but play with the affections of an innocent and too confiding girl, they have achieved a triumph, which fits them to be received into the highest ranks of human society.

On their meeting Harras greeted Hurdegen with all the familiarity of an old acquaintance.

" I am glad we have met," said Harras; " you are just come at a proper time to congratulate me on my good fortune. I have laid the first stone of the foundation of my happiness; and when I have gained the treasure you shall participate in it when I have done with it. The lily, I find, however, is not to be won by bribery, nor with a few pieces of gold; but I have already found an old experienced pander, who has laid a snare from which it will be a most extraordinary circumstance if she escape. The old widow Irmel can lie like a monk, when he swears that he never in his life touched the hem of the garment of a woman; and now my hopes are strongly excited, that on the following Sunday, when the vesper bell is ringing, I shall pluck a flower, one of the sweetest that is now blooming in the country. The time and place are all appointed in the lonely wood between here and Ebenstein. The credulous girl is flattering herself that she is going to be conducted to an old benevolent lady, who has taken a fancy to her, and who is to take her from her wretched hovel, to flaunt about in silks and satins, and ride in gilded carriages, and have a retinue of servants at her nod and beckon. The girl will no doubt at first put on the prude, and cry out that it is a shame and scandal; but never yet did I lay a snare for a girl, that she did not, after a little bustle and fuss, forgive me for all my sins. What—what is the matter with you? You look as pale as a corpse, and a few minutes before you were as ruddy as a new-blown rose. This is not the way to congratulate me on my good fortune. After next Sunday I will tell you where the roosting place of my turtle-dove is to be found. You would never look for such a beautiful pearl in such an ugly shell. Cheer up, my noble fellow! do not appear so downcast. If fortune does not smile upon you as it does upon me, your hour will come sooner or later; and if I can assist you in obtaining a beautiful girl, as I shall enjoy the happiness of obtaining, you may most willingly command my services."

"May you and your services," exclaimed Hurdegen, "be hurled together into the bottomless pit. Let me have no more of your familiarities. Keep your hands off my shoulders, unless you wish my dagger to find its way to your heart. I hold you for a base, unprincipled scoundrel."

"You are not the first man who has told me so," said Landsap, with the greatest coolness; "and I have heard the same from the lips of many a woman; and both have had the same effect upon me, as the humming of a bee. I know I am the object of envy amongst the men; and in regard to the abuse of the women, I never consider myself more certain of a woman than when she begins to vilify me."

"I have neither time nor inclination," said Hurdegen, "to listen to you any longer;" and with a look, in which anger and contempt were mingled, he proceeded on his way, swearing secretly, by all the saints in heaven and all the fiends in hell, to frustrate the intentions of his dissolute friend with the most zealous perseverance.

Landsap looked at Hurdegen with the most visible emotions of surprise and astonishment; for he knew not what to make of the scene which he just witnessed. He could not entertain the slightest suspicion that the girl, whose seduction he contemplated, and for whose ruin he had laid a snare from which he supposed that she could not possibly escape, was in reality the very girl with whom Hurdegen found himself to be deeply in love, and for whose possession he was now devising those measures by which his success was to be placed beyond the possibility of a doubt. Had any suspicions of this kind prevailed in his breast he would have known how to account for the conduct of Hurdegen. But Landsap fancied that the obscure and retired mode of life to which Gisela was confined, had kept her from the intrusive gaze of the libertines who visited the town of Baden during the bathing season; and he therefore flattered himself that he was the only one who had discovered her retreat, and that it was destined for him alone to pluck the beautiful flower which was blossoming in a desert, untrodden and unfrequented by the foot of man.

In the midst of these cogitations, and whilst he was standing almost as immovable as the "Pillar of Salt," into which the foolish wife of Lot was transformed, he was accosted on a sudden, by the Baronet Harras, with his round rubicund countenance.

"Hilloa! my good friend," exclaimed the baronet; "you appear to me almost as if you were in convulsions. As to myself, I could not have been more astonished if I had heard the little angels in heaven singing their matin songs, than I was just now, in beholding the sudden mental derangement of my good friend Hurdegen. Look! how he hastens there along, and fights the air with his arms, like a man in despair, or like one possessed with the devil. I can scarcely recover myself from my fright. Haste, follow him to his inn! These sudden attacks of the brain are not to be trifled with; my uncle died of one of these apoplectic fits; although, but a few minutes before, he spoke as rationally as a parson that is not drunk. Follow him, I say, and I will join you soon at the inn. The wine pleased me so well yesterday that I am disposed to try the same medicine to-day."

Harras spoke to him in such a commanding, imperious tone, that Landsap thought he had nothing else to do than to follow most submissively the instructions of the authoritative baronet. But if Hurdegen were really deranged, as the baronet had represented him, it was not a society into which he would willingly throw himself; nor did he exactly perceive what benefit could accrue to him in interfering with the affairs and actions of a lunatic. The conduct of Hurdegen had, indeed, appeared to him most strange, and not quite compatible with that of a man in full possession of his reason. But on the supposition that it might proceed from some sudden affection of the brain, he thought he was only performing an act of charity in following him to the inn, that he might be placed as soon as possible under medical assistance. He, therefore, very deliberately followed the steps of Hurdegen; but on his arrival at the gates his naturally churlish disposition obtained the scendency, and he questioned himself with wonder, on what account he had been induced to follow so blindly the orders of the conceited and imperious baronet.

"I will not execute his commands," said Landsap, to himself; "I will enjoy the beautiful evening in the open fields, and leave the moonstruck youth to his own whims and caprices. I will show the pompous baronet that I am not his donkey; and although I am not exactly entitled to be called Sir Ferdinand Scherer von Landsap, yet that, barring the title, I am just as good a man as he is. I have no objection to partake of his wine; and as long as he has a florin in his pocket, I will do my utmost to cheat him of it. But then it is an act of policy in me; I fill my paunch with his wine, and my pocket with his money, and he will not be the first dupe that I have sent home penniless to his bed. I'll go towards the wood, where, perhaps, I shall hear my pretty turtle-dove cooing for its absent partner. I'll soon stifle her cooing; and after I have taken the kernel, I'll throw the shell to Hurdegen, as a special instance of my regard and friendship for him."

On the other hand, Harras said to himself, how glad I am to be liberated from the company of that prying, curious, meddling fool. He tries to worm himself into the secrets of other people, merely to turn them to his own advantage. I have, however, sent him upon an errand, in which, if I'm not mistaken in the character of Hurdegen, he will come off with a broken head, or the point of a sword through his body. Hurdegen is not a man to be trifled with, and I could not have found a more seasonable opportunity of satisfying the grudge which I owe Landsap, than by despatching him on such an errand as that on which I have just now sent him.

Harras was disturbed in his reflections by the arrival of a posse of singular beings, whom he soon recognised to be a gang of gipsies, amongst whom were some men clad in the most grotesque style, and bearing the outward appearance of clowns and mountebanks. Amongst them was a man clad in a pilgrim's dress, who carried on his head a tin box, into which the casual passenger dropped his penny, as it was alleged that the alms were collected to liberate the souls of the damned sinners from purgatory, or for the use and relief of the necessitous pilgrims to the Holy Land. The passengers were told that for every penny they put into the box, they would be so many hundred miles nearer heaven, and the swindling pilgrim was not the first by many hundreds of the sons of Adam, who had extracted money from the pockets of his credulous dupes for holy and religious purposes; but which, in reality, was applied to the tampering of the epicurean appetite of the bloated priest, or to the gratification of other appetites of a more meretricious character. The pilgrim approached the baronet for the purpose of soliciting his charity, when they were not long in recognising each other.

"Who would have thought of meeting with thee, thou old scoundrel!" exclaimed Harras; "I thought, Saurbein, that thou hadst already taken possession of thy apartments in the devil's house."

"I am much obliged to you, most noble baronet," said Saurbien, "for the compliment that you have paid me; but I have been told that the measure of my iniquity is not yet full, and therefore I am not yet properly qualified for my future residence."

"It is a wonder to me," said Harras, "that you and the hangman have not been better acquainted before now."

"I have had rare good luck in the world," said Saurbein. "If I have ever been implicated in the carrying off of a nun, or emptying the coffers of an usurious miser, I have by some means contrived to slip my neck out of the noose."

"Are you a member of the most righteous and pious band of cheats and conjurors?" asked Harras.

"The Holy Virgin protect me from such an association," said Saurbein. "How can you expect that I should travel about the world with such a set of heathens? I have been for some time a pilgrim by profession. I collect alms for the penitent souls in purgatory, and for the impenitent pilgrims on the earth."

"Retire with me to the corner of the wood for a moment," said Harras; "I would have a few more minutes' conversation with you. I know you possess a particular knack of persuading people to act exactly in the manner that you wish them to do, and when you persuaded the Count of Waldburg to sell me his beautiful stud of horses for, comparatively speaking, a mere trifle, you rendered me a most essential service. You have it now in your power to render me another piece of service, although rather of a different kind. It is not a horse that you have now to obtain for me, but a fine beautiful girl."

"It is all the same to me," said Saurbein; "there is not anything in which there is so much cheating as in horsedealing, and in negotiation with girls; consequently, there is not anything from which a greater profit is derived."

"I have a project in my head," said Harras, "in which you cannot but succeed, as the

See page 16.

people are well-known to you whom you are to cajole. You were once in the service of that old spendthrift and debauchee, Gotz von Bachenstein."

"And a better service I never wish to be in," said Saurbein. "Kitchen and cellar were always open to me; and, at times, they were both under my superintendence. You may then easily suppose what a jovial life I led. Many a monk have I laid drunk at the steps of the monastery, and the holy fraternity threatened to excommunicate me; but I took the first opportunity of making them drunk also, and I heard no more of the excommunication."

" You shall find your old master again," said Harras; "tuck up your pilgrim's dress; follow me to my residence; victuals and drink, clothes and money shall be at your command, if you consent to perform what I require, and do it faithfully and speedily. If you do not, woe, then, unto your head!"

" Be not afraid, most noble sir," said Saurbein. "It is well known that you place no more value upon the head of a poor man, than you do upon that of a dog. But do you go on. I will follow you at a distance, for a tattered dress like mine will form a striking contrast with your splendid habiliments. In other respects we perfectly understand each other. To deceive Gotz of Bachenstein will not be a difficult task to me, as I have done it so often before."

Whilst these proceedings were going on at a distance from the town, Hurdegen had reached the inn, conducting himself more like a man bereft of his senses, than one who had the command of his reason. Alas! he met with little there to mitigate the violence of his ill-humour ; a few saddled horses were standing in the yard, and the riders, covered with dust, were employed in unloosening the knapsacks from the horses. The principal personage amongst these riders, a tall, stately man, with not a very prepossessing countenance and grey hair, approached Hurdegen, and, at a distance, tendered him his hand, without speaking a word. At last, Hurdegen exclaimed, with evident signs of astonishment,—

" By Heavens! my most noble Specht of Rubenheim! How come you here? It is a specimen of the most unexampled punctuality, and it deserves the highest commendation, that you should have taken upon yourself the trouble to bring the money that you owe me to Baden."

A very significant smile sat upon the countenance of old Specht, and he answered,—

" It is a very great misfortune that I am not the bearer of any person, and consequently that I come in my own person. Leiningen has not kept his word with me; Andlawer has taken no notice of me, as if he owed me not a single farthing; Nathan; the Jew, will not lend another farthing—and Issachar, half Jew and half Christian, the deuce take his mongrel breed! has for the last three months, been tantalizing me with empty promises. I had, therefore, no other alternative left, than, in God's name, to give my body in pledge to you, as it becometh a true and worthy gentleman."

It was some time before Hurdegen could so far collect himself, as to give any answer to the strange proposition, from his very conscientious debtor, whose unexpected defalcation frustrated all the hopes and plans which he had formed for the restoration of the property that had been consumed by the fire ; at the bottom of his heart he cursed his inconsiderate debtor, and the emotions that were passing in his soul were visibly depicted on his countenance. Rubenheim did not allow himself to be in the least perplexed, for, in those careless and faithless times, as was well known to the most unthinking borrower on the Rhine and the Necker, the melancholy, long-drawn out countenance of a deluded creditor was by no means an uncommon sight ; and, in return for the abuse and reproaches that were heaped upon him, he very coolly gave empty jokes, insignificant shrugs of the shoulders, and promises that were never meant to be performed. Such was the game that was this day carried on by Rubenheim, until Huredgen began to be more composed, and merely uttered a complaint, that, as he stood greatly in need of the money, he would be obliged to draw the sum required from the capital that he had invested at Strasburg, and which he had deposited there in case of any sudden emergency, or a fund for his future support. Rubenheim, in return for the reproaches and ill-humour of Hurdegen, said,—

" Would to Heaven I were in your situation! Your brother is notoriously one of the richest men in the country, and your uncle at Zavelstein also rolls in riches, and at the same time, must soon take his departure from this world. The gout will most probably very soon promote the octogenarian either into the paradise of heaven, or into the torments of an opposite place, and it is not to be supposed that, on his death-bed, he will forget his nephew."

" You speak like a child," said Hurdegen, ill-humouredly ; " were you not the Lord of Obenaus and Nirgendian, you ought to know, in the name of the Holy Trinity, that my brother is one of the greatest misers in the whole Roman empire, and that, for the sake of securing to himself a prominent place in heaven, he has bequeathed all his property to the monks. Independently of which, he entertains a decided aversion to me, and, although he is well known to be in possession of some extensive forests, he must not give me a log of wood wherewith to heat my winter stove. Besides, I lead the very devil of a life with my relations, and, although you have greatly deceived me, and that I am, for the time being, destitute of money, yet the evil is not so great but that it may be remedied. My property is yet large and extensive, and I have hitherto looked upon myself as the peculiar favourite of fortune."

With these words, Hurdegen assumed an attitude of pride and conscious importance, and he strutted up and down the room, puffed up with vanity and conceit. On a sudden, he became more calm, seated himself on a chair, and resting his head on his hand, said, in a deliberate tone,—

"My good friend, I wish my happiness were greater in two points. The first is, that the wound in my leg would be properly healed; and the second is—but you would not understand me, if I were to talk of love, and of a girl, whose coldness and reserve drive me to despair."

Rubenheim seated himself on a chair by the side of Hurdegen, and said, in a cool and indifferent tone,—

"The bath will heal the wounded foot, and time will lay a healing plaster upon the wounded heart. By my faith, if I had a wife, and my wife had a daughter, you should have her as your wife, and were you twice as rich, and I twice as poor."

"I believe you well; you are richly deserving of the appointment of the bishop's fool. In the meantime, however, I have no inclination to take a wife. I long for the love of a woman without the blessing of a priest."

"Then," said Rubenheim, "follow the example of your uncle at Zavelstein, who keeps a pretty housekeeper under his roof, and delights his eyes every day with the sight of a beautiful bosom, that never was made for the head of an old sapless trunk like your uncle's to rest upon."

Hurdegen sank into a deep fit of musing. On a sudden he sprang up, slapped his hands, and exclaimed, joyfully,—

"I have a thought that is worth a ton of gold. I will carry a plan into execution which never yet entered into the mind of man. Why should I trouble my head about trifles? Here I have been tormenting myself the whole of the day with fears and doubts, and the thought never struck me, that a clever roguish trick will bring me at once to the accomplishment of my design. You shall have a hand in it, my old Rubenheim, and, also, that old debauchee, my uncle, although without his will and knowledge. Lightning and hail! seeing that I lend you the money for a further period, you cannot do anything less than, out of respect and gratitude to me, act the part of a rogue for a short time. Give me your hand; then we'll try a bottle of champagne, and, afterwards, we'll set about our work."

"Agreed," said Rubenheim; "my throat is as dry as the crater of Vesuvius, and I am bound to render you every service in my power, and if I promise you my assistance, it is not done with the view of inducing you to grant me further indulgence, for you will be obliged to wait for your money, whether you please or not, and, therefore, I do not thank you for it. I, however, take a particular delight in a little roguery; and, were you to search the whole country for a hundred miles round, you would not find a cleverer head in the execution of it."

Hurdegen, highly elated, ordered wine to be brought. The two conspirators sat in close deliberation, with closed doors, until a late hour, and then retired to rest; the one excited by hope that his infamous plans were on the point of being realized, and the other rejoicing that he had succeeded so well in duping his credulous creditor.

CHAPTER III.

"There is a state of mind, when anguish keen,
For vices past, works on the heart of man,
And wrings it sore; till rising desperation
Remonsters quite his nature; then he spurns
The ties of blood—cancels all obligation
To which his mother bound him to her kind,
And is the image of the fiend that tempts him."

THE old Gotz, who had indulged to a greater excess in his libations of the bottle than his benefactor, Hurdegen, awoke at a late hour on the following morning, although not until he had been repeatedly called and shaken by his discontented wife.

"Are you not going to your work to-day?" said Margaret, in rather a placid tone.

"The devil take the service," said Gotz, "the inn and the host also. I have money enough to keep us for some time to come. I am sick of such continual toil and drudgery."

"Gisela has been spinning from daybreak," said Margaret, "and I have already sprinkled the piece of cloth, which we have laid on the grass to bleach."

"With all my heart," said Gotz: "let Gisela spin her convent cloth, in which she may idle away her time for the remainder of her life. Matters of that kind concern me very little. Do whatever you please; I shall not trouble myself about it."

"I wish," said Margaret, "that the cloth which we are bleaching were destined for my shroud."

"Perhaps it may be the case," said Gotz, in a most indifferent manner.

"It would be a relief to those sorrows," said Margaret, "which, in this world, will never cease."

"The grave," said Gotz, "generally puts an end to all things."

"I wish your words were verified in regard to yourself," said Margaret.

"It will come soon enough," said Gotz; "but there's many a flagon of wine will be poured down this throat, I hope, before that event takes place. The world is in better favour with me, since I have met with so good a friend as Hurdegen. I know his weak points, and, rest assured, I will not miss a single opportunity of playing upon them."

"Go! may God forgive you!" said Margaret, and left the hoary sinner to his own reflections.

Gotz put on his clothes, put Hurdegen's heavy purse into his pocket, and placed himself, with folded arms, in front of his hut, for the purpose of enjoying the warmth of the mid-day sun, in the same manner as was his custom at Hall and Dettingen, when in the superabundance of his riches, and the extent of the pomp by which he was surrounded, he fancied himself a king. His neighbour, the goatherd, just then, drove his goats past him, on their way to their distant pasture, and saluted him, saying,—

"You must have slept very soundly through the past night. You should keep a better watch, or the thieves will carry off either your goats or your girl."

Gotz eyed the goatherd with a contemptuous look, but the goatherd continued,—

"During the whole night some libertine fellows, full of wine, were prowling about your hut, and the ringleader was a tall, slender chap, who lodges at the same inn in which you officiate as one of the attendants on the bathers; had you not slept so soundly, you must have heard the music and their songs, which, at the very lowest, I thought was loud enough to wake one of the seven sleepers. They knocked gently at the shutter of your window, and tried to open the door, which appears, however, so have been well fastened within—and well for you that it was so, or you would most probably have had some visitors not very agreeable to you. I was suffering under the torture of the toothache, and looked out of my hut, wishing for daybreak, that I might hasten to the town for some relief; but not liking the game at which the dissolute fellows were playing, I sprang in amongst them, and dealt my blows most steadily amongst them, right and left. At first they attempted to play the bravo, and put themselves in an attitude of defence, and he who lodges at your inn most valiantly demanded who I was, and what business I had to interfere with them. You should have seen how the young fellows scampered away when they found that the goatherd was not to be trifled with, and that he was prepared to renew the visitation of his bludgeon upon their heads. Let me, however, advise you to guard well your hut and your daughter. Another time I may not have the toothache, and may you not find your nest robbed of its turtle dove."

The goatherd drove his goats onwards, and Gotz drew his fur cap deep over his face, and muttered between his teeth,—

"There will not be any peace until the girl is out of the house; she shall go this very day to the convent at Strasburg, or whithersoever else she pleases. Must I take upon myself the office of a watchman merely on account of her pale, melancholy face? I know not what the young fellows can see in her. She is certainly what may be called pretty, and there may be something about the girl that fascinates the young fellows, but let her once become the tenant of a convent, and I warrant ye they'll soon forget her."

He determined to enter the hut, and vent his ill-humour upon his daughter by the most abusive epithets, but he was diverted from his purpose by beholding his benefactor Hurdegen crossing the stile, accompanied by an elderly, stately man, who appeared to assume a high degree of dignity and importance.

Gotz welcomed his benefactor with a friendly temper, and Hurdegen said,—

"Yesterday I was agreeably surprised by an unexpected visit, and one, my worthy

Gotz, which may be attended with considerable advantage to you. The visitor is no less a personage than my uncle, who lives at Zavelstein, near Teinach, an unmarried, childless man. He entertains the strongest affection, and I have no secrets which I would not confide to him. It is also his opinion that it is high time that you retrieved the honour of your name, and, in the meantime, he makes you the offer, until times be more prosperous with you, to give your daughter the situation of housekeeper at his castle."

"That will I do with the greatest pleasure," said the pretended uncle, assuming an air of the greatest condescension; "your daughter shall find a most comfortable home. I have not many servants, and no children who might be apt to ruffle your daughter's temper, and make the situation uncomfortable to her. I am myself quite happy and content if my affectionate nurse provides my supper for me, pours out my wine, plays in the evening with me at draughts, and keeps order and regularity in my house."

Gotz made a profound bow, and answered, in the most friendly manner,—

"You do me much honour, Herr Von Zavelstein; and, at the same time, receive my hearty congratulations at the excellent state of your health. It must now be about thirty years ago since I saw you in the retinue of the Count Ulrech, and you appear quite as strong and as vigorous now as you did then. I should have taken you to be older, but I must admit that my memory is very weak, and, since that time, I have seen so many people, that I am apt to mistake one for the other. In regard to the kind and condescending offer which you make me, I fear some difficulty will arise in carrying it into effect. It is the determination of my daughter to become a nun, and so to bid farewell for ever to the world."

"By the holy St. Augustine," exclaimed the facetious Zavelstein, shrugging his shoulders; "but I am truly sorry to hear such a report of your daughter."

"It is all nonsense about the convent," added Hurdegen, with great animation; "where do you find, in these degenerate times, a young and beautiful girl, of a noble family, ever taking the veil? Leave to the village girls the senseless task of singing psalms and muttering paternosters, and do not deprive your old age of the affectionate care and solicitude of your beloved daughter. It will be greatly to your advantage if she should one day bring a rich son-in-law into your house, by which it might be restored to its former splendour. And, in regard to my uncle, he will not neglect, in his last hours, to make an ample provision for your daughter, provided she conduct herself with kindness and fidelity towards him."

"By my oath, as a man of honour and renown," exclaimed Zavelstein, in a tone of the utmost confidence, and well adapted to allay any suspicion that might arise in the breast of Gotz; "she shall have everything that is mine upon the earth. I have not a child living; and, as to my nephew, what with his expectations from his brother, he will have quite a sufficiency to support him with credit and respectability, and he may perhaps marry some opulent heiress, and then he will not miss the property which I should have it in my power to bequeath to him."

The friendly expressions of Hurdegen and his pretended uncle gave great satisfaction to the old and credulous Gotz, who was anxious to get rid of his daughter under any circumstances which could be attended with advantage to him; and, after reflecting for a moment, he said,—

"Well, my noble gentlemen, I will call the girl, and the business shall be settled at once, for I am no friend to procrastination in matters of this kind."

"Not so hasty, old friend," said Hurdegen; "a matter of this kind should not, in my opinion, be determined upon hastily. Consider that the future happiness of your daughter depends upon it; and, as she is the principal personage in the affair, take all becoming time to consult with her on the subject. My uncle will remain in Baden until to-morrow, when he will take the first opportunity of calling upon you for your answer."

"Let it be so understood, my dear nephew," said Zavelstein; "I have no particular business to detain me at Baden, having seen you in good health, and in a fair way of recovery, as far as your wounded leg is concerned."

"In regard to myself, old Bachenstein," said Hurdegen, in a free and familiar manner, "you must allow me now to take my farewell of you. Business of importance calls me to Strasburg, to which I shall travel by Zurich, as the physician has this day prohibited me from making any further use of the Baden waters. As soon as I am perfectly recovered, I shall join the armies in the Netherlands, so that it is most probable you will never see me again."

"Never again!" ejaculated Gotz, with astonishment and chagrin, for he thought of the many golden crowns which it was his intention to transplant from the pockets of Hurdegen into his own.

Hurdegen guessed, without much difficulty, the precise thoughts that were then uppermost in Gotz's mind, and he continued in the same tone of familiarity and good-will,—

"Be not, however, afraid that I will not perform the promises that I made to you ; my worthy uncle shall be the circular of my wishes in your behalf."

"Most willingly, my dear nephew," said Zavelstein.

"So long, therefore, my worthy fellow," continued Hurdegen, "that you conduct yourself with propriety towards my uncle, you will find in him a steady and faithful friend. If you act up to his desires, you will find him always disposed to assist you in any of your undertakings. Whatever you do for him you have done for me, and whatever he does for you, it is done in my name and for my sake."

"Be it so, my good nephew," said the hypocritical villain ; "you know I have much, and, whenever I render this good man or his daughter a service, I shall do so out of pure remembrance and affection for you."

Gotz was sensibly affected by this extraordinary display of disinterested kindness, and he said,—

"You deserve, my worthy young man, to be king of the Roman Empire. Will a drop of wine, or a morsel of the costliest brand be relished by me, when I think of this miserable and painful farewell? Where is my Margaret, where is my Gisela, that they may join me in my prayers for your future health and happiness?"

He called aloud for the females, and they immediately made their appearance. Margaret exhibiting all the signs of an unsatisfied curiosity, and Gisela, with a countenance indicative of grief and melancholy.

Gotz now, with all the exaggeration of a thoughtless gabbler, repeated everything that the kind and benevolent Hurdegen had done for his impoverished house, and how much it was to be deplored, that their benefactor was about to leave them, and that Margaret and Gisela were now sent for to undertake the painful task of bidding him farewell.

With a sincere grief, Margaret tendered Hurdegen her hand ; but it was with the greatest reluctance that Gisela could be brought to offer him even a finger.

The fire of the most ardent passion was raging in the breast of Hurdegen, but his countenance assumed a hypocritical coldness, and in a solemn, admonitory tone, he said to Margaret,—

"I have no great reason to boast of either the reception with which your ill-humoured daughter has favoured me, or the farewell which she has just given me ; but nevertheless, so strong is the interest that I take in all that concerns you, that I hope you will profit by my advice, not to place the slightest confidence in the promises which that widow Irmel made to your daughter yesterday ; they are nothing less than falsehood and deceit, the allurements of a mean and dastardly seducer, Scherer von Landsap. Be upon your guard against him, as well as against Harras, for the shame which they would bring upon you, would inflict upon me the greatest pain, even if I had no feeling at all for your daughter."

"It would have been as well," said Gisela, with a scornful look, "if you had kept your advice to yourself. I know what to do with the widow Irmel, without your undertaking to instruct me."

Margaret lifted up her finger in a threatening attitude, but Gotz broke out in the most violent passion.

"Hell and thunder!" he exclaimed, "the girl cannot keep a bridle upon her tongue! it is not possible to restrain my temper with her. Oh, thou ungrateful hussey," he continued, addressing himself pointedly to Gisela, "thus to treat the kind, good-hearted gentleman, who has assisted us in our necessities, and who at the moment of his departure is desirous of giving us a proof of his kindness towards my family."

Hurdegen made a signal to the old man to hold his tongue, and the uncle said, with an air of great importance,—

"Let matters rest according to the present arrangement."

On which the two confederates shook Gotz cordially by the hand, and directed their steps towards the inn.

Lutz was already standing at the door with the horse of his master and his own already saddled. The host was standing close by, with his cap in his hand, and expressed his sincere regret on losing so good a guest.

"I shall perhaps very soon return," said Hurdegen, in a light-hearted manner ; "how can I help it, that the waters do not agree with me?"

The host made a low obeisance, and according to the custom of hosts in general, he hoped he would recommend the sign of the Bald Stag to any of his friends who might find it necessary to have recourse to the waters of Baden for the restoration of their health, or for the purpose of recreation and amusement.

"Let me, however," said Hurdegen, "recommend to your particular attention my friend, Herr von Zavelstein, who intends to prolong his stay with you for a few days; let me, however, inform you, that it is his wish to remain incognito. It is not his intention to make use of the waters, nor to enter into the amusements of the place. He is a man of considerable rank and fortune in his own country, and were it to be made public, that a man of his rank and station were in Baden, he would be so annoyed with visitors, that his residence in the place would be actually annoying to him."

The host undertook to say, that the wishes of his late guest should be most punctually fulfilled; and Hurdegen once more ascended to the apartment which he had occupied during his stay at Baden, in order that he might have a few minutes, private conversation with his confederate in a work of villany.

They were no sooner alone, than Hurdegen said,—

"The success of our plans now depends entirely upon you, old Specht, my worthy uncle of Zavelstein. My accusing conscience would not endure the penetrating look of Gisela, which to your impudence would have been an easy task. Continue to feast the imagination of the old man with promises of money, and the doating mother with the hope, that you may one day be induced to offer the girl your hand and fortune as her lawful spouse. If then in the presence of the girl you enact the part of the man of virtue and piety, and if you call in to your aid her filial love and duty, then must success be ours, and our victory must be complete. In three days I shall return clandestinely, about midnight, like a thief, and I shall bring a sufficient sum to give the last blow, if necessity should require it. If it be the will of God, you will already have carried off your prize, and I will meet you at the appointed place. Let what will happen, the girl shall be mine, and I will then think seriously of healing my body, when the wounds of my heart are cured."

"Do not destroy your health," said Specht, "by over-fatiguing yourself on your journey to Strasburg. Take your time, for you may depend upon me. I will do everything which the necessity of the case may require. I will wheedle the girl from her father's house, and then he may inquire for her at Zavelstein. It will be the business of your uncle to send him about his business with a flea in his ear. Before, however, you depart, leave me a little money. You know that I must counterfeit the man of fortune, and yet my pocket is as empty as a charity box in the nave of a cathedral."

"Your pocket," said Hurdegen, partly in a jocose and partly in a serious tone, "is like a fathomless vortex, it draws as much as it can within its circle, but never restores any portion of it again."

He, however, shared the contents of his purse with his worthy confederate, and mounting his horse he took the road to Strasburg.

Whilst the snorting horse carried along his rider full of hope and expectation that his villanous plans were on the eve of realization, his prospects were not of the most flattering kind in the hut of his intended victim.

In the little household there was nothing but strife and contention. Gotz had lost not a moment in imparting to his wife and daughter the generous and disinterested offer that the pretended Herr von Zavelstein had made him; and Margaret was delighted with the fresh prospect of future fortune and happiness. It was the opinion of the poor mother, that if her daughter became a nun in the Convent of the White Sisters, it was tantamount to laying her in her grave. It was her wish that her child should enjoy a more cheerful and pleasant life, and such a life her residence at Zavelstein appeared to promise her. But the obstinacy of Gisela was the rock on which the exhortations of her father and the entreaties of her mother were wrecked.

"Anything, any place in the world," exclaimed Gisela, with the utmost emotion of anxiety and displeasure, "anywhere but at Zavelstein. My whole soul hangs upon a convent, yet will I relinquish it, if it will give you pleasure to see my future life embittered by accepting the post of a menial servant girl; but never, never will I go to Zavelstein."

"Thunder and fury!" exclaimed Gotz. "Why not, then, to Zavelstein? In the name of all the saints, why not there, where you have such a comfortable and respectable home provided for you?"

"You know not," said Gisela, wringing her hands, "the awful feelings with which I am oppressed—you know not what a chilling shudder creeps over me, when I think of the individual from whom all this misery proceeds. I have a dread—I feel an abhorrence for all men; but indescribably horrible are my feelings when I think of the Herr von

Sperbeneck. Remember well the words which I am now about to utter—his pret charity will be our ruin; his money will bring a curse upon us. His bounty, in the unfortunate hands of my father, who dissipated our inheritance—who squandered our patrimonial estates—oh! I shudder at the thought of it; I will not participate in the ill-gotten treasure. This money shall not be applied to my equipment; I will not be indebted to Hurdegen for my future support. Did I not behold a cool spirit lurking in the eye of the old uncle? What business have I in a house of wickedness and dishonour? I will rather beg the place of a scullion in the hospital at Lichtenthal. I would rather be driven from the house, with my father's curse over me, like my poor brother. I would beg my scanty morsel of bread on the highway in distant lands; I would rather follow a being wholly unknown to me, than the promises or directions of those men who fancy they have a right over us, because they have, in the bloated pride of their charity, bestowed upon us a few pieces of their accursed silver."

"Oh, thou holy Mother of Grace!" exclaimed Margaret, crossing herself, "do thou defend us from such ungrateful doings. How audaciously and presumptuously the girl speaks. This is thy work, thou wicked and sinning father! Misery has deranged the intellect of our Gisela."

"The fiend of pride has done it all," said Gotz. "It is the itching after monks, and ave-marias, and paternosters, that has driven the girl mad! To bawl out in the choir her kyrie eleison—to nibble at the toes of the saints—to make little Jesuses of wax—to banquet in the refectory—to lazy away the time from morning to night—to allow her hands to be submissively kissed by her father and mother, and perhaps to be instructed in certain things by the monk in the confessional. These are the things for which the wayward girl longs for. With this view, will she dash our hopes of future comfort to the ground; to satisfy this depravity of taste, will she reject the handsome offer which has been made to her of a settlement for life. Shame upon the profligate girl! Oh, that in this moment some angel, or some spirit of hell—I care not which—would appear amongst us, and carry thee through the air above, or through the earth below, that we might be rid of thee for all eternity!"

Gotz had scarcely finished speaking, than the door opened; then a lean, haggard countenance, on a scraggy neck, projected itself into the hut. Gisela gave a loud scream; and, overcome with fear, concealed her face with her hands. Margaret crossed herself, and, by the motion of her lips, it could easily be told that she was muttering a paternoster. Gotz, however, although equally struck with astonishment, still possessed sufficient presence of mind to measure the form from head to foot, which now stood erect in the middle of the hut. It was a lean, skeleton figure; his legs, in size, resembled those of a stork. A brown jacket, patched and threadbare, covered his body, around which was clasped a leathern girdle, to which appended a knife and an empty money-bag. A close cap, edged with fur, fell so deeply over his forehead, that not a hair was to be seen. Straggling eyebrows, and a greyish, pointed beard decorated his face, which bore the impress of a naturally deep and glossy cunning. The man carried in his hands a broad-brimmed hat, which had evidently weathered the storms of many a winter, and over his arm he carried a cloak, covered with dust and dirt. The impression which the form of this uncouth and grotesque creature made upon all present was certainly not the most favourable; but, in the mind of Gotz, a singular confusion of agreeable reminiscences arose, as he examined the stranger more minutely, and at last recognized, not only in his voice, but in his features, his former steward of the kitchen and cellar, Saurbein.

"The blessing of God be with you in this house!" said the new guest, with the most friendly voice that he could assume.

"May I be stricken with St. Vitus's dance!" exclaimed Gotz, "if I do not recognize in you Hans Saurbein."

"Yes," exclaimed Gisela; "that is our late steward, Hans;" for she remembered well the time when, as a child, she sat on the knee of Saurbein, and received from his hand many a dainty bit from the pantry.

"You are most welcome, Saurbein," said Margaret, who remembered with a melancholy joy the many humorous stories which the steward was wont to relate whilst in her service.

Gisela, without being solicited, brought a stool for the welcome guest; and Margaret made a hundred apologies that she had no dainty victuals to set before him, but that to whatever she had in her cupboard he was most welcome.

"It was not formerly so with us," said Margaret; "and that, Saurbein, you know well. Our pantry was always full of good things; in fact, it was often a matter of wonder to me, how we contrived to consume them all."

"It was not the mouths within," said Saurbein, "so much as the mouths without. The beggar never went without his satchel full from your door, and, in assisting the needy, I knew that I was but acting up to your own generous and charitable dispositions. Your name was spread far and wide for deeds of charity, and I, as the instrument of the administration of that charity, have reason to be proud of those days; for, if it be true

See page 29.

what the monks say, that our works follow us, I shall have a large balance of good deeds in my favour, when the account of my life comes to be summed up at the great assizes."

During this hypocritical speech of the designing rogue, Gotz had been sitting in mute

No. 4.

reflection; for he had not entirely forgotten the character which his late steward bore during the term of his service, which was generally considered to be an odd mixture of cunning, duplicity, selfishness, and hypocrisy. Gotz, therefore, took the first opportunity that the garrulity of his wife would allow him, to request from Saurbein some information as to the motive of his unexpected visit, and by what means he had succeeded in discovering their retreat. Saurbein put on a most sanctimonious and demure look, and answered,—

"What does the faithful dog do when he follows the steps and course of his master? However late he may come upon the scent, he still finds it at last; and a faithful servant is worthy of being compared with that not less faithful dog. Thus I directed my nose to the ground, but it was long before I obtained the scent that I required; at last chance led me to it, and I have followed it to this hut, where, Heaven be praised, I have found you alive and in health, and which is by far the more agreeable to me, as I am the bearer of good intelligence to you."

Gotz bestowed upon his old servant a nod of his approbation; and Margaret, whose curiosity was strongly excited to ascertain the nature of the good intelligence of which Saurbein professed to be the bearer, interfered with her importunity, saying, in an eager tone of voice,—

"Now—now, Saurbein, let us hear all that you have to tell us. It is so seldom that news of a favourable nature ever enters this miserable hovel, that when it does come, it is trebly welcome to us."

Saurbein prepared himself in the most formal manner for the communication which he had to make; he adjusted his dress with all the precision of a parson who puts his canonicals into their proper place and order before he begins to expound the meaning of a passage, which has perhaps no meaning at all, but such as he is pleased to bestow upon it. He stood erectly before his former master, whilst Margaret placed her two elbows on the table, and, with almost breathless anxiety, awaited the result of Saurbein's intelligence. Gisela sat on a stool close to her mother, and she seemed as if she were thinking not of the things of this world, but of those of another one. At last Saurbein, having placed himself in a becoming position, said,—

"In the first place, let me offer you the most kind, sincere, and hearty congratulations from your worthy and pious step-sister, Adelheid, at Ulm."

"How! what!" ejaculated Gotz; "a congratulation from Adelheid; had you informed me that you had brought a bull from the pope, appointing me a cardinal, my astonishment could not be greater."

Margaret had scarcely any time to express her surprise, for she fell almost senseless in the arms of Gisela. Embarrassed and full of doubt, irresolute and fearful, Saurbein looked upon the pale form of Margaret, and it struck him at the moment that, as the villanous plan which he had in view might end in a tragical manner, it would be more advisable in him to take his departure, than await the issue of his base and villanous project. In the meantime, however, Margaret slowly recovered, and taking hold of the hand of the false and designing Saurbein, she stammered,—

"Oh! blessed be thou, and I praise thee with my whole soul, thou angel in human form! Yes; my prayers have been heard, my hopes have at last borne the much-wished-for fruit. I have had a presentiment that matters would take the present turn, and that our misery was not to be of long duration."

"Mother!" exclaimed Gisela, "what are you thinking about? Are you dreaming or waking, that you talk such incoherent words?"

"Do talk rationally," said Gotz to his wife, "and let not Saurbein depart hence with the impression that his late mistress has become a fool."

Margaret appeared to rouse herself from her temporary stupefaction, and turning to her husband, said,—

"I will now confess all that I did a few weeks ago, when our wants were so great that we knew not where to obtain a morsel of bread. One day when I was in the market-place, at Baden, I met Letebfritz, the grocer, who informed me that he was about to travel to Ulm, on matters of business, and then, on a sudden, I remembered my aged and austere aunt, Adelheid, who so long and so often has rejected our petitions for relief with contempt and scorn. Notwithstanding, however, these repeated refusals, I determined to make another attempt, and I, therefore, selected Letebfritz to be the bearer of a note from me to our relative, and which was written by the worthy father confessor, Henry, and to which I affixed my cross; but, since that time, the reverend man has been committed to his grave, and my secret was buried with him; but the germs have sprouted and borne good fruit, and an early crop, as I could not entertain the hope of receiving an answer until the return of Letebfritz. And do you not, my worthy Hans, bring me an early answer to my request, and one that far exceeds our expectations?"

Saurbein gave an affirmative answer by a significant nod of the head, and taking advantage of the favourable turn which this unexpected statement of the foolish woman gave him, like a skilful general, who considers the battle as lost, but who suddenly obtains the victory by an unexpected blunder of the enemy, he said,—

"Your conjecture, my worthy lady, is perfectly true. I come in the name of your worthy relative, the Lady von Diessenhaven, and am the bearer of help and reconciliation to you. Time has at last mitigated her rancour, and, in the loneliness of age, in the solitude of her widowhood, she looks around for some congenial hearts, by the kindness of which her passage to the grave may be made smooth to her; and where could she look for those hearts with greater chance of success than amongst her relatives? As a pledge of her friendly intention, she sends you, my Lady of Bachenstein, this valuable wreath of roses; and to you, my Herr von Bachenstein, she sends this golden chain; and to her beautiful cousin there she sends the most pressing invitation to hasten to her to Ulm, there to close her eyes, and to inherit her property. She, however, requests that the utmost expedition may be used in the fulfilment of her wishes, as she is very weak and tottering, and, consequently, she cannot depend upon her life for a single day. Therefore, she commissioned me, who hold a situation in her house, to hasten to Baden, and to bring her hence to her, if you will grant her permission to accompany me. I have a vehicle in readiness at the sign of the Goat; and, if we depart to-day, we shall to-morrow fall in with a retinue of merchants, at Pfortzheim, who make that town one of their resting-places, and then we shall be able to travel to Ulm under safe conduct. If, therefore, your daughter consent, and you be willing, and if you place the fullest confidence in your old servant, your present wretchedness will be quickly turned into joy; and I have further to inform you, that I am commissioned to invite you, on the feast of St. Michael, to visit your daughter in the city of Ulm, and that you shall not return without some substantial proofs of the bounty and kindness of your worthy relative. It is the wish of the worthy lady, by the sight of her beautiful and amiable niece, to be fully reconciled to her parents before a personal interview takes place."

If, according to the dictum of the astrologers, the position of the stars be favourable, the rogue has often greater luck than the man of sense and virtue, and the man without principle who boldly and recklessly dashes into the commission of an act, setting all honour and honesty at defiance, will often arrive sooner at the goal than the prudent and considerate man, who stands hesitating on the threshold of an action, and fearing that, in the execution of it, he might commit an offence against the principles of morality and virtue.

There were three consenting parties to the proposition of Saurbein; in the first place there was Gotz, to whom his daughter was a heavy and insupportable burden in the house; Margaret, who, in the invitation of her relative, saw her most sanguine expectations realised; and Gisela, who was willing to accede to any proposition, so that she might escape being sent to Zavelstein; and thus, although the reasons for giving their consent were all different, yet not the slightest hesitation was observed in bestowing the most implicit confidence in the plausible representations of the villain. They regarded his appearance as an incontrovertible sign of the interference of Providence in their behalf; they looked upon the fidelity and integrity of their old servant, and, consequently, their consent was given without the slightest murmur or hesitation. An hour had scarcely elapsed before the scanty wardrobe of Gisela was packed up; the blessing of the father did not detain her long, and the mother, who had undertaken to accompany her daughter to the vehicle, postponed the long litany of her pious counsel and admonitions to beguile the time as they travelled on to the inn where the vehicle was in waiting. Saurbein, who was all zeal and officiousness, promised, in the most solemn manner, to take all possible care of Gisela, and was so pleasant and accommodating as to squeeze out a few tears as the last moment of parting arrived, and the unsuspecting victim of a most diabolical plan was surrendered into his hands with all the assurance that the happiness of her future life was established.

CHAPTER IV.

" Yet ere thou rashly urge my rage too far,
I warn thee to take heed. I am a man,
And have the frailties common to man's nature;
The fiery seeds of wrath are in my temper,
And may be blown up to so fierce a blaze
As wisdom cannot rule."

GOTZ was left alone in the hut, with a light heart and a smiling countenance, rubbing his hands with all the satisfaction of a man who had just experienced a favourable turn of fortune; and he was determined, on this evening, to enjoy himself with an extra glass of genuine Hockheimer. He therefore beckoned to him a shepherd's boy, who was playing at a short distance from his hut, and sent him to the nearest house where a bottle of the sparkling beverage could be obtained; and it was no sooner in his possession than he seated himself at the table to recreate himself with the glorious prospect which the future held out to him, and to devise those schemes by the accomplishment of which he would be enabled to appear again in the world in all his former splendour and importance. He was highly delighted with the source of prosperity and affluence which had so unexpectedly opened itself for him at Ulm, and which promised him for the future a rich and permanent harvest. Still, however, it would have been highly gratifying to him if he could have extracted a few more golden crowns from the purse of Hurdegen; but he found himself not a little embarrassed when he thought of the Herr von Zavelstein, to whom he had in some measure promised his daughter. The worthy and honourable gentleman had promised to call upon him for his answer relative to the acceptance of the situation which he had offered to Gisela, and, as he had no doubt that he would keep his word, he began seriously to reflect in what manner he could extricate himself from the dilemma into which he was thrown by the departure of Gisela from his house. He had, however, scarcely entered upon the consideration of his embarrassment, than a violent knocking was heard at the door, and, on Gotz opening it, the Herr von-Zavelstein presented himself.

If Gotz, who had just finished his second bottle, were verging nearly to a state of intoxication, the pretended uncle was not much better. His snuffling nose and his ruddy cheeks betrayed that he had been performing his oblations to the merry god, and he was just in that situation, half drunk, half sober, that does not render a man exactly unconscious of his actions, but nevertheless exposes him to the wicked designs of any one who might be disposed to take advantage of his temporary weakness. After the usual salutations had passed, the stately gentleman turned himself round and round in the room, and his inquisitive eye appeared to examine every part of it.

" Halloa!" he exclaimed, " where is your sweet and beautiful daughter? Is she gone out to sing her love-sick ditty to the moon?

" ' She's like a rose that blooms in May,
And throws its fragrance round;
With her o'er all the earth I'd stray,
In love's enchantment bound.'

The wine of the worthy host at Baden has made me poetical. But, tell me, where is your daughter? The brightest jewel is wanting in your crown, when your daughter is not at home."

" Oh!" said Gotz to himself, " is it so situated with the old gentleman? I must extort something more from him, before I fully declare my mind to him."

The cunning Specht continued,—

" Holloa! thou old broken-down knight, how is it with thee and thy daughter? When shall I carry her to my dovecote?"

Gotz swallowed hastily a glass of wine to conceal the wrath which the repulsive familiarity of the counterfeit Zavelstein excited in him, and he answered with a great degree of cunning and duplicity,—

" Matters must take their own course. Rome was not built in one day; and with God all things are possible. Girls are by nature changeable—the true symbol of the weathercock, pointing one way to-day, and another to-morrow. Stop until Gisela herself declares what her wishes and intentions are."

"Understand me well, Gotz," said Specht; "I take not my departure hence until I have obtained her consent from her own beautiful lips. The girl pleases me well, and if you will allow me, I will drink a glass to her health."

Gotz filled the glass of his artful and unprincipled guest, and said,—

"May you flourish like the vine that gave us the generous wine, and may you remain my friend as truly and faithfully as your nephew has been, of whose assistance I now stand most particularly in need, as a clamorous creditor torments me night and day."

"You are like a sieve," said Specht, "that holds not a single drop, and were it of the heaviest gold. You cast a longing eye to the purse which hangs by my girdle, like the sacrilegious thief after the holy tabernacle. For thy daughter's sake I would most willingly comply with your avaricious disposition. Nevertheless, as you are a true-born knight, it must vex you much, and you must feel yourself degraded in your own estimation, to be always receiving gifts. The bestowing of a gift, if it be too long continued, tires out the giver as well as the receiver. Place, however, some confidence in my generosity and riches. Let us play at dice until Gisela's return. We shall thereby cheat old Time of his leaden pace, and we can at intervals quicken our flagging spirits by our visitations to the bottle. You may be scarcely said to run any risk; for, by my honour, I swear that I am one of the most unlucky gamblers in the whole Roman empire."

With what secret delight did Gotz listen to these words! How his fingers itched to have again the handling of the dice, to which they had been long a stranger. Now did he think, with a smile, of the many nights which he had passed at the gaming-table, with alternate success and loss, but always with renewed joy and licentiousness. The golden crowns appeared actually to dance in his pocket, and Specht had already drawn from his the fateful cubes, spread his glittering coins on the table, and, by way of proving the truth of his ill-luck, made a throw with the dice, and threw the lowest triplet.

"Ah! by the holy Benedict!" exclaimed Gotz, "but I can throw better than that," and with an impatient hand he unloosened the strings of his purse.

One throw led to another, and the game was soon at its height.

"Let me see," said Specht jokingly, "if your money be good," and threw a main.

Gotz threw also, and won, and Specht laid a fresh stake on the table. Gotz covered it with his stakes, and, before they threw, the two gamblers swallowed a bumper of wine. They played for some time with alternate success, until, on a sudden, fortune appeared wholly to have forsaken Gotz; he lost at every throw; and, in less than half a hour, Gotz had not a single crown-piece in his purse. Almost frantic, he emptied the bottle into his glass, and made apparently one swallow of it. Specht, on the contrary, flushed with his success, was in the highest possible state of excitement; although, at the same time, he was far more sober and collected than his opponent.

"A plague upon the money," he said; "I value it not—let us play again!"

Gotz, with distorted face, pointed to his empty purse that lay upon the ground.

"Never mind that," said Specht; "I will lend you some money on your word as a knight."

"Be it so," said Gotz; "lend me twenty crowns."

Specht counted out the money, and in three throws he had won it all back again.

In the madness of the reckless spirit of the gambler, Gotz continued to play, until, as the last desperate act, he staked his own person, and those of his wife and child, against a hundred crowns. He lost; and he and his family were now, according to the laws of the country, the property and vassals of the winner.

In speechless horror Gotz sat with his head resting upon his hands, and wished that sudden death would come upon him. He might have betrayed his best friend; he might have broken his most solemn vow, and the injury might have been repaired; but the consequences arising from the damnable passion of gambling appeared to him irrecoverable. On Specht observing him sitting almost in a state of insensibility, a prey to the bitterest anguish, he clapped him heartily on the shoulders, and said—

"Rouse yourself, Gotz; you have not fallen into the hands of a heathen; you shall receive the best of treatment from me; and if your daughter answers our expectations, why, it is not improbable that, like a prisoner of war, I may give you your liberty in return."

The words of Specht spoke daggers to the heart of Gotz, and he stammered,—

"Oh! noble sir—you know not ——"

The voice of Margaret was now heard without, and immediately afterwards she made her appearance, and said, without immediately paying any attention to the fictitious Herr von Zavelstein:—

" Our girl is now under the protection of all the angels! The vehicle has already gone before, towards the mountains, and my feeble feet would not allow me to walk so far. I bade my dear child farewell at the gates, and repaired to the cathedral, where I have been praying ever since for the health and happiness of my Gisela. You will not, I am sure, be angry with us," continued Margaret, addressing herself to Herr Von Zavelstein; "for, deeply as we are indebted to you for the proud offer which you made us, of taking her into your service, yet no doubt whatever can be entertained that she will feel herself happy under the roof of her aunt."

" Thunder and lightning!" exclaimed Specht, who appeared as astonished as if he had just fallen from the clouds. " What is this I hear? What kind of joke is this that you are playing with me? Is Gisela no longer an inmate of the house? Oh, thou consummate rogue," he continued, turning to Gotz, "thou shalt suffer for this scandalous imposition."

Gotz very discreetly held his tongue, for which very wise action he was actuated by two motives; first, from a dread of his exposing his late conduct to his wife, and, secondly, from a fear of offending his new lord and master, who had obtained a sovereignty over his person, and who, in consequence, might condemn him to the most menial and degrading offices.

To Margaret, however, the conduct of the pretended uncle was all an enigma, and she said—

" Why should you express yourself so harshly against us? Can you censure a father who to-day, for the first time, has not stood in the way of his daughter's welfare? We are certainly under obligations to you, sir, but I would not have you forget, that we are, like you, born of noble blood!"

" What is the old woman gabbling about?" exclaimed Specht. " By the great toe of St. Francis I swear that you shall pay dearly for this trick which you have practised upon me. You belong to me: every inch of your skin—every hair of your head is mine; you are my property—father, mother, and daughter; and if you do not place her immediately in my hands, as my lawful property, I will ring such a peal about your ears, that you shall be deaf hereafter for the remainder of your lives. Why do you stare at me so, old woman? Do you think I am mad, or that I know not what I am talking about? ask your husband, there, the foolish dolt, whether he has not gambled away himself, you, and your daughter—his nobility and his armorial bearings; in fact, ask him if he be not my vassal—you, and your daughter; and you shall deliver her into my hands, or I'll crack your bones on the rack!"

" Gambled us away!" exclaimed Margaret, with an air of unbelief, but still in the utmost excitement of anger: " I will not believe it; I would give my husband credit for the commission of the most outrageous actions; but to risk his family, his wife, his daughter, his nobility, on the hazard of a die—to that extent, I never could have suspected that he would have carried his iniquity. Speak, thou wretch! is it true?"

Gotz gave a significant shrug with his shoulders, which was confirmatory of the statement of the fortunate winner.

Margaret could not support herself any longer, and, uttering a piercing shriek, fell upon the ground. Her screams thrilled through the ears of all present, when the villanous Specht, silently rejoicing at the power which he had now obtained over the person of Gisela, took up his mantle, and throwing it over him, said, in an authoritative tone,—

" Let me hear no more of this whimpering and howling, but listen to what I have to say to you: see that your daughter be brought home again, to-morrow at the latest; then I will take you with me to my castle; but if you do not fulfil my commands, I will bring the magistrate with me, and you shall be committed to prison, until you conform to my demands. I look upon you as a set of vile, unprincipled impostors; but, remember, you are mine!—and my treatment of you will depend upon your conduct. To-morrow you will see me again."

He rushed out of the hut, leaving the tenants of it in a state of horror and despair; and, foaming with rage, he retraced his steps to the town. The charms of Gisela had made a deep impression upon him; and, although he pretended to be the advocate of Hurdegen, he was, in secret, plotting those schemes by which he would obtain possession of the girl, and his extraordinary good fortune at dice had brought him nearer to the consummation of his wishes than his fondest expectations could have anticipated. Wine and resentment made his blood rush impetuously through his veins, and, as he considered his claims upon the parents of Gisela to be inalienable, he formed the most extraordinary projects, which he was determined to carry into execution, provided they did not comply with his demands in producing Gisela on the morrow. His entrance into the inn, however, made a most extraordinary change in his conduct; for on crossing the court to proceed to his apartment, to his most unaccountable surprise he encountered Hurdegen, whom he believed to be in Strasburg.

"How! what!" exclaimed Specht. "Can I credit my eyes? is it you in reality, Herr Hurdegen von Sperbeneck?"

"It is either myself or my ghost," answered Hurdegen, good humouredly. "I went no further than Strasburg, where the provost of the place advanced me what I required, and, therefore, I hastened my return. But tell me, how fares it with Gisela? Is everything in proper order? Is the beautiful treasure in our possession?—and, if so, when will it be delivered to you?"

The impatience of the lover had the immediate effect of bringing Specht to a state of sobriety, and in his head gave birth to the most glorious prospects. He therefore resolved to outwit a rogue by acting like one himself; and from the disaster of his merciful creditor, Hurdegen, in having lost Gisela, to establish the foundation of his own happiness. He therefore placed himself in an attitude of defiance before Hurdegen, framed his mouth to a scornful laugh, stroked down his beard with the utmost complacency, and said,—

"Most certainly is everything in order; but, perhaps, not exactly so as you would wish it. I have seriously reflected upon the business, and considered it under every possible shape, and I have further considered that it is not right that you should have everything in this world. I have a desire to possess something also, and Gisela is the very jewel that pleases me."

"Are you drunk, deranged, or possessed with the devil?" exclaimed Hurdegen.

"Neither the one nor the other," exclaimed Specht, with the greatest coolness. "Good luck and the dice have bestowed upon me their blessings. The old dotard Gotz staked his Gisela against my twenty crowns, and I won her, with himself and his wife into the bargain. Did you ever win such a treasure, Herr Hurdegen, with three spotted cubes of ivory?"

A volley of curses issued from the mouth of Hurdegen, but Specht laughed at his anger, and declared his intention at break of day to carry Gisela away.

"Dastardly wretch!" exclaimed Hurdegen, overcome with passion. "You dare not do it; you cannot do it."

"Do you mean on account of the debt I owe you?" said Specht, with a scornful look. "One word only, and Landsap will advance me whatever money I require, if I only consent that the girl shall sleep with him for one night. She is mine; I have won her, and I can do what I please with her."

"By the holy sacrament!" exclaimed Hurdegen, "but I'll not endure such damnable insult. Have a care of thyself, thou fiend of hell. I will cite thee before the margrave; he will neither sanction nor admit such devilish work. A nobleman cannot transfer himself and his family to another; you cannot traffic with a knight as you would with a common peasant."

"Indeed!" exclaimed Specht, with a contemptuous look. "Is he the first in Germany who has gambled away his body? And what is his nobility? Did he not break his escutcheon, when he took to the rubbing sponge and followed the ignoemployment of a common servant at the baths? But do just as you please; do not let me pretend to interfere with you. Lodge your complaint, if you think you can derive any benefit from it. In the meantime, I will throw the whole brood of the Bachensteins into prison; and I do pray you, have the goodness to inform the margrave of the mean and scandalous trick, which, taking advantage of my poverty and a few florins that I owe you, you hired me to commit."

This last keen insinuation of Spech, was a home stroke upon Hurdegen. He grew suddenly pale, gnashed his teeth, and stamped the ground madly with his feet; but, with a bold and resolute hand, he caught hold of Specht, and prevented him leaving the room.

"Stop," he said, scornfully, but not without some complacency; "thou art a malicious scoundrel, a profligate sinner, who, for the sake of a little money, wouldst destroy thy own father; but so it is with the world. Fortune favours the villain to the injury of the honest man. I cannot consent that Gisela shall fall into your hands. Tell me the price which you require for her. Speak to me without prevarication, or, should it cost me my life, I will stab thee to the heart with my sword."

With a ghastly smile, Specht repulsed Hurdegen from him, and said,—

"You would not surely assassinate me, when we can settle our matters in a more amicable way. Do you think that I am more friendly inclined towards Landsap than towards yourself?"

"Come," said Hurdegen, with the greatest impatience; "I want no circumlocution. Come to the point at once. What are your terms?"

"I know," said Specht, "what Landsap would give for the girl. You would not surely think of giving me less; and especially when I have it in my power to transfer her over to you as your lawful property."

"I am not a dealer in human flesh," said Hurdegen; "but," and he pointed to his sword, "you remember what I said. Declare your terms, or this night your soul shall be in hell."

"In the first place," said Specht, "you must cancel my note-of-hand for the sum you lent me."

"Well," said Hurdegen; "and secondly?"

"Why, secondly," said Specht, in a decisive tone, "it is necessary that I should take my departure from the place with all possible expedition. You know that, to further your designs, I have assumed a name and character that do not belong to me, and as you were the instigator of that scheme, I dare say, for the sake of your reputation, you would not wish to have it known—and known it must be, if I remain in the town; but how am I to get out of it, without the means of defraying my expenses?"

"Have done with this useless palaver," said Hurdegen; "come to the point at once. What further do you require of me than the cancelling of the note-of-hand?"

"I shall require," said Specht, "a sufficient sum to defray my travelling expenses— say one hundred florins,—for which I will resign to you all my claims on Bachenstein and his daughter. I do not think your own brother could behave with greater liberality to you."

"Contemptible wretch!" said Hurdegen, biting his lips with vexation; and, taking a small memorandum-book from his pocket, he took from it the written acknowledgment of Specht, and tearing it into pieces, he threw them in his face; and then having counted out the required sum, he handed it over to him, with his peremptory commands that he should instantly leave the city. Specht declared himself most willing to obey the command, and crept out of the room highly pleased with the booty he had obtained.

Hurdegen now called, in an impatient tone, upon his servant to procure a torch, and to accompany him a small distance from the town. Lutz recommended his master to be careful of his foot, which had become considerably inflamed by his journey, and he ventured to propose to him to defer his intended excursion until to-morrow. Hurdegen was, however, resolute, and would not hear of the slightest delay, for he considered every moment now to be thrown away which he did not employ in obtaining Gisela her freedom. He, therefore, insisted upon Lutz complying immediately with his orders, and in a very short time the master and servant had gained the outskirts of the town, and with all possible haste directed their course to the abode of Bachenstein. It was not long before they came in sight of the three birch trees which overshadowed the humble dwelling of Gotz, and on approaching it a faint light was seen twinkling from the window, and a female voice was heard uttering the most bitter complaints, between which a rough surly voice called upon the mourner to desist from her croaking and her grumbling.

Hurdegen knocked loudly at the door, and the light of his torch illumined the whole of the miserable apartment.

"Heaven preserve us!" exclaimed Margaret, "it is the officer from the margrave;" and Gotz and his wife shrank from Hurdegen as if he were a ghost. He, however, paid little attention to their alarm, but called out, in a loud voice,—

"I bring you your liberation from the vassalage of him who gained possession of your persons by treachery and fraud. Be not any longer dispirited, and drive away all grief and melancholy from you. I hope, Gotz, it will be the last imprudence that you will commit, and may I always succeed in averting the threatened danger from your heads."

"What angel is it," asked Margaret, sobbing, "that conducts you back to us?"

"Has your intercession pacified your cruel uncle?" asked Gotz, who had slowly recovered from his confusion.

"Talk not to me about my uncle," said Hurdegen, with an emotion of shame. "A rogue has deceived both you and me; he has, however, transferred all his rights and claims to me, and I most willingly relinquish them. You are free, for the sake of your misfortunes; but, more properly speaking, for the sake of Gisela."

With these words, he cast his eyes round the apartment, released himself from the warm and grateful congratulations of the aged couple, and inquired,—

"Where is your beautiful daughter? Call her, that I may feast my eyes with the view of her charms. I will no longer conceal it from you, that I love her; but that I have to repair a great outrage committed against her. Shame and repentance have completely transformed my heart; I fully justify her on the anger which she exhibited towards me, and the consequent contempt with which she treated me. Hitherto, I have only sought her for the gratification of my passions; but now I ask her of you as my lawful wife, to rescue her from the infamous snares which are laid for her, and thereby reconcile her with myself."

See page 35.

Gotz and his wife scarcely comprehended a single word that Hurdegen uttered, so unexpected did this projected courtship come upon them. Margaret at last exclaimed, in an anxious tone,—

"Oh, that Gisela were here!"

"Heavens!" exclaimed Hurdegen, with dismay. "What am I to understand by those words?"

Before Margaret could give an answer to the anxious question of Hurdegen, a fourth person appeared in the apartment, in whom Margaret recognized the tradesman, Eitelfritz, who, with his package on his back, stood at the entrance as if indisposed to enter; he, however said, in a rough, unmannerly voice,—

"I am just arrived from Ettlengen, and must reach Steinbach before midnight; because, to-morrow it is there market-day. As I found your door open, and heard voices within, Dame Margaret, I thought I would just call to let you know that your letter to the lady at Ulm arrived too late. She was buried on the Friday before the Fast of St. John. I now return you the letter unopened. Farewell; for I have not a moment to lose."

The cool and apathetic messenger took his departure, but the surprise, the alarm, and the despair, which he had brought into the hut by his afflicting intelligence, now exceeded all bounds. From the curses of the father, from the piteous lamentations of the mother, Hurdegen acquired the knowledge of the real situation of affairs, as well as the manner in which he had lost Gisela, and the deplorable victory, which the most scandalous deception had obtained. He rose from his seat like a lunatic, when the aged couple threw themselves at his feet, imploring him, in most pathetic terms, to restore to them their lost child.

"If the impostor has carried her over across the mountains," said Hurdegen, "I will follow him to his haunts; but I will previously chastise the scoundrel from whom this scandalous imposition has originated. I know him well, and most bitter indeed shall be his punishment."

Hurdegen rushed out of the hut with the quickness of the lightning's flash, so that his faithful servant, Lutz, could scarcely keep up with him. On his arrival at the inn, the host, who was half asleep, not being willing to retire to bed until the return of his guest, was astonished at the wild and incoherent conduct which his guest displayed, and implored him to mitigate his rage, soliciting to know if his interference would be of any use to remedy any injury or affront that he might have received.

"I want the man," said Hurdegen, "who occupied my apartment; the villain who has deceived me as no man was ever yet deceived."

"Do you mean Herr von Zavelstein?" asked the host.

"The same," exclaimed Hurdegen, "or him who gave himself out for such. The devil will have him one day, but I should like to give him a foretaste, whilst he is in this world, of what he has to expect in the next."

"Ah!" said the host, with a shrug of his shoulders, "he left the house and the city about half-an-hour ago."

Hurdegen struck his forehead with his clenched fist, and exclaimed, "May he be doubly cursed; but I have myself to blame that the villain has escaped my vengeance. In leaving the city he has but fulfilled the orders which I imposed upon him. Know you the route which he has taken?"

"It is a question I cannot answer," said the host. "It would not become me to inquire of my guests whither they are going."

"I believe not," said Hurdegen, sarcastically; "for were you to inquire, I believe some of them could not, or would not tell you." Turning abruptly from the host, he called loudly for his servant, and he ordered him without the least delay to saddle the horses.

"At this hour of the night?" said the host.

"Make no inquiries," said Hurdegen, "and then you will have no falsehoods told you. Before I go, however, I have an account to settle with one of your guests," and he hastened immediately to the apartment occupied by Landsap, at the door of which he knocked as if he would break the panels of it.

The unsuspicious tenant very deliberately opened the door, and Hurdegen rushed into the room like a maniac, to the evident alarm of the drowsy tenant, who at first believed that he was attacked by some robber or assassin.

"Where is Gisela?" cried out Hurdegen, in a most passionate tone. "This very moment is your last in this world, unless you confess the truth."

"How do I know," answered Landsap, "anything about Gisela? Are you again seized with a fit of madness? Leave the room, and do not disturb me with any of your mad tricks. Look for Gisela yourself; I am not her keeper; and trouble me not about your girls. I got into a squabble about one yesterday, when I was so soundly thrashed that I was obliged to be put to bed."

"May thy lies suffocate thee!" said Hurdegen. "You are one of the accomplices in the carrying off of Gisela; speak, then, perjured dog, or my sword shall make thee; whither have thy minions carried Gisela?"

"To the devil for what I know," said Landsap; "and if so, depend upon it I do not intend to follow them, even if she were a hundred times more beautiful than she is. I leave such feats as these to be accomplished by yourself."

"Do you intend to turn me into ridicule?" said Hurdegen, drawing his sword, and aiming a blow at him; "take that for your senseless ribaldry."

Landsap parried the blow with his arm, but a severe wound was inflicted on his elbow. The wounded man cried aloud for help; the guests and the domestics were all put into commotion. From all quarters were heard the cries, "Murder! seize the villain! Drag him before the magistrate! Let not the laws of the baths be broken! Let the villain suffer with his head."

Alarmed at the uproar, and forcibly expelled by the host, Hurdegen fortunately reached the court where Lutz was in waiting with the horses, and having quickly mounted one of them, and rushed towards the gates, the old decrepid watchman stretched forth his hand to take hold of the bridle of the horse, so that he might not be deprived of his toll; but, with his clinched fist, Hurdegen gave him a sturdy blow on his head, which laid the watchman prostrate on the ground, and Hurdegen pursued his course without further molestation.

CHAPTER V.

"Thou hast prevaricated with thy friend,
By underhand contrivances undone me;
And, while my open nature trusted in thee,
Thou hast stepped in between me and my hopes,
And ravished from me all my soul held dear:
Thou hast betrayed me."

THE clear fresh morning broke upon the town of Gernsbach. Saurbein leaned on the bridge, not far from the inn, known by the sign of the "Star," and allowed the cool drafts of air to play around him, which came from the mountains over the turbid waves of the River Marg. However comfortable Saurbein might find the situation which he had chosen, yet he was evidently restless and uneasy; his look was directed to the right, then to the left, and more particularly towards the steep street which led immediately to the gates of the town.

Under the ever restless eye was, however, a still more restless brain, in which some strange and discordant thoughts were whirling about, and tormented by doubts of the most painful nature. The spendthrift vagabond had already accomplished many a trick; he was smooth and glossy as an eel, and, like it, unrestrained in its course by an adverse wind or an impetuous stream, but never had he glided so smoothly through a roguish trick as through that which he had just accomplished with the Bachenstein family. Here in his present posture had he waited and watched until the midnight hour had struck from the tower of the church, and then, after an hour's rest, as soon as the first flush of day was on the eastern horizon, was he again at his post, casting an anxious look around, buoyed up every moment with an inspiration of hope, only to have it taken from him the next moment by the positive reality that all his expectations were false and groundless. In vain did he direct his eyes to a particular quarter, notwithstanding the most solemn promises that had been given to him. Neither the hero of the adventure, nor the patron of the rogue, the Baron von Harras, condescended to make his appearance. His beautiful game slumbered thoughtlessly in the skilfully constructed net, but the hunter appeared not to take it away. The applause which he hoped for, the wages that had been promised him if he succeeded in his act of villany, were by far too long in coming to satisfy the avaricious disposition of the grasping rogue. He already observed with chagrin and mortification how the doors of the houses were gradually thrown open—how here and there one of the citizens projected his head out of the window to ascertain the state of the weather; how the servant girls crept lazily along to the wells, and the shepherd blew his horn at the corner of the street, for the purpose of collecting the cattle to lead them to the pasture.

Everything was in activity and motion in the inn, but not a vestige of, not even a message from the baron. On a sudden, Saurbein perceived a beggar coming down the street, who belonged to that class who run vigorously and stoutly when they think they are not seen, and who hobble through towns and villages as if they were afflicted with a severe sickness. The shoes of the beggar were covered with dust, which was a sign that he had already on that morning travelled some distance.

"Help a poor beggar," said the impostor, as he stood before Saurbein, who, as he threw a halfpenny into the beggar's cap, said,—

" Whence come you, my poor fellow ?"

" I rose from my straw this morning in the dark," said the beggar, " and am just come from Baden, where I was confined with sickness for two days."

" Heard you of anything new that has happened in the city? did you see a horseman or a carriage on the road?" asked Saurbein.

" I saw a horseman, indeed," said the beggar; " but he was no longer on horseback. He lay in a miserable plight at the Teufels Kanzel, as he had been thrown by his horse, and some peasants were about to carry him on some boards here into the town."

" Is he a resident of Baden, or a poor man?" asked Saurbein.

" He is a stranger in the country," said the beggar; "but I think that he would rather have been foot-bound up here at Gernsbach than at Baden. Yesterday there was an alarm of murder in the city. A young gentleman was seriously wounded, and a watchman at the gate was knocked down by the same person, for which guilty acts they have taken the Baron Harras into custody, who, unfortunately, was seen in the vicinity of the place, and he was immediately declared the culprit, although he solemnly declared his innocence. It is, however, my firm belief, that the man who was thrown from his horse is the real culprit, and he ought to be thankful to the saints who have saved him from the power of the margrave."

Saurbein assumed a most woeful countenance, and looked so insolently and audaciously at the beggar, that the latter hurried across the bridge as fast as his pretended feebleness would allow him, instigated by fear that Saurbein might demand his halfpenny back again, and, perhaps, give him in return some hearty blows.

Saurbein in his heart cursed his unlucky stars, that had brought him into such a predicament, nor in his imprecations did he spare the Baron Harras, whom he looked upon as the cause of all his misfortunes. With a vacant stare he looked upon the waters as they flowed through the arches of the bridge, not knowing what course to pursue, or how to extricate himself from the predicament in which he found himself.

" Here I am," he said, " with a millstone about my neck, and what shall I do with the girl? The devil himself knows what has happened at Baden. I dare not go back with the girl, but I have no other aim nor purpose in travelling further with her—I am completely at my wit's end, and am not much better off than the rider, whose horse laid him prostrate on the ground."

Saurbein slowly retired under the gateway of the inn, and at the very moment the peasants entered, carrying the wounded gentleman on their shoulders.

" This is the best inn," said one of the peasants; " there is good cheer to be had, and, therefore, we cannot do better than leave the gentleman here."

As they passed under the doorway, the wounded man, whose countenance betrayed pain and anxiety, fixed his eyes upon Saurbein, and said, in a feeble voice,—

" I remember thee, thou old pious beggar, in thy pilgrim dress. Tell me, hast thou not seen a beautiful girl, who has been carried along this road by villains? I gave thee lately a piece of silver for the sake of the soul of my father; but a ten times larger sum will I give thee, if thou wilt candidly give me the information for which I so ardently long."

Saurbein remembered well the piece of silver which had been dropped into his begging-box, when he was in his pilgrim's dress; his safety was, however, of greater consequence to him than his gratitude, and he shook his head and swore that his eyes had not beheld any such object as had been represented to him.

The wounded man, who was no other than Hurdegen, gave a heavy sigh, let his head fall on his breast, and scarcely gave an answer to the host, who at that moment made his appearance to offer to the well-dressed gentleman all the accommodation which his house could afford. The golden spurs on the boots of the stranger—the sparkling jewels on his bosom—the heavy massive golden ring on his finger, inspired the host with the expectation that he would be richly rewarded for the exercise of his Christian compassion; and in the retired part of the country in which this inn was situate, a knight or a nobleman was a bird of so rare an occurrence, that when it did appear, it was in general most unceremoniously plucked. For this purpose the providential host set all his domestics in motion; the best rooms in the house were appropriated to the reception of the stranger; the grooms of the inn were sent in all directions to look for and to catch the runaway horse; and a few bottles of wine and some silver crowns amply repaid the peasants who had carried the precious load into the inn.

Whilst the wounded gentleman was carried up the stairs by about twenty officious persons, which could have been performed equally as well by two or three, there stood behind the banisters, concealed from every view, a curious and anxious spectatress, who had been disturbed in her morning prayers by the noise in the house; to ascertain the cause of which she had crept from her apartment. From her hiding-place she saw distinctly and clearly the wounded man, and she dropped down on her knees, as before the Holy of Holies; but not in reverence and placid devotion, but in the utmost terror and alarm. Her heart beat tumultuously, and she moved not from her position until the crowd had entered the apartment with their burden, and had closed the door after them. She then suddenly raised herself, flew down the steps with the agility of a fawn, and cried out,—

"Hans, Hans! where art thou?"

Saurbein heard the voice of Gisela, and threw himself hastily in her way.

"What is the matter with you?" he cried. "By your cries the people of the inn will be led to think that some one is murdering you."

Gisela, in the wildness of her emotions, grasped his hand, looking with fear and alarm towards the stairs, and said,—

"Come—quick! let us be gone—we must away from this place—not a moment is to be lost!"

Saurbein, irresolute and undetermined, rubbed his forehead, as if he were trying to collect his scattered thoughts.

Gisela, however, became more importunate, and said,—

"Tarry not a moment. Do not appear as if you were half asleep. I am lost if he sees me!"

"He! who?" exclaimed Saurbein. "There is no one here who can harm you."

"There is—there is!" exclaimed Gisela; "my enemy is in the house. Come—come, I say—away—away!"

Saurbein, almost dragged along by Gisela, was on the bridge before he was well aware of it. His conscience, which had been almost cauterized by a systematic adherence to a life of vice and profligacy, attempted now to make its voice attended to, and he said, in a hesitating tone,—

"I must inform you that the carriage which we expected to meet with yesterday, on the road, has not made its appearance, and I much fear ——"

"Fear nothing!" said Gisela; "am I not hale and stout? Where is the road to Pfortzheim? Let us proceed on it without delay. Be not afraid that you will have to leave me behind you. I feel as if I could walk a hundred miles; and the idea will encourage me, that every step that I take removes me further from the ruin that awaits me, if I protract my stay in this place."

Yielding to the importunity of Gisela, and tormented by his own irresolution and the painful consciousness of the dilemma in which he was placed, he pointed to the hills on the opposite banks of the river.

"The road which you see yonder leads to Loffenan; if you are willing, we will wend our way to yonder village, and we shall there, perhaps, meet with the thoughtless fellow who has been driving about in the world, Heaven knows where, without waiting for us at the appointed place."

"Quick—quick, Master Hans!" said Gisela; "the morning air blows upon us refreshing and invigorating, and we shall be in the village before we are well aware of it."

"Perhaps, on our way thither," said Saurbein, "you will relate to me the cause which has influenced you so strongly to hasten your departure from this place?"

"Expect not any such explanation," said Gisela, "from my terrified lips. Perhaps, in Ulm, under the protecting roof of my aunt, I will confide to you what now so painfully and so terribly afflicts my soul."

"In Ulm!" repeated Saurbein, lost in thought, whilst his lips quivered as if they would pronounce some words of a dreadful import. "Thou simple child," he said, "whose confidence is still as firm as the rocks of those mountains, wouldst thou wert in Ulm, or in Hungary, or in Turkey—anywhere but here! I should then have a burden less upon my shoulders, which my evil star now imposes upon me."

As they now proceeded hastily along in silence, the steps of Saurbein became more nimble and active, whilst the example of Gisela expedited the journey, and it so happened that the travellers reached the village of Loffenan before the sexton had tolled the bell for the morning service. From the eminence, at the foot of which was situate the village, looking down into the valley of the Murg, Gisela breathed more freely and tranquilly, and, composed and resigned, she seated herself on a stone by the roadside, whilst Saurbein entered one of the huts of the village, for the purpose, as he pretended, of making some inquiries about the carriage.

The sun shone with all its splendour on the valley at Gisela's feet; the birds carolled their matin song from the woods—over the meadows and the corn fields, the bees and the butterflies wantoned in the pride and glory of their existence, and strengthened, in the warm beams of the morning sun, their wings, benumbed by the dew of the night. The bells of the village sent forth their monotonous sounds, and from all sides of the mountain, from villages and monasteries, the chanting of the metal tongues vibrated on the listening ear, and at last the bells from the gloomy Gernsbach joined in the morning chorus, inviitng the devotee to her matins.

Gisela felt her heart most wonderfully affected—partly from the joy of life, and partly from the longing after the solitude of a convent, which appeared to her as the highest happiness of the terrestrial state. She felt like the splendid archangel, Michael, after from the golden clouds of Heaven he had hurled Satan and his rebellious crew into the abyss below. Hurdegen, whom she feared and abhorred like Satan himself, lay in the gloomy town at her feet, bound as it were in chains, and in the grave; around her brow, however, played the glory of the triumph—the consciousness of freedom and virgin pride expanded her bosom, and animated it with joy and confidence. Glorying in her victory, she looked down with feelings of contempt on the ignominy of the hut in which she had lately resided—on the depravity of her father—on the feminine pusillanimity of her mother, and on the wretched snares which had been laid for her youth and innocence. She repeated the oath which she had frequently sworn in the silence of the night—never to be the wife of a man—to hate every man, and only to strive after the crown of the holy bridegroom.

In the meantime, Saurbein returned from the village with a slow and tottering step, seated himself by the side of Gisela, and said, evidently under a state of embarrassment,—

"It is now past all doubt that the fellow has scandalously deceived us. Not a horse nor a carriage has been seen, and the worst of all is, that the rogue has not only gone away with the vehicle, but has also taken with him all the money with which I trusted him. What is now to be done?"

"I know not," said Gisela, after a moment's consideration; "my father gave me a few crowns at our parting, which I now willingly give to you; but still, great is my fear that they will not be sufficient to bear our expenses to Ulm."

Saurbein weighed the money in his hand, put it into his pocket, and said,—

"The journey is long, and this small sum of money will not be sufficient. If you be willing I will return to Baden and obtain a further supply from your father."

"You would not leave me alone?" said Gisela, with an emotion of fear.

"Then," said Saurbein, "go yourself; or, if you will, I will take you with me."

"I will neither go alone nor with you," said Gisela. "I am satisfied in having escaped the dangers which this morning awaited me. Not for all the treasures of the world will I again pass through Gernsbach, where my seducer is lying in watch for me. Not on any account would I again see my parents, from whose fate I am separated for the world. You were in general able to devise the best measures under any sudden or unforeseen calamity. Now put your ingenuity to the test; all that I can say is, conduct me to Ulm, and my aunt shall richly reward you."

The old rogue was secretly vexed that Gisela so pertinaciously refused him every opportunity of betaking himself off; yet he knew not how to account for it, but he felt himself as if bound by a magical power to Gisela. The beauty and determined resolution of the girl had a most irresistible influence over him, and it grieved him to expose her innocence to the snares and dangers by which she was surrounded. In deep reflection, he rested his head upon his hands; but some time had elapsed, and he appeared as undetermined as at first. At last he said,—

"We may defer an evil, but it is not thereby removed. Chance, perhaps, will assist me out of the predicament, and, should that not be the case, I can to-morrow, or the day afterwards, forsake the girl; for the world is large—the sun shines here and everywhere, and I am not very particular as to the road which I must take. I know not one that leads to a home, therefore I'll throw a feather into the air, and whichever way the wind drives it, in that direction will I pursue my course."

Encouraged by these deceitful and vicious thoughts, he said to Gisela,—

"I am acquainted, indeed, with the road over the mountains, through the Black Forest, and over the Alb, which will render our journey shorter; and, if we be good and vigorous pedestrians, will soon bring us to Ulm. The road, however, is rough, inhospitable, and almost impassible for a tender maiden like yourself."

"What matters it, Master Hans?" said Gisela. "I will run with you for a wager. I have no dread of the midnight hoar-frost, nor for the mountain stream, nor for the path less forest, nor a nightly lodging in the dilapidated and roofless barn. Everywhere is my guardian angel with me, and from the earliest infancy I have learned to endure the worst that could befal me, after my father had squandered away our riches and estates, and trampled the honour of our house in the dust. Be not, therefore, discouraged on my account. The hunger and thirst which we suffer here below, will be a thousand-fold repaid in everlasting bliss in the heavenly mansions."

Saurbein put on a most contemptuous look; for he thought, when he fancied to himself the everlasting life, not so much of its blessings and its joys, as of the hot and fiery palace of the rich man in the gospel. When, however, he cast his eyes upon the confiding Gisela, whom he had so often played with on his knees, whose inheritance he had assisted in destroying, a voice of thunder seemed to sound in his ear, " Forsake not the girl, hoary sinner, if thou wouldst not taste the torments of those sulphurous fires which Satan is preparing for thee." He therefore arose, as if suddenly inspired by a hidden power, and said,—

" In God's name, Gisela, let us immediately pursue our journey, and with a stout heart ascend the Tobel. I will carry your portmanteau on my back, and I will take care that we shall not be in want of money, if you will promise me not to put on a wry face, let me commit whatever actions I may."

" You will not become a thief, I hope, Master Hans," said Gisela.

" Not exactly that," said Saurbein. " He, however, who is lashed with the whip of necessity, is not in general very scrupulous as to the actions which he commits. In this country it is only by cunning and artifice that a penny is to be extracted from the pockets of the people; and, you may believe me, there is no great harm in the trick which is often played."

Saurbein determined to illustrate his ambiguous words by an example. On his passing the houses of the village, with his companion, he let the cloak, which he had tucked up, fall as low as his feet: girded his body round with thick cord, and sang, to the utmost pitch of his voice, one of his pilgrim songs. The effect was instantaneous. The women came to the threshold of their doors, or drew aside the little windows, and cast a curious eye upon the wanderers. Saurbein saluted them on every side in the most friendly manner, without allowing himself to be disturbed in his song, and at last a woman came out of one of the houses, and asked, in a voice of sympathy,—

" Whence come you, my good man, with the pretty girl?"

Saurbein answered the woman, in a humble manner, but in a soft and gentle tone of voice,—

" We come from the Rhine, my good mother, and are on a pilgrimage to Rome and the Holy Land, on account of our sins. The girl is my daughter, who accompanies me in my pilgrimage, in fulfilment of a vow of a good and pious woman; for it is permitted, and it is well done, to undertake the fulfilment of a vow for a Christian who is prevented from carrying it herself into execution."

" May the saints bless you!" said the woman; " and if, on your arrival at the Holy Land, you will pray for my poor Werner, who is with the army of the count, in Flanders, I will willingly bestow upon you this gift."

" The thanks of my grateful heart be given to you," said Saurbein, " and you may rest assured that the prayers shall be said, as if yourself or your son made a pilgrimage to Jerusalem."

In this manner Saurbein passed from house to house, and great and cheering was the success. Silver and copper were thrown into his cap; the pockets of the counterfeit pilgrim were filled with good and substantial victuals; the monasteries of Werrenalb and Tranenalb supplied the pilgrims with hot and nutritious soup; the travelling countryman gave them his last piece of bread, in order that prayers might be put up at Jerusalem for his soul.

" How do you like the trick?" said Saurbein, with a smile, to his companion, as they sat at mid-day under the shadow of a beech tree in the Tobel.

Gisela answered, prudishly,—

" Your actions are those of a false prophet, and are by no means pleasant to me. We are, however, under the pressure of necessity, and on my arrival at Ulm I will have some masses said, that the poor people may have justice done them, and we have our sins forgiven us."

Saurbein bit his lips maliciously, and, after a moment's reflection, Gisela said,—

" One thing has been made clear to me by your mode of action, of which I always harboured some suspicions; namely—that you men are all as false, as mean, and selfish, as the hypocritical dragon of the abyss below. Your most pious and sanctified smile is not to be trusted—your most honourable word is nothing more than a falsehood, and you violate the dea rest and most holy sanctuary."

"One would think," said Saurbein, "that you had been inhaling the atmosphere of a monastery during the whole of your life. I can remember the time when you were very different."

"The circumstances of life," said Gisela, "were then different with me. I was surrounded by pomp, luxury, and abundance—I had no time for reflection, and, what is more, I scarcely knew what prayer was. I have now been long a pupil in the school of adversity, and I have been therein taught not to depend upon the fleeting happiness of the world, but prepare myself for that of another."

"Why," said Saurbein, with an air of sarcasm, "you speak like a very abbess."

"And why should I not?" said Gisela. "In these wicked and degenerate times, the employment of the woman ought to consist in nothing more than in the choir and the altar, to solicit the compassion of God. Still I am convinced I was not born for a mean and lowly condition; there is in me a spirit of ambition, which I cannot quell: and if the kingdom were now in existence, of which the olden traditions tell, and which was once founded in Bohemia by a host of pious girls, I would immediately hasten thither, and seize the lance and the sword; for I would still be rather the foremost in the battle, than pray on my knees before the altar."

"Your aunt," said Saurbein, "will, indeed, be proud of you, and bless the nurse who suckled you with lion's milk."

A tear glistened in the eye of Gisela, and she said, in a kind and supplicating tone;—

"Blame not, I beseech you, the nurse and guardian of my youth, the good and pious Sister Cecilia, who, in the convent of Lichtenthal, taught me prayer and virtue. In her lap I consoled myself at the disgrace and downfall of my parents, and on her grave I vowed to remain faithful to her instructions. Were she not now in her grave, I should not be obliged to accept of a residence in the house of my aunt; I should long ago have bidden farewell to the world, and I should now be sitting amongst the haughty nuns of Lichtenthal, who refused me admittance after the death of my benefactress."

In a melancholy mood, Gisela rose from her seat, wiped the dust from her feet, and directed her steps towards the place where the path led down the mountain into the defiles of the Black Forest. With indifference she turned her back upon the glorious prospect which presented itself to her view. The beautiful Rhine spread its blue waters in the valley, and the horizon was bounded by the distant mountains of the Wasgau; and she felt herself as happy as the timorous deer, when in a short time she saw herself surrounded by the dark and gloomy fir trees, and her feet sprinkled by the foaming mountain torrents. The shadows of the wanderers were growing longer and longer; darkness was setting in apace as they arrived at the small town of Wildbad. The brazen trumpets sent forth their clanging sound, and the shrill fifes sent forth their merry noise from the different houses.

"What is the cause of all this music?" said Saurbein to a boy who was standing on the road.

"Our most gracious Landgrave of Hessen has arrived at the baths, and gives a ball to his tenants," answered the boy.

The eyes of the old glutton sparkled with joy. He simpered and clapped his hands; but Gisela said, rather peevishly,—

"What are you thinking of, Master Hans? Do you still long for music and wine? Heaven forbid! You may enjoy yourself as much as you please in Ulm, but at this town, under our penniless circumstances, it becomes us to shun the world. I would rather sleep in towers inhabited by the owls and bats, than in the gorgeous apartments of Babylon."

"I wish," said Saurbein, whose patience began to be exhausted, "that some barefooted Carmelite had put all your whims into a sack, and carried them to the witches on the Yberg. A thought just struck me, that a good meal, and a glass of generous Rhenish, would refresh and invigorate my old exhausted body, and now you desire that I shall proceed with you into the forest, and find my bed on the ground, like a poacher, if we should not be so fortunate as to fall in with a hut, where we can find some rotten and musty straw."

"Can I help it," said Gisela "that your body is weak and decrepid? I detest the dance, that senseless whirling of silly people, making themselves only objects to be laughed at. Are you my master? or, rather, are you not my servant? Were I to inform my aunt how you have presumed ——!'

"Your aunt," said Saurbein, in a surly tone, "won't have much to blame me for," and followed immediately the order of the imperious lady, and, with a forced submission to his fate, he led the way out of the town.

The path led through an almost impassable wilderness. The tumult of the town and the clangour of the instruments by degrees died away, and instead of the torches from the bell-room of the Hessian landgrave, a sickly star now and then illumined the path of the wanderers. The ascent of the mountain was steep and difficult, without any intermission,

See page 43.

and the path seemed gradually to lose itself, and then to wind amongst rocks overlooking the steep declivities below. Saurbein relinquished all hope of reaching the hamlet of which he had been speaking. A gurgling noise was heard in the front, which, on examination, was found to proceed from a babbling spring, which lavished its riches in the lonely solitudes, and with its waters refreshed only the thirsty stag. A herd of these wild animals broke on both sides through the underwood, seeking their safety in flight, from the intrusion, as they supposed, of their murderous enemies.

"Here shall be our resting-place," said Gisela; "I am quite exhausted, and my tongue is parched. The night is not cold,—the foliage of the trees will protect us from the wind, and in this lonely spot no murderer can be lying in ambush for his prey."

Saurbein looked anxiously around him, and that look soon lost itself in the darkness which was at his feet, and in the gloom of the fir trees above his head. He then whispered to Gisela, "This is a horrible place. How cruelly have you played upon my old age, in enticing me so far from an hospitable inn. I grant you we may be safe here from robbers and murderers; but, instead of the timid deer which we have just now chased away, a bear or a wolf might pounce upon us, or a wild boar with its deadly tusks."

"Offer up your prayers to your holy Mother," said Gisela, "and confide all your ways to her; but if that be not satisfactory to you, let us keep watch alternately. Lay yourself down—close your eyes, and I will undertake to drive away the bear or the wild boar. When you awake, for the sleep of old age is generally not of long duration, then you shall watch over me."

The benignity and kindness of the fearless girl affected deeply the coward rogue, and he said, in an honest tone, "Sleep if you can. Were I to attempt to sleep, my fears and my alarm would not permit me. May the Lord protect you in your sleep, as I will do with my poor human power." Thus saying, he took her cloak, and covered Gisela with it, who laid herself with all becoming modesty on the moss. With infantine simplicity Gisela repeated her evening prayer, offered her companion the hand of amity and confidence, and soon fell asleep. Saurbein sat close to her, and reflected with serious and anxious attention on the occurrences of the day. He asked himself, what bound him so firmly to the cause and fortune of this girl; it was to him a matter of wonder how he, who had acted so faithlessly and treacherously towards all the world, could have remained so long true and faithful to Gisela. He attempted to discover or to conjecture what would be the consequence were he to get rid of his companion; but his conscience always told him that it would be to his misfortune were he to separate from her. So great is the power which youth, which the open and confiding candour of innocence, exercises even over a hardened heart. The girl appeared to him to be a treasure, which he was bound to preserve even against his will, and the immediate vicinity of that treasure was even sacred to the sinner. The deep-drawn respirations of Gisela dispelled the anxiety from his breast, and rendered him partaker of the confidence with which the virgin innocence of Gisela was protected as with a coat of armour. It was not the first time for many a year that the rogue recalled to his memory the happy, jocund days of his youth—those years in which he was good and pious, in which he was unacquainted with deceit and knavery, and in which he had never yet averted his look from that of a good and honourable man. In his thoughts he repeated the stories which his anxious and affectionate mother once related to him, as well as the advice and paternal admonitions which his father gave him when he set forth in the world as an honest and respectable member of society. Further, however, he ventured not to live over again in his memory the days of his youth, because there was not in that recollection anything to cheer or console him. His mind now became gloomy and overcast with the clouds of a painful and precarious future; estranged from the world, despised and shunned by the virtuous part of it, and hated and feared by the guilty portion, his days were spent in a miserable vacillation between hope and despair, amidst wretchedness for the present hour, and dread for the future.

When Gisela laid herself down to sleep, the heavens were without a cloud, the stars shining brightly on the virgin form of Gisela, as she lay in the sleep of innocence—visions of future bliss dancing around her, and happy in the bliss that a smiling Heaven poured upon her. On a sudden the sky became overcast, and heavy turbulent clouds were seen moving from the westward. Not a star was any longer to be seen, and the heart of Saurbein quaked with fear when he heard the thunder growling at a distance, and a faint flash shot across the horizon. He had been told in his youth that God speaks to the heart of man in his storms, and he now fancied the time was come when he was to be spoken to, and he shuddered at the thought of the awful sounds which he might perhaps be doomed to hear. The tops of the trees which an hour before shot their spiral cones in the air, unmoved by a breath of wind, now bent before the force of the surly blast; the thunder now sounded like the discharge of heavy artillery, and the forest was illumined by continuous flashes of the lightning. Not a drop of rain had yet fallen, but the storm passed majestically over the forest, to pour down its torrents of rain in some distant valley. Whilst the heart of Saurbein was terrified with the violence of the storm, Gisela still slept soundly and tranquilly as a child, and Saurbein now thought it was a favourable opportunity for him to leave her, and he rose from his seat for the purpose; but he cast a look upon her, and his heart immediately failed him. Nor was his mind wholly exempt from the many superstitions that at that time prevailed, especially in the part of Germany where these scenes were enacting. The mountains were at no great distance which were supposed to be the chosen abode of Rubezahl and all his attendant witches, sprites, gnomes, and warlocks; not a rustling was heard in the air, but it was occasioned by some witch careering on her broom: not a shriek was heard but it proceeded from some sprite, who was playing its pranks with some village maid: there was not a spark of phosphoric light shot from some stagnant bog, but it was immediately converted into a light, carried by some imp to lure the traveller to his destruction. It was, therefore, rational to suppose that the mind of Saurbein, surrounded as he was by objects calculated to instil fear and terror even into the stoutest heart, the three principal of which objects were silence, solitude, and darkness, was not under the immediate influence of superstition; and as it was a current belief in the country, that the witches and the ghosts entertained a peculiar respect for a sleeping virgin, he looked upon Gisela as a kind of guardian angel, and that were he to remove himself from her society, he would immediately become the object for some mischievous and malicious imps to play their tricks upon. The principle of self, therefore, prompted him to remain; he had, however, no one to speak to, and that circumstance annoyed him not a little; but then he knew there was a charm about a sleeping virgin, which was never attempted to be broken by either spectres, witches, or sprites, and, therefore, were he to awake her, those dreaded beings would be absolved from all respect; and as it was a settled opinion with him, that they knew he was a great sinner, they might seize the favourable opportunity of punishing him for his transgressions. As he could not talk, he attempted to pray, but his tongue refused him the service. In proportion, however, as the firmament became pure and serene, his fears subsided; and as the stars became paler and paler from the growing light of the day, his heart revived, and greatly was he rejoiced when Gisela awoke, wondering in her own mind how she could have slept so soundly throughout the whole of the night. She had been dreaming, she said, of a dark and gloomy life, full of pain and misery, but which, in the end, was illumined by the sun of peace and joy. Saurbein in secret envied her the repose which she had been enjoying, as well as the cheering prophecy of the dream. No friendly star, he thought, would shine upon his after life; no tear would be shed over his grave. He would fall like the leaf from the tree in autumn—unheeded and unknown; and, perhaps, like the leaf, to rot away upon the spot where it has fallen.

They now proposed to resume their journey, but they had not proceeded far, when, to their great surprise, they found that in their mountain resting-place they had had a neighbour, of whose proximity they had not the slightest conception. A youth of about fifteen lay in the shade of a large detached piece of rock, and slept as soundly as if it were under a canopy of gold in a palace. His long cloak of black stuff denoted him to be a student; his head, partly covered with his small cap drawn deeply over his forehead, which was encircled by golden locks, rested on a small bundle containing his apparel, and at his side lay a small guitar.

Gisela stood overcome with surprise, and looked attentively upon the sleeper. She then said to Saurbein,—

"That is a pious countenance, the contemplation of which pleases me much. It seems to me as if my guardian angel lay before me asleep in the form of this youth, and was now resting himself from the watch that he has kept over me."

"Nonsense," said Saurbein; "the most wicked scoundrel has frequently a very pious and devout countenance when he is asleep. Let us be going. I am weak for want of rest; all my limbs are shivering with cold. Let us, therefore, hurry along, that I may set my blood in motion."

Gisela still stood almost immoveable before the youth, and scarcely could she bring herself to leave him. It was only the fear of disturbing his rest that prompted her to desist from awakening him; but Saurbein continued to importune her to proceed on their journey, to which she at last unwillingly consented; and as she left the place, she often turned her head to take another view of the sleeper, until the darkness of the wood completely concealed him from her view. With a heavy sigh she then said,—

"Whithersoever the youth may wander, and whatever may be his pursuits, he will prosper in the world, for the Lord is certainly with him; and were he to join us in our pilgrimage, I should consider myself free from all danger and injury."

"Folly! superstition! bigotry!" muttered Saurbein to himself, and marched along, evidently chagrined and in ill-humour with everything about him. They, however, soon arrived at a village, where a substantial breakfast refreshed the travellers, and put Saurbein into rather a better humour. They then proceeded on their journey without any particular accident or adventure, but also without much conversation; for as Gisela was on her part occupied with all kind of thoughts, so had Saurbein also recovered his usual tone of mind, and in secret he was revolving in his own thoughts how he could carry the resolution which he had formed into execution, of forsaking Gisela, and with the little money which he had still in his possession, return to his usual haunts and his accustomed licentious mode of life.

CHAPTER VI.

"I hate all praise,
Given or received; we have enough within us,
The meanest vassal or the loftiest monarch,
Not to add to each other's natural burden
Of mortal misery, but rather lessen,
By mild reciprocal alleviation,
The fatal penalties imposed on life."

IT was midday that the wanderers stood on the edge of the beautiful valley of Nagold. The towers of Caln stretched themselves at their feet, and Gisela proposed that they should enter the city, and rest themselves for the day. Saurbein, however, suddenly seated himself on the grass, and said—

"It is not possible for me to go a step further. I am fatigued, and all my limbs are aching. I feel as if I should faint; I, therefore, beg of you, my good girl, to see if you can find a spring, or a cottage, from which I can obtain a draught of water. My tongue is cleaving to the roof of my mouth with thirst."

When Gisela saw her companion so exhausted, her heart was moved with compassion, and she took a pumpkin flask, which Saurbein carried along with him, and made the best of her way through the green underwood in search of the strength-restoring draught. She took particular observation of the direction in which she walked, collecting some wild strawberries which abounded in the woods, and casting her look in every quarter for a cottage, where the desired refreshment was to be obtained. At last her ears caught the joyful sound of a murmuring rivulet; with joy she hastened towards it, and, having filled her flask, she began to retrace her steps, rejoicing in her heart that she had succeeded in obtaining the desired relief for her companion. Her surprise, however, was boundless, when she could not find him at the place where she had left him. He had disappeared, as if he had been carried away by one of the witches of Blacksberg, and he was not only gone himself, but he had also taken with him the knapsack with all the money. Like a person in a dream, Gisela stared around her, and she fancied that she might have mistaken the place where she had left Saurbein; but the more she examined it, the more she was convinced that she was right—there was the little knoll on which he had been sitting—there was the birch tree against which he had been leaning, and in the sand were the marks of his hobnailed shoes.

"Whither is the old man gone?" said Gisela to herself. Not the sound of a footstep was to be heard, and no other answer was given to Gisela's anxious cry than the monotonous chirping of the birds brooding in the bushes. The wretched girl felt all her firmness gradually diminishing; her limbs quivered, and the miserable consciousness that she was alone, a stranger amongst strangers, a weak and defenceless girl in a land of vice and iniquity, paralysed all her powers, and rendered her incapable of all resolution and exertion. After a short interval, she appeared, on a sudden, to rouse herself. She ran to the right and the left, backwards and forwards, in the wildness of despair. She penetrated into the thickets, where the adder alone leaves its slimy track, and the lizard holds its solitary court. Louder and louder she cried, "Master Hans—Master Saurbein—where are you? Are you playing your jokes with me?" No answer, however, was returned. The louder her cry, the more depressing was the silence. On a sudden—her ear could not deceive her—she heard some steps at a distance, and doubted not they were those of her companion. Nevertheless, she hastened towards the spot whence it now proceeded, and, to her great joy, she heard the sound of voices, and in the next moment she felt herself seized by the rude and sturdy grasp of a man, and as she, overcome with alarm and terror, turned her head, she saw herself in the power of two charcoal burners, who stopped her with the utmost rudeness, and uttering the most vehement curses.

" Have we got you at last?" said one of them, a tall, black fellow, with sparkling eyes. " Have we caught you at last in the fact, thou scandalous woman, who, for a long time, hast been stealing our wood?"

" The pitcher goes to the well till it is broken," growled the other, a bandy-legged fellow with a bushy head. " All resistance now is vain; come along with us that you may receive the punishment that is due to you."

After her first alarm was over, Gisela looked in an undaunted manner in the face of the two men, and answered boldly—

" You are mistaken in the person—I am not a thief. Lead me to the magistrate in the town, that my innocence may be made manifest."

This unexpected appeal made the fellows hesitate. They looked at each other as if perplexed with doubt, and the bushy-headed fellow said, rather pacified,—

" You swagger much about your innocence, my fine young lady. Do you belong to the town—and what business have you alone in the wood?"

" I am here a stranger, my good people," said Gisela; "and but half an hour ago I lost my conductor, an old meagre man, whom you have perhaps encountered in your way?"

The bandy-legged man shook his head incredulously, and said, with a satirical simper—

" What silly, senseless talk. You ought to be ashamed of yourself, to wander about with a grey-headed man in the forest, when matters might be more comfortable with you!"

" Hold your tongue, with your scandalous talk," said Gisela, in a firm and passionate tone.

The fellow, however, who had spoken thus indecorously, gave a nod to his companion and said,—

" Come with us, my fair maid, and we will lead thee where thou wilt find thy friend."

During this conversation they had proceeded imperceptibly some way in the forest, when they stood suddenly still on a black and parched place, on which an enormous charcoal kiln was burning. Not a sound was heard in the neighbourhood but the crackling of the wood, and not a soul was to be seen but the two begrimed fellows, and the road which ran on the other side of the kiln was, at the time, wholly free from passengers. An indescribable dread came over Gisela, as she cast her eyes around her.

" What have I to do here?" she asked, in a trembling tone.

" You shall have your meals with us," said the man with the bushy head, at the same time chucking Gisela in the most familiar manner under the chin. " You are beautifully fair and handsome—not whiter is the new fallen snow! You must be a tender morsel for such sooty fellows as we are!"

" Keep your distance, demon!" said Gisela, who repelled the impudence of the fellow with the most determined resolution.

The bandy-legged fellow, however, held her fast, and said, in an impudent tone,—

" Such conduct does not become you. You shall either give us your kisses, and we will then hold our tongues about your suspicious calling, or we will hang a bundle of twigs about your neck, and drag you as an object of shame to prison!"

" By the holy saints," said the other, and rushed furiously upon Gisela, "the prison is too good for such girls. If you do not yield to our wishes, we will throw you head over ears into the kiln, and after you have been there for half an hour, you will not have many sweethearts after you!"

The two savage fellows took hold of Gisela, and dragged her along to carry their scandalous threat into execution, but her piercing cries rent the air, and from the adjoiniug road a strong masculine voice called out,—

" Hilloa! What's the matter there?"

The two savages stood, in an instant, like statues, and released their hold of the almost exhausted Gisela. Panting for breath, she stood for a moment to recover herself, whilst the charcoal burners hastily seized their pokers and began to work at the kiln, as if they had not committed the slightest outrage; when, on a sudden, a tall, lean, grey horse came trotting towards the kiln, on which was seated a man of a meagre, haggard appearance, clad in a white ticken coat, a cap of felt upon his head, with the brim turned downwards, such as is worn by the peasants. His legs were covered with enormous boots of brown leather, and in his hand he held a sturdy whip, full of rugged knots. As he approached, Gisela perceived a long sword under the coarse cloak of the rider. His horse was caparisoned in a true knightly style, and the spurs generally worn by person of high degree glistened behind the silver stirrups.

" Hilloa!" exclaimed the gentleman, in a louder voice, and cracking his whip in a threatening manner. " What are you about, you ruffians? Why, by all the saints," he continued, casting a look of astonishment on Gisela, "I will venture my salvation that you wretches contemplated some injury to the defenceless girl!"

With these words he gave each of the charcoal burners a couple of smart lashes with his whip on their backs, and they appeared as tame and patient as two sheep, saying that they meant not the slightest harm to the girl, and whatever they had done was merely out of sport, and were she to accuse them of any outrageous action, or say anything to their disadvantage, it ought to be looked upon as nothing more than a malicious falsehood.

"Well," exclaimed the gentleman, in a passion, "my whip has one good effect—it has opened your mouths. But now, my pretty girl of the woods, it is your turn to speak. Speak without any reserve, and if the scoundrels have maltreated you, they shall suffer for it."

Although Gisela felt a secret dislike for the coarse language, the uncouth manners, the staring eyes, and the repellant features of the old gentleman, yet she hesitated not to inform him, in as brief a manner as possible, of the infamous charge that had been laid to her, and the scandalous treatment which she had received from them. At every word that she spoke the old gentleman nodded his head, as if in approbation, adjusting, with a smile, his long white hairs behind his ears, and fixed, almost immovably, his large staring eyes on the pearly teeth and ruddy lips of the interesting narrator.

Gisela having concluded her narrative, the old gentleman turned, with his mouthful of curses, to the charcoal burners, and exclaimed, in almost childish passion,—

"I have a great mind to dismount and lash you with my whip that the blood shall run down your backs, ye d—ble bears of the wood. Attend to your kiln, that your work may be done properly; but meddle not with innocent girls, who travel on the road on their business, and who are not made for you."

As the old gentleman now swung his whip again in the air, in a threatening manner, and spurred his horse towards the trembling savages, Gisela caught hold of the bridle, and begged of him to spare the men, and to allow her to walk by the side of his horse until she was safe out of the wood. The old gentleman desisted, therefore, from inflicting any other punishment on the fellows; and with discontented countenances they begged Gisela to pardon them for their misconduct, and wished the marshal, as they called him, good day, and all prosperity to him.

"That is a most extraordinary circumstance," said the marshal; "the man cannot, like Elisha, have been carried up into Heaven, or was it his intention to commit upon you an irreparable injury."

"I cannot believe that," said Gisela; "the old Saurbein had no reason nor provocation to injure me in any manner whatever."

As the marshal heard the name of Saurbein, his countenance betrayed the most evident signs of anger and chagrin, and he d—d Saurbein!

"Hans Saurbein! by all the saints! But the scoundrel is well known to me, for I saw too much of him when he assumed the character of a veterinary doctor in my stables, until one night he rode away with one of my most beautiful horses. Poor creature, you have indeed been in bad hands, and the scoundrel intended to bring thee to a bad end, from which he will not escape himself. Nothing but deceit and falsehood come out of his mouth. Depend upon it you will never see him again." And he now began to repeat a long catalogue of Saurbein's misdeeds and impositions, which he had already practised in Coln and Nagold, and even in Stutgard and Ulm, and the catalogue appeared to be so endless, that tears rushed into the eyes of Gisela, and her heart was most sensibly affected, for no doubt now whatever rested upon her mind, that she had been the dupe of a most consummate scoundrel.

"May all the saints be gracious to me!" she said to herself, and crossed her hands in a disconsolate mood over her breast. "What will now happen to me? What will be my future fate? I would still rather die on the spot than return home; but still, whither shall I direct my course?"

The marshal now said to her, with unassumed courtesy and kindness,—

"I am an old well-disposed man, and pretty children can wind me round their finger. Accompany me to my castle, you shall find everything there to contribute to your happiness and comfort. I am in my seventy-sixth year, therefore my life is a sufficient voucher to you that the offer which I make you does not proceed from any wicked design on your innocence."

Gisela knew not what answer she should make to this offer, and as the marshal repeated it to her in an urgent manner, she at last answered, after considerable hesitation in her manner,—

" If your house, noble sir, be not at a great distance, and if you have a wife at home, I will most thankfully accept from you lodging for the night."

The marshal laughed heartily within himself, and answered,—

" If you will accept a seat on my horse, in an hour we shall be at home, and my house-keeper will give you a hearty welcome. To-morrow we will have some further conversation with each other."

This speech, in some degree, pacified the alarms of Gisela, and as the marshal stopped his horse, and offered her the foremost place on the saddle, she raised no further objections to accept of the offer which was apparently given to her with so much good-will. It was, however, a revolting sensation to her as she felt the long arm of the rider round her waist; but, helpless and destitute as she was, she resigned herself to her fate, calculating that the ride would not be of long duration.

The town of Coln now lay at some distance behind them, and the journey went on pleasantly along the smiling valley. The rider and his fair companion encountered various bands of people—fishermen, hunters, and peasants, who lived in the black forest, and a number of gabbling, talkative women, who, with bundles of sticks or baskets at their back, were directing their course homewards. The men in a most respectful manner took off their caps, on encountering the good old gentleman in his ticken coat, who in his turn saluted them in a most friendly manner, giving them now and then a few lashes over the shoulders, in all the playfulness of second childhood, and who, although the smart might have been excessive, did not seem in the least disposed to resent the unexpected visitations which they received from the knotty whip of the rider. To the women, who placed themselves on the side of the road, staring with the eyes of curiosity and wonder on the extraordinary spectacle, he addressed himself, in a joking and familiar manner, jeering them either about their sweethearts, their love of matrimony, or their constancy to their husbands, and maids and wives laughed at the facetious feeble old man; and now and then he received in return an equivocal remark, which was partly complimentary to him in beholding him in the society of a young and beautiful girl, and partly sarcastic in attaching a motive in the acquaintance of his fair companion, which did not well accord with his years. These jokes and sneers were, however, by no means pleasing to the modest Gisela, and still less did she relish the suspicious looks which the women cast upon her, and the half expressed jeers and banterings which she was obliged to hear at times when the rough trotting of the horse rendered her seat uneasy. She, however, bore it with patience, and more especially as the marshal suddenly struck into a steep road at the side, bordered by groves and meadows, and thence ascended a lofty hill, on the summit of which uprose the stately battlements of a nobleman's castle, the windows of which were burnished by the rays of the setting sun.

" There is my residence," said the marshal, pointing to the castle. " That is Zavelstein, where I hope, my pretty maiden, that you will find a comfortable home."

Gisela thought she should fall from the saddle on the stony road, as the marshal pronounced these words. The very house, to escape which she had undertaken the long journey to Ulm ; the house, which a melancholy presentiment had pictured to her as the most dangerous abode for her, now lay before her, and she was to enter its gates as a guest, under circumstances of a most extraordinary and mysterious nature. She, however, allowed not her fear to be made known by any premeditated or unguarded expression; nor would she put a single question, which might disclose the suspicions which literally racked her breast. With the most torturing anxiety she awaited what fate had in store for her, feeling herself incapable of escaping from the power by which she found herself entangled.

A servant, with a broad escutcheon on his coat, hastened to meet the marshal, as he approached the drawbridge. " Hilloa! Lips," cried out the marshal, " how is all at home?—Have the apartments of the castle been fumigated?—And is Hubert quietly deposited in his grave?"

" Yes, most noble sir," answered the servant; " he can now lay claim to a greater space of ground than ever belonged to him before in this world, and I do not think there are many who will be very desirous of disputing it with him. God grant him a joyful resurrection."

" Amen !" ejaculated the old marshal; " I only wish he had not just taken it into his head to die in my house. He knew that I cannot bear a corpse in my castle."

During this discourse, the horse had crossed the drawbridge into the court, where two lazy fellows, in the livery of the marshal, were in readiness to hold the stirrup whilst he dismounted, during which they looked upon his fair companion with wonder and astonishment. The marshal having alighted, he said to one of his servants,—

"Master Thomas, go and tell Matilda to prepare the best entertainment in her power I have brought a companion that I hope will be welcome to her."

Thomas hastened to ascend the winding staircase; but as Gisela, under an emotion of the most painful alarm, cast her eyes to the windows above, she beheld, standing at one of them, a fine, well-grown female, rather splendidly attired, who, with a scowling brow and indignant look, viewed the scene beneath, and in a few moments exclaimed, in a shrieking tone,—

"I have been long waiting your return, sir; but what kind of a visitor have you brought to the castle?"

The marshal appeared to shrink within himself at the manner in which he was accosted on his return, gave a kind and courteous nod to the lady, thrust his companion, as it were, clandestinely up the stairs, and said to her, in a low confidential tone, as she ascended,—

"Be not afraid, my good child; behave with politeness and courtesy to Matilda. She is hasty in her temper, and is haughty and austere in her demeanour, but, with good words and kindness, she is very easy to be managed."

Was it the expectation of the things that were to come, or the cutting coolness which reigned in the vaults of the castle, that the bosom of Gisela felt itself painfully contracted, and scarcely allowed her breath to follow the lord of the castle? Gisela assisted herself, in her ascent, by clinging fast to the bannisters; but that which she saw as she ascended was not calculated to allay her apprehensions, or reconcile her to the fate that awaited her. She beheld a maid servant, who was cleaning the stairs with a besom, and could scarcely put one foot before the other on account of the chains with which her feet were bound, and the clanking of which was sufficient to strike terror into any female's heart, much more so into that of Gisela, in whose mind the most trivial circumstance was likely to make a most serious impression, and to plunge her into the most painful contemplation of the fate that awaited her. The marshal and Gisela had now arrived at the first landing-place, when some heavy groans struck their ears: and, in one of the recesses of the windows, Gisela perceived one of the servants suffering the most cruel torment in a kind of stocks, in which his feet were confined, whilst his hands were tied behind him, and who no sooner beheld the marshal than he implored his mercy and compassion.

"Poor devil!" said the marshal, in rather a tone of pity; "who has placed this man in the stocks?"

As he said these words, the doors of one of the apartments flew open, and with her arms a kimbo, and the air of a bravado, Matilda stood before the marshal, and said, in a commanding and authoritative tone,—

"Who else has done it but myself? and I will do it again under similar circumstances. I'll teach the impudent fellow to open his mouth against me, and to fill the head of his master with a thousand lies about me. I have condemned him to the stocks until the setting of the sun, and I should like to see the person who would attempt to release him."

The marshal, evidently embarrassed, shrugged his shoulders, and turned his back upon the servant; and Matilda stepped aside to let the marshal enter the apartment. But, as he encouraged his companion to enter before him, Matilda placed her corpulent body in the way, and said, under the excitement of the most violent passion,—

"Who is that girl?" and, addressing herself to Gisela, she said, "what business hast thou here?—thou lookest just like some vagrant who hath known how to impose upon the compassion of the worthy marshal, and, for aught I know, thou may'st deceive him still further."

Highly exasperated, but in silence, Gisela retreated a few steps, and cast a look of the most profound contempt on the insolent woman. For a moment the marshal appeared to recover his usurped authority, and he exclaimed with a voice of thunder, that made Matilda shrink back aghast,—

"Have I not had enough of your insolence—or how much longer am I to endure it? —Make way, thou red-tailed dragon, or thou and I shall have a tilt at each other; the weapon of which shall be a knotted whip, such as I now hold in my hand."

As the entrance into the apartment was now clear, the marshal took Gisela by the hand, and led her in triumph into the room, which, in elegance and splendour, was not to be equalled. It was easy to be perceived that, in the castle, an invisible hand directed the interior economy of it; the wainscoting was so bright that the passing forms were almost as clearly reflected on it, as if it were a mirror. The coat of arms, with their variegated colours, shone brilliantly from the windows; the golden ornaments of the ceiling sparkled most beautifully, as if they had been only made a few days previously, and not an atom of dust was to be seen on the painted floor; the round table in the middle of the room was covered with a snow-white cloth, which was edged with a fine tin of the dishes, and the steel of the knives and forks, were as bright as silver. A sumptuous meal stood on the table, and near the seat appointed to the marshal stood a bottle of sparkling wine.

This order and elegance imparted to Gisela as much delight and satisfaction as the reception of the malicious housekeeper had given her pain and anxiety. She remembered the stately refectory at Lerhtenthal, and the fleeting dream of her youth, when her father was still in possession of his castle, as beautiful, and still more beautiful than that in which she was now sojourning. Her bosom agitated by the most conflicting feelings, she allowed herself to be handed by the marshal to the table, placing her exactly opposite to himself.

See page 45.

A prey to the bitterest rage, and yet wisely holding her tongue, fearing the sudden ebullitions of the marshal's temper, Matilda stood in the back-ground, and in her passion played with the silver chains of her damask stomacher.

The marshal seated himself with apparently great self-satisfaction on his downy cushion, and said, without bestowing a look on Matilda,—

"You kick up a fine rumpus, Matilda, when it is my will to bring a guest into my house; therefore I will not allow you to sit at the table; you shall wait upon us. I rather think that that iron, stubborn disposition of thine is still to be broken. Come, carve the venison, and help my guest to the choicest bits, for there is something noble under her mean and peasant dress; and I will wager that she is of far nobler blood than thou art, thou haughty Jezebel."

Without raising any objection, Maltida obeyed the orders of the marshal, and with a trembling hand, and a countenance flushed with rage, she proceeded to carve the joint, first helping the marshal, then Gisela, on whom she cast a stolen look, which fully betrayed the rage that was passing within her. She then, with a huff, placed herself a few paces behind the chair of the marshal, and squeezing her hands together, as if she would crush her fingers.

The viands, although they were good and savoury, pleased not the lovely Gisela. She had no appetite to eat, for her feelings were wrought to too great an intensity to admit of her partaking of any enjoyment in the repast that was spread before her. The marshal attempted to play the part of a man careless and indifferent of the objects around him, although the conduct of his housekeeper was anything but pleasing to him. With his own hand he poured the sparkling wine into Gisela's glass, and shook her hand significantly, as she rejected the intoxicating juice, and with all the courtesy which was natural to her, and in a tone bespeaking kindness and gratitude, she requested of Matilda a glass of water.

The grace with which she preferred the request affected the housekeeper, notwithstanding the obdurate character of her disposition, and she hastened to obtain the required beverage from a little fountain that was playing in the corner of the room.

The marshal then said to Gisela, in a harsh tone,—

"How can you demean yourself by allowing the ugly creature to bring you a glass of water; and do you not entertain some fear that she may, in the malice of her disposition, mix some poison with it?"

"I have not done anything to injure or affront her," said Gisela, in a manner quite composed; "independently of which, I place the greatest confidence in a woman's heart."

Gisela had scarcely uttered these words, than bitter tears shot into the eyes of the passionate Matilda, and she said, in a vehement tone,—

"That is too much, Herr Segbold. Have I deserved to be so maltreated by you, whilst all my actions are directed for your good? Am I an ugly creature? Am I one likely to be guilty of mixing poison in the draught of one who never injured me? It is not given to us to be all as beautiful as our blessed mother; and for a long time I have been sufficiently handsome for you, and have never yet been guilty of mixing poison, however severe and numerous may have been the affronts that have been heaped upon me from every quarter."

Her words were, by degrees, lost in sobs, on which the marshal appeared to be restless, and moved his chair backwards and forwards, as if his seat were uneasy to him; but being somewhat appeased by Matilda's complaints, he said,—

"Well, well; be only kind and good. I did not mean any ill in what I said. If you will give over weeping, and promise to conduct yourself properly, we will be as good friends as we were before. I grant that my anger is easily excited; and, therefore, you should not exasperate me; knowing my weakness, you should not play upon it. You should be kind and hospitable, and try to curb your damnable jealousy, which even shows itself when my dog fawns upon me. A jealous woman is generally a fiend; and I am not anxious to encourage the breed of that sort of creatures in my house; I would rather extirpate every one that dared to show itself under my roof. Now, Matilda, I shall say no more, so dry your tears, and seat yourself by my side, and enjoy merrily and cheerfully whatever Heaven has sent us."

On Matilda perceiving that the marshal had, on a sudden, changed his mode of conduct and his behaviour towards her, she became as docile and as supple as a leech, brought with the greatest readiness and goodwill the night-cap of the old gentleman, and his dressing-gown lined with fur, and his shoes of felt, and appeared unwilling to desist from her attentions until the comfort of the old gentleman was confirmed in every particular, when she seated herself between Gisela and her master, with satisfaction expressed in her countenance, and apparently an unfurrowed brow, as if nothing of an unpleasant nature had happened in the house.

Segbold now became extraordinarily merry, played all kinds of childish tricks, which are too often practised by a bachelor of seventy-two years old; addressing himself particularly to Gisela, he praised the fidelity and the honest services of Matilda, and said at last, joking to the latter,—

"O, thou red, purring cat, thou didst then really think that I had bought myself a young wife on the highway. But what if I tell thee that I krow nothing of the handsome girl, further than that her name is Gisela, and that she was forsaken by that scoundrel Saurbein, who stole my beautiful chesnut-horse."

Matilda, with her eyes directed on her plate, cast from under her dark eye-lashes a look of suspicion upon Gisela, and was in a great measure pleased with the candour and simplicity which sat on the maiden's brow. The suspicion which she at first entertained, that the lord, her master, departing from the ways of propriety and decorum, had introduced a new lady-love into the castle, began to subside, especially when Segbold, the sharer of her garrulity, being opened by frequent applications to the bottle, gave a circumstantial account of all the momentous occurrences of the day, at the conclusion of which she said, in a very becoming and discreet manner,—

"Christian charity is acceptable to God. This house is much at the service of the young lady, and everything which stands in my humble power to render her comfortable. I am but the servant, and my master has only to command, and my duty teaches me to obey."

"I will not be long a burden to you," said Gisela, placing her hand in that of the false and malicious Matilda; "the goodness of the Lord of the earth is too great to me, and the residence in such a noble mansion becomes not a poor girl like myself, although by birth I am as noble as the proprietor of it."

An air of incredulity sat upon the countenance of Matilda; and Segbold, in a most inquisitive and pressing manner, importuned his guest to disclose her family name. Gisela, however, answered with great humility,—

"Spare me the painful task of relating to you the misfortunes of my father, and attribute it not to my pride that I have made mention of my noble birth. It was merely my wish to give Miss Matilda to understand, that I am no wandering vagabond girl, and would rather die than be a burden upon good and compassionate people."

"By the holy St. Ursula!" exclaimed Segbold, "but the girl speaks as if she had been accustomed to preach from the pulpit. By my soul, a common person could not speak in this manner."

"Did you not make mention of an aunt who resides at Ulm?" said Matilda, in an artful and cunning manner. "You are not far from the road that leads to it; you will soon arrive at the banks of the Danube."

"Ah! ah!" exclaimed Segbold, eagerly, and casting a look of love upon Gisela. "There's no hurry for such matters. Let it be considered as a settled matter, that the young lady be made as comfortable in my house as circumstances will admit, and until it be her pleasure to depart; of that, however, we will talk to-morrow, or the day afterwards, or perhaps in a month, or even in a year. I have neither wife nor child; I will make no provision for my reprobate nephew, the dissolute vagabond, the unprincipled spendthrift, whose whole business of life appears to be the seduction of innocent girls. Promise me, my fair stranger, not to speak again of departure, or of bidding farewell to us before our acquaintance has scarcely begun."

"That will depend upon circumstances, noble sir," said Gisela, almost inattentive to what the enamoured dotard was saying. "Grant me only tranquillity in some retired chamber in which I can pass the night, not in sleep, but in prayer to Heaven, that in its goodness it would point out to me whether I should proceed forward in my journey, or return to my home."

"You shall proceed no further," said Herr Segbold; "you shall remain here, and that is my determination. By the great toe of the pope, but I know how to manage obstinate people. For miles round about I must tell you, that people tremble before me—you had a specimen of that with the charcoal-burners. You must learn to fear me. For thirty years I have played the despot in this castle, excepting now and then that I have, like a fool, placed myself under the government of a woman. Eh! Matilda—what say you to that? Fools only are governed by women. I am not governed by women, therefore, I am not a fool. Eh! Gisela, my pretty maid, what say you to that?"

Gisela now perceived that the power of the wine began to exert its influence in the weak head of the old man, and she became, therefore, importunate in her request to be allowed to retire to her bed-chamber.

"Immediately, my fair lady," said Matilda, in rather an ironical tone, but apparently with the utmost courtesy. "I occupy a gloomy, great chamber, and you may share it with me. I suspect that we shall become very intimate; and the society of a modest, well-behaved lady like yourself, of which pleasure I have hitherto deprived myself, out of love and regard to my worthy master, will tend to make the time appear less tedious upon my hands."

With the guile of the serpent she threw her arms round the neck of the unsuspecting girl, who thought she had excited the sympathy of her adversary, who, in a few moments afterwards, conducted her out of the apartment.

In the meantime, the taper had been placed on the table, and Segbold, after he had received the sincere good night of Gisela, directed his eyes for some time to the door by which the beautiful apparition had disappeared; and he began to dream of a new source of happiness which might spring up for him in the deep wintry snow of his age, like a late but an unfading rose. To rear and cultivate this rose for himself appeared to him to be one of the most desirable of things; in fact, as an actual necessity of his life. He, however, felt a secret dread of the female sentinel with the flaming sword; and he, therefore, felt himself highly elated when Matilda entered in a more friendly and merry mood than in which she was generally wont to show herself. The artful hussy approached the old dotard, and said waggishly, holding up her finger in a threatening attitude,—

"This is against our agreement, old Father Segbold; but as it appears that you have imbibed an affection for her, I will also love and thank you for my new assistant."

"Thunder and lightning!" exclaimed Segbold, in a doubting tone, "are you serious, Matilda?"

"As true, my dear man," answered Matilda, "as that I gave some money to the servant whom I ordered to be put into the stocks, and took the chains off the legs of Eliza, merely out of joy at the arrival of our new guest."

"I am grateful to Heaven for it," said Segbold; "but do not let the bird escape out of the cage; and I hope that you will live like two turtle doves together. I shall sleep well to-night, Matilda, because we have to-day been on such extraordinary good terms with each other. Come, lead me to my chamber; since my ride this morning, that infernal gout has been trying where it can make its lodgment good. Is everything fresh and healthy in the castle? I hope no one else will take it into his head and die, and drive me from my castle."

"By no means," answered Matilda. "Everything is fresh and wholesome, and may you live long, as you are my joy and my staff."

"Thanks to thee for thy good wishes, sweet Matilda," said the elated dotard. "I will think about augmenting thy legacy. I have given enough already to the monks, and if they want to procure the intercession of the saints of Heaven for my safe and speedy delivery from purgatory, why, I doubt not, sweet Matilda, but thou wilt assist them."

"Certainly, oh, most certainly, dear, good man," said the hypocritical serpent; "if I can assist you out of purgatory, depend upon it, you shall not remain there long."

"Everything that I possess," said Segbold, "with the exception of this castle, which, for the sake of the honour of the family, I have bequeathed to my nephew, will at my death belong to you."

"And I will share it with Gisela," said the artful fiend.

"And wilt thou do that, my darling?" said Segbold; "why, you anticipate my fondest wishes. A long time may not elapse before the parentage of Gisela may be discovered; a rich man may then perhaps take her as his wife, and then everything which belonged to me and which in your goodness you shared with Gisela, will again revert to you."

"I will not, however," said Matilda, "be bought by any one. I will live like a widow —like one whom you have left alone in the world."

"Ah!" exclaimed Segbold, "therein I recognise your true, your faithful heart. It's now you will cherish and nurse me well until my death; but do not let Gisela escape."

"Do not trouble yourself on that account," said Matilda; "depend upon it, she will not run away. I warrant you that when she awoke this morning she never expected to sleep at night in a castle like this. I wish you may not be deceived in the opinion that you have formed of your new guest. The company of charcoal-burners was an odd kind of place to find a modest or a virtuous girl; but time will show. But it is time you were in your bed, my dear master."

It was the general custom of Matilda to talk the old man asleep; but on this night no such narcotic appeared to be necessary, for he had no sooner laid himself snugly between the sheets, than he called upon Matilda to give him her nightly blessing, which was a kiss, as he thought, from her pure and unpolluted lips; and, having again committed Gisela to her especial care, he fell asleep.

Matilda, being assured that the enamoured dotard was fast asleep, lighted her lamp, and on tiptoe left the apartment to proceed to her own dormitory. On the stairs she encountered the marshal's valet, Ulrick, a stout, vigorous man, who was bringing to her the keys of the castle, according to the regulations of the place, and in return for the ponderous load which he delivered to her, she gave him an affectionate kiss from her supposed unpolluted lips.

"The old fool is asleep," he said, in a whisper; "I will follow you, my love."

"Not to-night, Ulrick; the upstart girl that Segbold has brought into the castle sleeps in my apartment."

"Who is this stranger girl?" asked Ulrick.

"The devil himself knows," said Matilda; "but the old goat is enamoured of her, and that is quite enough for me to put a speedy termination to the matter."

"You are a wise woman," said Ulrick; "the person who gets to windward of you must be a confounded clever person. But get rid of the nuisance as soon as you can, that we may pass our nights as usual."

"Depend upon it," said Matilda, "I have made my arrangements. The creature does not sleep many nights under this roof, and had I not a particular end in view, do you think that I would have been tormented with such a bedfellow as she is?"

"Not I, indeed," said Ulrick, with a smile, "when you could have obtained one more agreeable to you."

Matilda in a playful manner placed her hand on the mouth of her favoured swain, and having affectionately embraced each other, they retired, not very well satisfied, to their respective apartments.

On Matilda opening the door of her apartment, she was struck with astonishment on observing Gisela standing at the window, which she had thrown open, looking down on the vast depth below, at the foot of which the tall fir tree looked like some diminutive birch.

"Why are you not asleep?" said Matilda, in an abrupt and surly tone.

"I have been conversing with God," said Gisela, and pointed significantly towards the heavens, in which the clear full moon, surrounded by its host of stars, swam like a silver swan on the dark blue sea. Matilda appeared to be very little affected by the solemn spectacle of the night, and turned in an abrupt manner to Gisela, and said, in a half-suppressed tone, but therefore not the less imperious and threatening,—

"Allow me, now," she said, "to speak openly with you. I am not one who fights about the bush—I generally come to the point at once; and I now tell you that you and I shall not agree here together. Whatever conceit you may have in your head, or whatever may be the plans which you may expect to carry into execution, depend upon it, you will find yourself disappointed. Herr Segbold is a weak, foolish man, easily led away by a pretty face, and soon deceived by an artful hussy; but I will soon put an end to such proceedings. One of us must give way; and as I am determined not to do it, you shall be obliged to do it; and no time shall be lost about it—it shall take place to-morrow, and that, too, before the last fowl has gone to roost. I'll not have any fuss nor hubbub about it—the whole business shall be done quietly and secretly; and should you presume to return, I will have thy back scourged, and I will send thee forth a vagabond; and if that be not sufficient to tame thee, I will have thee placed where neither sun nor moon can shine upon thee; and if I be obliged to kill thee at last, I know how it can be done, and no soul on earth shall know it. Have you heard what I have been saying to you?"

It was the expectation of Matilda that Gisela would fall upon her knees before her, and sink to the ground with alarm and fear. No such circumstance, however, took place. The whole stock of ferocity and barbarity, as well as of insolent abuse, which Matilda possessed, was in some degree rendered wholly ineffective by the cool tranquillity and undisturbed presence of mind with which Gisela looked her enemy full in the face; and still higher rose the astonishment of the she-tyrant, when Gisela, with the greatest composure and collectedness, answered,—

"You may spare yourself your threats; not one of them was necessary, for I had previously determined what I should say to you, and what I had resolved to do, and which appears exactly to coincide with your wishes. I was not five minutes in this house before I was devising the means by which I could leave it. I am by no means anxious, as it may perhaps be your belief, for the friendship of the Herr von Zavelstein, and still less for the situation which you occupy in his castle. A more solitary and tranquil life is my destiny, and I require no other friend than the God in Heaven. I have even now been holding converse with him, and since that moment the most extraordinary thoughts have entered my mind."

Matilda stood opposite to Gisela, and knew not what opinion to form of her. She had hitherto been accustomed to rule over the menials of the house with a rod of iron—to find them all obsequious to her will, and to throw themselves at her feet, rather than excite her anger or displeasure. Now, she had met with something quite new and uncommon, and from a quarter where she least expected it.

There was something in the conduct and demeanour of Gisela which possessed a kind of overawing influence, and there was a power of fascination about her which, struggle as she might against it, she could not withstand ; and she listened to what Gisela had to say with an attention bordering on respect and veneration.

" I have considered," said Gisela, " how the great Lord of the creation exhibits himself with so much goodness towards all those who call themselves his image. The sun shines with an equal warmth upon the good man as upon the roguish Saurbein, who deceived me. The moon throws a light equally upon the drunkard, over his bowl, as upon the modest tenant of a monastic cell, who leaves his hard and unenviable bed to join the midnight hymn to the mother of our Saviour. It is our duty to imitate the everlasting compassion, as far as it lies within our power ; to reward our enemies by kindness and amity, and to love those who persecute and hate us. Therefore, to you, Matilda, who are persecuting me without any valid reason for it, to you will I impart the secrets of my life, in order that the scales may drop from your eyes, and you may know against whom you have threatened to raise your malicious and guilty hand."

With the greatest composure, and without the slightest reserve, Gisela related to her astonished auditor the afflictions of her short life, her hatred to the nephew of the marshal, now rendered more inveterate, since she had been made acquainted with the wicked design which he had contemplated against her. She then related her flight from her father's house, and the resolution to which she still adhered, notwithstanding the mysterious disappearance of her conductor, of proceeding to her aunt at Ulm ; and should she be treated with severity or unkindness, rather than suffer disgrace, to enter as a lay sister into any convent that would receive her.

The undissembled confidence with which Matilda saw herself honoured, without in the least deserving it, stung her to the heart, although she felt herself flattered by it. She acknowledged that she was in the wrong, declared her sorrow for it; but, nevertheless, she hesitated not to turn everything that she had heard to her own advantage. She increased in the most cunning manner, by the most extraordinary narratives, not one of which was, perhaps, founded in truth, the hatred which Gisela had imbibed towards Hurdegen, as well as the dissatisfaction which Gisela had expressed at the conduct of the marshal.

Matilda represented herself to be an unfortunate woman, who had been seduced, who bitterly repented of the fault which she had committed, and, in return, left no means unemployed to make the most ample remuneration for the crime which she had committed, by the performance of a good action whenever it lay in her power. She therefore considered it to be her most sacred duty to offer her hand to Gisela as a pledge of her determination to promote her wishes to the utmost possible extent, saying it gave her the most unfeigned satisfaction that a most favourable opportunity just then presented itself for accomplishing the purpose which she had in view. She had heard that it was the intention of the miller in the valley below, a most worthy and respectable man, to depart to-morrow for Pfullingen, in a carriage fit for the accommodation of a traveller. Gisela might most safely confide herself to his protection, and she would take care that everything should be provided that could render her journey comfortable and pleasant. From Pfullingen it would be an easy matter to obtain a conveyance to Ulm ; and if Gisela did not find matters in that city exactly conformable to her wishes, or that, on her arrival at Pfullingen, she might change her mind, and not proceed to Ulm at all, she had it then in her power to second the views of Gisela, for she knew a convent exactly according to the wishes expressed by Gisela, and her admission into which would be easily accomplished for her by the interest and intercession of Matilda.

" To what convent do you allude ?" asked Gisela.

Matilda replied, with a devout air, and her eyes directed to the ground—

" It is the Convent of Gnadenzell, of the Benedictine order."

" Where is it situated?" asked Gisela ; " and how comes it to pass that you are able to procure me admission into it ?"

" The convent," replied Matilda, " is situated on the Alb, in a most retired part of the country, exactly according to your wishes, very much resembling the caves in which dwelt the first and most reverend hermits. The prioress, however, the holy Mother Richardi, is my sister."

" Your sister !" exclaimed Gisela ; " then let us not cease to wonder at the dark ways of the eternal Providence, which places your sister at the head of a holy flock of lambs, whilst you are the housekeeper of an old, dissolute dotard."

Matilda found it necessary to squeeze a few hypocritical tears from her eyes, and sighed, beating her breast.

"One has already entered Heaven here below, whilst the other has plunged into the death of sin. It is, however, my hope, that the blood of the Redeemer has also flowed for me; that I shall also one day escape the snares of death; and it is my wish to close my terrestrial career in the holy house over which my sister presides."

With an emotion of conscious virtue, Gisela exclaimed,—

"Why will you not do to-day what, perhaps, on the morrow the devil will prevent you? Cut off from you those golden ornaments—those silver spangles and chains—this gorgeous silken attire. Leave everything behind you that is offensive to virtue, and follow me to Gnadenzell. There shall not be any distinction between us; we shall be as sisters, and edify each other by our example."

Matilda felt herself partly alarmed at this proposition, and partly she felt herself tempted to cast the whole force of her ridicule upon the innocent enthusiast; but she stifled the scorn with which her throat was filled, covered herself with the shield of duplicity, and answered, with a tone of melancholy,—

"How willingly, my dear Gisela, would I follow you, but my absence would prove the death of the marshal. Is it not my duty to attend upon the sick-bed of him in whose happiness and joys I have participated? The interval between his final departure from the world is already a golden season of probation for me; and, purified from many spots and blemishes, I shall one day leave this house. You are, however, one of the blest—an unspotted angel on earth. Promise me, at least, to be the bearer of a note, which I will write to my sister. Her thanks will reward you for the trouble when mine can be of no value to you. I will go, and return immediately, and I will arrange everything that can make your journey agreeable. Let not such a gloom hang upon your countenance. You shall not stand indebted to me for anything; you can repay me for everything from Ulm—that is, if there be anything to repay."

Matilda hastily left the room. She had, although with some degree of humiliation, obtained a speedy victory over the enemy. The malicious smile with which she seated herself to indite the letter, appeared to indicate as if she had it in her contemplation to bring down a still heavier blow on the head of her whose cheerful innocence and unshaken fortitude caused her so much vexation.

Whilst Matilda was thus employed, Gisela sank into profound meditation. It was repellent to her to accept of any assistance or favour from her. Nevertheless, the reality always stood before her.

"I must away; I will never return; there is no choice left for me."

And then the image of Gnadenzell, with its deep, sequestered retirement, played so vividly before her imagination, that she almost forgot her aunt in Ulm, and she already saw herself habited as a nun in the holy walls.

Daylight had scarcely tinged the eastern sky, when Gisela, conducted by the treacherous Matilda, stepped out of the castle of the hated and dreaded Zavelstein. The honest miller, having received his instructions and his bribe, through the hands of the confidential valet, was by times at the appointed place at the foot of the castle, and vowed, as her travelling companion tarried in ascending the carriage, to take all possible care of her, as a good and honourable man. After a cool and monosyllabic farewell, the carriage drove off, and a few hours afterwards, Matilda, with a woful countenance, informed her master, that the ungrateful Gisela had found the means of effecting her escape, and that it was not worth the trouble to make any inquiries after the vagabond girl.

It did not take many words to dissuade the old childless man from encouraging any further the whim with which he had amused himself on the preceding day, and which tended rather to her shame than her credit; and, if Segbold soon forgot Gisela, in her turn, Gisela was not long in forgetting Segbold, but only in so far as his person or his character was concerned; for, in regard to the circumstances connected with her short sojourn at Zavelstein, they were never erased from her memory; and when she recalled them to her mind, she felt a cold shudder come over her, as if she were witnessing some horrid scene, on which her ruin depended. A new life, however, now opened upon her —a new world presented itself to her, and she was angry with the horses that they did not go at a quicker rate, but crept up the mountain, slow and panting, a pace by far too slow for her impatience.

The miller and Gisela had dismounted, out of humanity to the brutes, which had a heavy load to drag up the steep ascent; and Gisela, being somewhat in advance, soon came up to a black figure, who, leaning on a thick walking-staff, appeared to be tired with the ascent of the hill. The devout countenance of the youth, his auburn locks, and his student's dress, were not wholly unknown to Gisela. The sleeper amidst the rocks, when she was in company with Sauibein, stood before her, and she saluted him in a familiar manner, as if he had been an old acquaintance. The friendly salutation of Gisela was highly pleasing to the student, and soon created between them that bond of cordiality, which, in general, exists between persons who are travelling on the same road.

"Whither are you going, my good young man?" asked Gisela.

"To Pfullingen," was the answer.

"I am going thither," said Gisela. "What is your name? and what is your profession?"

"My name," answered the youth, "is Jacob Spittler Goppinger; I am a clerical student, and am just on my way from Hirschaw, where the abbot richly rewarded me, as he was so well pleased with the music of my guitar."

"You appear fatigued, poor youth," said Gisela.

"I am fatigued," said the youth, "and glad, indeed, I should be if you could let me ride in your carriage."

"Most willingly," said Gisela; "if the miller have no objection."

At this moment the miller came up to them, and heard the last words, when he jocosely said,—

"Get up, my young monk; your dignity will not add much to the weight; and, when we are fatigued, you will, perhaps, play us a tune. I have heard that some horses are very fond of music, and, perhaps, mine may be of that number; if so, they will go the quicker for it."

The hill having been surmounted, Gisela and the student mounted the carriage, and, discussing on various subjects, they proceeded on their way to Pfullingen.

CHAPTER VII.

" Then leave him to his conscience;
It is a scorpion, sent by Heaven itself
To fix on hidden crimes—a slow still stream
Of molten lead kept dropping on the heart,
To scald and weigh it down. Believe me, love,
There is no earthly punishment so great
To scourge an evil act as man's own conscience,
To tell him he is guilty."

IT was a beautiful season of the year, when everything was flourishing in joy and luxury. The golden ear of corn hung heavy and full; the vines promised an abundant crop; the branches of the trees were breaking with the weight of the fruit. Thus there was joy and merriment in village and in town, and the wine and the corn that had been hoarded, most lavishly consumed, as the bounty of Heaven appeared to have provided so liberally for the future. Notwithstanding the favourable prospect, all was not well constituted in the country; for, although the peasant and the farmer might sleep in peace within the four walls of his cottage, yet he could not always travel in safety on the highway, and many under the sky of Wurtemburg lost both life and property by the nightly highwaymen, although the utmost attention was paid by Count Eterhard to maintain peace and tranquillity in the country, and to see that the laws were justly and impartially administered. Thus it frequently happened, where the foresight of the government could not prevent the commission of a crime, that it was obliged afterwards to interfere with the axe or the halter of the executioner, so that blood was frequently shed, and it was not always that the guilty blood was shed. In those troublesome times neither word nor faith was held; an oath was no longer sacred, and in every quarter crime and guilt arose like a great field overgrown with weeds.

For the purpose of applying the sickle to such a crop of thistles, twelve true and good men, natives of the village of Pfullingen, of the holy Roman empire, assembled under the blue canopy of heaven, whilst the sun was shining; and, in the open highway, according to the custom of the countries of the German nation, the staff officers, with their staffs, sat in a ring; but, on the steps of the council house, was elevated the chair of the chief magistrate of Urach, and he pronounced judgment in the name of the emperor, and the powerful lords of Wurtemberg. Two secretaries sat on either side, and, at the barriers, which surrounded the place, were the bailiffs, and the thief-catchers and their followers, as well as the officers who attended upon the chief magistrate, and the officers of justice in their imposing armorial coats, carrying the flag, the sword, and the rod of death; and, in their turn, called upon those to enter the ring who had any business to transact in it. Around the barriers a numerous crowd was collected, citizens of Pfullenger, gentlemen and tradesmen of Rentlingen, peasants from the banks of the Alb and the vallies, and many of the inhabitants of Ehnengen, the merchants of Rentlengen, market people and carriers, for the business that was on this day to be transacted, was to them of great and paramount importance At a respectable distance from the people stood the executioner, with his assistants and his instrument of torture, awaiting the sentence, by which his services would be required.

See page 56.

After the horn had sounded three times, and the drum had been beat, the chief provost read aloud the ordinance of their gracious liege; the officers of justice cried silence to all the four quarters of the wind, and no one ventured afterwards to move; neither the noblemen within the barriers, nor the daring boy on the corner of the roofs of the houses. The streets were closed with chains, and not a horse nor carriage dare pass through Pfullengen whilst the tribunal lasted. The chief provost then ordered that the accused should be brought forward, and, from the council house came forth a pale young man, with flaxen hair, and the down scarcely upon his chin. His hands were tied behind his back, and the constables placed him in the ring, unloosened the bandages which confined his hands, but appeared to take every necessary precaution to prevent his escape. The chief provost now gave a second signal, and the accuser and the witnessess came within the barrier to substantiate the charge against the prisoner. The first was a man dressed in deep mourning, the second was a tradesman of Ehnengen, and the third was a gamekeeper, in the Carthusian monastery, at Guterstein. The two latter were wounded, and had several bloody scars on their head.

The first accuser delivered his evidence under the obligation of an oath and his honour, as a gentleman, namely,—

"That he was a native of Dressenhoven, on his return from Ulm, where he had buried his father's sister-in-law, on his way to his own residence, at Wotenlop; that a few days ago he arrived at Urach, and that he had there sent his horses forward on the road, whilst he himself went on foot to St. John, having made a vow there to hear a mass for the poor soul of his aunt, in purgatory. A poor, honest man, from Ehnengen, the same who now stood wounded at his side, accompanied him on his pilgrimage without any risk or danger. They, however, little suspected, in their journey from St. John, to be attacked by some robbers, who placed their lives in the greatest jeopardy, which took place as they were passing through a wild and inhospitable part of the country, when these men rushed from a wood, and, with murderous weapons in their hands, robbed them of their money. Nor would they have escaped with their lives had not the honest gamekeeper—sent, it would seem, by God—arrived at the critical juncture, who laid one of the robbers prostrate on the ground, and, after a hard struggle, compelled the other two to save themselves by flight."

The tradesman from Ehnengen, after having the oath administered to him, confirmed the previous evidence, exhibited his wounds, and swore by all the saints, that the man, who was immediately afterwards captured in a wretched hovel, at Pfullengen, and who was now at the bar as a prisoner, was one of the robbers. In this he was confirmed by the gamekeeper, who added, "that the highwayman, who was killed, was a person unknown in the country, but who, no doubt, would be very easily recognised; whilst one of those who escaped, was no other person than the dreaded Wildherr, the chief of the gang of robbers, who for some time had been committing the most alarming depredations throughout the whole of the country."

At the close of the evidence, the three witnesses called upon the magistrates to pass the severest sentence upon the delinquent, as a lesson to his confederates, that they were not to carry on their atrocious crimes with impunity.

After a long pause, the chief magistrate turned to the accused, and said,—

"Who are you? What is your name, and whence do you come?"

"I was christened Heinz," said the youth; "and refuse to give you any further information."

"As you refuse," said the magistrate, "to give to these wise and learned men any further information touching your birth, your origin, and occupation, I will do it for you. You are, my honourable friends, all acquainted with the house of Stahlerk, not far from Wolzelfengen, a noble mansion, where heretofore an honourable family resided. At this time, however, it is the residence of several decayed noble families of different names, the character and renown of which stand not very high in the country. They, indeed, carry their coats of arms, wear open helmets, keep well stocked dovecots, according to the ancient German custom. Their indigence obliges them to cultivate their fields during the six days of the week; and, on the seventh, they parade pompously to church, clad in their scarlet cloaks. There is, however, a report current in the country, that the produce of the fields is not sufficient for their support; that their house is falling daily more and more into ruin, and that it is difficult to conceive how they manage with honesty and integrity to support the pride and haughtiness of their outward demeanour, to hold their banquets, and to lead a life of riotousness and profligacy, such as is notorious throughout the whole of the country. One of these wild and profligate youths now stands before you, the descendant of a very respectable family, of the name of Schlaif. Considering that he was ashamed here publicly to declare his name, so ought he to have been ashamed of committing the robbery of which he now stands accused. Or do you still deny, Heinz von Schlaif, do you still obstinately deny the act of which these creditable men now accuse you?"

"I do deny it." said Heinz.

"That which aggravates your deed and your obstinate falsehood, is the suspicion that you are in association with the terrible robber, who, by the audacity of his acts, renders these vallies scarcely habitable. His name is an abomination, as his deeds have been long a scandal and a disgrace to the country. It is rumoured that he has often found a refuge in your house, and that you and several others have frequently accompanied him on his predatory excursions."

" I do not know Wildherr," said Heinz.

The gamekeeper of Sutenteen here interfered, and said, " I will pledge my salvation that that young man was one of the robbers who attacked us: I recognised him immediately; I saw him as distinctly at that moment as I do now, and also when I met him on the Airhelberg, and he granted me my life."

" You ought, therefore, to be ashamed of yourself," said Heinz, with particular vehemence; "that you vilify him in return for your grateful thanks."

" But how then do you mean," exclaimed the magistrate, thinking that he had entrapped Heinz; " that the gamekeeper vilifies you, seeing that you deny that you were present at the robbery ?"

A murmur of approbation ran through the assembly, and all present expressed their astonishment at the acuteness of the magistrate. Heinz, for a short time, maintained a sullen silence, the blood rushed into his face, but he soon answered with renewed composure:—

"I was not present at the robbery. I know not these people, nor do I know Wildheer."

" What do you say to my rosary that was found in your possession ?" asked Diessenhoven.

"And the box of balsam that belonged to me," said the tradesman of Ehnengen, " that was found in your pocket ?"

"And your concealment in the hayloft to which you were traced ?" exclaimed the gamekeeper.

" I wished to pay a visit to a girl, and was obliged to conceal myself from her in ended bridegroom. In regard to the rosary and the box, I bought them of a Jew, to make a present of them to my sweetheart."

"In that house," said the judge, "there is no sweetheart for you; it is a public-house of ill fame, the knavish hostess of which awaits her sentence in prison."

The magistrate waited for some time for a satisfactory answer from the prisoner ; but as he forbore to give any, he said, rising from his seat,—

" By virtue of the power vested in me, I sentence the hardened offender to be stretched on the wheel, until he speaks the truth, and declares the names of his equally guilty confederates."

Mainz shuddered, as he heard the preliminary sentence, and seemed anxious to say something, but he suddenly checked himself, bit his lips, and allowed himself to be conducted away by the constables. The doors of the council-house closed behind him, and the executioner, who was followed by his assistants and a few of the members of the tribunal. The people followed the criminal with their eyes, and the magistrates were about to rise from their seats, when a grey-headed man forced his way through the barriers, and threw himself on his knees before the chief provost.

" You see before you," he exclaimed, wringing his hands in despair, "a nobleman at your feet; but I am not ashamed of the disgrace, provided you will grant me your compassion. I am the father of the unfortunate youth, now suffering the torture of the rack. I am a poor man, and have two daughters and a sick wife to support with the sweat of my brow. I gain my livelihood from the stoney ground which fell to my lot, when, with the other inheritors of the district, I took up my residence in the dilapidated house of Stahlerk. My girls spin for the people, my poor Heinz fells the wood in the forest, and drives our lean cow, which is obliged to drag the plough, instead of giving us nutritious milk in a warm stable. Have compassion upon me, a broken-hearted man. I know nothing of the commission of any crime; on the contrary, I call God to witness the innocence of my son Heinz. He cannot be a thief nor a highwayman. He is, perhaps, thoughtless and volatile, a libertine, one who at night is addicted to forbidden ways. But, most noble and learned sirs, know you whence the evil originates? Know you why the sons of good and respectable people in this neighbourhood fall into ruin and disgrace? The scandalous monastery at Offenhausen makes them rogues and libertines, renders them lazy and indolent, and, instead of being respectful to their parents, are insolent and supercilious. It is there they have their rendezvous, carry on all sorts of games with the profligate monks, and make their secret assignations with the wanton, God-forgetting daughters of the holy St. Frances. If it be your wish, noble sirs, to strike at the root of all the evil, direct your extirpating power against that den of profligacy. Give me, however, back my son, that I may not expire with hunger and shame."

The bold and bitter speech of the old man made a deep impression on the minds of the magistrates; the chief provost, however, answered him with a shrug of the shoulders,—

"God is justice, and we administer justice according to our unbiassed conscience. The sword is not placed in vain in the hands of our wise and upright prince; and when grace and clemency have no effect, then must the severity of the law be visited upon the hardened offender. May the God of Heaven console you, poor old man. There is not a father who sits in this assembly, that does not sympathise in your grief. But pay particular attention to your own actions, and reform your mode of life before the rod recoils from the head of your son on your own grey and scanty looks. Report speaks not well of you, and you will not pretend to say that the nuns of Offenhausen have also seduced you into the paths of wickedness? Leave the women of the convent to answer for their own iniquities, for which it is the intention of the chancellor of our gracious liege and master to call them severely to account. Attend to your own welfare and to the future prosperity of your other children."

This interlocution, the greater part of which was only heard by the magistrates, but which was chiefly drowned by the tumult of the restless crowd, was suddenly interrrupted by the doors of the council-house being thrown open, and Heinz appeared, borne almost in a lifeless state by the executioner and his assistants, having bravely overcome the tortures of the rack. The deplorable sight of the tortured youth frightened the father away, and, covering his face with his hands, he was lost amidst the crowd. On the other hand, the crowd pressed tumultuously towards the ring; and the windows of the houses, which for a time had been unoccupied, were now again filled with spectators in almost breathless anxiety, and influenced by the most painful curiosity. In the inn, known by the sign of the Holy Angel, facing the council-house, the ingress and egress of the people resembled a bee-hive, and the casual spectator would have supposed that it was fair time, so great was the crowd employed in eating and drinking, and in loud and idle talk; and so great were the noise and hubbub, that a person could hardly hear what his neighbour was saying to him. Every moment fresh guests arrived in the rooms of the inn, chiefly strangers, who had left their vehicles standing in the streets that were barricaded, and who had entered the house by a back door. The throng was indescribable, and the modest and the diffident could find neither a place at the table nor at the window, nor any victuals to satisfy their hunger.

Thus leaning in a corner stood a beautiful girl, with a bundle in her hand, and close to her a youthful clerical student, with his guitar concealed under his cloak, who said to his companion,—

"I think we should have acted more prudently to have taken up our quarters at the baker's house where the miller stopped. We shall not be able to earn a single penny here by my music, and you appear to be very weak and faint. I know not what is going on before the magistrates, and should the beheading of a poor criminal take place, we should feel ourselves in a still more dreadful condition, although we might not exactly witness the flowing of the blood, nor the headless trunk writhing in agony."

"My good Jacob," said Gisela, with a trembling voice, "I would most willingly take our immediate departure from this place, if I knew exactly whither to direct my steps. Who will advise me whether it be better to introduce myself at once to the prioress, and solicit her advice, or to request of you, when you visit your master in the convent, to deliver the letter to the prioress, whilst I prosecute my journey to Ulm?"

"To Ulm!" exclaimed an elderly, corpulent man, who was sitting close to her at a table, before his bottle of wine. "I am a native of that place, and I will convey you thither, if you be good and honest people."

"You may depend upon that," said Gisela; "the lady, the widow of Diessenhaven, is my aunt, and has promised to provide for me."

"Poor child," said the man, with a look of rather contemptuous pity, "I would advise you to return immediately whence you came, for you will gain but little by going to Ulm. The old avaricious woman has been dead for some time; and that part of her property which she did not bequeath to the hospital has been taken possession of by her cousin, on whose account the tribunal is now sitting at this place; an ill-natured man, as stingy as the old woman, who was most lavish in his abuses and his curses, because he found less than he expected."

The man now turned away from Gisela with the utmost indifference, and began to talk with his neighbour, and, as it was evident that he did not intend to trouble himself any further about her, a tremour came over her whole frame, and she whispered to the young student,—

"That is a hard stroke, indeed; and Saurbein has most scandalously deceived me.

My only hope and salvation are now to be found in the convent; and, if there be no objection on your part, we will depart immediately, before any further calamity befals us."

" I am ready," said Jacob; " I should think that the distance we have yet to travel now cannot be great."

At this moment the host passed close to them, and Gisela, in a mild and timid manner, inquired the road that she was to take, by which she could arrive at Gnadenzell, without risk of any danger.

The host put on a sorrowful look, measured the strangers from head to foot, and then said, with a malicious smile,—

" What business have you in Gnadenzell, my pretty girl?"

Dispirited by the laugh of the host, neither of them ventured to give an answer to him, and he continued, with a bitter sneer,—

" You are on the right road at an early age, you silly creatures. Make all possible haste, that you may enjoy the society of the virtuous and pious ladies. Take the road there to the right hand, that leads to Honan, and then every rogue and scoundrel will tell you the road to Gnadenzell."

He then turned to some of the guests who were drinking, whispered a few words in their ear, and pointed to Gisela and her companion, on which they all burst into a loud fit of laughter, which so exasperated Gisela, that she beckoned Jacob to follow her; and having with difficulty reached the outside of the house, they soon found themselves on the road to Honan.

Chagrined and mortified at the rude and uncourteous behaviour of the host, they made the best of their way through the tumultuous crowd, and were glad to turn their backs on the inhospitable house, as well as on the avaricious cousin, and the bloody tribunal, the horrible ceremonies of which filled their innocent hearts with fear and horror.

In the meantime the bell sounded solemnly from the tower of the church, and all the spectators round the tribunal took off their hats, for the magistrates were then engaged in prayer to God, that he would enlighten their minds, that the sentence which they had to pass might be founded on justice, tempered with mercy. A deep silence reigned over the whole place, and not a word was heard, as the chief magistrate again appeared, accompanied by the other members of the tribunal, and in a solemn voice pronounced the sentence :—

" In the name of the emperor, and our most gracious lord and liege, the Count of Wurtemberg, that seeing that thou, Heinz von Schlaiz, setting aside our paternal admonitions, and even under the torture of the rack hast persisted in thy denial of the charge imputed to thee, and hast refused to disclose the names of thy confederates, we, the judges, and magistrates, do hereby condemn thee, although in mercy we spare thy life, that thy left foot and thy right arm be cut off by the common hangman, as a punishment to thee, and a warning example to others; and, further, that thou be banished from the country, under the penalty of thy head, if thou ever returnest; and may God reform thy sinful soul. Such is our sentence."

With a heartrending cry, the father of the condemned youth fell to the ground, whilst Heinz himself leaned, almost annihilated, on the shoulders of the assistants of the executioner, who supported him. As, however, the hangman approached him, Heinz cried aloud, so that it was heard by the whole assembly,—

" May the retribution of God fall on my judges on their death-bed, for this cruel sentence; and here on earth may the vengeance of God fall on the witnesses who have sworn falsely against me. Woe and damnation be upon their heads!"

A terrible voice was immediately heard amongst the assembled people, exclaiming,—
" Amen!"

An unaccountable commotion ran through the whole assembly; for no one knew immediately by what mouth the awful word was pronounced; but in a few moments a hundred voices cried out,—

" It was the voice of Wildherr—Wildherr has sworn it. God be gracious to the judges and the accusers."

Deeply were the magistrates affected, as they rose from their seats, and they whispered to each other,—

" Woe to us and our children. The young sinner has pronounced our doom."

The chief provost then said,—

" Of what consequence is such a trifling word?"

One of the eldest of the judges answered,—

" You are ignorant, sir; but we know too well that Wildherr never pardons, and that, in condemning the criminal, we are ourselves condemned to death."

A secret shudder came over the chief provost; he, however, departed not from the dignity of the judge, and entered the council-house, saying,—

"What is written is written."

He was followed by the magistrates, and a private council was held, in which it was determined to postpone the execution of the sentence, and to despatch a messenger to the Castle of Arhalm, where the count was residing, in order that, in his wisdom, he might determine whether, under the peculiar circumstances of the case, it would be politic to carry the sentence into execution.

Whilst the blood-thirsty people, ignorant of the postponement that had been commanded, were dreaming of the mutilation of the malefactor, some of them crowding along the streets, others talking on the house-tops, others drinking in the public-houses, the father of Heinz hastened, with an expedition far byond his years, through the village of Unterhausen towards the wild defile in the mountain, on the steep declivity of which the house of Stahlerk was built. It lay in the shadow of the ruins of the former edifice, more towards the depths of the hollow way, and was constructed chiefly of the fragments of the former castle. It was an irregular building, and and had arisen by degrees according to the accidents of chance and necessity. The rustic arch of the gateway could scarcely bear any longer the weight of the upper story, the window openings of which, like dark holes, looked upon the hollow way. The window-sashes hung corroded by the air on their rusty hinges; the stairs were decayed and defective; the roof was full of holes; and not less ruinous; nor unguarded was the barn in which the collected families who resided in the house deposited the scanty produce which they obtained from the fields which they cultivated, which, barren and inhospitable as they were, lay up the hill, and chiefly within the boundary-walls of the castle so that the barley now grew where formerly the horses of the lord of the castle grazed, and the plough formed uneven furrows between ruins and thistles, where formerly the youths and the maidens danced in the heyday and jollity of their life. Nothing more was necessary; by casting a look in the abode, and the property of the resident of the house, to arrive at once at the conclusion that want there held dominion, and poverty presided at their table in all its gaunt wretchedness.

The people pursued a kind of gipsy life, the scorn and the terror of the surrounding prosperous farmers, even where the latter were frequently obliged to bestow a tenth of their produce for the support of the inhabitants of Stahlerk. This, however, was done from a prudent and political motive, for they considered it better to give a little, than perhaps to be robbed of the whole, for there were some who hesitated to bestow their proportion, and the consequence was, that not a night elapsed but that some of their corn or fruit was carried away, and all attempt at redress was in vain; for, in those cases, the whole of the inhabitants of the house entered into a confederacy, and the bitterest revenge was exercised against those who had dared to summon any of them before the magistrate to answer for their delinquencies.

Of all the families who resided in the house, old Schlaiz and his relations obtained the greater portion of the bounty furnished by the farmers, for they feared him more than any other of his confederates. His hypocrisy and cunning were not deeper and more profligate than his anger and resentment were hasty and dangerous; and he was scarcely ever known to pronounce a threat which was not very soon afterwards carried into effect. That which he could not execute himself was accomplished by his son, and when he could not execute it, there were his two sisters who were always ready at hand to spread confusion and mischief to the utmost extent of their power. They certainly spun and wove when they had anything to spin and weave, and they gathered herbs and fished in the Erhatz, but they were also dexterous thieves, and committed here and there such extraordinary actions, that in some parts of the country they were looked upon as witches. In such actions they were greatly encouraged by the mother, who, having lost the use of almost all her limbs, was unable to leave the house. When the young ladies returned to their home at night, they groped their way to the miserable bed of chaff on which their aged mother lay, and related to her with a malicious joy all that had happened to them during the day, what they had caught in the river, or what they had stolen or begged; and then they received their instructions from their able preceptress how they were to carry on their nefarious proceedings for the future. On Sundays, however, no one could recognise them to be the same persons: decked out in the most gorgeous apparel, they sat before the door of their dilapidated dwelling, with their hands resting on their laps, relating to each the most romantic tales, of which love, of course, was the most prominent subject; or they sang some of their beautiful national airs, or romped and joked with their sweethearts, of whom each had found one amongst the residents of the house, although, in their formation, nature had forgotten to mingle a single particle of beauty, and their general appearance was disfigured by want, disease, and a life of the most wretched profligacy and debauchery.

On this momentous day they were sitting before the door, although it was not a holiday, and their haughtiness and superciliousness were humbled, and their look was more anxious than bold, as they directed it afar off, looking out for a messenger from Pfullingen.

The distant mountains were already covered with a violet mist, as the elder of the girls exclaimed,—

"By the blood of St. Januarius, but I see our old father coming hurrying along. Alas! he is coming alone, and our Heinz is not with him."

In a short time the old Schlaitz stood before them, halted, exhausted as he was, at the entrance of the house, and half stifled with anger and grief exclaimed,—

"It is now all over with us, ye women; they have now deprived Heinz of a leg and a foot, and to-morrow we shall have our own throats cut."

A horrible scream issued from the lips of the daughters, who rushed violently into the house, and conveyed the dismal intelligence to the bedridden mother, whose weakness would not allow her to join in the general tumult, but her eyes were drowned in tears, and she stammered, with a feverish convulsion of her lips,—

"Our fate, then, is determined, and you must henceforth look for your dwellings in the woods. As far as myself is concerned, set fire to the roof over my head, that my body may be rather reduced to ashes than that it should be a prey to the bloodhounds of Pfullingen."

The dismal intelligence had not long circulated in the house, than all the inhabitants of it—young and old, great and small—assembled in one of the dilapidated halls, to intermingle their curses and maledictions with those of the exasperated Schlaitz, who exclaimed, in the wildness of his rage,—

"Should we be lost, we should be obliged to endure a death of hunger, or expire on the gallows; or, should we be driven into the wide world, houseless and unbefriended, let revenge, in its most hideous form, be our precursor!" With these words, he left the women in their distraction, drew a young man aside, of an audacious and repulsive character, and said, "Hear me, Lamparter. Heinz was your friend, my eldest daughter is your sweetheart. You, I know, will grant me your assistance. I know that you are acquainted with Wildherr, and that you have at night accompanied him on some of his predatory excursions. I have that information from Heinz himself. The last hope of my paternal heart rests on that man, whose example has brought my son to his present miserable condition. Conduct me to Wildherr this very day—not a moment is to be lost. I will not shed a tear until Wildherr has sworn to me to lift his arm in revenge for the sufferings of my son!"

Lamparter hesitated a moment, and then said,—

"Consider, old Marten, that you are already an object of suspicion. I consider that it would be more prudent in us to remain tranquil for a time. Wildherr knows well what he has to do."

"Well," said the old man, with dissembled anger, "I will myself return to Pfullingen, and stab the chief magistrate dead in his bed!" On saying which, with a threatening mien, he exhibited a long dagger, which he had concealed under his cloak. This resolve of Marten, formed in the madness of his despair, shocked the rugged nature of Lamparter, and he said,—

"Rather than you should go hence with such a resolve upon your mind, I will do as you require of me. Let us, however, depart immediately. Throw your great coat over you; the distance is great for your aged limbs, and I am not yet certain where we can immediately meet with Wildherr."

"I will not shrink from your side," said Marten. "Rage and revenge have made me young again." Thus saying, he threw over him his thick weather-proof coat, and followed his active leader according to his promise.

On their way they were obliged to pass through the village of Anterhausen, and the road leading to Honan was still thronged with men, returning from Pfullingen They were conversing freely about the tribunal, about Wildherr, and the condemned malefactor, whose case they considered as decided. They abused the executioner for not carrying the sentence into effect before the view of the public; and, in several places, small knots of people were seen repeating the most marvellous stories of robbery and murder. Marten wished to tarry amongst the crowd to gain all the intelligence in his power respecting his son, but Lamparter dragged him along, saying,—

"This is no place for us; let us hasten past them; strike into the path to the right over the meadows, which leads to yonder mountains."

Marten did as he was bidden, and they hurried along the green, wet with the morning dew. By degrees the sound of the streets no longer reached their ears; and, on a sudden, they came in contact with a man who in the twilight was stalking over the field like a goblin. A short whistle from the mouth of Lamparter made the stranger halt, and say a few words in a particular jargon, on which he continued his course.

"We are on his track," said Lamparter, with an air of satisfaction. "The chief is resting himself in his summer-house, and we shall soon be in his presence."

A quarter of an hour had scarcely elapsed, during which they had been climbing the mountain amidst bushy and almost impenetrable underwood, when they arrived at a place, in which it was completely dark, unbroken by a single luminous object, except the streaks of white sand between the dark furrows formed by the mountain streams in spring and autumn.

"We are now at the place," whispered Lamparter, and uttered a cry like a wild bird as it screams in passing over the forest. Silence reigned for a few moments, and then a hollow voice sounded from above,—

"Who calls?"

Instead of an answer, Lamparter repeated the former cry; and, in a short time, a rustling was heard among the branches, and fragments of rocks and stones rolled down into the abyss, and immediately afterwards a huge black figure presented himself, leaning on a mountain staff, and, stopping a few paces from Lamparter, said, in a commanding voice,—

"What is the matter, ye fellows? Answer directly, or I will cleave your heads in twain!"

On Lamparter mentioning his name, the man became rather pacified, and said,—

"Who is with you?"

"The father of Heinz," answered Lamparter.

"What is his business here?" asked the man.

Lamparter called upon Marten to declare his business, when the old man said,—

"If thou be Wildherr, open your heart to the sorrows of a father!"

"Let me have no howling nor whimpering," said the man; "I cannot endure it. What dost thou require of me?"

"My son is unfortunate," said Marten.

"I know it," said the man.

"His blood flowed by the hand of the executioner," said Marten; "and his fate is far worse than if he had been beheaded."

"It was his destiny," said the man. "What have I to do with it?"

"It was in thy service," said Marten, "that the misfortune has befallen him."

"A misfortune of that kind may happen to every one," said the man. "I have always shared everything honourably with him; nor can he say that I am indebted to him a single farthing."

"On the rack," said Marten, "he did not betray thee."

"May the devil thank him for it," said the man. "A noble-minded fellow will always keep his oath, and he be stretched on a hundred racks."

"You augment my sorrow," said Marten. "Your breast appears callous to compassion."

"How can I help it?" said the man. "What have I to do with thee? and, above all, let me have no insolent words from thee."

"If you could not save my son," said Marten, "will you not revenge his sufferings? —'tis the least you can do."

"Revenge is a most significant word," said the man, "but you come too late. I have already provided for it. But then, old fool, why disturbest thou me here? Could I possibly have been nearer to you than I was at Pfullingen. I could have touched you with my hand."

"Oh," said Marten, "who can recognise thee under thy hundred disguises? but I never thought I should have to search for thee in thy haunts. I was always angry with my son and this man, who will be my son-in-law, for embroiling themselves in such dangerous undertakings. But I come to offer you my arm in the work of revenge."

"What can I do with thy trembling hand?" said the man. "Go home, and go to bed; to-morrow all will be done."

"How?" exclaimed Marten, vehemently; "you will, also, think of the convent, in your anger?"

See page 61.

"What convent?" asked the man.

"The convent of Offenhausen," answered Marten, "where my son was seduced from the paths of virtue, and sent alienated hence from my power."

"Thou cowardly thief," said the man, "who hadst a son who is by far too good for thee. The boldness of Heinz was worthy of a noble fellow; he went boldly to work, whilst thou carriedst on thy pilfering in secret. Say not a word about Offenhausen; it is an excellent school, some bold and enterprising men are there brought up for use; but how came your son's sentence to be mixed up with the innocent nuns? His last request shall be fulfilled on the judges and witnesses. This night it shall be fulfilled on his accusers. I will spare the judges for a few days, that the agony of death may visit them tenfold. Are you now satisfied?"

"When you command," said Marten, "I must hold my tongue. One favour, however, I ask of you."

"What is it?—be quick, old gabbler," said Wildherr.

" Send me to the bedside of the accursed crew," said Marten, "who mutilated my son; let me, also, plunge the dagger into their breasts."

"With all my heart," said Wildherr; "you will not have far to go. As soon as the scoundrels have been captured, they will be brought hither; the liars have dared to implicate me in the business, although not one of them ever set their eyes upon me. They shall, however, have that satisfaction in their last hour; and, if you feel an inclination to try your dagger upon one of them, I will not raise any objection to it. In the meantime, ascend that path; I will follow you. Hold hard by the projections of the rocks, and take care you do not fall; it will cost you your neck. If any one call to you, stir not a step until I have answered. Forwards, thou old curmudgeon of a thief."

Whilst Marten, with unsteady and tottering steps, crept up the steep paths, Wildherr sent Lamparter to Pfullingen, for the purpose of collecting information, and, having bidden him use all possible expedition, he followed the steps of the revengeful father.

CHAPTER VIII.

" How fierce a fiend is passion! with what wildness,
What tyranny untamed, it reigns in woman.
Unhappy sex! whose easy, yielding temper
Gives way to every appetite alike;
And love, in their weak bosoms, is a rage
As terrible as hate, and as destructive."

OVER the green forest of the mountain of the stars, came on gently and gracefully the blue night, and its silvery, sparkling stars looked down with a friendly light on the mountain valley, which, one great continued forest, stretched itself from the village of Khlostetten, as far as the mountain which is called after the stars of Heaven. Solitarily and alone, as if they were the only beings in creation, Gisela and Jacob, the student, trod along the road, and their hearts beat joyously in happy anticipation that they were on the point of arriving at their destined goal. At a rapid pace they passed through the villages, on the banks of the Echitz, and they had ascended the pathway, leading to Honan, scarcely stopping to put a question to the peasant boy, who came out of the woods, or a shepherdess, as she sat spinning by her flock. Having reached the summit of the hill, they stopped to rest themselves; and, from the fragment of the rock, on which they were sitting, they saw a glittering cross on the top of a steeple, projecting from the dark foliage of the trees, and, although they were not certain whether their imaginations were not deceiving them, yet quicker and quicker they directed their steps towards the place, as if it were the haven where all their troubles were to rest.

"It is about the time," said Gisela, looking towards heaven, "that the nuns should ring the vesper bell, for night is growing on apace," and, as if it had almost waited her bidding, on a sudden the melodious sound of the bells vibrated on her ears; a joyous signal for devout and pious souls—a welcome salutation for the weary pilgrim.

Notwithstanding the exhaustion caused by her long and tedious journey, Gisela flew rather than walked towards the outlets of the wood, and she clasped her hands in the fulness of her grateful joy, when she beheld in reality the convent, at a short distance from her. A green meadow stretched itself like a carpet of velvet, from the wood to the convent, through which ran a small rivulet, on the banks of which was the mill which ground the corn for the use of the holy sisterhood. The meadow was soon crossed, and, full of anxious expectation, the pilgrims halted at the ancient chapel, from the portals of which, the mother of all grace, erected under a canopy, with the child Jesus in her arm, and the sceptre of the world in her hand, welcomed the pious pilgrims to the holy place.

"Before we knock at the gate of the convent," said Gisela, with a pious elevation of mind, "we will enter the house of God, pronounce our prayers, and listen to the sweet harmony of the brides of Heaven."

The bells just then ceased to sound, and the shudder occasioned by the sanctity of the place came over the kneeling pilgrims, who, after having bestowed their first look upon the altar, expressed their wonder that they should be alone in the dark and gloomy church. They not only saw themselves alone, not one being present, who, like them, were anxious for the blessing of the altar, but even in the choir all was still, and at a distance were heard the wooden soles of the female bell-ringer, who was retiring into the house.

"It appears to me," said Jacob, in a doubting tone, "as if all the residents of the convent were dead," and the heart of Gisela misgave her when the silence of the grave was around her, instead of the sweet and melodious tones with which, about the hour of the evening, her ears were wont to be enraptured in the convent at Lichtenthal.

A long and disheartening pause ensued. At last some steps were heard at one of the side doors leading into the church; and a nun appeared, clad in a white habit, dragging after her her black cloak with its ample folds, and rattling the bunch of keys which she held in her hand. She appeared overcome with astonishment to behold strangers at that hour of the night in the chapel, and having eyed them most minutely from head to foot, she said, in a coarse, masculine voice,—

"Leave the place; the gates of the church are about to be closed; let me have no delay; your presence here is an intrusion."

Gisela approached the nun with great humility, kissed the hem of her garment, and said,—

"That she was come to deliver a letter to the holy mother, the abbess."

"What is that to me?" answered the nun; "your place is outside the gates of the convent. Knock, and it will be opened to you. There is no access here for you into the convent."

The nun pointed in such an authoritative manner to the gates, that the weary pilgrims were obliged to obey, without putting any further questions. The doors of the church were closed hastily after them; but, notwithstanding their repeated knocking, the door of the convent was not opened. Once, indeed, a dark, forbidden countenance appeared at the grated window, and inquired the business of the strangers; but before an answer could be given, the information was given that the sister who had charge of the door would soon make her appearance, and the repellant countenance immediately withdrew. The keeper of the gate, however, came not, and Gisela sat with her companion alone and dispirited; and was not able to form any conjecture as to what the result of their visit would be. It was now evident to her, that there were some living beings in the convent, for, from time to time, a confused noise was within, as if proceeding from the voices of a considerable number of persons. At one time, some doors were heard to be thrown to with the greatest violence; then at another time, a loud, obstreperous laugh was heard; then some sounds like music were heard; then the jingling of glasses was heard; and at one time, it appeared as if some rude and indecorous persons were chasing each other along the passages.

"To what sort of a place are we come?" said the student, whose composure began to be not a little ruffled, and in whose mind some suspicion arose not very favourable to the characters of the place; but Gisela knew not what answer to give him; but at the same time, the sneers and the contemptuous expressions of the host of Pfullingen, rose like an evil spectre before her soul.

The darkness of the night was coming on apace; the light of the stars became more vivid; the trees in the burying-ground sent forth a rustling and mysterious sound. Behind them, on a sudden, a gate, which they had not perceived, was suddenly thrown open, and Gisela and her companion remarked that several horses were led forth, and followed by riders, who were evidently intoxicated, and who, having mounted their horses, shouted and laughed, and with a loud noise and tumult, galloped away. The gate was then immediately closed, and the pilgrims still sat in the porch wholly unnoticed, and their minds by no means at ease at the scene which they had just witnessed. They again ventured to knock at the door; but the result was as before. To increase this doubt and anxiety, a man suddenly entered the porch with a hasty step, who appeared to be a sportsman, with his fowling-piece on his shoulder, and a bugle-horn at his side. Without taking the slightest notice of the two pilgrims, he gave a thundering knock at the door with his fist, on which the gate-keeper at last made her appearance, and in a screeching voice, demanded to know who dared to make such an obstreperous noise.

"First come, first served," said the sportsman, good-naturedly, and thrust Gisela towards the window, by which she delivered her letter; and in conjunction with the student, who inquired after the father vicar, expressed her humble petition to be admitted.

"Have patience," said the nun; and taking the letter in her hand, returned into the convent.

The sportsman muttered a few impatient sentences to himself, and leaned against the pillars of the porch with folded arms, casting up his eyes to the star-bespangled heavens. Impelled by curiosity, Gisela fixed her eyes upon him, and was greatly struck with the serious and earnest expression which sat upon his countenance. It was one of those faces which carry the expression of command—a high, prominent forehead—bushy eyebrows over sparkling eyes, and a finely formed Roman nose. A dark beard covered the lower part of his face, whilst his upper lip was covered with thick moustaches. In other respects his form had nothing very peculiar about it—it was not particularly large nor powerful; and yet it appeared as if the man himself cared not for the whole world, and with the same cold-blooded indifference would command a giant or the slender greyhound, which was outstretched at his feet. Gisela, at the moment, wished that she was a man, that she might converse with the stranger. In the meantime the gate-keeper returned, opened the gate, and said, in rather a more friendly tone,—

"Come in, my good girl; and you, also, my worthy student; a lodging is provided for you in the convent."

The happy pilgrims, rejoicing in the success of their application, having crossed the threshold, the door was immediately closed, and the nun presenting herself at the grating window, said to the sportsman who was waiting without,—

"Who are you? Have you brought any recommendation with you?"

"I have lost my way," said the sportsman, "and crave your hospitality. I bring not any recommendation with me, as I am an entire stranger in these mountains."

"Then," said the nun, "pursue your journey in God's name. This house is not a place of refuge for vagrants."

"Indeed, most holy sister," said the sportsman, "you mistake my character; I belong to the suite of the count—am one of his chief gamekeepers. Is not that sufficient recommendation to me?"

The repulsive indifference of the nun was now changed almost into direct contempt, and she answered,—

"Heaven preserve you, my good man! Our house is not adapted for such a guest as you are. What would our holy father abbot say, were we, at this time of night, to admit strangers into our sacred edifice? No, no. Pursue your journey; the moon shines brightly. If you take that road to the right, you will in a very short time arrive at Kholstetten, where, for money and civil words, you will be able to obtain whatever accommodations you may require."

The nun shut the window, and drew the shutter over it; but she listened for some time behind the grating. Her ears were at first assailed by a short loud laugh, then a shrill whistle, and at last the hasty steps of the man, as he took his departure. The nun, however, as she conducted the two pilgrims across the passages, said, in a low tone,—

"We can easily dispense with such customers. Heaven defend us from such spies and eavesdroppers from the court of the count, who already interferes too much in the affairs of our house. God bless all such cunning fellows; they will not gain their point with us."

They had just now reached the kitchen door, from which the bright reflection from the kitchen fire shot a gloomy light into the passage, when the nun said, haughtily,—

"Go into the kitchen, my good people. Seat yourselves by the fire, and some refreshment will be provided for you. Our most holy mother and the reverend vicar are at present engaged in important business; and when it is completed she will send for you." With these words she ascended the stairs, and, rather abashed, Gisela and Jacob entered the kitchen.

On the spacious hearth an immense pile of wood was burning, surrounded by iron saucepans and enormous kettles, which were suspended from the top by chains and hooks, and from which a savoury smell filled the whole of the kitchen. Before the fire a whole sheep was roasting, and different kinds of pastry were placed before it, for the purpose of keeping them hot.

"Is this the sorry fare of a convent?" said the student to himself, as he beheld the luxuries and dainties with which he was surrounded.

The cook, a corpulent lay sister, who sat at the head of the spit, bestowed a friendly nod upon the student; and the superintendent of the kitchen, a short, ugly nun, with her gown tucked up, who sat near the pillar close to the dresser, in a comfortable armchair, gave Gisela a hearty welcome, and invited her to seat herself by the fire, and make herself quite at home. A mean and petty curiosity appeared by no means to be prevalent in this department of the convent, for the officials of it appeared to be well accustomed to strangers. Servants of all kinds were observed running to and fro, with splendid dishes, and other ornaments for the table; in fact, there was every indication of a sumptuous banquet; and Gisela, in a very diffident manner, inquired the cause of it. Mother Anna, the fat superintendant, answered, with a smile,—

"To-day is the birthday of one of the benefactors of the convent, and therefore we should do wrong not to celebrate it."

The lay sister tendered a small goblet of wine to Gisela, who felt herself revived by the heat of the fire, and the stimulating quality of the beverage of which she had been partaking. Mother Anna approached the student, and in an apparently affectionate manner stroked his downy cheeks, saying,—

" You pretty youth, you have got a guitar; play us, then, one of the tunes for which, I make no doubt, many a love-sick girl has given a hearty kiss, and many a cook has cut you off the best slice from a reeking joint. I love to hear a song, for it sometimes reminds me of the days of other years, when I was a gay and happy being, with God's world to roam in, free as the birds of heaven. The nun may carry outwardly the look of contentment and resignation; but depend upon it, there is a wound rankling within, for which there is no cure in this world."

Gisela looked at the nun from head to foot, and was surprised to hear such sentiments issue from the lips of one whose countenance bespoke happiness and contentment, and she said,—

" Is not a holy house like this an asylum from the miseries and afflictions of the world?"

" The world is not so bad as people represent it to be," said the nun. " Crime and vice will convert a heaven into a hell; and it is not in a house like this that virtue and innocence are always to be found. But play us a tune," said the nun, addressing herself to Jacob, apparently anxious to change the subject of the conversation.

Jacob required not a second bidding, and he played such a merry roundelay, that all the servants, including even the corpulent superintendent, placed themselves in a circle, and clapping their hands with joy, began to dance to the great and culpable profanation of the holy place.

Gisela, however, took no part in the unhallowed joy; nor did a man, who sat on a stool at a corner of the hearth, cowering over the fire, his hands resting on his lap, and now and then beating time with his foot. He was far advanced in years, with a weather-beaten countenance; a grey beard covered his chin, on his back he wore a ragged cloak edged with faded fur, and on his head was a huge velvet cap, such as is worn by the Jewish rabbins. It was evident that he was not here at home. His pilgrim's staff lay on the ground by his side, his leathern cape was studded with shells, and in his hand he held a large book, from which hung ribbons of various colours. His countenance on a sudden assumed an expression of gaiety, as the student played a particular tune, and looking up at Gisela, he said, with a foreign accent,—

" God takes delight in mirth, and blessed are those who can taste of mirth; but they are born under a particular star, and under such a clear sign of heaven, was thy spiritual brother born."

Gisela gave a nod of her head, as if giving her assent to the remark of the old man; but a kind of shudder came instantly over her, for she observed, but a few paces from her, a pale, death-like countenance, like that of a spectre, which projected from a crevice in the wall. She thought at first that the countenance was nothing more than the work of her inflamed imagination, formed of streaks of lights and shadows on the wall, or that it was one of those strange formations which in those times were erected in churches and convents by the caprice and whim of the architect; but the more intensely that she directed her look to the crevice, the more distinctly she beheld the pallid countenance, the crooked, projecting nose, the grinning mouth, and the sharp-pointed skull, from which depended long, black, matted locks.

The merry song still sounded from the guitar, when the cook gave a loud scream, exclaiming,—

" Poppele—Poppele! where art thou? Dost thou not see that the fire is almost out? Bring some wood, thou lazy churl."

Like some unearthly hobgoblin, the creature that was called crept from his hiding-place, where he had been reposing, and from which he had excited such an extraordinary degree of alarm in the breast of Gisela by his hideous countenance. The most abusive epithets were bestowed upon the wretched attendant of the kitchen, who appeared to be a lean, haggard being, in whose cheeks scarcely a trace of youth was to be deciphered. He was habited in a wretched dress of the coarsest stuff, to which, in a most ridiculous manner, several calf's tails were appended. His feet were bare, his arms naked, his gait bent and slow.

" Be quick, thou laggard!" exclaimed one of the servants, whilst the lay sister took a knotted whip, which was hanging on the wall, at the sight of which a trembling appeared to come over the whole of the frame of the miserable wretch, and brandishing it over his head, he fell on his hands, and, like a beast, crept on all fours out of the kitchen. In a short time he returned, bending beneath a load of wood, which he threw down on the hearth, for which he was rewarded by a loud, scornful laugh from the cook. A piece of black rye bread was the reward for his exertion, which the creature greedily devoured, seated on a stone which was near where Gisela was standing. Gisela attempted to move his seat further from her; but he caught hold of her dress, and said in a snarling, almost childish tone,—

"Be still, holy sister Hailwig; you do not disturb me. I must suffer whatever is imposed upon me."

"Of what is the fool talking?" said the cook, who placed herself with her arms akimbo. "He speaks to you, fair lady, as if you were an old acquaintance."

"And he is in the right, after all," said Crescentia, the lay sister, after casting a most scrutinising glance upon Gisela. "If we were to change the convent dress for that which the young lady is now wearing, we might almost take an oath that our good mother Hailwig was sitting before us."

As if in chorus, the remainder of the women agreed in the remark; and some of them exclaimed,—

"Poor mother Hailwig—poor mother Hailwig! Would that she were here."

Poppele said, addressing himself to Gisela in a confidential but a humble tone,— .

"I like you the better that you are not Hailwig. You are far more welcome to me as a stranger. Mother Hailwig once called me a monkey, and God has visited her severely for the injury which she has done me; for I have searched for her in every quarter, and cannot find her."

"Be quiet, thou stupid dolt," said the cook, threatening him with her uplifted hand. "Thou shalt starve for three days, if thou presumest again to mention her name."

The wretched, degraded creature rolled himself on the ground, as if he were a huge hedgehog, raised his hands, in an imploring attitude, above his head, and then laid them upon his mouth, as if he would make a vow never to open his lips again. An indescribable fear and melancholy were portrayed in his sunken, distracted look, and an emotion of compassion appeared on a sudden to influence the conduct of the lay sister, who, by way of extenuation for his conduct, said,—

"We ought to make some allowance for the poor fool; he is an inheritance of the convent; some creature that has been sent into the world without the sanction of the priest, or, perhaps, he was found on the highway. I am ignorant, however, which was the case."

"It's all a falsehood; a wicked invention," whispered Poppele to Gisela.

The lay sister continued,—

"We have often great trouble with him, when the wind changes, or when the day and night are equal, or when there is snow in the clouds. Then is he roguish, rude, and silly."

"Oh, how she lies; how she slanders me!" whispered Poppele, in the same tone as before.

"At other times he is peaceable and obedient," continued the lay sister; "but it is a fortunate thing, that he is only mischievous with his tongue, and not in his actions, and there is one delusion which appears to occupy the whole of his thoughts. He has the folly to imagine that——but I just now hear the bell sounding from the refectory—our most immaculate mother with the nuns, and the worthy guests of our house are about to seat themselves at the table."

Now all was noise and bustle in the kitchen, jingling and rattling of plates, servants hurrying to and fro, going and returning from the refectory with the full and empty dishes. There was every indication of the holding of a sumptuous banquet, which, in the opinion of Gisela, did not well accord with the austerity and self-denial of the monastic life; after some time Jacob was ordered to attend in the refectory with his guitar, and Gisela found herself alone with the extraordinary creature, who had so powerfully excited her attention. After a pause of a few minutes, he said, in a bitter, scornful tone, "I pay for all this; I cannot endure either music or wine; there is, however, no end to this carousing and banquetting, and when it is over, the cry is always, Poppele, do you pay for it?"

"How so, thou extraordinary being?" said Gisela, casting upon him a look of compassion.

"Alas!" answered Poppele; "you must naturally be ignorant how matters stand in the house; but they have taken everything from me; a heritage greater than the pope possesses, or even the emperor." With these words, which he uttered with great ardour and vivacity, he stood erect as a lance, extended his pale and shrivelled arms before him, and then drawing, as it were, a large circle with them, he said, in a bold and determined tone, "All the land which you see here around you, is my inheritance; they have taken it away from me, and of my vast and princely property they have left me nothing but the bench of stone on which I sleep, after having toiled and laboured during the whole of the day in this hateful service; teased and tormented by these shaven women, these magpies, who, with their white habits and black trains, stalk in triumph over the graves of my forefathers, and daily and hourly offend the Lord their God by their scandalous practices."

Poppele folded his arms, and, with a mysterious air of importance, directed his look to Gisela, and then to the aged pilgrim, who had just resumed his seat by the fireside. He then seated himself at the feet of Gisela, saying, "I will not yet tell all I know; they think that this mode of life is to last for ever; let them think so, I care not for it. Let me only find the hidden treasure, and then there will soon be an end to these women of Baal; until then I will carry a double face, and rejoice that they do not know where the money is buried that belongs to me."

He leaned himself contentedly by the fireside, and, with the eye of a hawk, watched all the motions of Gisela, who had the greatest trouble to refrain from bursting into tears. In the meantime, the stranger pilgrim had risen from his seat, and said, with his finger pointing to Poppele,—

"Truly, no benignant star, no friendly sign watched over the cradle of that creature. So fall happiness and curses from the houses of the heavens on our heads here below. We sleep on the bud and know it not. Nevertheless, they are the poorest on this earth to whom it is given to read the future destiny of man, and to trace it in the track of the stars. Still will that destiny be fulfilled. Therefore, thou idiot man, show me the palm of thy hand."

"What art thou?" asked Poppele, without changing his posture.

"An astrologer," answered the pilgrim.

"You are a fool, old man," said Poppele; "how canst thou find in my hand the stars which thou requirest?"

"The raillery of folly wounds not my soul," said the pilgrim: "as a slave amongst the heathens, I learned, during the course of many years, amidst the sleepless nights in the desert, the language of the stars, as it is there to be read in the brightness and purity of the heavens. At the same time, I learned from the sages of those countries, the manner in which the constellations of the heavens display themselves in the hand of man. Come, give me yours, without fear or alarm, that I may tell thee what thou wert, and art, and shalt be."

"If such be thy intent," said Poppele, "come and try thy art;" and he placed himself in such a position, that the astrologer could obtain a sight of the palm of his hand.

Gisela touched him gently on the shoulder, and said, "Thou weak-minded creature, suffer thyself not to be made a fool of. That which comes from the heathens is the work of the devil; it is only the finger of God that directs the course of our life."

Poppele, with a discontented air, and a ridiculous grimace, directed his look to Gisela, without altering his position, and said, in a hasty tone,—"Do you then know who interests himself about me? I have often dreamt that God has forsaken me; therefore, let me hear what thou hast to say, old heathen, and speak without fear."

The importunate prophet had, in the meantime, not averted his look from the hand of the foolish youth. He frequently shook his head, and consulted his book, on the parchment leaves of which all kinds of extraordinary and grotesque figures met the gaze of the credulous creature. The old astrologer took the cap from his head, and said, in a deep, sepulchral tone,—

"In this hand a most extraordinary destiny has drawn its circles and its lines. I am not able to arrive at any positive definition respecting it; yet one thing I distinctly perceive, that the many cross and ramified lines of life converge from all ends into a crown, which is sometimes worn by princes of the highest degree."

The countenance of Poppele became on a sudden animated by the expression of the purest joy; he rose haughtily from his seat, and clapped the prophet rather rudely upon the shoulder.

"Thou art my man!" he exclaimed; "I see thou hast learned something, and were not Poppele so miserably poor, thou shouldst go home laden with riches. A crown! Ha! ha! ha! It belongs to me—on my head it ought to be placed. I will show you who I am!"

Poppele hastened to the place where his stony bed was fixed, and soon returned with a dirty piece of parchment, on which the form of a king was to be seen, miserably cut in wood, as it lay on the bed, or on the tombstone, covered with a cloak or mantle, but with a sovereign crown on its head, and in its hands the sceptre and the imperial globe.

Heaven alone can tell by what means the parchment came into the possession of the poor idiot; but, with a haughty air, he pointed to it, and said,—

" Look! such am I; and as such they must one day lay me in my grave, if God listens to my prayers, and restores me to my exalted state, as he has now been pleased to humble me."

" Oh! what a distraction! what a deplorable phantasy!" said Gisela; and the astrologer stared at the inspired youth with open mouth. Poppele, however, answered quickly, sinking immediately from his assumed haughtiness to the bitter and galling feelings of the slave,—

" Truly it is no distraction, it is no idle phantasy, thou good angel, and thou shalt hear what the spirit related to me, and look not upon it as an idle tale."

He seated himself, with his feet bent under him, on the edge of the hearth; placed his forefinger on his nose, like one who had a riddle to expound; and said, in a monotonous tone, as if he were repeating his litany,—

" In former times—yet it is now a long time ago—and the heathen reigned in Rome, there was on the spot where we are now standing—ye, the guests, I, the slave of the shaven women—yes, there was on this place, I tell you, a great city, and many men dwelt therein; and they had a king whom they obeyed; and the city was called Offenhausen. According to the report of some, the city stood further up the mountains, and was called Hazingen—but it is not true. Offenhausen was the name of the city, as it is now of the convent—for Gnadenzell has been long a heap of ruins, and it has become a den of devils. There was also an emperor in the German country, who held his court at Hohenstaufen, and he had a longing after the throne of the heathen at Rome, as he was lazy and indolent upon his own. And he commanded the lords and barons of his land that they should accompany him on his expedition; but the lords and the barons were not inclined to fulfil the wishes of the emperor, as they were comfortable at home, and had no desire to enter into a contest with the heathen; on which the emperor grew angry, and placed the lords and barons under the ban of the empire, that, instead of being lords, they should be vassals—vassals and slaves, such as I now am, although it was not for a long time afterwards that I was born. Vassalage, however, is painful, and it became highly displeasing to the lords, so that they entered into a council with each other, and humbled themselves before the emperor, and acknowledged the transgression they had committed. The emperor condescended to bestow upon them his pardon; but he imposed upon them a penance, that they might know how to conduct themselves for the better in future. He therefore said to them,—' Behold the king at Oppenhausen, how rigidly he sways his sceptre over the country and over the people, and cares not a tittle neither for me, nor for you, his neighbours. Go and set fire to his castle, and take possession of the city; burn it, and level it to the ground, and, on its ruins, build a convent for seventy-two holy virgins. Then shall grace be awarded to you, and unpunished shall be your flagitious conduct.' On the lords and barons hearing this sentence of the emperor, they hastened immediately to obey his commands. They slew the king, drove his children into distress and misery, and, of the ruins of the city, they built a village, in the immediate vicinity of which they erected the convent, to which the name of Gnadenzell (cell of grace) was given. And not many years elapsed before they said to each other,—' What shall we do with the village in which the men still reside, whose pale and downcast countenances continually accuse us that we brought death upon their fathers and mothers? we will go thither, and raise bad reports about them in the country, as if they were wicked people, and we will proclaim that the judgment of God will fall upon the sinners.' And they went, in fulfilment of their resolution, and, in the first place, they destroyed the character of the poor people, and then their bodies, and afterwards burnt the village to the ground.

" The nuns of the Convent of Gnadenzell sang a hymn of praise on the occasion; but there was no grace for any one except the corpses which already slept in the grave, and for the Church of St. Panoratius, which was obliged to be left standing, because every one died who touched it with their finger. But do not believe that this is a tale of fiction which I have now related to you; and, in the next place, do not believe that I am a fool who thus speak to you. I am in reality the grandson of the murdered king, and the spirits of my ancestors wander about every night, and they have vowed to me that their souls cannot find any rest, until the fate of the cruel women of the convent be accomplished, and the treasure be discovered on which I am to erect my golden throne."

" And the treasure! where, then, does it lie?" asked the astrologer, in apparently a simple manner, after Poppele had finished his recital.

Poppele answered artfully, and with a smile,—

" Ask the constellations and the moon—but no star shines in the bowels of the earth, and a chaste virgin must be present, or he who digs for the treasure will be torn to pieces by a black imp of hell."

The astrologer nodded his head significantly backwards and forwards, twinkled his eyes, and said,—

"You are more of a rogue than a fool; and thou givest thy services only in this holy house that thou mayst meet with a chaste virgin, in order that the injunction of the spirits of thy predecessors may be fulfilled."

See page 69.

Poppele appeared as if a cold shivering came over him, and he answered, partly in a droll and partly in an angry tone,—

"Ha! ha! I am freezing with cold. The chastity of this house is the very plague! These maidens who sit at the table in mummery and sin—who raise their voices to the highest pitch in their bacchanalian songs, but who seldom visit the choir—may the Lord have mercy on their souls! But I know what I should do, were I the Lord."

The eyes of Poppele rolled madly in his head, he distorted his mouth in a hideous manner, seized the burning coals which were lying on the hearth, and hurled about him ashes, flames, and fire. He then attempted to cool his singed hand with his breath, and, with a most discordant tone, attempted to join in the song which was sung by the company in the refectory, and which was not a little at variance with the sober and demure customs of the convent. Gisela stopped her ears with her hands, and the astrologer stalked up and down the kitchen like a stork in its most clumsy and unwieldy manner. It appeared, however, that an end was put suddenly to the banquet, for an unusual bustle was heard in the refectory, and all the servants and nuns were seen hurrying and skurrying about, as if something unusual had occurred. The voice of mother Anna was at last heard, exclaiming—

" Keep a good watch—extinguish all the lights—no noise nor talking—the servants of the count and his hunters are coming from the mountains, and in the house everything must be as silent as in the grave."

These directions were most punctually obeyed. The convent appeared as silent as if all its inhabitants were dead, because they were perfectly practised in the art of dissimulation, and could, accordingly as the occasion required it, appear most holy and demure, whereas, in reality, they were the most flagrant of sinners.

In the meantime the sound of the hunters' horns sounded cheerily over mountain and over vale, mingled with the barking of the dogs and the tallyho of the hunters. A loud knocking was heard at the gate of the convent; but no answer was returned, as if all the residents of it were asleep in their beds. The hunters, therefore, proceeded on their way, and Gisela knew not if the banquet would not now be continued. To her great joy, however, the kind and sympathetic Crescentia appeared, who conducted her to a small cell, in which was a bed, hard but clean, and here she reposed herself to sleep, which, after so much pain and fatigue, visited her like a comforter, or a benevolent intercessor between the past and the future. So slept the tired Gisela, guarded by strong iron bolts, which Crescentia had particularly enjoined her to draw, not knowing to what intrusion she might be subject.

CHAPTER IX.

——————————————" Excuse
A woman's frailty; when she once has loved,
Strong is her passion—and, howe'er suppressed
The smothering embers, still the flame bursts out,
And strives to climb above our just resentment."

THE chanticleer of the convent had already announced the approach of day, portending, according to the opinion of the good women of the country, the certainty of a rainy day, when Gisela arose from an unrefreshing sleep. Her first emotion was that of surprise, for she could not easily conform herself to her new habitation, as she had been dreaming of her father's hut, and of the careworn forms of her parents, who stretched out their hands towards her, exclaiming,—" Daughter—daughter! why hast thou forsaken us, and why dost thou not return to us from thy long sojourning in a strange country?" It occupied her some time to collect her scattered thoughts, and regulate the reminiscences that crowded upon her, and to find even the slightest comfort in her narrow and contracted cell. Having, however, overcome the most grievous of her cares, like a decent and decorous maid, she adjusted the pallet on which she had been sleeping, brushed off the little dust that had fallen upon the few articles of furniture that were in the room, drew back the bolts of the door, and, with cautious eye, looked out upon the long and dreary passage.

She listened for the sound of distant footsteps; but all was still in the convent. She then fell upon her knees, unobserved by any one, before the crucifix of her cell, to stammer her morning prayers to her God in heaven. She then opened the little window, which was immediately under the roof, in order to inhale the sweetness of the morning air, and to take a view of the surrounding country. She found that her cell was situate in the hinder wing of the convent, with a prospect towards the mountains and the extensive gardens belonging to the establishment, which were surrounded by lofty walls, terminated by verdant hills, the acclivities of which were steep and almost inaccessible by human footsteps.

The faint beams of the sun, the precursors of a rainy day, fell upon the now deserted place. The forests stood in their natural blackness on the hills; the meadows, with their stubble, had a dreary and disheartening aspect; and in the rank and wild bushes of the garden the song of the merry bird was seldom heard. From the further depths of the garden the monotonous murmur of a rivulet might be heard, and at a distance the ear could catch the sound of a water-mill, where the flour of the convent was ground.

Gisela felt herself happy in this depressing silence, and, amidst her sighs, she cast her eyes to Heaven, thanking it, with a grateful heart, that she should be permitted to wear the bridal dress of her Redeemer in a place so well adapted for holy meditation. Leaning, with her hands folded, out of the window, in order that she might take a more extensive view of the garden, which was partly concealed from her view by the projecting corner of the building, she on a sudden heard a slight noise close to her, and, in a moment afterwards, she saw Crescentia, who, in the most friendly manner, wished her a good morning.

"I hope you have slept well," said the lay sister, with a smile. "May God make your rest pleasant and beneficial to you. How do you like our solitude? After the long journey which you have completed, this valley must appear to you as a prison."

"By no means, most worthy sister," said Gisela. "The hermits build not their huts in cities; for it is only in retirement from the world that the way to grace is found."

Crescentia put in another smile, and pointed to the distant landscape. She then continued,—

"Look, my dear sister; those meadows have been bestowed upon the convent by some generous benefactors, and from yonder forest is obtained the wood that is necessary for the use of the convent. You can, however, there see the Sternenberg, which is situated opposite to the Aichenhald, and also a portion of the Hoppenhald, so called from a notorious robber, who for a long time carried on his criminal acts in that part of the country. I cannot remember it, but our venerable mother, Eustatia, has often beheld the terrible man, when he came from the caverns of the Alb, to offer up his prayers in our church; for he was a very pious man, paid all due homage to the saints and the holy convents, confessed his sins, and received absolution for them. For a long time, however, no intelligence whatever has been received of him, and the conjecture runs that he died somewhere in a lonely part of the forest, or, perhaps, that he has fallen a victim to the revenge of some one whom he deeply injured. Safety now prevails in every part of this country, and it is only beasts of prey that prowl round the walls of our convent."

"It's better," said Gisela, "to have wild beasts as your neighbours than bad and wicked men."

Crescentia continued. "It is a pity that the whole of our garden cannot be seen from this place; but I will take the first opportunity of showing you every part of it. Notwithstanding the keenness of the mountain air, our fruit and vegetables thrive luxuriantly, and our tulips and our hyacinths are as beautiful as those at Honan. There are also some pleasant shady retreats in the garden, to which we often retire, and hold conversation with each other. In the sultry days of summer are these retreats most pleasant and delightful, for the source of the rivulet is in the neighbourhood, and flows in three streams from the rocks. It is here that the sisters of the convent bathe, when the moon shines through the thickness of the foliage, and all around them is in sleep and silence. Indeed much more pleasant are the silent recesses of the garden than the cemetery, of which—there, on the left—you can see a portion. There, deep—deep under the surface—lie the mouldering bones of the old inhabitants of Offenhausen, and the report is current in the country, that frequently at night the graves fly open, and the ghosts of the wicked sinners rise from them, and, in long rows, dance, hand-in-hand, amongst the rustling trees. God grant the poor souls a joyful resurrection, and not less so the deceased bodies of the nuns, who sleep in the vaults of the church, as we are all sinners in the eye of the Lord."

Having uttered these words, Crescentia appeared for a moment to be lost in deep reflection, but suddenly collecting herself, she said,—

"I had almost forgotten to inform you that our most reverend lady prioress is desirous of seeing you. She gave me her order to conduct you to her."

"I will obey her order," said Gisela; and, in joyful expectation of the happiness that awaited her, she followed Crescentia.

They descended the creaking and rotten staircase, which threatened every moment to fall to pieces under their feet; they passed the conversation-room, the door of which stood open, and in which could be seen some lazy, ill-favoured women, who apparently were clearing away the remnants of the regale of the preceding evening, and who appeared to be more fitted for the hut of a blacksmith than for one of the holy houses of the Saviour. In a few minutes they arrived at the door which led to the apartment of the prioress. They knocked, and it was opened by a servant, who directed them to the end of a gloomy passage. Here another door presented itself, which was opened by Crescentia, who went first into the presence of the prioress. In a few minutes she returned and ushered Gisela into the room, who was astonished to behold the elegance and splendour with which it was furnished. Luxury appeared to pervade every department of it; on the tables stood the most exquisitely carved vases, in which were placed the most odoriferous flowers, filling the whole of the room with their delightful fragrance; window-curtains of the most costly damask descended from the ceiling; the doors were hidden by curtains of scarlet cloth, richly embroidered; and the floors were covered with the richest carpets of some foreign manufacture, said to have been brought as a present to the convent by some pious pilgrims, who had returned from a pilgrimage to the Holy Land. In an arm-chair, her feet resting on velvet cushions, sat the prioress, a fat, mangy dog resting on her lap; and on one of the arms of the chair sat a huge black cat, which, like the prioress herself, appeared to be well-fattened with the dainties of this world. The prioress did not deign to rise from her seat as Gisela entered, but welcomed her with a friendly nod, but at the same time accompanied with a degree of *hauteur* that was well calculated to make the new visitant feel that she was in the presence of her superior.

The very reverend Mother Richardis, or, in other words, the prioress, bore a very great resemblance to her sister, Mechtild of Zavelstein; the same handsome countenance—the same blooming cheeks—the same dangerous eyes, on whatever masculine heart their powers might be exercised—and, much more than all, the same passionate expression of the countenance, combined with the pride of one who has been accustomed to govern and command, and who, at the same time, is certain that her power will be obeyed. Her fine and slender form was habited in a white dress, of the most exquisite texture, and a cap, white as the mountain snow, covered her forehead and her cheeks. Over the whole was thrown, in a tasteful manner, the black cape and mantle, beneath which shone the glittering cross, imbedded, as it were, on the white scapulary. The beautifully formed and delicate hands of the prioress were employed in adjusting the hair on the back of the dog, and in a voice which was perhaps never equalled for sweetness and harmony, she said,—

"Are you, my child, the bearer of this letter, which my sister has written to me?"

"I am, most reverend lady," replied Gisela; "and await your commands."

The prioress fixed her dark expressive eye upon Gisela, and it was a look which penetrated to the very soul of the embarrassed girl. Surprise, pride, and a parasitical friendliness were mingled in it. It was a probation which Gisela could scarcely endure, for she felt a terror which she could not account for; and although there was almost an angel's form before her, yet she thought she could read that a devil dwelt within it.

The prioress, at last, broke the silence. "The contents of the letter, my daughter," she said, "giving me every particular concerning you. My beloved sister has recommended a modest and a virtuous lamb to my paternal care, and would that the power of us poor worms of the earth were always equal to our will. What shall I say to you, my beloved daughter? It is the highest merit—it is the most superlative virtue of a virgin soul, when it renounces for ever the iniquities and temptations of a deceitful and wicked world; and we poor sisters of the convent are more than disposed to support and encourage so pious and exemplary a resolution; but, my dear Gisela, you enter this convent at a most unfortunate period; the crisis of all things appears to be at hand. The mighty ones of the earth tread the disciples of Christ under their feet; and we poor, weak, powerless women are particularly unable to contend against such a preponderating power. You will not find, my daughter, much peace within these walls; but I fear much bitter affliction and misery. Have you well considered the eventful step that you are about to take? Has the world no charms for you? Do not your parents weep for you and deplore your loss? Do you feel no anxious longing to return; and is your bosom an entire stranger to the joys of home? Have you not a mother?"

Gisela felt a sudden emotion thrill through her whole frame at the mention of her mother; but she soon collected herself and said, "My father is dead to me, and my mother has long been accustomed to the thought of our separation; and whatever my fate might have been in the world, must I not, sooner or later, perhaps, have been obliged to leave my father's house. If the bride must part from her mother, in order to follow her husband, why should she hesitate, when she has to follow the celestial bridegroom?"

The prioress bestowed upon Gisela a nod of her approbation, appeared for a moment to be lost in thought, and then, with the most extraordinary expression of art and cunning in her eye, she said, "And it is not, then, the longing after a husband, which may one day make you repent of having taken upon yourself the severe and self-denying duties of a nun?"

"I speak the name of a husband with disgust," said Gisela, in rather a quick and passionate tone.

The prioress smiled and continued: "Does not a wounded heart speak within thee? you are young, not devoid of beauty and grace,—has no one approached you who has deceived you; whose ingratitude and baseness have forced from you the vow to hate th whole race because one has been inconstant to you?"

"I am a pure and virtuous girl, most holy mother," said Gisela. "I have no transgressions to repent of; I have no ungrateful nor inconstant lover on whom to fix my hatred."

A most expressive smile sat upon the countenance of the prioress, and she said, rising majestically from her chair,—

"You promise, my daughter, to be a light and an ornament of this house; but what, after all, if I should refuse to receive you? The Count of Wurtemberg, our lord and protector, is highly exasperated against us, and we poor sisters of the convent are unable to discover the cause of it. He has already forbidden us to receive any more sisters into our house, nor to allow of any sister taking the veil, and, in the fulness of his wrath, he threatens us with greater punishment and severity."

"Then, holy mother," said Gisela, "let me serve in the convent as a servant, until matters assume a more favourable aspect."

"You speak, my daughter," said the abbess, "of a change of our condition for the better, and that the future will be more favourable to us; but we have not any such hope to cheer us. The end of the world is approaching. The swords of the lords of the earth destroy and slay the faithful servants of the Almighty God. Our holy father at Rome is far from us, and he beholds, with weeping eyes, how one stroke after the other falls heavily upon our holy mother church. Oh, woe! woe! What the fury of the mighty one leaves untouched, is destroyed by the venomous tongues of the impious people. It matters not that we lead a quiet and exemplary life, and that with walls, and bolts, and bars we conceal ourselves from the world; still are we calumniated and vilified—we are abused and scandalized throughout the whole of the country. The count at Uzach appears to give his sanction and encouragement to these evil and scandalous reports, and we have no other weapons to contend with him than gentleness and patience. Hast thou, during thy pilgrimage, never heard of any of those malicious and unfounded imputations upon the holiness and [virtue of our lives? Are there not numerous tales afloat in the country of our banquetings, of our luxurious mode of life, of our deviations from the path of virtue and chastity, and of the shameful neglect of the service of God and the holy church which is to be daily witnessed within the walls of Gnadenzell?"

"I cannot remember," said Gisela, "that any such reports ever reached my ear."

"Thou art, indeed, a most fortunate one," said the prioress, "that thou hast not heard the hissing of the snakes; but truly, my daughter, we are most infamously traduced. The most trivial event, the most innocent occurrence, nay, our very righteousness itself, do the spirits of darkness take advantage of, in order that they may lash us with their merciless scourges. What should we poor women be, directed, as we are, to teach charity and alms, without the aid and compassion of good and pious benefactors? How natural it is that the good and generous souls often pay a visit to this wretched abode in order that they may see what use we make of their charitable gifts; and further, how natural it then is that we should attempt to render their short sojourn amongst us as comfortable as possible, more especially in these times, in which we are compelled by necessity to look out for patrons, protectors, and friends? This it is which the malicious, calumniating people call holding banquets and revels, and leading a wicked and dissolute life; and finally, if we no longer perform the appointed service at midnight, if we but seldom sing in the choir, and shorten, as much as we can, the holy services of the day, it is all done in pursuance of the orders of our bishop, who by such a silent interdict wishes fully to expose the grief that must be naturally felt at the decline and ruin of monachism, and the unjust and unmerited treatment which the convents receive from a licentious rabble. Ah, my beloved daughter, never attach any belief to the censure and calumny of mankind; show thy profound contempt for the malicious and uncharitable judgment of the world, and place thy confidence only in the words of thy mother and God-devoted priests."

"I will follow your instructions in all things, holy mother," said Gisela, and imprinted a fervent kiss on the hand of the prioress.

"Now, my daughter," said the prioress, "return to your cell, and prepare thyself by prayer and fasting, and during the whole of the week in solemn and holy meditation, when I will then make known to thee what the convent and myself have determined upon in regard to thy future settlement amongst us. Strengthen thyself in thy solitude with the belief that we have it in our power to unbind what the count has bound, and, on the other hand, to bind what the count may wish to unbind."

This speech appeared to the zealous disciple of the convent a pledge of salvation, placing her hope upon it, as upon the blessing of the sacrament, she respectfully took her leave, in order to enter upon the thorny path of her ordeal, as she had been ordered by the prioress, on whom she wished to confer the sovereign power over her in this world.

The prioress, on Gisela leaving the room with downcast head and folded hands in the attitude of submission and humiliation, followed her with her eyes, at first with surprise and astonishment; then, with a furrowed brow, and an expression of the deepest contempt.

"Thou silly creature," she said, in a most scaring tone, stifling to the utmost of her power the serious and solemn voice which spoke within her in favour of the beautiful girl who had so enthusiastically devoted herself to the service of her Redeemer; "poor, silly thing," she said, "thou'lt soon be made wiser."

She then repaired to her dressing-table, opened her box of jewels, looked at herself with secret pleasure in the glass, drew from under the folded veil the beautiful ringlets of her hair, which hung from her temples to her bosom, admired herself again in the glass, and whispered to herself,—

"Do I not look charmingly? shall I not please him in my present dress?"

Without any formal announcement, the door flew open, and two nuns rushed into the room, and surprised the prioress at her pleasing occupation—one of them, rather of a middle age, having a bold, sharp, and rather repulsive countenance; the other, still younger than the prioress, and beautiful as a Hebe in the hours of her spring. Both appeared to be of a lively disposition; the principal thoughts of their mind leading to other things than crucifixes and senseless images; and not only in their actions, but in their dress, overstepping the limits of their holy profession. The finest camel-hair cloth, the smoothest silk, decorated the persons of these mendicant nuns; their feet, instead of wooden soles, were covered with the most costly furs; and over their head was thrown a veil, fantastically but most tastefully arranged. The ugly hands of Medora were concealed by the most beautiful gloves, ornamented by glittering and splendid rings. On the other hand, the beautiful Renata, full of vanity and voluptuousness, displayed her beautiful neck and snow-white bosom, in spite of her cowl and scapular. In the jocund days of Easter, they would have been taken for dissolute women, who wished to carry on their jokes and pranks in the garb of a nun. Noisy and indecorous as two courtezans, they ran up to the prioress, embraced her with the utmost fearlessness, and, giving the wink to each other, they drew up the curtains which hung before the recess in which the prioress slept.

"Am I not in the right?" said Renata, with a smile, and making some significant gestures to Medora. "Our holy lady understands her business well, and lets the war-hawk fly away at the earliest dawn, before the envious bats return to their nests."

Medora shrugged her shoulders, and broke out into a fit of loud laughter.

"What is the matter with you, ye hairbrained women?" exclaimed the prioress, without making the slightest change in the adjustment of her head-dress.

"Think only, most holy mother," exclaimed Renata, with a bold hilarity, "that Medora, with her calumniating tongue, wished to persuade me that Oesterlein was still in his comfortable lodging, and sleeping away the precious hours of the day—the bold, intrepid knight—in the lap of a chaste and virtuous nun!"

"Our thoughtless sister," said the prioress, "shall be placed under discipline."

Medora, however, uttered her complaint in a half-playful and a half-angry tone,—"All pleasure," she said, "is now driven from me, since I discovered, most unexpectedly, our mother stewardess with her beloved Holdarstock in the granary."

"You have been properly punished for it, sister Medora," said Renata. "Our eyes should not be everywhere; and if they will be prying into forbidden places, they will often see what is not agreeable to know. Thus, you may say that my eyes have seen what they ought not to see, and that is, how the sturdy, manly Hug crept out of the cell of sister Medora, just as day was breaking."

"Thou shameless hussy!" exclaimed the prioress, raising her hand in a threatening attitude.

"We are all sinners," said Medora, with a feigned show of repentance, whilst her eyes sparkled with desire and passion.

"May the hard-hearted saints forgive us!" said Renata, "as well as the Mother of God of Lindenholz, when she anoints our sister Gertrude so finely with olive oil when she has to weep before the people."

"Do you not know, you thoughtless fools," exclaimed the prioress, "that although punishment may have for a time a hobbling gait, it still frequently overtakes the most rapid rider?"

"I pray you grant me absolution," said Medora, in an ironical tone, and kissed the hand of the prioress.

Renata took the other hand of the prioress, shook it like a love-sick swain, and said, in an arch, roguish manner,—

"I pray you, pretty little hand, to grant what we poor creatures ask. Beat us not, but pray for us. Look, Medora, what beautiful fingers, soft as down, pure as crystal—the tips so rosy, and the nails so beautifully transparent. There, holy mother—there is a white spot on one of them—it is the sign of good fortune. Tell me, beloved mother, is not a child a pleasant thing to you—the offspring of your secret love?"

The prioress burst into a loud laugh.

"You are a clever prophetess. Do you know the boy, and how he is called?"

"Brown hair, black eyes," said Renata.

"Respecting his name," said Medora, "the holy mother of a chaste and virtuous convent ought to have the most beautiful and the most holy that is to be found in the calendar."

"You are full of your jokes to-day," said the prioress, rather flattered than displeased with the remarks of her virtuous companions.

"But why did he depart so early?" said Renata. "Had you been quarrelling?"

"There is not any anger," said the prioress, "where there is love. The gallant fellow is, however, gone, either towards Pfullingen or Reuthugen, in quest of information that may be useful to us. There is a storm hanging over our heads, and we must be found prepared to meet it."

A slow and lazy step was now heard before the door, and sister Anna, the superintendent of the kitchen, projected her broad, greasy face into the room, saying,—

"The breakfast is ready; will you hasten to the chapter-room?"

"We will follow you, most worthy cook," said Medora. "What have you got to-day for our refreshment?"

"The most savoury soup," answered the cook, "that was ever made, with some of the most savoury remains of yesterday's feast; there is, beside, a noble goose, well stuffed and roasted, and a fat capon, the inside of which is lined with sausages. The old and venerable father at Guterstein could not possibly have fared better when the Pope allowed him to eat meat during lent."

Amidst jokes and laughter, the nuns and the prioress betook themselves to the appointed chamber, in which it was their custom to take their meals, when they had any business to transact, or subject to discuss which they wished to keep a secret from the listening servants in the refectory.

The prioress, with some of the nuns, had seated themselves, when the former exclaimed,—

"But where are our remaining sisters—why come they not to their morning meal?"

"Oh, Santa Maria!" exclaimed sister Anna, "I have forgotten to ring the bell;" and whilst she hastened to the belfrey to pull the rope, there glided into the room a pale, emaciated figure, and which, in silence, seated itself at the bottom of the table.

The nun, apparently wo-begone, and borne down by a weight of grief, had fastened a mourning band to her scapular, and in the fold of the kerchief that covered her bosom was a faded nosegay. She gave a heavy sigh as the prioress, in a tone of sympathy, said,—

"How do you find yourself, sister Agnes? Is there not any end to your sorrow?"

Without waiting for any reply from the disconsolate nun, Renata said, in rather a satirical tone,—

"I cannot understand how, from the love of a common vagrant, your eyes can be always overflowing with tears, like a little well in the spring. Heinz was certainly a dapper youth, but a wicked young fellow, who never passed a dovecote without stealing some of the fledglings, nor the window of a pretty girl without stepping into it."

"May God forgive you for your falsehoods!" sobbed Agnes. "May that, however, never happen to you which has happened to me! I know, however, that since the poor fellow was condemned in Pfullingen, my life is a burden to me, and a stone round my neck in the milldam would be preferable."

"Shame upon you!" said the prioress. "Are you not now a member of this convent?"

"My father's conscience," said Agnes, "is laden with the sin in having driven me into this house. I cannot, however, help it. There, leave me to myself, and let those throw the first stone at me who dare to do it."

"What a foolish, thoughtless speech!" said the prioress. "What if it had been heard by the ears of a stranger? I impose silence upon you, and let your tongue utter no more such senseless words. We are all mortal creatures, prone to and full of sin; but this whining and pining on sin is a shame and a scandal, and cannot be allowed.   Put away that mourning hood and that faded nosegay, or you shall be confined to your cell with bread and water."

Agnes raised her weeping eyes, and, with a bitter and reproachful look, pointed to the luxuriant ringlets of the prioress, to the exposed bosom of Renata, and to the glittering rings of Medora; and then, in obedience to the orders of the princess, laid her mourning hood and her decayed nosegay on the bench. In further obedience to the commands of the prioress, she attempted to eat, but she could not; and the kind-hearted Anna, from a motive of compassion, handed to her secretly some spice-nuts—a kind of dainty, with which the pocket of the superintendent of the kitchen was in general pretty well stored.

The bell at the convent gate was now rung most violently; and, with one accord, the nuns rose from their places, instigated by their curiosity to ascertain the cause of the ringing. "It is sister Simplicia," they cried, "with the sumpter ass. Now we shall hear and see something new, and have something that will excite our laughter."

CHAPTER X.

"I've made
A study of thy sex, and found it frail.
The black, the brown, the fair, the old, the young,
Are earthly minded all; there's not a she,
The coldest constitution of her sex,
Nay, at the altar telling o'er her beads,
But some one rises on her heavenly thoughts,
That drives her down the wind of strong desire,
And makes her taste mortality again."

MORE resembling a dwarf than a full-grown woman, sister Simplicia made her appearance, conducted by a lay sister, in the chapter-room. Under one of her arms she carried an enormous bundle of flax, and under the other several pieces of worsted stuff of various colours. Over her shoulders she had thrown a violet-coloured altar-cloth, and on her back she carried a small basket, filled with various kinds of domestic utensils made of iron, copper, and brass. A leathern bag, well filled, was suspended to her girdle, and in her countenance was impressed the signs of the highest self-satisfaction—or, in other words, a proud, stupid consciousness.

The active mendicant was received with every expression of joy, for every month she sallied forth to lay her contributions on the poor inhabitants of the villages and the cottages, in order that the devout and pious sisterhood of Gnadenzell should not suffer from want.

The alms that had been extorted from the charitable and the good were triumphantly displayed, and the worthy sisterhood secretly congratulated on the estimation in which they must be held, if a criterion were to be formed from the number and value of the gifts, which consisted of candlesticks, forks, salt and pepper-boxes, leather, wool, sundry pieces of ham, beef, and smoked sausages; and in numerous little packages, carefully fastened round with thread, were to be found the pecuniary benefactions, which varied in value according to the rank and circumstances of the giver. It fell to the lot of sister Anna to unlead the ass, laden with all kinds of provender—flour, butter, bacon, peas, cheese, and other good things, wherewith to repel the thoughts of hunger and want from the minds of the worthy sisterhood.

Seated behind a full goblet, not of water, but of sparkling, generous wine, sister Simplicia, like a victorious general, received the hearty congratulations from her holy sisters, for the able manner in which she had executed her commission, and she contrived to give a full relation of all that had happened to her during her absence from the convent. The simplicity of the good woman was so well known throughout the convent, that the recital of her adventures was eagerly sought for as a source of fun and merriment to the whole of the auditors. She therefore began as follows :—

"Great was my joy as I rose from my prayers yesterday morning, that I had put on my right shoe first, for I thence concluded that I should be successful in my peregrination, and bring my ass well laden to our holy house. It must, however, be remembered, as an important circumstance, that the ass brayed most piteously, and shook her left ear with violence, which was a certain omen of stormy weather; but still, in matters of that sort, the cat is more to be depended upon than the ass; but he lay snugly in a corner,

See page 83.

and scratched his head now and then, which was a certain sign that we should receive a visitor.''

"Yes, yes, sister Simplicia," exclaimed the nuns; "the cat prognosticated truly; we have had a visitor—a right merry visitor—one of true flesh and blood.''

"With these good omens," continued sister Simplicia, "I set forward under the safe guidance of our Lord Jesus. I sneezed three times, as I led the ass through the gate, which was an excellent sign; but it was still a far better sign when the merry huntsman, Hug, met me with his dog, and directly afterward a man who had a terrible squint, having with him a red-haired girl. I also met some pigs, but they directed their course across the Alb, to the Carthusian Monastery, and the white-coated monks may put what signification they please upon the drove of pigs.

"I directed my course to Gomadingen, and drove my ass at its quickest pace, and I rang my bell most lustily, although I knew that in the stingy place there was not a crumb of bread to be had. Nevertheless, I enjoyed the sport, to see the women putting their heads out of the windows, thinking that the ringing of my bell signified that the holy host was passing by. I heard the abuse that was heaped upon me; but I still continued to ring the bell, and in this manner I arrived at the cottage of old Adam's widow, who, being a godly soul, threw some good things into one of the ass's panniers. My ass liked the hay of the widow, and I enjoyed her good fare, and, so strengthened, I reached Steingebroun.

"I knew that village to be the residence of very pious people, who, before they dispense their charity, do not scornfully ask why the nuns of Gnadenzell go prowling about the country as a gang of beggars; but they immediately hasten to their larders, to empty them of their good things for the benefit of our holy sisterhood, for which good and charitable deed I am certain that the Lord will grant them a joyful resurrection. I proceeded on my path most merrily, and my ass began to sweat under his load, when, on a sudden, my nose began to itch, which signified that my anger would be excited, and my right eye smarted, which signified that I should cry, and, to crown my misfortunes, my knife fell to the ground, and the blade stuck upright in it. This was a certain sign of trouble and vexation; and so in reality did all these things come to pass, for, in the middle of the wood, I met a fellow in green clothes, and a fur cap on his head. He was talking seriously to himself, and looking right and left, as if he had lost something. My heart instantly misgave me, when I recognised the coat of arms which the hunter wore. It was the hateful hunting horn, and the stag's horns of the Count of Wurtemburg. I drove my ass respectfully to the side of the road—drew my cowl over my eyes; but whom do the minions of a count leave without molestation? I was obliged to hear such language that made my ears tingle. In a moment he was joined by some more huntsmen.

"'Hilloa!' exclaimed one of them; 'whither art thou going, little dwarf, with thy ass?'

"'Oho!' exclaimed another; 'by all the saints, it is one of the impudent nuns of Gnadenzell, who would make the world believe that they are as chaste as when they were born.'

"'Nothing but hypocritical vagrants,' exclaimed a third, ' who deserve to be burnt at a stake.'

"I began to count a hundred, and thence back again from a hundred to one, which I know to be a preventative against the rising of one's anger. One of the fellows was impudent enough to pull off my cowl, and said, maliciously, ' A pretty little monster,' and something more, which I will not repeat."

The nuns burst into a loud laugh, and began to jeer their sister upon the conquest that she had made.

"On a sudden," continued Simplicia, who was not to be deterred from continuing her recital by the sneers and jokes of her evil-minded sisters, "a man stood before me to whom all the rest paid an uncommon degree of homage and respect, although he was on foot; but a man, in a splendid livery, was leading his horse behind him. He cast upon me an ill-tempered look, and I now knew him to be the count, from the extreme bushiness of his beard, which is more like that of a thief than of a nobleman; and he said at last to me, in a gruff, surly tone,—

"'Whence come you?'

"'From Gnadenzell,' I answered.

"'How long have you taken to vagabondizing about the country, like the Jews?' he asked.

"'Our poverty is the cause,' I said.

"'I will put an end to your trade,' he said, and combed his beard with his fingers. 'You women deserve, every one of you, to be put into the stocks; you are a positive nuisance to the poor people. I tell you, old one, that some of you are not any better than the Swiss girls, whom the peasants take home with them at night. You shall hear from me soon.'

A murmur of discontent ran through the whole pious community, but Simplicia heeded it not, and continued,—

"I begin to think that the reputation of our convent does not stand so high as it did some time ago. I, however, arrived safely at Engstingen, when——"

Ronata pulled Simplicia slily by the arm of her dress,—

"How is my little fellow at Meidelstatten—did you see him when you were there? is he in good health?"

"As safe and sound," said, Simplicia, "as if he was the son of a count; and if the money be regularly paid for his support, the boy will thrive and do well. Martha, who has the care of him, says that the children out of the convent thrive better than any others. I made the best of my way to Holzelfingen, whence I am the bearer of many salutations to the convent."

" Heard you anything of sister Hailwig?" said the prioress.

" Oh, yes," exclaimed the nuns with one accord; "did you see our poor sister? Is everything over with her, and will she soon return to us?"

" The saints alone can tell," said Simplicia. " Why the affair lasts so long with her; the poor woman is not yet brought to bed, but she still is as beautiful as ever. The dress that she now wears becomes her well; she looks almost like a queen in the fulness of her beauty. God grant it may soon be over with her."

A confused murmur ran through the chaste assembly, and the noise was at length so great, that they heard not the hasty tread of a stranger, who in the court-yard had dismounted from a foaming horse, and who, after saluting Crescentia in the familiar manner of an old acquaintance, he, without any further ceremony or invitation, made the best of his way into the convent. As if a thunderbolt had driven him through the ceiling, so stood he on a sudden amidst the nuns seated at their breakfast-table. He was welcomed by all of them, and by the majority received with every token of surprise.

" Eh, eh!" exclaimed the prioress, " what brings you hither?"

Renata welcomed him as her cousin, and said,—

"Whence come you? God be with Sir Truchsess von Bichishausen."

" I pray you give me a draught of your wine," he said, seating himself in the most familiar manner by the side of the prioress; " my stay here will not be long; nor should I have paid you a visit at all, if Ostertag von Friedingen had not requested me to deliver a message to the worthy lady prioress."

" From Ostertag do you come?" exclaimed the prioress.

" But why, cousin," said Renata, " are you in such a hurry?"

" I do not wish to be arrested," said Truchsess.

" Who is then in pursuit of you?" asked Renata; " what crime have you committed?"

"A mere trifle, after all," said Truchsess. " The Lord of Ehinger gave a ball at Tubingen, and the fool would send an invitation to some wild profligate students, and one of them behaved insolently to a beautiful girl whom I had solicited as my partner. I did not long hesitate about what steps I should take; so, taking the fellow coolly in my arms, I threw him out of the window into the street, by which he broke some of his bones, and particularly his neck. The fellow, it is true, was nothing more than a Frank, and therefore of not much use in the world, but the count appears to entertain a particular affection for strangers in his new university, and so, as I broke the neck of one of the students, I am to have mine broken in return by the hand of the executioner. I therefore made a precipitate retreat, and am now on my way home, although I should have been perfectly safe at Rheutengen, from its peculiar privileges; but there are some people there who are not friendly disposed towards me, and, therefore, when I have once crossed the Lantor, I am safe from the constables of Tubingen."

" What a serious misfortune it is upon you, my dear cousin," said Renata.

" A fig upon it," said Truchsess, " I'll spend my time at home in hunting deer, bears, and wild boars. The storm will soon blow over, and I shall perhaps return to Tubingen; but," addressing himself to the prioress, he said—"Ostertag decrees me to inform you that the count is now at Ochalm, and it is determined that the chancellor shall come as suddenly and unexpectedly upon you as the cat comes upon the mice."

" Oh, gracious Heavens !" exclaimed the prioress, " what shall we do?'"

" The misfortune and the disgrace of poor Hailwig are now well known to the whole of the court at Urach. It is intended to take you by surprise, and to prove that to be true which you have hitherto denied. No excuse will be admitted, and you will be commanded to produce Hailwig before the chancellor, dead or alive. Your discipline, your solitary confinement, and all your mummeries will be strictly investigated, and your future existence as a house of religion will depend upon the disclosures that will be made. It is the intention of Ostertag to pursue his inquiries at the court of the count, and he will send me as his messenger when he has any important information to convey to you."

The prioress had listened in silence to the not very welcome intelligence; but, on a sudden, an unusual vivacity appeared to sparkle in her eyes, and, with a smile of triumph, she clapped her hands, and said,—

" We are armed as with steel and iron. Fortune, in one of her own freaks, will help us through our trouble and embarrassment; she shall give us the victory, and laugh at the hoary chancellor, who thinks to catch us, like a badger, in the trap."

" God grant that may be the case !" said Truchsess.

The prioress gave a particular signal, and the nuns ceased from talking, arranging themselves in regular order on either side of the table. The prioress then, in a solemn tone, addressed them,—

"A severe hour of probation is about to overtake us, and, therefore, let the customary rules be observed in the house, so that the strictest order may be maintained. I recall all dispensations that I have granted to you, and send your tongues to the silence of obedience."

She had scarcely uttered these words, when she determined to set the first example to the holy sisterhood. She concealed her beautiful ringlets under her veil, and her countenance assumed all the gravity which became the most immaculate mother of a holy flock. The nuns followed her example. Plates, dishes, and glasses vanished from the table, and in a moment the community appeared to consist of devout and decorous nuns, instead of the dissolute and abandoned women, who, but an hour before, had been carrying on their scandalous pranks in the same place.

Truchsess could not exactly understand whether all these proceedings were the effect of earnest, or merely done in a joke. He, however, saw that his company could be easily dispensed with, and therefore took his leave as quickly as possible of his pious hostess, on the ground that it was necessary for him to provide for his own safety. Renata accompanied him with great stiffness and formality to the convent gates, and then returned to take a part in the solemn deliberations of the holy sisterhood.

The prioress stood at the head of the table, and said,—

"We will not speak of the causes by which a gradual alleviation of the cruel and severe rules of the convent must be introduced, nor will we speak of the extent of paternal power, by which many of us are condemned to the austerity of a monastic life, nor of the poverty by which many good and virtuous are driven to seek an asylum within these walls. In these perilous times, when it appears that all restraints and shackles are to be removed, it would be the extreme of folly in us, were we to persist in maintaining that to which we are subject. Our most dangerous enemy, who has sworn to watch our proceedings, and to visit us with his vengeance, is Count Eberhard, the elder—he who in his younger years was a confirmed libertine, addicted to every species of debauchery; who was a scourge and murderer in the country—will now attempt to play the part of the rigid moralist, and accuse us of crimes, because we are naturally of a free and merry disposition. It is now his pleasure to carry his bold threats into execution, and to his shameful love of revenge, he adds the crime of hypocrisy and the falsest artifices. It is his intention to come upon us by surprise, and, in the midst of our simple and virtuous life, to strike us to the ground.

"Let us, however, show him that the wisdom and cunning of the woman is superior to the wit and artifice of the man. The mildness and clemency of your prioress have hitherto permitted you to live according to your own pleasure, and now and then to strew a few rosy leaves on your thorny path. Let the count, however, find you on your bed of thorn—immersed in prayer, labour, and repentance. Let no sound, no step henceforth betray the liberty and the freedom which has hitherto prevailed in this house. Let everything be removed to some obscure place, which could in any manner bear witness against us. Let all your comfortable clothing, your fine linen and apparel, and the most simple ornament be instantly removed from your cells; then, with a bold front, and a head erect, we will confront our accusers. I now excommunicate, and put under the ban, the tongue which would betray to our enemies a single circumstance which would bring shame, or injury upon our community. The misfortune of our sister Hailwig, her weakness, the too natural fruit of hereditary sin, is taken advantage of by our persecutors, as a pretext to overthrow our house and destroy all our rights and privileges. He thinks to annoy with his challenge to produce before him our unfortunate sister. He thinks, perhaps, of bringing back those horrible times when a fallen sister of a convent was closely imprisoned, and suffered to languish and pine away with want, instead of treating her transgression with indulgence and love, and leading her back to virtue by the word of kindness. But confusion, shame, and ignominious blight from these walls shall await them. Let the chancellor come when he will, and the count along with him; they shall find our sister Hailwig in the midst of us, and their very hearts shall burst with rage and passion."

The nuns were rather puzzled to account for the latter part of the speech of their worthy prioress; for it was well known to all of them that sister Hailwig was in that particular situation, that she could not be exhibited to the chancellor or the court, or to any other man whatever, excepting to the individual who had been the cause of her temporary retirement. The prioress was well able to read these doubts and suspicions in the countenances of her immaculate flock; and Renata, more bold than any of the rest, exclaimed,—

"You will not dare, most holy mother, to place our unfortunate sister in the presence of the chancellor and the court. Would she not be a living proof of the truth of the infamous reports that our enemies have circulated respecting the laxity of our conduct?"

"Hold your tongue, you foolish woman," said the prioress. "What business have you even to make an allusion to the laxity of conduct in the holy house? Do you suppose I should be a fit and proper person to hold the reins of authority in the house, if I did not know how to provide a remedy for every disaster that might befall us? The saints, I know, will support me in my endeavour to rescue this good and holy house from the attacks of its impious enemies; and have not my prayers to the saints been heard? and have they not sent to our house a maiden, whom they have selected as bearing the closest similarity in countenance and outward deportment with our sister Hailwig, in order that we might be saved from the snares of Satan and his infamous crew? A maiden of noble birth is enthusiastically attached to a monastic life, and implores, as the greatest blessing that can be conferred upon her, to be received into our holy sisterhood. It is her very enthusiasm that is a guarantee to me for her implicit obedience to all my commands and instructions; and, as I take upon myself the arduous task of preparing Gisela for the part that she has to play, I forbid all and every one of you to offer the slightest interference or interruption to her in her devotions, or to interfere in any manner whatever with her mode of conduct, however strange and singular it may appear. Our honour, our salvation, our rights and privileges, and our existence as a religious community, depend upon the success of the plan which I have now in my head, and which I doubt not the holy saints will enable me to carry into execution. I am by no means ignorant that there are many in this holy house who entertain a secret dislike for the superior of it, as well as for many of their holy sisters; but, under the present alarming circumstances, when ruin appears to be hanging over us, it is my order—and I will go further, and say that it is my request—that all private resentments and all personal dislikes may for a time be quelled."

"Amen, amen!" responded the holy sisters of the community.

It is impossible to relate how long the speech of the prioress would have lasted, had it not been suddenly interrupted by the entrance of the vicar of the convent. The holy father was a fat, bloated, corpulent monk, his countenance well studded with carbuncles, and his jolly, rubicund nose was a prominent voucher that his visitations to the cellar were frequent, and his libations copious. It was whispered amongst the holy sisterhood that he had enchained the affections of one of them; and he, in return, from a spirit of gratitude, had bestowed his upon her. Of the result of those affections, the records of the house of Gnadenzell are silent; and, therefore, in Christian charity, let it be stated that the love of the jolly friar was purely platonic; and that he, from a sense of his professional duty, attended more to the salvation of her soul than to the gratification of her earthly passions. On the present occasion, it was evident that the potations of the holy father had been rather deep; for, instead of walking in an erect and dignified posture into the room, as became a minister of the holy Jesus, and an expounder of his doctrines to a numerous flock, he stumbled into it, making certain eccentric motions, which demonstrated that there was a confusion in his brain, which charity and liberality might attribute to indigestion, but which truth would ascribe to the influential fumes of a spirituous liquid. Astonishment might certainly have some little share in the eccentric motions of the reverend monk; for he started with surprise when he beheld his holy flock in so decorous and respectable a condition. The monk was, however, more inclined to be humoursome than to be serious and devout.

"Well, beloved sisters," he exclaimed, "praise be to Jesus, what are you all about? Are you holding a court of inquiry; and, if so, who is the delinquent? If a hundred kisses be the punishment that will be inflicted, I offer myself as the executioner."

The prioress was, however, by no means disposed to understand the joke of the holy friar, and said,—

"If any punishment is to be awarded, let it fall upon you, you negligent and careless shepherd of an oppressed flock."

"To what do you allude, holy mother?" said the unruly vicar, who was known by the name of Belzer in his monastery.

"Because," said the prioress, "several new complaints have lately been made against you."

"Indeed!" exclaimed the monk; "you know, reverend mother, that we are all prone to sin, and that by nature we are full of vanity."

" That is a lesson," said the prioress, " that I hear, or ought to hear, every day, from the pulpit. But whither did you go to early this morning?"

" I paid a visit to my reverend brother, at Gomadingen," replied the monk, " who gave me an excellent banquet, because I took Jacob with me to amuse him with his instrument."

" It is for these banquets and this riotous living," said the prioress, " that you, day after day, neglect your duty."

" Do you not know," said the monk, " that it is a part of my duty to support the internal man?"

" And," said the prioress, " it is the only duty that you properly fulfil. Know you the situation in which we stand on account of your criminal negligence? Do you not bring suspicion and trouble upon our holy house? No mass is celebrated—no sermon is preached; the faithful in the neighbourhood find, indeed, the sacrament in our church, but no priest to offer it."

" The world is about at an end," said the holy friar, " for the prieress of Gnadenzell has been reading me a lecture about holiness, duty, and such like mortal things; but are you serious in these reproaches?"

" Serious with my reproaches!" exclaimed the prioress. " Never was I more serious; and I have still more bitter reproaches to make."

" Then," said the holy father, " either you or I must be mad."

" You bring our house into disrepute," said the prioress. " The tongues of the scandal-mongers are wagging day and night against you. How can we expect any alms or benefactions to be given, where there is neither mass, confession, nor sacrament?"

" Let me hear no more of your nonsense," said the holy father; " and consider, what has been long our custom—service on a Sunday; that is quite enough for Gnadenzell; the peasants would otherwise forget how mass is celebrated."

" Reflect upon your own words," said the prioress. " You are an unworthy member of our holy church; impious, profane, and full of sin; and, if you continue in these unrighteous paths, we will apply to the bishop to give us another vicar."

" With all my heart," said the holy father; " then he shall also give me a fresh stock of nuns; for you are as insufferable and odious to me, as you have declared that I am to you."

A deep murmur of discontent ran through the whole community; but the countenance of the monk was inflamed with anger, and he continued—

" It is yourselves, ye loose and profligate women, that have brought your convent into disrepute. It is no longer called Gnadenzell, but a brothel, a house of prostitutes. Of what use is it that I should give myself much trouble about you, as you are all hastening to the devil as fast as you can, like your predecessors? Is this your gratitude for my secrecy and my assistance? If I should take it into my head to open my mouth, why, there is not a head in the place, the hairs of which will not stand as erect as the bristles of a hedge-hog. You ought to be poor—poor and destitute; but it is only in the bath that you are naked and poor. You ought to be obedient; but you are so only when you are at the dining-table, when the plates and dishes rattle, and the goblet passes round. You ought to be chaste; but to talk of a nun of Gnadenzell being chaste, it is like talking of the mercy of a wolf. Oh, by the holy cross! give not yourselves so many airs, and behave yourselves as if the angel of repentance had suddenly got into you. You are all black sheep—pitch black, and you will remain so, if you were to use the scrubbing-brush of purification from morning to night. I'll now make the best of my way to the count at Urach, and open his eyes to all your infamies and abominations."

This threat on the part of the irritated monk had the desired effect, for the language of the prioress became immediately changed; from the tone of insolence and defiance, it was now changed to that of submission and supplication. The nuns knew well, for reasons best known to themselves, what a zealous advocate and champion they possessed in their holy vicar, and, therefore, they unanimously requested the prioress to desist from any further abuse or vituperation of the reverend father. The prioress, therefore, said to the vicar, in rather a more friendly tone,—

" Be not angry, holy father, and continue to live amongst us in peace and amity; but I would have you consider that the vengeance of the count is ready to fall upon us, and, therefore, wait, in the due performance of your holy office, until the storm has blown over, instead of wandering about to the residences of your brethren in the Lord Jesus, and filling your belly with their dainties and their luxuries."

" Why should I not do it?" said the holy father, with a smile; " you know that I entertain a strong affection for all of you, and that I always shut my eyes when anything appertaining to the masculine gender shows itself in your chaste and holy house. Have I not immediately absolved every one of you who may have wandered into a different path than what is pointed out to you by your rules and discipline? Have I not shut my ears to the cries of certain little things partaking of the human form who, by some accident or circumstance unknown, have been found within the walls of your holy house? In return for this indulgence and connivance at your sins I require that I may not be molested, and that I may be master of my own actions. I am partial, I need scarcely inform you, to a regular life, and to live one day as I do on another, and that regularity principally consists in satisfying my hunger whenever nature requires it, and not only my hunger but my thirst also. Now, with you it is wholly a different thing; to-day you are living in luxury and superfluity, and to-morrow you are without a crust of bread; but as long as there is a loaf in the larder, or a bottle of wine in the cellar, you'll consume the whole of it, without thinking of the morrow. Why should I not pay a visit to-day to the holy father of Gomadingen, whose kitchen and cellar are always well supplied, and with whom I am going to sup to-night on fowls and ham and a larded hare?"

"Then," said the prioress, "betake thyself off to Gomadingen."

"And why not?" said the vicar. "To-day it is too late for mass, and as for the vesper, why, some one else may perform my duty."

"May I ask," said the prioress, "your motives for coming hither to-day? for all the good that you have done for our famishing souls you had better have stopped away."

"I will tell you, holy mother," said the vicar, "the son of one of our holy fathers lies very ill of a fever; the doctor and the witch have both prescribed for him, but all in vain. On a sudden I thought of the astrologer who visited you yesterday, and who told your Poppele his fortune so exactly. Where is the vagabond? Sister Benedicta, call him into my presence."

"Of what are you thinking?" said Benedicta, highly vexed; "I shall not go after the vagabond."

Sister Anna, however, said,—

"As I was running out of the court-yard, I saw the wonderful man prowling about the burial-ground, apparently, to me, as if he were looking for ants' eggs."

"Ants' eggs, indeed!" exclaimed Simplicia; "he is more likely looking after the treasure that lies buried in the churchyard."

"Hold your tongue," said sister Barbara, "and let us hear no more of your foolish stories about witches, and ghosts, and apparitions. Have you not already deranged the brain of poor Poppele?—and yet you cannot hold your tongues."

"I want not to hear about your buried treasure or your apparitions," said the vicar; "go and bring the astrologer to me. I must away with him this very hour."

With great ill-humour Benedicta went in search of the astrologer; and, as the vicar opened the door for her, a piercing cry of distress sounded through the passages of the convent, which brought a paleness in the countenances of all the nuns. Sister Anna, amongst the rest, trembled with alarm, and exclaimed,—

"Oh, holy mother! it just now occurs to me. Oh! that my memory should be so weak and treacherous. I now remember, that since yesterday at noon we have totally forgotten our sister Damath. She must almost be literally dead with hunger. I will hasten to her."

Sister Anna waddled out of the room, and the cry of distress somewhat subsided, when it was succeeded by a loud exclamation issuing from the throat of a nun calling for help and assistance; and the whole sisterhood, who, full of alarm, had rushed into the passages to ascertain the cause of the exclamation, beheld the astrologer running with the utmost haste towards the gate, and hurrying from it when he found it closed, then sprang into the flower-garden, and then through the lower arcade, over the wall into the great kitchen-garden.

In the arcade, however, against one of the pillars, was leaning Poppele, in deep vexation and chagrin, and to whom the nuns cried out,—

"Hilloa! hilloa! Poppele—Poppele; catch the thief—stop the vagabond!"

Poppele immediately rushed through the arcade, followed the track of the astrologer, and caught him just as he was climbing over the wall—wrestled with him for a time, and at last a part of the garment of the astrologer was left in the hand of Poppela, who with a strength not to be expected from his years, climbed over the wall, and fell on the opposite side.

Several of the nuns and subordinates of the establishment beheld the extraordinary scene; and to the majority of them a hubbub and confusion of the kind were nothing new nor surprising. The politic prioress, however, despatched Crescentia to the cell of

Gisela, for the purpose of preventing her leaving it in order to make some inquiry relative to the noise and tumult which were then heard throughout the convent. Gisela was in reality listening at the door of the cell; and on Crescentia appearing, she inquired, in an anxious tone, the cause of the disorder. In a tone of great indifference Crescentia answered,—

"It is a mere trifle, my dear sister. The uproar is entirely caused by that idiot Poppele, who, when the moon is at the full, keeps the whole of the establishment in a state of alarm with his maniac pranks."

Gisela knew that the moon was at the full; she knew, also, that lunatics at that particular period are ungovernable and untractable; and believing the story of Crescentia to be true she shut the door of her cell, and returned to her devotions.

CHAPTER XI.

" Yet no attribute
So well befits the exalted seat supreme,
And power's dispensing hand, as clemency.
Each crown must from its quality be purged,
And pity there should interpose, when malice
Is not the aggressor."

COUNT EBERHARD, the prince and ruler of the country, had, according to his custom, risen at an early hour, and was parading up and down the saloon in his princely residence, at Urach. His valet cautiously and respectfully opened the door, to admit the ingress of the prefect, who approached the prince with all the fawning servility of the courtier, making his obeisance at almost every step. The count folded his arms, and looked the prefect full in the face, with an expression of anger and displeasure, saying—

" You constables and bailiffs, you keep fine order in the country. It is only two days ago that I was obliged to take up my quarters at night in one of the thieves' dens; and is it in this manner that you administer the laws which I have enacted? It is my wish that my subjects, after so much trouble and distress, should be in the enjoyment of peace; and yet the robbers and highwaymen fix their quarters in the mountains and the vallies, as if they possessed am undisputed right to the territory; and, what is more, they presume to issue their threats, and to carry those threats into dreadful execution, if the sentence that has been passed upon one of their accomplices is carried into execution. What is the cause of all this disorder in my territory?"

" Most honoured lord," said the prefect, with great composure, " I cannot be held accountable for the negligence and misconduct of my brethren in office. I would have you remember how this country has been dreadfully scourged by sanguinary wars and intestine commotions, and, consequently, how impossible it is at one blow to destroy all the obnoxious objects which have sprung so luxuriantly from such a protracted system of murder and rebellion."

" I have heard before of these excuses," said the count, " but they are by no means satisfactory to me. The prince and his servants are not to pass the day in sloth, and idleness, and negligently to expect that from the future what must and ought to take place immediately. I will, therefore, suffer no longer that tardiness and negligence which are so injurious to my subjects; do you regulate your proceedings accordingly."

The prefect made a low bow, but said not a word.

The count continued,—

" Of what use is it to pass sentence, whether it be severe or not, without knowing how to carry it into execution, unintimidated by the threats of a human being? It is true, the heart of the judge may bleed when he is obliged to have recourse to the sword of the executioner; but there are cases in which mercy would be a crime, and a relaxation of the sentence incompatible with law and justice. The people, indeed, are well-disposed, faithful, loyal, and obedient; but they are uncultivated, stupid, from antiquated prejudices and superstitions. But, on the other hand, they take immediate advantage, so soon as the reins are not held tightly over them."

" It shall be the pleasure of my life," said the prefect, " to see your commands, most honoured sir, carried into execution, and I believe I may say the same of my brother officers; but, allow me to inquire to what determination you have come in the case of Heinz von Schlaitz?"

" Have you," said the count, " in accordance with my orders, had the young rogue conveyed hither?"

" Your orders have been rigidly obeyed, most noble sir," said the prefect.

" Then," said the count, " let him be brought before me.   I will question himself, and, from his conduct, I will determine whether I shall place my signature to the sentence, or if I shall lend a willing ear to the petition of those that have been robbed."

The prefect left the room, and made a signal to the constables who had Heinz, laden with chains, in their custody, and, in a few minutes he was brought into the presence of the count.

See page 87.

The head of the young man was resting on his breast, his looks were directed to the ground, and his whole frame appeared to be in a state of wild commotion.

The count looked steadfastly at him for some time without speaking a word.   At last he said, in a mild and composed tone,—

" Take his chains off; it is not proper that he should appear in such a state before his prince.   Every one ought to be able to raise their face to their prince and judge with confidence and freedom."

The chains were taken off the hands and feet of the criminal, and he said in a subdued tone,—

"I thank you, my lord, for the temporary comfort."

"Stand upright, like a man," said the count.

"I cannot, most noble sir," said the culprit; "the rack at Pfullingen has weakened and disarranged my joints."

"Pity it is," said the count, "that justice required that thy tender age should be visited with so much agony. Thou art so young, and yet so depraved, so obstinate and unrepentant, thou wouldst not make any confession, although screw was turned upon screw, and club upon club fell upon thy joints, whilst thou wert stretched upon the rack. That is most wicked; a boy like you should yield to friendly admonition, to kind and indulgent treatment, seeing that repentance is a becoming virtue, even in the most hardened criminal."

"But, my lord," said Heinz, "no such words as you mention were spoken to me; I acknowledge that I am a dissolute young man, but, on the other hand, let me tell you, that my ears and my heart can easier be led and influenced by kindness than my tongue and my body by all the severest torments of the rack."

"It is something in your favour," said the count, "that you acknowledge your depravity. How has that been brought to pass?"

"The silence and darkness of the dungeon," said Heinz, "have had a salutary influence over me. I have been so accustomed to freedom, fresh air, and an active life, that I could not but deplore having, by my crime, forfeited such inestimable blessings."

"What induced you," asked the count, "to commit the crime of which you now express your repentance?"

"Poverty, most noble, sir," said Heinz, "and the desire to please my sweetheart."

"How so?" asked the count.

"My sweetheart is unhappy," said Heinz, "because she is not free, and dare not be mine. In order to dissipate her grief, I wished to make her some presents; but we are miserably poor, my relatives as well as myself; and I, therefore, stole what I could not honestly obtain."

"Who is your sweetheart?" asked the count.

Heinz made not any answer, but shook his head.

"Who were the accomplices in your theft?" asked the count.

Heinz spoke not.

"What connexion had your theft with Wildherr, the bandit, and wert thou associated with him?"

Heinz again shook his head, but made no answer.

"You abuse my patience, young man," said the count; "you cannot place any great value upon your future fate. I do not place much confidence on your repentance, as you are deficient in sincerity."

"I cannot, most noble, sir," said Heinz, "bring myself to confess more than my crime."

"Tell me, then, at least," said the count, "something about your residence, your father, your mother, and sisters; your relations in general; what sort of a life you have led, and whether you have been morally and virtuously educated."

"You are asking me about things, my lord," said Heinz, "with which you are previously acquainted; but spare the son who loves his parents the unpleasant task of answering your question."

"Truly, Heinz," said the count, "there is something better in thee, than what one would expect from the crime that you have committed. A heavy responsibility is attached to your father. I have made a dangerous acquaintanceship with him, and I know too well that he has nothing of man belonging to him but the form; for his love to thee is nothing more than the impulse which belongs to the beast, when it stretches out its claws, and whets its tusk for its young ones. You dishonour a noble name, and are a stain upon your family; I will take care that the nest shall be destroyed."

"It is already done, most noble, sir," said the prefect, "according to your orders; but we found nothing, but, as it were, the dregs. The desperate thief, Ganerbon, had suddenly betaken himself off; old Schlaitz never returned, and the sisters only of the young vagrant remained for the purpose of attending upon their bedridden mother. A guard has been set on the house by the authorities of Pfullingen.

"You appear," said the count, "to be much concerned about your family; but do you think at all about your own fate? What if I, enraged at your pertinacious silence, were to issue my orders that the sentence which was passed upon you at Pfullingen should be instantly carried into execution?"

"That you will not do, most noble sir," said Heinz, with the greatest composure.

" How!" exclaimed the count. " You perhaps suppose that I am intimidated by the threats of the chief of the banditti. Know, mistaken youth, that I know not what fear is, and that I would carry your sentence into execution, even if the hoary villain stood behind me with his uplifted sword; or perhaps you think I should spare you from gratitude, because the rogues did not kill me when I fell into their hands. I consider myself under no obligation whatever to the villains; for if they did not wound nor injure my princely head, they only did that which the God in Heaven commanded them. Why, therefore, should I not do, young man, whatever it is my pleasure that shall be done to you for the commission of your crime?"

" Because," said Heinz, with great humility, " your sense of justice will not allow you. You have been so long pleased to hold this discourse with me—to let me remain so long in your presence, that I consider myself secure of my life and my limbs; knowing, as I do, that you are a most gracious prince, and not to be compared to the savage beast of prey, that cruelly plays with its victim before it kills it."

On hearing this speech, the count clasped his hands, and said, in a tone in which astonishment and pleasure were mingled,—

" There stands that miserable creature, with the utmost confidence before his judge, and preaches to him how mercy and forgiveness belong to the virtues of a prince; but is not the prince also a man, and ought not clemency to be practised by every man? But then, ye thieves and highwaymen, have you a proper comprehension of peace, mercy, and forgiveness? Well may it be said that the human heart is an unfathomable ocean, in which what is good and bad are mingled; in which the monster sleeps close to the pearl, and in which the storm rages one moment, and the next the sun shines into its depths. Thus do we offend God, and defy his grace and mercy; thus do we deeply afflict our father and mother, and reckon upon their everlasting love; and in the end, in spite of all the Lord God bestows his mercy, and the love of the parent never ceases; and I also will be compassionate, and remit the severe sentence that has been passed upon you, and, in your lonely cell, give you time for reflection, if you will repay my princely clemency with unfeigned repentance and true confession."

Heinz was about to throw himself at the feet of the count; but the count turned away from him with a repulsive motion. The constables led the culprit gently away, whilst tears of gratitude fell from the eyes of the young delinquent. The prefect, however, under the influence of deep emotion, said to the bystanders,—

" Behold a wolf, whom the goodness and judgment of our worthy prince has converted into a penitent man! God preserve us our gracious prince, whom Heaven has sent to rule over us!"

The people joined in one accord in praise of the prince; for, in truth, he was worthy of the dignified station which he filled; and in the perilous times in which the events of this history are supposed to have happened, a just and merciful prince was a phenomenon seldom to be seen.

The count was about to return to his private apartment, when, casting his eyes accidentally into the court yard, he perceived a well-known figure, who was standing under the archway, seeking shelter from the rain, and apparently impatient for the hour when access to the prince would be allowed. The man was dressed in a faded court costume, and bore about him all the signs of poverty and distress. The count, however, opened the window, gave a friendly nod with his head, and cried,—

" Good morning to you, Herr von Sperbeneck. You have chosen bad weather to make your appearance at court. If you have any business to transact with me make no ceremony. I will be at home to you. I do not suppose you will require a long audience."

The visitor made a very low bow, and with an assumed consequence bent his steps to the flight of steps leading to the great hall. He, however, arranged his dress as carefully as he could, concealing the tattered parts, and carrying his hat, which was full of holes, under his cloak, so that it should not be seen by the count.

On entering the apartment in which the count was standing, the latter said, in the greatest good humour,—

" You are, indeed, Herr von Sperbeneck, a most unexpected guest. Has anything particular occurred; is your life too monotonous for you in your lonely castle, or are you in search of a place at court? Tell me candidly what it is of which you are in search."

Herr von Sperbeneck was rather embarrassed, and said, with great diffidence,—

" You are pleased, your honour—you are disposed to pass your jokes on my poverty and wretchedness. How could I take an office at court, when I am more of a peasant than a nobleman? My wife and my six children, for whose support and maintenance I have to provide, are the best of all persons to drive pride out of my head. The times grow worse and worse; a man of straw, like myself, must go along with the stream, I must swim wherever the fancy or caprice of others compel me; and, after all, I get nothing but bruises and hard treatment."

"You make a great mistake, Sir Anshelm," said the count; "are not your riches publicly spoken of, and are you not compared to the rich man in the scriptures?"

"All falsehood and calumny, my lord," said Sir Anshelm; "it is the most infamous report that was ever circulated against a man in my situation; the people amuse themselves in chatting about land and estates, silver and gold, and leave me to be pillaged by beggars and robbers, to say nothing of our neighbours, who, actuated by envy and malice, expose us to be insulted on every occasion, and to be accused of crimes and faults of which we are wholly innocent."

The count assumed a serious countenance and said,—

"You are considered, Sir Anshelm, to be a very rich man, but very stingy and penurious. If, however, you be not the first, I will not, nor can I then believe the latter affair. A miser is odious to me, and I consider it a pleasure to be your friend. What can I do to serve you?"

Anshelm collected his thoughts, and began with that prudence and circumspection, which throw every word into the scale before it be spoken. "There are three points, most noble lord, which I wish to submit to your consideration, and I will be as brief as possible, as I do not wish to waste my time unnecessarily, and I know that your time is of the highest value to you. In the first place, I have a brother who lives at Arach, possesses a farm, which has been lately greatly damaged by fire, but which he has now offered to sell me the transfer. Although I have very little to spare for the purchase of farms, yet, out of pure affection for my brother, I have not any objection to have the injured property transferred to me, provided, most noble lord, that it meets with your sanction and approbation."

"And why not, Sir Anshelm?" said the count; "a peasant has it in his power to purchase an estate without any appeal to me; why then not you, whom I esteem as my neighbour? But what has happened to your brother? I remember well at the festivities at Treves, he was in the suite of the Duke of Burgundy. He was considered a very brave swordsman, and very near receiving the honour of knighthood. He was reproached as being frivolous and thoughtless, and a confirmed spendthrift; but they are qualities that are often to be found in the bravest of men. How is he now?"

Anshelm gave a deep sigh, shrugged his shoulders, shook his head, and said, in a broken voice,—

"It is his unbounded extravagance, and his propensity to duelling, which have reduced him to necessity, have been the cause of great trouble to me, and have now compelled me to trouble you with my petition. In order to be cured of his wounds, he went to Baden, fell into dissolute and profligate company, has been guilty of several very unpardonable acts, squandered a great deal of money, and at last has got himself into a serious scrape, by having struck a nobleman with his sword, for which he has been obliged to fly the country. In consequence of which the Margrave Christopher has put the most stringent laws of Baden into execution against him, by which he is declared an outlaw, and his rank and nobility taken from him. He has now sent his servant to me from Gernsbach, where he is confined by illness, and should he return home, I should be under great apprehensions for him to eat of my bread or to drink out of my cup. It is true I am his brother; but, as the father of a family, I have a heavy load upon me. I am disposed to maintain him, but I am not in a condition to support him as a sick and helpless man. Under this serious dilemma I have ventured, most noble lord, to make this appeal to you, that you may be pleased to appease the anger of the margrave, your illustrious friend, and solicit him to restore the goods and property belonging to my brother, which were seized by his orders at Baden, that he will remove the stain that has been placed upon his escutcheon, and reverse the sentence of outlawry. You will then, I hope, most noble lord, not let the dissolute youth escape without a serious lecture, and that, instead of being a burden upon my limited income, he shall either sell or pledge whatever property he may have remaining, and with the wreck of his fortunes return to the Netherlands, or wherever else it may be, seeing that he can no longer do any good in his own country, but bring scandal and disgrace upon his family and relations."

Count Everhard looked upon the affectionate and considerate brother with the eye of displeasure, and in rather a hasty tone said to him,—

"This is a fine story about your relation; but it is useless to spend many words about it. I will write to the margrave to send me all the particulars of the transaction, and if your brother has been guilty only of a juvenile indiscretion, or a mere act of youthful imprudence, my intercession, considering him in the character of a brave and noble soldier, may be of great use to him. He shall then go whithersoever he pleases, and were it even here at my court; but, depend upon it, I will dissuade him from being a burden to you in your castle, or to partake of any of your bounty or provisions."

The miser saw too well through the expressive meaning of these words, and was most profuse in his thanks to his gracious prince for the offer of his arbitration, and proceeded to enlarge most piteously on the trouble and vexation which his brother Hurdegen had caused throughout the whole of the country, when about a year ago he paid him a visit. In order to work still more powerfully upon the feelings of the count, who listened in rather a careless manner to the voluble relation of the miser, he continued,—

" Discontent and confusion appeared, alas! to have taken up their abode in our ancient house. The father is continually at variance with the mother, the mother with the children. One brother is quarrelling with the other, and the sisters cannot give each other a kind or friendly word. Every one has a wayward will of his own, which is not agreeable to the others; and I know of only one day in which we all sat together in amity, and apparently contented with each other. It was the marriage day of my two sisters, who married at the same time, and to two excellent and stately men were they married. In order to celebrate this double marriage, as well as the journey which my brother Hurdegen was about to take to the Netherlands, my two other brothers, who are now in peace in heaven, came to the paternal house, and we seated ourselves happily and contentedly at the table. To be sure the father was missing; he was gone, on account of family quarrels, on a pilgrimage to the Holy Land, and authentic intelligence has reached us of his death."

Anshelm stopped for a moment to give vent to a deep, hypocritical sigh. A heavy frown came upon the countenance of Everhard, and he appeared as if he were struggling with a painful reminiscence.

Anshelm then continued,—

" In consequence of the absence of my father, my mother sat at the head of the table, and shone, as in the days of her youth, in all the pride and glory of her superlative beauty, of which, most noble lord, you must have heard, if, indeed, at that time your eyes may have not beheld her. She was, indeed, an angel of a woman."

Anshelm made again a sudden pause, as if dubious whether he should proceed; but the count, whose eyes glistened with an extraordinary fire, and whose cheeks were suffused with a deep crimson, said,—

" I remember her well, Herr von Sperbeneck; but proceed, and come to the point as soon as you can."

" Thus was my mother," continued Anshelm, " in the roseate time of her youth, and we, her offsprings, whispered to each other, pleased with the joy and satisfaction which my mother displayed, that she looked more like a girl of eighteen than the mother of a family. With an eye beaming with pleasure she counted her children and her daughters' husbands, and she found that there were five knights at the table; and one in particular who, on account of his bravery, would one day be entitled to wear the golden spur. She spoke with maternal pride of her sons and her blooming daughters; but, on a sudden, she became silent, wept bitterly, and said, she was not worthy of so great an honour. She then left the table, shut herself up in her chamber, would not allow any one to see her, and when at night the brides and bridegrooms came to the door to ask her blessing it was discovered that she had left the house; not a trace of her was to be discovered, and up to the present moment no tidings whatever have been received of her."

" No tidings received of her!" repeated the count, leaning in one of the recesses of the windows, and apparently lost in thought; " no tidings whatever did you say ?"

" None whatever, my noble lord," answered Anshelm; " we conjectured that the poor woman may have lost her way in the forests or may have been murdered by the banditti, as she took her ornaments and her jewels with her. Thus was our house of joy turned into one of the deepest mourning."

Anshelm covered his face with his hands, as if he were immersed in grief, and the count appeared to be overcome with the violence of his emotions. On a sudden he appeared to collect himself, and said,—

" Had you not a third affair to communicate to me, Sir Anshelm ?"

" It is but a sequel to the former part of my narrative," said Anshelm. " Our mother, indeed, is lost to us; but yet it is with the greatest astonishment that I have heard the intelligence, that a man has shown himself in these quarters, who gives himself out to be our father, and has actually been acknowledged as such by the minister at Owen. It is true he has not shown himself at my castle, in which he has done well; for the man cannot possibly be anything else than an impostor; since our father, according to the most authentic intelligence, departed this life either at Joppa or Rama. It is, however, well-known that such falsehoods and impositions have a great effect upon the credulity of the people, give rise to idle and malicious reports, and disturb me in the peace of my house. Who can tell the extent of the villany that may be concealed in this fabrication of the sudden appearance of my father, and whether my ruin and destruction have not been contemplated by the wicked scoundrels, who in order to injure me have brought this impostor into the country? It is a matter worthy of our consideration; if our true, our legitimate father were by some miracle to be awakened out of his grave and to appear before me, demand his property and reduce me and mine to beggary; but still more vexatious and scandalous would it be were we to receive a shameless impostor into the house, and, as it were, behold him trampling upon our legitimate rights. Therefore, most honoured lord, do I petition you that you will be pleased to issue your commands to all your prefects, constables, and other functionaries to take into custody the wandering vagabond; inflict upon him a summary punishment, and drive him over the frontiers of your territory."

"My orders shall be issued accordingly," said the count, after a little reflection; "and if your presumed father be caught we shall then institute the proper inquiry and deal with the matter accordingly. Neither yourself nor the humblest of my subjects shall be unlawfully disturbed in the possession of their property. But, after all, be not so very anxious about the matter. Who can tell but that you have been imposed upon? Every one has his enemies, and it is not in your power always to guard against their evil practices, and their treacherous designs. Thus I have lately gained information that Ostertag von Friedingen, who is continually involved in quarrels and disputes with me, has been lately seen at Achalm and even here at Urach. I cannot suppose him to be wandering about in this quarter without some specific design; and candour and integrity are often defeated by duplicity and subterfuge. For yourself, return in comfort to your house, I will do for you whatever stands in my power."

Sir Anshelm made a most profound obeisance, and was ushered out by the chancellor of the count, who informed the count that he was perfectly in readiness to proceed to Gnadenzell on his mission of examination into the crying and scandalous abuses and mal-practices which had taken place in the convent.

"Use all possible expedition, my worthy chancellor," said the count, in a most determined tone. "There is not any necessity for reminding you that the utmost severity is a part of your duty. The *ruse de guerre* that has been planned against the insolent and audacious women must this time be crowned with success, and the scandalous disgrace which the pious mother Hailwig has brought upon the convent, as it is reported, must necessarily put a stop to all clemency and mercy. You are well acquainted with the resolution that I have taken; do you execute it with zeal and fidelity, for you are the herald who is to pave the way for the venerable sisters of Pforzheim, whom I have appointed to reform the depraved and dissolute convent."

The count, with these words, dismissed his plenipotentiary, and whilst the latter was giving the necessary instructions to his secretary, one of the pages hastened with the utmost speed from the prince's residence to the hotel, known by the sign of "The Crown," and, in a moment afterwards, a stately young man sat on a horse before the door, and galloped away, reckless of all surrounding objects, towards the Seeburger valley, which leads to the Alb. This rider was no other person than Ostertag von Friedingen.

<hr>

CHAPTER XII.

" ——————— The land of Golgotha,
Inhabited by none but by the dead,
Except some airy shadows, and they're silent.
* * * * *
I see a strange confession in thine eye;
Thou shak'st thy head, and hold'st it fear or sin,
To speak a truth."

THE weather had been for some time exceedingly tempestuous. The rain inundated mountain and valley; the hail broke down the flowers of the garden and the corn in the fields; and the sun had scarcely peeped out for a moment from behind the turbulent clouds, than the sluices of heaven were again opened, pouring their torrents upon the already deluged earth. A short truce had taken place in the war of the elements, but on the summits of the mountains still rested black threatening clouds, the precursors of the approaching storm.

During this uproar of the elements, sat in the house below Stahleck two watchmen, good, simple citizens of Pfullingen, yawning most uncomfortably at each other, and overcome with listlessness and *ennui*, mingled with no little portion of chagrin, at the changes and violence of the weather. Their javelins rested, like themselves, in a state of inactivity against the wall; and after the lapse of a quarter of an hour, one of them said to the other,—

"Are we not stupid fellows—worse even than blockheads—to sit here in this idle manner, and keep watch over an empty nest? The rogues have flown away, and we may rest assured that they will not very soon return to their home. No one will carry away the old gouty woman, and the ugly wretches, her daughters, will in the end bring some trouble upon us, as they are said to be in league with the devil, and we all know what kind of tricks he is apt to put into the heads of women."

"You are a very learned man, Master Kreidenweiss, and your words are those of wisdom and understanding," said the other dutiful guardian; "besides, the head of the police forgets us wholly in this tedious watch that we have to keep, and our trade suffers most severely. Your skins will be tanned in a most slovenly manner, and my customers will give their orders to some other shoemaker for the articles of which they may stand in need, whilst we, the principals, are here left to perish with hunger. Our stock of pro·visions has been long since consumed; the wretches have scarcely a crust to gnaw at, ⌐ σ the rainy weather is so terrible in this solitary hole."

"My advice is, Father Staigle," said the other, "that we betake ourselves off with all becoming expedition; and we will call at my cousin Steinberg's, who gives a feast to-night, on the christening of his child. The good things that will be there set before us, will do us good after this lent that has been forced upon us; and, having arrived at Pfullingen, we will let our high constable know something of our mind, for keeping us here in a state of starvation, looking at each other like two cats in a garret. Let him send two of his idle constables, who have not any other business to attend to than run after the prostitutes, and then take a bribe from them to set them again at liberty."

"Be it so, Father Kreidenweiss; we will pick up our things, and steal away from the place unnoticed. Before the scoundrels are aware of our retreat, our discharge will, perhaps, have arrived from the police·office."

The tanner and the shoemaker soon carried into execution what, in their wisdom, they had resolved upon. Like ghosts, they skulked out of the dilapidated house, and hastened with all possible speed to reach the village, before it began to rain again; and it was their opinion that they had effected their departure from the place unnoticed and unknown. Such, however, was not the case. Elizabeth, one of Martin's daughters, concealed behind an oaken partition, had overheard the whole of the council of war, which had been held between the worthy guardians, and sprang full of joy to her mother and sister, in an upper apartment, carrying with her the joyful tidings of the flight of the honest citizens of Pfullingen.

"What a pity it is," she said, "that we did not know it when your sweetheart was talking to you this morning at the window. We would have detained him, and, perhaps, seen our father again."

The mother, a cunning and artful adviser, said in a hurried tone to Lamparter's sweetheart,—

"Quick—quick, Appel; put out the signal on the roof. I will wager a trifle, that one or more of our poor fellows are still lying concealed in the ruins of the old castle, and they will not lose any time in informing the remainder that the coast is clear."

Appolonia followed the instructions of her mother with the greatest good will, climbed up into the dilapidated granary, and thrust a large besom of birch, fastened to a long pole, through a hole in the roof. The signal could be easily seen from the ruined castle, and, in a very short time, a voice was heard from the stables of the castle, that echoed over the mountains.

After the lapse of a short time, Lamparter, like a frightened fox, skulked by the house, and Appolonia gave him a friendly nod. He then summoned all his courage—was no longer in fear of any snare that might he laid to entrap him, and, highly delighted, he repaired to the bedside of the gouty mother, and thence into the arms of his beloved. In a kind of savage triumph, he said,—

"It is fortunate for the two poor devils from Pfullingen, that they took their departure of their own accord. In another hour, it is a question with me, whether they would ever have seen Pfullingen again, for Nickel has just now informed me that Wildherr himself is on the road hither, with the intention of taking shelter from the inclemency of the weather in this very house. There are four or five noble fellows in company, and they would not have made any great fuss about the necks of the two worthies of Pfullingen."

A malicious joy shone on the countenances of the mother and the daughters; for it was a matter of regret to them that the two victims had so fortunately escaped the fate that awaited them. The danger which impended over their heads, should the watchmen of Pfullingen not return to their homes, was, in the opinion of these vicious women, not to be held in comparison with the joy to be witnesses and assistants in a work of blood. Elizabeth supposed that it alone would be a source of consolation to her, that she should at last behold the dreaded Wildherr face to face, and Appolonia complained that she had not proper provisions in the house to set before so distinguished a guest; but her mother, mistress of her profession, reminded her daughter that an honourable highwayman, as soon as he enters the house of a friend, brings the provisions along with him, so as to pass a pleasant day.

Lamparter ascended the heights every quarter of an hour, cast a wary eye around him, and at last brought the joyful intelligence that the gang which he had mentioned was then in the immediate vicinity.

In fact, they were soon seen coming, with a cautious step, in the direction of the Hardborg, and made their formal entrance into the hut, midst torrents of rain. First came Nickel, the spy and scout. He was followed by Walzfrieden and Dornhan, who had in their charge a man who was wonderfully and grotesquely clad, and scarcely able to walk, from the excessive fatigues he had undergone. Next came the chief of the gang, Wildherr himself, conducted by Martin; and the rear was brought up by Scheidenhart, one of the bravest of the gang.

The bandits were bent on murder, and wondered when they found the door open, and nothing on which their daggers could be employed. Whilst the fellows uttered their complaints at the disappointment, or passed their coarse and indecent jokes upon it, Martin, with tears of passion, and threats against all the world, embraced his family, and Nickel pryed into every part of the building, to see if there was not some secret snare laid for them. Wildherr had seated himself comfortably by the fire, which was always kept burning, in order to soften the frosty air, which penetrated through all the chasms and crevices of the dilapidated house.

"It is well," said he, casting his gloomy look around him, "that we are spared the butcher's work. We were obliged to have a shelter, let it cost us what it would, because the Pfahlburgers examine all the caves which have hitherto served us so excellently for our places of resort. Your house, old Martin, is not a very comfortable one. I am not in the least surprised that your cowardly companions left the place so unexpectedly, when they had so much filth under their noses. It is not much worse in the open forest. Are those girls your daughters? Which of the two is your sweetheart, Lamparter? Poor fellow, some little time will elapse before your marriage-day arrives. The imprudence and folly of Heinz are the sole cause of your misfortunes. No one ought to allow himself to be taken."

"Who can control his destiny?" said Martin, in a tone of chagrin. "Give us the means, Wildherr, of either revenging his fate, or rescuing him."

"If he were now at Pfullingen," said Wildherr, "he would soon be at liberty; but the dungeons at Hohenurach are too strong to be forced, and the guards are particularly strict, under the immediate observation of the count. Heinz, however, still lives, and is in good health; and, therefore, as yet, we are no great losers. Therefore, let me hear no more of your complaints. And now, my companions, open your provision-bags, that we may have something wherewith to satisfy our hunger. Come, ye women, begin to roast and boil, and then we will have a glorious feast. The greater the anger of heaven in its storm, the merrier I will show myself, as well as all those who are my companions. By the great toe of the Pope, if we had a fiddler here, and some fine, buxom girls, we would have a dance, even under the nose of the prefect of Pfullingen, and all his shabby hirelings. A man who is pursued by the harpies of the law is nowhere so safe as just before the threshold of the executioner, for no one thinks of finding him there."

In pursuance of the commands of their leader the bandits opened their knapsacks, and a rich display they made of the produce of the forest. Nickel was sent to a distant village to procure some wine, and the whole of the family assisted in preparing the feast. Wildherr, however, appeared to be soon tired of the scene before him; he hung his coat, that was saturated with the rain, before the fire, gave a signal to his favourite Scheidenhart, and retired with him to a distant part of the room. He then leaned against a projecting post, folded his arms across his body, staring vacantly before him, and said, after a short silence, to his companion, who was anxiously waiting for the communication Wildherr had to make to him—

"I cannot endure," said Wildherr, "the look of those devilish women. Old Martin, with his family, appear to be the very scum of human society; and the young thief in the dungeons of Hohenurach, is the best of his race. But, as to the rest, by my soul, I believe it, that they would sell their very God for a few florins."

"They are a bad race," said Scheidenhart, shrugging his shoulders. "I warned you of them—you should never have allowed Heinz to join our gang. Sooner or later, we were sure to have the whole blessed family as a burden upon us—that was most easily

See page 99.

to be foreseen. Place not the least confidence in that old rogue, Martin, who can laugh and cry at the same moment—who can fondle over you one minute, and curse you in the next. And, above all, place not the least faith in Lamparter, because he is courting one of the daughters of the old scoundrel."

"I acknowledge it," said Wildherr, "that you have given me repeated warnings, but when one gets into a labyrinth, it is not always an easy matter to find the clue to guide us out of it. My life, Scheidenhart, has become a burden to me."

" Nonsense," exclaimed the astonished Scheidenhart, with a smile.

Wildherr, however, continued—

" Pleasant as it is to live as your own master and king—to do whatever you please, and to leave undone that from which you cannot derive any pleasure, still it often comes across my mind that there must be something extremely enviable in the life of an honest man. Tell me, my brave youth, how these singular thoughts have crept into my mind. For some time I have compared myself to a tree in the spring, redolent with wholesome sap, from which the blossoms are to spring, but while the buds are preparing to burst, the rude frosts of the night destroy them, and the time will come when the tree will wither away, and has borne nothing but false blossoms and abortive fruit. Is not that a miserable condition, Scheidenhart ?"

" Ho, ho !" exclaimed Scheidenhart; " what strange megrims have come into your head ? Would you gather grapes, where you have sown nothing but tares? Truly, not one of us was nursed in the lap of fortune or we should not perhaps have followed our present dangerous trade. Necessity, Wildherr, was our preceptress, when the whole world turned its barb upon us. Have we been cast out and rejected, that we might diffuse blessings around us ? No; we bring the battle and the sword, and wounds are our roses. That which is refused us we take by force, and we eat our bread in bitterness. It is impossible for man to be subject to greater troubles than we endure. We know what will be the last fruit that we shall taste—and that is death. And you Wildherr, whose strength and courage have made you our leader, are you the first to waver, and to wish for a better life ?"

Wildherr laid his hand on the shoulder of Scheidenhart, and looked him full in the face.

" We know each other," he said. " Cowardice is a thing of which we know not even the name; but how can I help it that my blood will sometimes move most sluggishly, and then some dismal thought creeps into my mind ? I am still the lover of freedom—of unbounded liberty, for which we have to contend from morning to night; but I know not how to account for it, a most inexplicable feeling has taken possession of me. Perhaps it is mere listlessness, or a disagreeable longing after something, but what that something is I cannot tell. Perhaps I am ill—my powers have become relaxed, and I am fit for nothing but to sit at home and help the women to spin."

" Come," exclaimed Scheidenhart, with a smile, " out with what you have got to say."

And Wildherr answered with the simplicity of a child, which formed a singular contrast with the greyness of his hair.

" I will tell you," he said, " there are three things which I would have. In the first place, I desire to lead a merry, jovial life, and in ease and comfort, without any exertion to await what the day will produce, and the future will promise."

" That is to say," said Scheidenhart, " you wish to enjoy the luxuries of life."

" In the second place," said Wildherr, " I long for the sacrament of penitence and the body of our Lord. A medicine of that nature would methinks cheer me up and refresh me in the world."

" A most extraordinary wish," said Scheidenhart; " for my part, I have no great inclination for such a medicine."

" In the third place," said Wildherr, " I would take a wife."

" Take a wife! What! would Wildherr, the bandit, purchase a wife? Are you mad? Verily, some evil spirit must have practised its sorcery upon you, to impregnate your mind with so strange a thought. A son of the forest—either flying like the hunted deer, or savage and cruel as the beast of prey—talking of a bride and marriage ; of courting and matrimony! In faith, if it be necessary to distract your mind, I will sally forth, and bring to you the most skilful conjuror or the best musician that I can find. I will drag him hither, so that he may give you some amusement."

" You are rather bold in your remarks," said Wildherr ; " one time jocose, at another full of your threats. Let me, however, advise you not to be so profuse with your reproaches ; or, perhaps, I shall seek for my amusement in the shedding of your blood."

The hint was quite sufficient for Scheidenhart. He became suddenly pale, and he answered, with downcast eyes,—

" Well, well, do not trouble yourself; I will say no more. According, however, to my thinking, your wish is mere child's play. One bold stroke can fill our coffers, and you can then retire in comfort to some distant land. Your naked dagger can force the trembling priest to give you absolution, and to favour you with the sacrament ; and as to a wife, you have nothing to do but to issue your commands. There are hundre who are quite ready to jump into the matrimonial bed."

" By all the saints," exclaimed Wildherr, with a smile, " I am fully aware of the truth of what you say, but an every-day woman will not suit me. I would not be indebted for my riches to the commission of a crime; nor to a threat for the sacrament; nor to the favour of a woman from her loose course of life. You know well that I never yet embraced a girl. I always felt a disgust for your dances and your debaucheries. It is only the purest dove that can satisfy the desire of the hawk."

Scheidenhart shook his head, and said,—

"You have three difficult points to obtain, Master Wildherr; I am very curious to know how they are to be carried into execution"

A confused noise now arose in the room where Martin and the other bandits were carousing. It appeared that a dispute had broken out at the fireside; and, in order to obtain peace, Wildherr stepped amongst the disputants, and he saw one of the daughters of Martin, her eyes sparkling with the fire of passion, grasping the tired stranger by the throat, who had arrived with the gang, and with her fist threatening to strike him, whilst the bandits stood by laughing at the scene.

Wildherr rushed to the assistance of the old man, exclaiming,—

"Peace! peace! what is the cause of this tumult?" and this exclamation was no sooner heard from the mouth of the dreaded Wildherr, than the female vixen desisted from her violent conduct, and a heavy book fell from the hand of Martin, which he had carried to the hearth for the purpose of throwing it into the fire.

"What have they done to you?" said Wildherr, addressing himself to the trembling stranger in the grotesque dress.

"I fell asleep," said the stranger, in a simple, anxious tone, "and I dreamt of black birds, when these people awoke me, and called me a sorcerer; they would have scratched out my eyes, and thrown my treasure, the book of the stars, which they took from me, into the fire."

"Is this true, ye vermin?" exclaimed Wildherr, and cast a terrible look upon the members of Martin's family.

The old woman, shaking her palsied head, muttered some unintelligible words, but Elizabeth cried, in a croaking voice,—

"What business has the old sorcerer in our house? we have already misfortune enough upon our shoulders; let him exorcise the devil out of the house if he can."

"And," said Apollonia, "have not my mother's pains been on the increase, ever since the imp of hell came into the house?"

To which Martin added, "I found this cursed book under his cloak. The very signs in it will bring a curse upon the house."

"How!" exclaimed Wildherr; "you dare to maltreat a man who stands under my protection, and you rob him in your very house, you scandalous wretches; every one of whom, if I wish, I can burn to ashes; haste, begone out of my sight. I'll bear the sight of you no longer. There is room enough for you under the roof. Betake yourselves off to another part of it; a pig-stye is good enough for such a brood. Turn them out, it is Wildherr who commands you."

The old woman howled; the daughter trembled; and Martin foamed at the mouth with rage.

The companions of Wildherr lost not a moment in fulfilling the commands of their leader, as the only reparation they could make for the fault they had committed; and it was a curious and rather a laughable scene to behold with what dexterity and expedition the whole of the family were driven out of the room, and obliged to take up their quarters in a cold, cheerless apartment, in which there had not been a fire for many a year, and in which in a few minutes sounded the cries and wailings of the imprisoned family.

The door of the room was no sooner closed upon the abandoned wretches, than Wildherr said to Lamparter,—

"I hold your roguish head as a pledge for the security of those people. Woe unto you and them, if only one of them crosses out of this house, or if they meditate any treacherous act, I will teach you to pay proper obedience and respect to me, your leader. Do you not see, you pitiful creatures, that into whatever house I go I consider myself, and act there, as the master. Away with you; and, if you value your life, be circumspect in your conduct."

Lamparter skulked away, full of chagrin and vexation, to condole with his sweetheart and her amiable relations. Dornhan was stationed as a sentinel before the thieves' hotel. Walzfrieden and Scheidenhart attended to the fire, and Wildherr addressed himself to the old man, who still sat trembling with fear.

"Be comforted," said Wildherr, "not a hair of your head shall be injured. I consider it a piece of good fortune tha chance has brought us together, for I am partial to wise people; and I believe in the stars and their presages. I will never part from you provided you will act faithfully and honestly towards me, and tell me the fate that impends over me."

The astrologer gave a friendly nod with his head, and with a trembling hand turned over the leaves of the book, as if he wished to convince himself that no part of his treasures had been taken from him.

Wildherr, contemplating the extraordinary figure with a superstitious awe, said, in a milder and friendly tone,—

" Tell me by what means you understand to prophesy the fate of man ?"

" From the stars, the hand, and from dreams," answered the astrologer.

" You are positively certain," said Wildherr, " of the truth of your art ?"

" Art never lies," said the astrologer.

" You are, then, a rich and powerful man ?" said Wildherr.

The deep sigh which broke from the bosom of the astrologer, as he let his head fall upon his breast, and directed his eyes to the ground, gave a direct negative answer to the question of Wildherr.

Wildherr, however, continued,—

" Explain to me, then, why you, to whom the signs of the heavens, and the thoughts of men, are made manifest, so blind with fear and anxiety, were so severely flogged, when, at Sirchingen, you fell into the hands of my companions ?"

" I was terrified at a ghost," said the astrologer; " and I possess not any power over ghosts."

" A ghost !" exclaimed Wildherr; " I never yet saw a ghost; but still I believe in them, because I am a Christian, and have been told and believe in a heaven, and a hell, and a purgatory, from which the poor souls now and then return to the earth, if God gives them permission. Where did you see the ghost which so alarmed you ?"

" At Gnadenzell, in the convent," answered the astrologer.

" What had you to do in the convent?" asked Wildherr.

" I was resting there on my pilgrimage," said the astrologer; " and was in search of a treasure that there lies buried in the cemetery."

" Ah!" exclaimed Wildherr, " who disclosed to you the existence of the treasure ?"

" An idiot boy—a juvenile prophet," said the astrologer.

" Do you, then, place any faith in idiotcy?" asked Wildherr.

" It is universally known, throughout the east," said the astrologer, " that the voice of God is heard from the mouth of the insane. Independently of which, a dream has confirmed to me the truth of the idiot's information."

" And you place your confidence in that dream?" said Wildherr.

" Dreams," said the astrologer, " have conducted me through life, like a leading-string. A dream was the cause of my marrying—that was many, many years ago. I left my house and home—my wife and children—in order to visit the promised land. It was a dream that announced to me my liberty from the hands of the infidels. Sleep never deceived me with the images which it held before me."

The old man sank into a deep silence, and Wildherr reflected on the words which he had just heard, and his sound common sense, although in some degree under the influence of superstition, opposed itself to the language and the prophetic wisdom of the astrologer. Actuated, therefore, by the spirit of curiosity, he said,—

" Have you, then, seen the treasure at Gnadenzell ?"

" With the eye of the spirit," said the astrologer. " It lies under the third beech tree, on the left hand of the site, on entering the cemetery, five yards beneath the surface of the earth, and, above it, lies the corpse of a man, who was long since buried at Gnadenzell. By the side of the treasure, however, sits a black dog, and must be got rid of by prayer, as the skeleton of the resident of Gnadenzell, because it is a cursed corpse. For this purpose an immaculate virgin is indispensable, and she now resides in the convent."

A smile came upon the countenance of Wildherr.

" The women of Gnadenzell," he said, " are not very celebrated for their chastity."

The astrologer nodded three times with his head, and said,—

" I speak the truth when I say, that the immaculate virgin is now in the convent who is selected for the accomplishment of this important act. She arrived at Gnadenzell the same evening as myself, and a dream has confirmed all I have now told you."

" The virgin being there," said Wildherr, " why did you not take up the treasure ?"

" I was driven away by the ghost," said the astrologer.

" A man who is in search of a treasure," said Wildherr, " should not be a coward—he should not be afraid of the devil himself."

The poor, simple man looked anxiously around him, and said,—

" You know not much about these things; but I can assure you that the ghost at Gnadenzell is, in reality, more terrible than the devil himself. May God release the poor soul; but, as it still wanders upon the earth, it so torments me with burning fangs that I hastened across the ocean; and now it persecutes me afresh, although its outward covering is long since mouldered to dust, and will not remain in the place that is pointed out for it. And yet I have not committed any great sin, and have scarcely visited my own house, so that I might not unexpectedly offend the incensed soul."

" My good old man," said Wildherr, " you talk most incoherently. Perhaps your brain became a little deranged, or you dreamt with your eyes open. Whither do you roam?—what is your name?—and who are you?"

" You do not understand me," said the astrologer; " but God knows who I am. But I would forget my own name, and, until my death, be a stranger in my own home, if only the evil spirit would be at rest, whose terrible form forced me to seek an asylum amongst robbers."

" Be composed, old man," said Wildherr; " no harm shall here betide you, and in time you will place greater confidence in me."

With these words Wildherr left the old man to his own reflections, and went to Scheidenhart, who, with a smile on his countenance, had listened to the whole of the discourse.

" Now," said Wildherr, in a half whisper, " what do you think of our wonderful companion?"

" In my opinion," said Scheidenhart, " the old man has got the water on his brain; but there is something more in him than we are aware of, and the secret may be productive of great good to us, for from the folly of the tenth man, the eleventh prospers in the world. But now, is it not clear to you that you know the place where two of your wishes can be realised—the treasure, which you have only to dig for in the ground, and the chastest of all virgins."

Wildherr could not refrain from laughing at these remarks of Scheidenhart, and said, that in reality his inclination had been for some time directed towards a nun, and that he would go to Gnadenzell, if it were only to pay a visit to the sweethear tof the unfortunate Heinz.

Walzfrieden was busy turning the spit at the fire, and cried out,—

" The meat is quite roasted enough. Let us seat ourselves, and once more feast like noblemen."

On a sudden a man rushed into the room, wet through with the rain, and covered with mud, like one who had returned from a long journey; and as soon Wildherr saw him, he set up a shout of joy, hastened towards the stranger, embraced him, and said,—

" Hunerkogel, my dear brother, and are you so soon here again, you expeditious messenger? An angel must have conducted you hither, because you have found me out at once, and in a place where you certainly would not have looked for me."

" Nickel was the angel," said Hunerkogel. " I wandered about Nobellooh and Sommerhuttlein, but all in vain; the officers of the police and the executioner were constantly at my heels. At Wechsel, below the valley, I accidentally met Nickel; and here I am, Wildherr."

" Quick, my noble fellow," exclaimed Wildherr, rather impetuously, and taking the messenger to the further end of the room; " open your mouth without reserve. Quick as has been your expedition, spread the honey which you have collected on my thirsty tongue. What are the people—the beloved people—doing? Are they in good health? Do they often think of me? Did you give them my little present, and did they send me a kiss for it in return? Answer me quickly. Do not stand there as motionless as if you were a statue in a church. My heart beats with anxiety to hear what you have got to tell me."

Hunerkogel was for some time unwilling to speak; but being importuned strongly by Wildherr, he said,—

" You might have spared yourself the expected joy, and me my weary and blistered feet. The people have all run away, and the crawling serpent leaves a stronger mark behind it than I have done. Not the slightest information could I obtain respecting them. No one knew, or would not know, anything about them—so, full of vexation and chagrin, I retraced my steps homewards."

Wildherr had no sooner heard these words than his courage appeared on a sudden to forsake him: his blood seemed to stand still, and his power of speech was gone. He seated himself on the nearest bench, folded his hands between his knees, hung down his head; and it was not until a tear started into his eye, that he gave a heavy sigh, and said,—

"Oh, ye saints, and thou, Jesus, befriend me!"

He now solicited Hunerkogel to impart to him some further intelligence, when the latter placed his mouth to the ear of Wildherr, and they spoke in so low a tone to each other, that neither the astrologer nor those who were sitting by the fire could distinguish a single word.

Scheidenhart then said to Walzreiden, in a plaintive tone,—

"The meat is roasted enough; but I know who will not eat of it with an appetite."

As they were consulting together as to the best means of raising the spirits of their leader, to whom they were all greatly attached, Lamparter rushed hastily into the room, and immediately afterwards he was followed by Dornhan, who said,—

"The wind blows in the direction of Hansen, and we can distinctly hear the sound of drums at a distance."

"Drums!" exclaimed Scheidenhart. "Wildherr, do you hear that drums are heard in the valley?"

Wildherr, however, paid little or no attention to what was said, so deeply was he immersed in his grief, but gave a repulsive signal with his hand, as if he commanded them to be silent; for Hunerkogel was still speaking to him like a father confessor.

Another messenger now arrived, it was Nickel—panting for breath, but bringing with him neither bottles nor glasses; but he was a true messenger of Job.

"Pack up—pack up!" he exclaimed. "We must away into the mountains, or into the forest. The count has issued the strongest orders to wage war against us. Two hundred florins are placed upon the head of Wildherr, and pardon and reward are promised to him, even if he belongs to the banditti, who will betray his leader. The order has been read at the church doors—the prefect has put the whole of the police under arms, and the drums of alarm are beaten in all the villages."

With a terrible curse, Wildherr awoke out of his stupefaction, and said,—

"Is this the manner in which the count repays our obedience, and our mercy for his princely head, that he will not grant us any peace or rest? We will then light the torches for our blind persecutors, so that they may be shown the proper path. I have a heavy account to settle with him; and, should certain persons escape our sword, we will set their castles in flames. Up, up, my companions; take your dinner as you go along, but follow me quickly into the forest, from which we are just now come. He who is my friend, let him not remain behind; and to you, my brave Scheidenhart, I confide this aged man."

The bandits, whose inclinations always led them either to battle or to flight, followed their leader with the utmost expedition, whilst Scheidenhart threw the old man, like a sack of feathers, on his sturdy shoulders, and bravely carried him away to the forest.

Lamparter and Martin delayed their departure for some time, when the former said, ill-humouredly,—

"What's now to be done, Appolonia? I must leave you. We are obliged to follow Wildherr, in order that our lives may be safe."

To which Martin added, with the smile of the fiend,—

"Yes, children; we must follow him, in order that we may destroy him. Do you suppose that he shall not pay dearly for having been the instrument of bringing our Heinz to misery and imprisonment; and, moreover, for having despised yon poor woman? Do you suppose that I will not take the advantage of the price being set upon his head? In the meantime, farewell my wife and daughter. If the hangman drags you into the dungeon, do not despair; we will liberate you and Heinz with the head of Wildherr, and found the fortune of our house on his scaffold."

CHAPTER XIII.

"Not even the high anointing hand of Heaven
Can authorize oppression, give a law
For lawless power, wed earth to violation,
On reason build misrule, or fastly bind
Allegiance to injustice."

THE rapid rider, Ostertag von Friedengen, need not have put spur to his horse, nor have applied his whip so frequently, for still he would have arrived sooner at the Convent of Gnadenzell than the chancellor of the count, who, with his attendant, the Father Wendelen, from the monastery of the Blue Monks, and the two secretaries, who were the usual attendants on the counsellor of the count. The mules, indeed, went at an easy pace, but the learned gentlemen were not accustomed to ride in wind and tempest. With every torrent of rain that fell on the mantle and the hood, the patience and activity of the riders gradually became less and less; and when they arrived at the Alb, where the rain became snow, and hail roared and bellowed, against which it required a stouter heart than theirs to contend, then there was not any end to the murmurs and the complaints. Father Wendelen, whose eyes had been greatly weakened by a severe illness, felt in them the most smarting pain, when the sleet and the hail dashed into his face. The chancellor did nothing but sneeze and cough, and in his heart he wished the count had been at the top of the Blocksberg, or at the bottom of Rubenzahl's subterranean cavern, rather than he should have dispatched him in such inclement weather to transact a piece of business for which there was not any immediate necessity, and for the accomplishment of which a person of less consequence than himself might have been selected. In regard to the two more juvenile secretaries, they concealed their red noses under their cloaks, and thought and said to each other, "I wish I was in the Golden Lion at Urach, where there is such excellent wine, and where the guests are served by pretty girls; what have we to do with a set of refractory nuns? I suppose they have only been doing what nature taught them, and now they are to be punished for it. Punish nature for it, and not those who are obliged to follow her laws."

There is very little doubt that what the secretaries were bold and perhaps imprudent enough to say to each other, was in reality the present opinion of the chancellor and his coadjutor, Father Wendelen; but for the best of all possible reasons, they kept their opinions very wisely to themselves. The chancellor wished himself at his writing desk, and Father Wendelen in his cell, and leaving the dissolute women of Gnadenzell to repent of their iniquities as soon as they might find it convenient. It was, perhaps, rather a laughable scene, though not exactly so to themselves, to see the holy cavalcade buffeting the rudeness of the elements, and glad they were when the cupola of the convent of Gnadenzell burst upon their view. If there were any truth in the reports that had been so industriously circulated in the country, the cellars of the convent were well stocked with wines, and the larder amply supplied with all the good things that the forest or the river, the field or the garden could furnish; therefore, in anticipation, they saw themselves seated at a table groaning under the weight of dainties and luxuries, and their spirits exhilarated by frequent potations from the foaming goblet.

Onwards rode the plenipotentaries, wet to the skin with the rain, and delighted were they when they heard the hoofs of their mules trampling over the stones of the fore court of the convent.

Benedicta was looking through the grating, and when she beheld the human quartet about to enter the court, she exclaimed in a tone of anger and indignation,—

"In God's name, continue your journey; we have no means for your accommodation. The ladies of the convent are about to partake of their mid-day meal, and we have received the strictest commands from Count Eberhard, of Wurtemberg, not to allow a person of the masculine gender to enter the convent."

On hearing this, the chancellor threw open his cloak, that the golden chain of office might be seen, and his splendid inkstand pendent from his girdle. They were articles, he thought, which would strike respect and reverence into the breast of the nun, who had so rudely and unceremoniously accosted them.

Now Benedicta was a shrewd, cunning woman, and very little doubt can exist that she had the cue given her how to act on this occasion. She therefore said,—

"How can you expect, whoever you may be, that we should be induced by four men, of whom we know not anything, to open our doors, and therefore thereby expose ourselves to the wrath and vengeance of our noble prince; whom may God for ever bless?"

"Amen!" responded Father Wendelen; I can assure you we are wet to the skin, are very hungry, and beg of you to show your kind hospitality; and I am certain you will not deny our request, when I tell you that we are sent by the count. Therefore, open the door for us, without any further ceremony or hesitation, or we shall be obliged to use force to effect an entrance."

Benedicta answered with the greatest humility,—"Heaven defend us from such an act of violence; but highly culpable should we be to drive the ambassador of our noble lord and prince from the threshold of our door. Our house, and all that is in it, are at your service. The door shall be immediately opened."

While the porteress was rattling with her bunch of keys, drawing back the heavy bolts, and making the keys sound within the locks, the ambassadors of the count had alighted from their mules, fastened them to one of the rings of the gates, and whispered to each other, "We are come just at the proper time to take the profligate band by surprise, in their feasting and junketing, for it is not to be supposed that they can have foreseen our arrival."

With heads erect, and grave and solemn step, the ambassadors entered the gates. Benedicta made her most humble obeisance to them, and, as she soon discovered that there was a reverend minister in the group, as an obedient handmaid, she kissed his hand. This act was highly flattering to Father Wendelen; and as he beheld the capacious rosary on the girdle of the nun, he made a most gracious motion with his head, saying, "Truly is this house conferred to the care of a virtuous and pious overseer, and my daughter, in the name of Heaven, I give thee my blessing."

In the meantime, the bell had announced to the prioress that some visitor had arrived, and the conference room was immediately opened to admit the gentlemen; not a trace was to be seen of negligence, or of the dust arising from idleness,—everything was mean and poverty-stricken, but clean and neat.

The prioress met the ambassadors of the count with a grave and solemn demeanour; and the chancellor was struck with astonishment at the beautiful countenance of the prioress, which, however, was partly concealed by a coarsely plaited cap, as well as her slender, but finely proportioned form was hidden under the mean costume of the convent.

The chancellor was, on a sudden, seized with a most embarrassing cough. He looked at the prioress; but he would not have liked any one to have known why he looked at her. The prioress, however, was not in the least abashed, but said, in a firm and dignified tone—

"You are most welcome, noble sir; in the name of our holy mother, your visit is as a light to us in our deep abstraction from the world, and we await most submissively to know the business which has brought you hither, or whether we can in any way be instrumental to the execution of it; we sincerely wish that your visit may be of as pleasant a nature as it is unexpected by us."

"May it find you," said the chancellor, "properly prepared fully to justify yourselves, for we do not come here on a trifling commission."

"The will of the Lord be done," said the prioress, with downcast eyes, and a most humble demeanour, during which hypocritical farce the chancellor drew forth a long sheet of paper, and read the orders of the count, which he gave to his plenipotentiaries, to examine into the management of the convent, and to confirm or to negative the injurious reports which had been circulated throughout the country, complaining strongly of the want of order in the house, and the commission of many abuses, which went to strike at the root of the character and respectability of the establishment. Amongst other abuses were particularly mentioned the general decline of morals and the regular worship of God; the abolition of the separation of the choir from the remainder of the church, notwithstanding the strictest ordination of the council, the bishop, and the count; the wanton expenditure of money, of alms, and the revenue; and lastly, the accusation that but a short time ago one of the sisters of the convent committed a crime which deserved the most exemplary punishment.

With her head resting on her bosom, in an attitude of the deepest humility, the prioress listened to the perusal of these momentous charges against the character of her holy house; and when the chancellor had finished the last of his charges, she said, in an humble tone,—

"The malice of the devil is great, but our hearts are pure; and not a corner of it, and equally so, not a corner of the house, but what shall be opened for your inspection. Will you now repair to the refectory, most noble chancellor and our very reverend father? The sisters are now assembled at their midday meal; be pleased to share with us what we have, and what Heaven, in its goodness, is pleased to bestow upon us poor, persecuted, and calumniated women, and then act as it seemeth best in your eyes. Your secretaries, who, according to the rules of our house, dare not be admitted into the interior of it, shall be amply provided with food and drink to the utmost of the ability of our impoverished condition."

As she now proceeded to open the grated door, the chancellor and the priest looked at each other with eyes of astonishment, for they knew not what to make of the quiet and unembarrassed manner in which they had been received at the convent. More collected and appeased than when they entered the holy house, they followed the prioress, who preceded them with a stately and haughty step into the refectory, where the sisters were seated, silently, and with the utmost decorum, partaking of their meal with the

greatest humility, and listening to one of the sisters, who, with a sonorous and a melodious voice, was from the pulpit reading a chapter of the Holy Scriptures.

The entrance of the strangers occasioned not the slightest disturbance in the assembly; the reader, indeed, stopped, whilst the remainder of the females awaited the commands of the prioress in what manner they were to conduct themselves. On a sign being given by the prioress, they moved from the upper end of the table, awarding to the holy visitors the principal places at the top of it. The prioress then solicited the permission of her visitors to allow the reading of the Holy Scriptures to be finished, the consent to which was most formally given; on which the reader continued, whilst the lay sisters, with great servility, laid before the guests the victuals that were still remaining on the table. The frown of disappointment was, however, visible on the countenance of the chancellor, who had expected to find a well provided table, which, in the first place, was to afford him pleasure and recreation, and in the second, to furnish him with good ground and reasons for the reproofs which he had uttered relative to the luxurious mode of living which had been alleged against the holy sisterhood. In vain did he cast his eyes around him for some savoury dish wherewith he could gratify his palate; and, on the other hand, Father Wendelen, notwithstanding the keenest exercise of his impaired light, was not able to discover a single circumstance which could authorise him to make any charge against the nuns on account of the indecorum or the richness of their attire. The former could see nothing but a meagre soup of sour milk, with a scanty dish here and there of boiled peas, whilst the latter could discover nothing but clothes that had been patched and darned, the bosom most modestly concealed, and hoods over their heads of coarse lawn, under which appeared the most demure and sanctified countenances in which the greatest adept in physiognomy could read nothing but an expression of holiness and virtue. Instead of rich and exhilarating wine, which, it had been alleged, was the beverage of the holy sisterhood, the ambassadors of the count could only see pure spring water, whilst to the guests a nauseous sour beverage was given, of which they had no sooner tasted, than the whole of their faces became distorted, so odious was it to the palate. The chancellor spat it out again, and the holy father Wendelen followed his example, which the prioress no sooner beheld, than, checking her inclination to laughter, she said—

"You see, most noble chancellor, how we have been vilified; we are said to carouse and intoxicate ourselves with the juice of the grape, whereas we are content with the water from the spring and the beverage of which you have just now partaken; and I am pretty well convinced that your report to our gracious count will be, that it is not a beverage in the least likely to intoxicate us."

"Oh, no, no," exclaimed the chancellor and the priest, almost simultaneously; "so far from it intoxicating you," said the chancellor, "it is only custom that can reconcile you to it."

"Your words are the essence of truth, most worthy chancellor," said the prioress; "but you see to what we vilified sisters are obliged to accustom ourselves. And then to be accused of being a drunken flock—is it not most abominable, holy Father Wendelen?"

"Most abominable indeed," answered the priest; "and I can only say, if the report be not abominable, your beverage is."

"Alas!" said the prioress, "they are shocking times with us."

The reading of the Holy Scriptures and the dinner were concluded about the same time, when the nuns rose gravely and solemnly from their seats, and, one by one, left the refectory in becoming silence, and their arms folded over their bosoms. As the nuns passed in a kind of review before the chancellor and the priest, the prioress pronounced the names which they bore previously to their entrance into the convent, and that which they assumed when they were admitted into it; and as the reader, after she had closed the ponderous book, and had descended from the pulpit, the prioress, in answer to the inquiry of Father Wendelen, as to her name and circumstances before she entered the convent, said,—

"That is our good and pious sister Hailwig, who has been so scandalously calumniated to our gracious count. May Heaven forgive the unprincipled liar, her son, for having attempted to throw a stain upon such matchless purity."

The plenipotentiaries again cast their inquisitive and astonished looks upon the nun, and Father Wendelen invited the nun to come nearer to him; and this accordingly took place, the nun approaching him with the greatest modesty, her hands clasped beneath her scapulary, and her beautiful eyes directed to the shoes of the priest. For some time the reverend father fixed his eyes upon her, shrugged his shoulders, cast an expressive look towards the chancellor, and said,—

"Truly, that is sister Hailwig, as I have already seen her, as she a few years ago came with our most worthy mother here to Renthengen, in order to collect alms for the people of the Alb who were lying dangerously ill of the pestilence."

The prioress confirmed what the priest had said with a smile of satisfaction; and the chancellor, who at one period of his life was a great admirer of female beauty, said,—

"Most truly, reverend father, this virtuous sister has been most scandalously vilified. Chastity itself speaks in her every feature and in every part of her form; therefore we will make our report accordingly to the count, and the liar and the calumniator shall be brought to shame. Wicked indeed must that man be who could invent such a scandalous falsehood."

"Depart in peace, my dear daughter," said Father Wendelen. "Blessed are the pious, for neither hell nor those that are in it have any power over you."

The nun made an humble obeisance, and retired, after having, according to custom, imprinted a kiss on the hand of the prioress and the priest.

Rerharder was, however, no sooner alone with the plenipotentiaries than she began, with tears in her eyes,—

"Most reverend and worthy mediators, however strong we may feel ourselves behind the shield of our conscience and the divine protection, yet, after all, we are but weak, helpless women, exposed, without defence, to the attack of our enemies, particularly our gracious Count of Wurtemberg, who gives a credulous ear to everything that is said against us. How often have we implored him, with weeping eyes and bended knees, to be strict but still just towards us; but he has never listened to our prayer, but treated us with great severity and oppression. When will there be an end to such trouble and affliction to us?"

"This very day," said the chancellor and the priest; "fully satisfied with what we have seen and heard, we will now prosecute our inquiry further, and be your intercessor with our gracious lord, who is a lover and an administrator of justice. Do you be our guide, and fear nothing provided you walk in the right path."

The prioress took the keys again, ordered the stewardess to give her attendance, and proceeded to open every room, every chamber and every cellar in the house. The ambassadors of the count were surprised at the general order which prevailed in the convent, as well as at the industry of the nuns, who seemed all to be employed in different kinds of work; but more particularly than all were they astonished at the poverty which presented itself in the kitchen, the cellar, the granary, and the store room; on observing which, the chancellor could not refrain from exclaiming,—

"Verily, ye poor women, dreadfully have ye been calumniated. Instead of swimming in the oil of superfluity and abundance, want appears to be your cook, and difficult is it for us to comprehend how it is that you manage to live."

In answer, the prioress pointed to her tattered garment, and the stewardess did the same to the little wooden platters, from which the nuns ate their meals, and both exclaimed, that they should be starved to death but for the compassion and the charity of the good and pious Christians who supported them by their benefactions.

"The public voice forbids us to possess any property but what has been given by the founders of the convent; but that property has been greatly injured and diminished in value, on account of the numerous wars and the unfortunate disagreements of the Emperor Ludwig with the Pope, and the impiety of the laity. Then, to crown our misfortunes, the plague has broken out several times amongst us, destroying entire families, which has been the cause of strangers settling in the country, who bought houses and lands for a tenth of their value; and, from some groundless disputes and violence, have scandalously robbed the convent of Gnadenzell; first of a field, then of a meadow, and of a great portion of the forest, by which our supplies of fuel have been cut off. The severity of the Count of Wurtemberg, and the unjust suspicions that he entertains respecting us, have brought an additional calamity upon our holy house, as the doors have been shut against its benefactors, and who were obliged to withdraw their protection and patronage, on account of the strict orders of the count; independently of which, owing to the injunctions that no noviciates shall be received into the convent, we are deprived of the benefit of the sum that is generally demanded for their admission. Thus the greatest misery prevails in our house; so that neither myself nor the stewardess are able to stem the evil, and both of us are willing to resign our offices, so that others may be appointed to them who are more able to provide for the exigencies of the convent."

Whilst these complaints, full of bitterness, continued, during which frequent allusions were made to the rancour and malice which were daily and hourly exercised towards the unfortunate convent, the indignant prioress wandered with her guest through the cloisters, and the chancellor remarked in a corner of one of them, a flight of stairs, which led under a very low archway, and the termination of which could not be seen on account of the extreme darkness in which it was enveloped. From this darkness sounded, dismally and mournfully, the melody of a penetential hymn, sung by a plaintive voice. The ambassador started; Father Wendelen pointed significantly towards the dark and vaulted passage, and the prioress, knowing well the intent of his action, answered in a tone of indifference, and divested of all embarrassment,—

"There lives underneath a pious and devout penitent, similar to the hermit of the Pean desert, who has taken the resolution to pass the remainder of her life in a dark and gloomy cell, so that she may enter with greater joy into the golden mansions of heaven."

"Many such examples," said father Wendelen, "have been given of pious and holy women, in the early days of Christianity; but I did not expect to find any at the present day."

"Who is the woman?" asked the chancellor, in a most inquisitive tone.

"Mother Demath," answered the prioress, "an old lay sister of the convent. She had already entered upon the solitary penance that she has inflicted upon herself, before I took upon myself the office of prioress. There are now only two sisters resident in the house who were resident in it when the transaction took place."

The chancellor looked the prioress full in the face, and asked,—

"Is it true, most venerable mother, that the sister has immured herself in the cell, and condemned herself to such a horrible life voluntarily, and of her own accord? Not that I mean to impute to you the commission of such an extraordinary act of cruelty; but is it not possible that your predecessor may, by a too severe sentence for the commission of some fault, have condemned her to expiate that fault by a perpetual imprisonment?"

"By no means, most learned chancellor," said the prioress. "Would she, under the circumstances that you have mentioned, have been placed in the vault through which the people of the convent pass daily and hourly? But if you entertain any doubt upon the subject, 'twere better you questioned her yourself."

In the meantime the singing had ceased, and the prisoner in the cell had listened to the conversation that passed between the nuns and the ambassadors. The chancellor, in order to gratify his curiosity, descended the steps, trod slowly by the side of the damp and dripping walls, and at last, stretching his eyesight to the utmost, observed a heavy door, enclosed with iron bands, and fastened by enormous bolts. At the side of it was a small square hole, which could be covered in the inside by a wooden shutter, but which at times stood half open, so that the inhabitant of the horrible place could stretch forth her head, although it was concealed under a hood that was black and tattered. As she heard the chancellor approaching, as well as the steps of some other people, she asked in a coarse, rough voice,—

"Who goes there? Have you brought me my evening meal? and why have so many of you come?"

"Be composed, mother Demath," said the prioress; "these reverend men are members of the government, and would wish to speak with you."

"I will not speak with them," said mother Demath. "I desire I may not be disturbed."

"We are only astonished," said the chancellor, "at your pious firmness and perseverance."

"What is your astonishment to me?" said mother Demath.

"We would only ask you," said the chancellor, "if you intend to persevere in your present incarceration, and if your body be wholly dead to this world?"

"Dust to dust! We are ashes," said mother Demath. "May God preserve you!"

"What induced you," said the chancellor, "to adopt this horrible mode of life?"

"My sins," answered the nun.

"What is your name?" asked the chancellor.

"Demath," answered the nun.

"What was your name when you were in the world?" asked the chancellor.

"I have no longer any name belonging to me," answered Demath.

"Where was your home?" asked the chancellor.

The nun tried for a few moments to recollect herself. She then answered, in an abrupt tone,—

"Kirchheim on the Teck."

"Who are your parents?" asked the chancellor.

"I have not any parents," answered Demath.

"Any brothers or sisters?" asked the chancellor.

"All dead," said Demath. "Oh! do not torment me."

"You lead a melancholy life," said the chancellor, "and even if it be for the sake of Heaven. Will you not uncover your face?"

Demath slowly shook her head.

"Can we not offer you anything," said the chancellor, "by which the horrors of your situation can be mitigated?"

"Our worthy mother supplies all my necessities," said Demath.

"What can we do to please you?" said the chancellor.

"Betake yourself off," said Demath.

As, however, neither the chancellor nor the priest appeared disposed to follow the last instructions of the nun, she hastily closed the shutters of her window, and she was heard to fasten it with a bolt on the inside.

Full of thought, the ambassadors of the count returned to the cloisters, glad of being emancipated from the cold and damp air of the vaults.

"A true saint," said Father Wendelen.

The chancellor, however, who was more attached to worldly things than to those of priests and nuns, shrugged his shoulders, raised his eyes to Heaven, and, if it had been possible to read what was passing within him, the secret would, perhaps, have transpired—that he looked upon the whole scene as a pitiable piece of mummery, and an insult upon human reason.

The prioress, however, in the most complaisant manner, informed the priest that sister Demath, during the whole period of her voluntary imprisonment, had not infringed in the slightest degree the severe penance that she had inflicted upon herself. Father Cunrath, the confessor of the convent, who had been dead for some time, a strict and rigid disciplinarian, had prepared the penitent for the desperate step she had determined to take, and had given her the most solemn absolution. He was also the only one who knew of her birth and parentage, and had imposed the duty upon the convent of supporting her as long as she lived. She observed the most rigorous fast, ate no meat, drank no wine, and not one of her relations had ever made an inquiry after her. As the convent church is not far from her cell, in her thought she solemnizes the holy mass, listens anxiously to the sounding of the bell, and receives every month the sacrament of our Lord, which the vicar carries to her, as if it were to a dying person. Only once a week, when the cell is swept and cleaned, does she leave it, but then only in the night time; and conducted by a nun, she wanders about the garden of the cloisters, until the cell is made ready for her. Every one is prohibited, during her walk, from being in the garden; and her face was never known to be unveiled."

The chancellor expressed his opinion, that it was a kind of terrestrial purgatory; but that it redounded greatly to the honour of the sisters of Gnadenzell, that in the midst of their poverty they had so faithfully and so humanely executed the injunctions of the deceased Cunrath. To which the prioress added, in an acrimonious tone,—

"And thus it is with us, scandalised sisters of Gnadenzell. We do as much good as lies in our power; and yet it is the pleasure of the world to pelt us with the stones of their calumny."

"But, gracious Heaven!" exclaimed sister Gertrude, "why should we complain? Did not the cursed Jews oblige our heavenly bridegroom to wear the dress of shame? Did they not scandalize and abuse him, and yet he complained not? Why should we not follow his example? But let me inform you, most learned and reverend sir, that sister Demath is not the only creature which we, poor mendicant women, are obliged to support in our poverty and helplessness. The severe and rigorous count, who knows not anything of the burdensome penitent, knows as little of that miserable wretch who is there cowering over the kitchen fire. There, behold him!" pointing to Poppele, who, with his mouth wide open, was staring at the strangers, and made no attempt to rise or to salute them.

"You rude clown," said the prioress, and cast a look upon him, the sequel to which he knew would be blows and stripes, "do you know what you deserve?"

In order to escape the threatened punishment, the poor creature sprang suddenly up, bent his back like a timid animal, and attempted to take hold of the mantle of the priest, that he might press his lips upon it. He was, however, prevented from the commission of that act by Father Wendelen himself; but, in a mild and gentle tone, he said,—

"What is your name, my boy?"

"I am poor Poppele," answered the idiot.

An expressive look, however, from the prioress, told him that he had not given a proper answer; he therefore tried to correct himself, and said,—

"I am Poppele Frischhans, the son of the forester."

"How old are you?" asked the priest.

"That I cannot tell you," said Poppele.

The prioress made a sign to the chancellor that the intellects of the poor creature were in a deranged state, on which the priest gave him a piece of money, and proceeded on his way. The chancellor, however, said,—

"The face of the man shows no proof of his having been born an idiot. Did any particular calamity occur to him?"

"Who can tell?" answered the prioress, in a contemptuous tone. "The father of the miserable creature was a most confirmed rogue, a descendant of the celebrated robbers of the former village of Offenhausen. He has boasted a thousand times that his predecessors were the proprietors of the accursed village, the undisputed lords, and, as it were, the monarchs of the place. Their virtues were also the same as those of the old Frischhans. He had blasphemed, abused, and scandalised all the saints; also was it well known that he belonged to the gang of thieves who some years ago were the terror and the annoyance of the whole country. His hut was admirably adapted for his profession, being situated in the depths of the forest, which is not far distant from this place. When he was on his death-bed, he implored my predecessor, for the mercy of God, to take compassion upon the wretched orphan, and his prayer was granted, although he had injured the convent in every way in which it lay in his power. Since then the poor creature has been dependent upon us for his support. He is only fit to play the buffoon, as his only heritage is idiotism."

" Let us praise the Lord of Creation," said the priest, "that he has given to us the light of our sound senses," and bent his way to the door of the church, on the threshold of which the plenipotentiaries of the count were received by the vicar Helfer, in his full canonicals—his hair adjusted in a most priestly fashion, and on whose countenance was impressed reverence and humility. In order to conceal his coarse and vulgar German, he conversed with the ambassadors in the Latin language. In the meantime the bell in the cupola appeared to be rung by a violent hand, so quick and rapid were its intonations, and the masculine hand of Barbara ran wildly over the keys of the organ. The nuns hastened, one after the other, into the trellised choir, some praying faintly, and some loud, and at last the hymn broke forth, to the edification and devotion of the auditors. The voices at first sounded weak and timid, and the organist had much to do, with the thunder of her instrument, to fill up the chasms in the choral hymn; but a sweet, melodious voice sounded above all the dissonance and discord of the other singers; and so powerful was the effect, that the ambassadors inquired who the singer was.

" It is Mother Hailwig," answered the prioress, with a certain degree of pride.

The chancellor and father Wendelen said, almost simultaneously,—

" It is that chaste and virtuous maid of the Holy Virgin the greatest ornament of this holy house, instead of being a shame and scandal to it."

As they were about to leave the church, the prioress whispered to them in a conciliating and flattering tone,—

" Will you bear in mind your present praise and satisfaction when you appear in the presence of the severe and rigorous count? and pray to him that he will not henceforth expose us to the scandal of the world, and that if we have in any way sinned and transgressed, he will henceforth place the utmost reliance on our reformation."

" We will do as you have desired, most worthy prioress," said the chancellor; " and the opportunity is now presented to you how you can prove to the count that you are really in earnest to make every reparation for any sins that you may have committed, and some of which were wholly unintentional. In a very short time, perhaps to-morrow, some very pious and devout sisters will arrive here from Pforzheim, to complete, with Christian love, the work of your reformation. As long as you are obedient and submissive to them during their sojourn in your house, so may you be said to pay obedience and respect to the will and orders of the count. We will not fail to inform him of what we have seen and heard, and, in taking our leave, we thank you for your hospitality."

The countenances of the prioress and the stewardess underwent a most visible change, and assumed a most deadly paleness, when they were told of the unexpected arrival of the hated and odious female reformers. The prioress, however, knew well how to put a proper restraint upon her feelings. In sweet and honeyd words, she implored her guests to prolong their stay, or, at least, before their departure, they would partake of some refreshment. They had, however, had quite sufficient of the convent fare, and remarked that night was drawing on apace, that a lodging had been prepared for them in Munfingen, and most reverently recommended themselves to the prayers of the chaste and virtuous sisters of Gnadenzell. Whilst the ambassadors were under the gateway of the convent, the prioress exclaimed,—

" Fare ye well, ye worthy ambassadors of the count, and long may you live to be an ornament and a blessing, not only to us poor sisters, but to the country in general."

These good wishes, however, which were supposed to come from the heart, towards the individuals, as they mounted their mules, had, as it may be easily supposed, not the slightest relation with the safety of the equestrians, or the welfare of the count. On the contrary, if the count, the chancellor, and the priest, had in themselves formed a trinity, and were surrendered into the hands of Satan, the rejoicings would have been loud and great amongst the holy sisterhood of the convent of Gnadenzell.

CHAPTER XIV.

" Prevailing, powerful virtue!   Thou subdu'st
The stubborn heart, and mould'st it to thy purpose;
Would I could save them; but tho' not for me
The glorious power to shelter innocence,
Yet for a moment to assuage its woes
Is the best sympathy, the purest joy,
Nature intended for the heart of man,
When thus she gave the social gen'rous tear."

THE prioress, after she had given the necessary directions to the stewardess to prepare an excellent supper in the refectory, which was to indemnify the virtuous members of the convent for the restraint and the miseries to which they had been subject, during the visitation of the ambassadors of the count, hastened with all expedition to the church, and came into contact with the nuns, who were hastening from it, in order to recover themselves from the hard day's labour to which they had been subject. With wicked eyes, in which there was an expression easily to be understood by her to whom the look was directed, Medora and Renata gave a wink to the prioress, who said, in a tone of voice scarcely audible, " Is the pious sister Hailwig still to be found?" Renata answered in the affirmative with a smile, and Medora, by the most expressive gestures, turned into ridicule the devout simplicity of the novice. The latter was kneeling in prayer on her stool in the choir, and the prioress gave a significant wink to the organist, who was about to enter into a warm panegyric on the vocal powers of the beautiful girl who had lately come amongst them, to retire and leave her alone with the novice.

With great consideration she waited till the virgin had finished her devotions, she then approached her and said, in a maternal tone,—

" The angels in heaven will tune their harps and sing to the praise and glory of the Almighty; but do thou receive the thanks of an afflicted mother of a convent, who by thy aid has been saved and restored to her pristine importance and respectability. Your obedience has diverted a terrible storm from our house; you, my dear Gisela, have most ably enacted the part allotted to you and to those who have rendered assistance to an oppressed and persecuted community, the highest praise and thanks are due."

Gisela thanked the prioress for her complimentary observations, but a cloud came over her countenance, when she said, in a hesitating tone,—

" But what, holy mother, if it should be imputed to me as a sin that I lent myself to the commission of a fraud! It is the thought which torments my heart, and it is only from your lips and those of my confessor, that consolation can be restored to me."

" How can such a thought enter your mind, my dear daughter?" said the prioress; " is it not all for the honour and salvation of our holy church?" Can we be looked upon as criminals, when we attempt, by a Christian love and charity, to conceal the transgressions of a poor fellow-creature from the world? And in the present case there was not any crime, but merely an unfortunate occurrence, which the count, the governor of the country, has unwarrantably seized upon, to bring disgrace and infamy upon our house. It is true that our sister Hailwig lies extremely ill with her relations, and that is the whole of the matter; but had we not devised the innocent fraud which was of such essential service to us, the infamous falsehood that has been propagated would have been held as truth, and we should all have been dragged away to Urach, as accomplices in the crime; and even if Heaven—and it would not have acted otherwise—had brought the truth triumphantly to light, still the hostile count would never have restored us to our rights and privileges, but would have persevered in his injustice and hostility; we should have separated and dispersed into other convents, and never afterwards should I have had it in my power to be of service to you."

" Now, willingly do I believe in what you say," said Gisela, " as I have wholly surrendered myself into your hands; but still there is another doubt which torments me. Is it proper or allowable that I should wear the dress, as a confirmed nun, before it has been given to me by the bishop?"

" You know, my dear daughter," said the hypocritical prioress, " what I have promised you. In certain cases we are allowed the liberty from the Pope to bestow the dress of a nun upon a novice, even should the sovereign of the country forbid it, for such command is wholly illegal and unjust, if not impious. Therefore resolve to lay your vows as soon as possible before the priest, as I am possessed of the power to shorten the term of probation, according to my own will and judgment. Although you may pronounce your vows with closed doors, they are not the less valid and binding, and this I swear to you."

" I verily believe you, holy mother," said Gisela ; " but what will the sisters think of me? And what will they say of my sudden appearance amongst them as a confirmed nun ?"

" An obedient and dutiful sister of this house," said the prioress, " thinks and says only what her superior commands ; but let it be sufficient for you to know that they believe that you, at your home, have been inducted into all the forms and ceremonies of a conventual life ; and that, for private reasons, you have been obliged to leave your cell, and that you require merely to be here to renew the vows which you have formerly taken."

" I will follow most implicitly your will and order," said Gisela ; " and I have the fervent hope that I shall receive absolution ; but do use your influence with my future sisters, that they may receive me amongst them with kindness and affection. I have seen a few of them, who have treated me with scorn, others with chagrin and displeasure, and I have often been abused in the pulpit and the choir."

The prioress here assumed a plaintive tone, and after a deep sigh, and clasping her hands together, she said—

" You have there touched a tender point, which, however, cannot be concealed from you. The dignity of a prioress, my beloved daughter, is not a condition of joy or happiness, but rather a painful crown of thorns—a heavy cross to bear. It is but seldom that the lambs follow willingly the careful shepherdess ; for, alas! many are called, but few are chosen. We weak and erring creatures are apt to form the best resolves—swear the most solemn oaths—and yet there broods under the veil of obedience, the most perverse and obstinate head; and, under the scapulary, there beats the tempestuous and easily misguided heart. It is only the firm and courageous contest that carries away the palm, and many, therefore, depart this life, without ever having attained it. Envy, jealousy, and passion are wicked dragons, which the mild and gentle government of a prioress is not able wholly to destroy, if, indeed, she succeeds in restraining them. Even in this house there are few faithful and dutiful sisters ; should you find any of that character, attach yourself to them, your acuteness and penetration will soon enable you to discover them. Forgive those who envy you, because you can read and sing in the choir, what they have forgotten ; and, further, because you are good and pious, which they are not. Disorders and vexations of that kind are not of modern standing, and are occasioned by the present wicked world. I have fought and struggled against them with tears in my eyes, but all in vain. My last hope is fixed upon the reforming sisters, who will shortly arrive here, and whose zealous disciple I long to show myself; if only my example should prove of any avail to lead back the wandering souls into the yoke of discipline, and thereby lead them to the path of salvation."

Deeply affected by this edifying speech, Gisela thought of the quarrels and disputes, of which she had been witness in the convent at Lichtenthal, and she began to suspect that all is vanity in this mortal world, and she sighed for the arrival of the female disciplinarians, which the prioress had announced as speedily to take place, and which she considered to be the precursor of a more holy and blessed time. Her innate pride by degrees derived a pleasure in wandering in the path of dependence and subjection, and without reserve or intimidation to follow the leading star, which the prioress promised to be to her. For this reason the hitherto haughty Gisela shed the tears of confidence and obedience on the hands of the prioress, and prayed with the emotion of a thankful heart. Grant me your affection, most worthy, and save the tottering from falling. I will never lend my ear to the counsels of the wicked, who show themselves disposed to abuse me, and to scorn and vilify you, in order in the end that you may include me in the number of your faithful and devoted daughters."

The sincere and candid expression of genuine, unaffected zeal, as it flowed from the lips of Gisela, had so strong an effect upon the false and deceitful heart of the prioress, that in spite of herself, a blush of shame came over her cheeks, and she said in an embarrassed manner,—

" Weep not, Gisela ; forgive the weak and those that wander from the path of goodness and righteousness, and shut yourself up again in your cell until I come with the torch in my hand, to lead you to the altar, as a pure and immaculate bride of Heaven. It is only after the priest has consecrated you, that you can enter into communion with your holy sisters, amongst some of whom you will be as a rose amongst thistles."

As they now departed from the church, and each went a different way, Gisela towards her cell, and the prioress towards the refectory, the latter bitterly blamed herself for allowing herself for a single moment to be led away by the emotions of a simple girl. In her eyes, also, there was a smarting pain, as if from tears to which she had been unaccustomed; but she checked these salutary messengers of a contrite heart, dispelled all feeling and emotion from her countenance, cast behind her the menaces and compunctions of her conscience, and the heavy responsibility of having so inexcusably deceived a pure and virtuous soul, and with these unenviable feelings she joined the companions and the abettors of her life of vice and infamy.

The frivolous and evil-minded women, who a short time before were so abashed and timid, so hypocritically serious, now on a sudden threw off the mask of piety, and the

See p. 104.

reins of order and decorum. From the secret vaults of the convent was now again brought forward whatever could cheer and exhilarate the heart; the most luscious fruits, confectionary of all kinds, meats of the rarest and finest quality, and the most intoxicating wines. The glass went merrily round; they laughed and danced, the vicar dancing with them, playing all kinds of tricks and buffoonery, for which his corpulent frame particularly adapted him. The elder sisters were playing at draughts; the younger ones listening to the tales related by sister Simplicia, in some of which modesty and decency were wholly omitted. Jokes went round as if the gates of Paradise had just been opened; and scarcely a thought was bestowed upon the lady reformers who were on their way to the convent. The enemy had been overcome, deceived, despatched with their blessings and all the value that could be attached to them from the convent; and what cared then the victorious sisters of Gnadenzell for the morrow?

Sister Agnes, who, with her continual and deep-rooted melancholy, joined not in the excesses nor the debaucheries of the holy sisterhood, was, in a rude and peremptory manner, commanded by the prioress to repair to her cell.

"I shall not long be a burden to you," said the broken-hearted girl, as she left the refectory to converse alone with her sorrow.

To the surprise of some, but not to that of all, who gave a significant wink of the eye to each other, the prioress pleaded indisposition for retiring from the jovial scene, giving the stewardess instructions during her absence to contribute as much as possible to the mirth and happiness of her virtuous flock.

"Be merry, my children," she said, in a grievous tone, as she was about to leave the refectory, "and, to-morrow, we will hold a consultation as to the manner in which we shall receive the odious sisters of Pforzheim. I'll warrant ye we will lead them as good a dance as we have done the chancellor and his companion, the blear-eyed father Wendelen." Medora ran to the prioress, and whispered in her ear,—

"We shall not keep up late; the night is very bad, and our favourite guests will not be here;" meaning thereby, the young libertines who now and then paid a visit to the convent to meet with some sympathising hearts, and they generally found what they wanted. The prioress gave an ambiguous smile at what Medora had said, and again wishing them a pleasant evening, she directed her steps to her own apartment. The partition between the refectory and her own apartment was very slightly made, and she had scarcely closed the door, when she could hear some very malicious allusions and some coarse jokes on her pretended indisposition, as well as some very envious and uncharitable remarks on Gisela, of whom it was a mystery to the nuns whence she came or whither she was going; the prioress, however, cared very little for the tittle-tattle of the women, she had only her own pleasures to attend to, and at this particular moment there was only one care, one longing that affected her heart, and the longing was full of tenderness, the care full of sweetness and delight.

Secretly and stealthily as the timid deer when it ventures out of the forest to look for the bubbling spring, so crept the prioress in the twilight of the rainy evening towards her apartment, and she turned ill-humouredly round, when she heard herself called upon by Crescentia, and was obliged to stop to hear the purport of her mission.

"In the name of Christ," exclaimed the prioress, in an impatient tone, "what is now the matter?"

Crescentia answered, in a submissive tone,—

"Most worthy lady, it grows daily worse and worse with the old woman in her cell, the mysterious mother Demath. I see well what will be the upshot of all this business, I shall have my eyes scratched out; or I should not be surprised if I had my teeth knocked down my throat. Sister Anna has long since desisted from visiting her; and the burden now rests solely on my shoulders. Since the day when that curious simpleton, the astrologer, thrust his nose into that corner, mother Demath has become insupportable. She dreams about ghosts, and even about murderers who are circumventing her life, and then she is under a continual alarm that she will be poisoned, and she sighs ten times in a breath for her speedy death."

"God grant her a joyful resurrection," said the prioress; "she will not hold out much longer, and therefore be patient towards her.

"Most reverend mother," said Crescentia, "I will not make any mention that mother Demath, in proportion as she becomes more wretched in her body, she becomes more violent and malicious in her mind. I would accommodate myself to existing circumstances, if it were only on account of my sins, of which I have a great number to repent, but I am grievously afflicted for the soul of the poor woman, for never can she enter Paradise until she be purified and consoled. A powerful spiritual exhortation would do the poor creature a great deal of good, but I am not learned enough, and am by far too simple to preach to her of the glorious things of another world. To be sure, there are some of our sisters—but, lady prioress, you know well ——"

"Yes, yes," exclaimed the prioress, interrupting her, "I knew well what you would say."

"And with our worthy vicar," continued Crescentia, "I am afraid my trouble would be in vain."

The good-hearted lay sister sobbed as she uttered these words, for she was, in reality, in great trouble about the salvation of the soul of the incarcerated nun.

For the purpose, however, of ridding herself of the troublesome Crescentia, the prioress answered drily and hastily,—

"Be of good courage, sister Crescentia; I know a preacher who is exactly calculated for the maniac brain of the old Demath. From to-morrow, sister Gisela shall take upon herself the attendance of the troublesome woman, she will not then stand in need of spiritual exhortation."

Crescentia nodded her head, in token of her approbation, and said, in a tone of great satisfaction,—

"Yes, yes, that is the truth; sister Gisela is, indeed, an angel, pure as snow, whom the Lord in his boundless grace has sent to this house to be a blessing to it, and all its inmates. Pardon me, reverend mother, but we are a long way removed from attaining to the virtue of our sister Gisela; you know we are wading deeply in sin."

"Hold your tongue," exclaimed the prioress, in an angry and threatening tone; "how dare you speak of your superiors? do you long for the punishment of fasting and confinement in the vault, where you will be daily scourged? Quick, betake yourself off, or you shall feel the consequences of my anger and revenge."

Full of alarm, Crescentia retired, muttering to herself,—

"Oh, that my conscience were at rest; when shall we awaken from pride and folly, will Heaven ever grant us its pardon? will it separate the strayed lambs from those who have been the means of leading them astray? Take compassion upon us, O Lord, with thy precious blood, and send us sincere repentance and salvation."

In the meantime the prioress, full of rancour, arrived at her private apartment, fastened the door carefully behind her, and looked about the room; her dog came fawning upon her, and her singing birds were twittering in their cages, although nearly overcome with sleep in the twilight. The circumstance, however, which kept the birds awake, was a low melodious tune on a guitar, which stole from behind the curtains in the sleeping chamber of the prioress; it was a sweet and harmonious tune, as if played by the hands of spirits. The prioress was not, however, in the least alarmed at the apparition, but she drew the curtain aside, and breathed a tender welcome to the harmonist, who was sitting on her bed, in an attitude of manly beauty; the lamp that was concealed in a recess threw its faint light upon the form of a young man, in knightly costume, who was as comfortable and as much at his ease in his conventional hiding-place, as if the priest had given him permission to be the companion of its most holy tenant.

"You are then come at last, Rechardis," said the young man, assuming a discontented mien; and Rechardis, seating herself by his side, answered in a gentle and insinuating tone,

"Here I am, my beloved; your own dear love."

"The black animals that have lately visited you," said the young man, "have made the time hang heavily upon my hands; and I envied them that they were in enjoyment of the sight of your beautiful eyes, whilst I was here watching like a cat for its prey."

"They are gone, my beloved Vesterlein," said the prioress, in a smooth and flattering voice, and played with the ringlets of her lover, as they fell upon her shoulder; "let me now give you a thousand and a thousand thanks, for having been so valuable a herald to us. You cared for neither time nor trouble, so that you could protect and save your beloved."

"Am I not called in the country," said Vesterlein, "the bold Friedingen; give me only something of more importance and of peril to do for you, and will I not dash into it. Tell me where the house of your enemy is situate, and a firebrand shall soon be thrown into it. I will risk my neck and my life, and your convent veil shall be the banner under which I'll fight. I am not born to be a fox, my character partakes of the lion."

"One thing, then, I pray you," said the prioress, jocosely; "do not tear your poor lambkin to pieces."

Friedingen threw the instrument away from him, and clasped the prioress passionately in his arms, saying,—

"No, no, I will not tear you to pieces, but I will take you in my arms, carry you over mountain, and over sea; such is my determination; and that must happen if I am not to be driven to despair. You yourself have made me the offer; as a rash impetuous youth, I crept into the convent told to taste the forbidden fruit, and then after I had enjoyed the meal to skulk away like a bloated badger. But I can endure it no longer; I'm in your net, as in the magical hair of a mermaid; I cannot leave you; I cannot go without you; thou art mine, although the flames of d——n were burning before this chamber.''

The glow of the highest satisfaction beamed over the countenance of the nun, and she whispered in an amorous tone,—

"I will go with you into the hottest fire, and were even the breach of the rules of our order to be punished elsewhere by the torments of the d——d. I only long for a few years here in the world to enjoy with you a state of uninterrupted happiness; and if thy courage be unshaken, firm thy love, and thy arm strong, so will, ere long, the wreath of love be bound around our brows. Only give me your commands—the mummery—the hypocritical doings of a monastic life, are no longer to be tolerated. I hate and abjure them. I am not accustomed to have restraint put upon me in my enjoyment. I like to be free and unshackled."

"A convent life," said Friedingen, "may please the cold and frigid soul, to whom nature has given the temperament of the icicle; where there's passion, there must be life, and is a convent the place to enjoy it?"

"No, no, my beloved Friedingen," exclaimed the prioress; "your longings, your desires are near; and if you be prepared, I will follow you. Here my stay will not be long. The gratification of this silent place will soon be changed into gloomy severity and iron bondage. I will be saved before the storm lays low my hopes. Are your hands still tied, or cannot you yet be the master of your own free will?"

Friedingen heaved a deep sigh, a frown came upon his countenance, and he said,—

"I am still upon the same terms with my brother. I have little or nothing to expect from him; yet I promised him to fight out a battle for him, and to make a kind of excursion with him, which he intends to make into the country of our natural enemy, the Count of Wurtemberg. Perhaps I shall obtain some honourable booty. Perhaps my sister, who has bequeathed to me a small estate, will betake herself off to another world. If I obtain any riches, be they great or small, I will place thee on my horse, and fly into a distant land, amongst strangers, where the convent vow is never heard—where the ban of the emperor and the pope is laughed at. We will fly to the Bohemians, who honour the wine-cup, or to the rude and savage Hungarian. Nay, I will fly with thee even to the Turks, rather than renounce thee."

Rechardis filled him a goblet of sparkling wine, and said,—

"Drink, then, to the continuance of our love; and let me now tell you, that the poor convent woman can bring you a handsome dowry, and that we shall not go with empty hands."

Friedingen having drank copiously of the wine, looked the prioress full in the face, who on a sudden rose from her seat, and opening a small cupboard, she drew forth a casket of an antique and ugly make, but which, from its weight, she found it difficult to carry.

"Whilst my sister Merhthild," she said, in a confidential tone, "is awaiting with doubt and impatience the death of the old Zavelstein, in order to inherit his money and his property, I have, from the mouldering walls of this convent, without any great or extraordinary trouble, struck out a source of wealth, like Moses, when he drew the water from the rock."

With greedy hands Friedingen took hold of the casket, and in an ironical tone, asked if the treasure were concealed in it, which, according to the report of the country-people, lay buried in the cemetery of Gnadenzell.

The prioress shook her head, opened the casket with a rusty key, and displayed before the astonished gaze of Friedingen an assemblage of valuable articles, consisting of golden buckles, chains, necklaces, bracelets, valuable watches, pearl ornaments of the most exquisite colour and size, and a great variety of other jewels, which would not disgrace an empress to wear, and the majority of which were set with diamonds and other precious stones.

"What is all this?" exclaimed Friedingen, his eyes sparkling with delight; "to whom did the treasure belong, before it became your property? According to all appearance, it would seem as if you had been plundering the riches of the virgin of Altenotting."

"It is no such thing," said the prioress, archly; "I never take the jewels belonging to the saints. These riches are an inheritance of my predecessor, who, without doubt, thought as I do, that it would be more prudent and wise to retain them in her possession than to fritter them away for the wants and necessities of the convent. They constitute the fund which has been given to the convent for the care and support of the old, mysterious mother Demath, whom I wish the Lord would be pleased to take to himself, as soon as possible."

" Do you mean the old penitent ?" said Friedingen, " over whose birth, family, and life, there rests such an impenetrable mystery ?"

" The same," replied the prioress. " The secret lies in the grave of Father Cunrath; but what is that to us? What are to us the mysteries of the old visionary ? We nourish a sweeter mystery, like a tender flower; and in order to bring it to fruit and maturity, let the gold be applied which has been long forgotten by the whole world."

Friedingen weighed several of the jewels in his hand, and then said, after an attentive examination of them,—

" Some time must now have elapsed since these trinkets and jewels came out of the hands of the goldsmith. They are not worn at the present day so heavy, nor so elaborately worked. It would appear as if they belonged to some opulent wife of a citizen of Ulm or Augsburg, where the ladies, as it is proverbially stated, strut about like peacocks. See, I'm not wrong in my conjecture—here, close to the mark of the maker, stand, the fir cones of the city of Augsburg. May God bless the good women-for their piety and penitence, and send them a joyful resurrection."

" She is now in a very tottering, feeble condition," said the prioress ; "her life hangs by a thread; and in order that the soul of the poor wretch may be soon prayed out of her, I have appointed the pious monster, Gisela, to be her nurse."

" What !" exclaimed Friedingen ; " the superstitious, foolish girl—how does she deport herself—the immaculate virgin ? Has she shone for a time like a meteor, and dazzled the eyes of the stiff and ceremonious ambassador of Urach ?"

" The fraud succeeded most excellently," said the prioress ; " but still I am in a great dilemma how I shall be able to keep my word with the simple girl. We are expressly prohibited to receive a sister into the house ; and our vicar, who has been painted to the authorities at Urach as black as a crow, hesitates to add this one to the many kindnesses and civilities which he has already shown us. Nevertheless some plan must be devised, if it were only an illusion for the time, to satisfy the fool, and make sure of her silence. Then things may take their own course. I shall know how to get rid of her, and to render her wholly harmless as soon as she is completely in our net. My sister Merhteld has thrown her upon me as a burden, but she told me not to give her the most friendly reception, and I will willingly obey the injunction of my sister, as I hate and abhor her parade of virtue, her disgusting prudery, her stupid superstition, and the show of an extraordinary piety."

Friedingen burst out into a loud laugh—told the prioress she was jealous of Gisela, and said mischievously, " Why do you hesitate, when he who sits by your side can help you out of your dilemma ? If it be required to deceive an enemy, a Jew, or a fool—is there anything, let it be however mad and foolish, which Friedingen will not undertake? Let the Wurtemberger circulate his command with his trumpets and his drums. Leave the doubts to the priests ; but place your dependence upon me, and I will venture to say that I will make as good a nun of her as ever was made by a bishop."

" You make a nun of her ?" exclaimed the prioress, overcome with astonishment.

In a boasting tone Friedingen continued,—

" Yes, by all the lightnings of Heaven! I'll make a nun of her. The girl has never seen me, and I will be a bishop—a cardinal—a wandering missionary sent forth to convert the heathens. I will be a monk, priest, a vicar—I will be anything you please, so that you shall carry your point. Did I not once carry on the trade of a monk, and showed myself as the light and torch of the altar, until I took a fancy to the housekeeper of my cousin, one of the heads of the chapter, and felt a disgust for the breviary ? I have not yet forgotten my Latin nor the formulæ, nor the blessing, nor the chanting. As long as I have any leisure with my expedition against the count, I will carry out the trick for you."

" I do not understand you, you madcap," said the prioress.

" It will pass off well," said Friedingen. " You will only have the job to perform of making me a tonsor, and you can then fancy how willingly I appear again for a time in the garb of a priest, because you know well how greatly I am attached to spiritual things."

He kissed the lips of the prioress in the most passionate manner, and said,—

" Now, my beloved, without any contradiction, reward me with the staff and ring, and hold yourself as high as the pope, although you are more charming than the ancient father at Rome."

With amorous kisses the prioress disengaged herself from the arms of Friedingen that were thrown round her, opened the casket of mother Demath, took from it a heavy golden ring, and tendered it to her beloved, saying,—

" Here is the ring as a happy memorial of our love."

" And also," said Friedingen, " as the ring of our betrothment, and the ring of our constancy and fidelity."

He then took the goblet, held the ring before his mouth, and drank through the circle to the health and happiness of his beloved.　He then stopped for a moment, examined the ring more minutely, and said, in a satirical tone,—

" Look, look—here are the arms of my most illustrious friend, the noble Count of Wur-temberg, engraved upon it—the stag-horns, the fisher—oh, how beautiful.　With what Jew has the Honourable Prince of Hanse pledged this ring, until it came at last on the coarse fist of the Augsburger lady?　Much rather would I have drawn it from the stiffened hand of the count in a field of battle; but still I will prize it highly in memory of the living.　Certainly then, my beloved, you must give me another ring, a plain gold one, which signifies an everlasting bond—whereas the arms of the Wurtemberger announce discord, dissension, and a miserable end."

Instead of an answer, the prioress offered him again the ruby of her lips, and there was an end to the amorous discourse; nor were the dulcet tones of his instrument heard again in the convent,

---

CHAPTER XV.

" Thou hast prevaricated with thy friend—
By underhand contrivances undone me;
And, while my open nature trusted in thee,
Thou hast stepped in between me and my hope,
And ravished from me all my soul held dear!
Thou hast betrayed me!"

STRUGGLING with the most restless morning sleep, Herr von Sperbeneck lay tossing upon his bed, and with his groans awakened his wife, who was lying by his side.　She raised herself up in the spacious bed, seized her husband roughly by the arm, and, giving him a violent shake, exclaimed,—

" Anshelm! Anshelm! what the deuce is the matter with you?　For the sake of the Holy Virgin, awake—awake!"

In a few minutes the husband awoke, and he also sat up erect in the bed, gnashed his teeth, gave some very heavy sighs, and, in a piteous tone, asked for the towel, that he might wipe the perspiration from his forehead.　Then he said, in a tremulous voice,—

" That was, indeed, an awful dream, and day has not yet began to dawn!　Get up, Elizabeth, and light the lamp, that I may breathe with greater freedom."

The wife did as she was bidden to do, although the first beam of the morning began to peep through the windows, seated herself on the side of the bed that was ornamented with curtains and escutcheons, and, in an anxious tone, demanded of her husband what he had seen in his dream?　Anshelm pondered for a moment, and, leaning on the pillows, he began his narrative, which was, at times, interrupted by sighs, which appeared to come from the very bottom of his heart,—

" Alas! my beloved spouse, I cannot describe to you what I have suffered!　But was I not in good spirits, and merry, when I laid myself down to sleep? and yet listen to me.　It appeared to me, suddenly, that I contemplated myself from head to foot in a glass; and, behold! I was afflicted all over me with a malady, like a leper, and not a single part of my body was free from the nasty disorder, and some one hung a black cloth over my head, placed me on the threshold of my house, and said the bishop would come to fetch me, to thrust me into the bottomless pit.　From a distance sounded the bells, and a psalm was sung, so deep and hoarse as if it had been by a hundred aged priests.　I trembled through every limb of me with cold and pain, and my fear became greater and greater.　As the procession approached, with flags and torches, as far as could be seen in the valley—an entire chapter of pale choristers, at the head of whom was a grey-headed bishop, a silver mitre on his head, a black mourning mantle, and the dark-coloured stole, ornamented with silver skulls.　They formed a circle in front of my house, and my bishop pushed me with his hand, and told me to follow him.　And I did follow him with naked feet, and all the people made way for me a few paces, and blessed themselves when they saw me.　An old cathedral stood open, and before the choir was placed a double row of enormous lights, and I was placed in the middle of them, and a requiem was sung over my head, on which the procession again set forth, till they arrived at a burial-ground. They then pushed me into a deep grave, and the bishop told me that my leprosy was a curse of Heaven, and that henceforth I should be dead to the whole world. He then took three handfuls of earth, sprinkled it over my head, and said,—'Begone! thou old leprous man—begone! and think of thy grave!' He had, however, scarcely uttered these terrific words, when—— "

Anshelm stared, bereft of motion, straight before him, and his listening and attentive wife shook him again most violently, and said,—

" Anshelm, what is the matter with you? What are you staring at so strangely? Wake up—wake up, and finish the history of your dream."

Anshelm sprang suddenly out of bed, and said, in a hasty tone,—

" Go and awaken our boy, Andres. Do you not hear how he is tossing about in the cradle? And listen to the other young vagabonds—how they are snoring! Go and awaken them—day is fast breaking. I bless the day!"

Elizabeth left the room muttering to herself, to pacify the unruly little one, and to awaken the others, and the knight knelt before the image of the patron of his house for the purpose of saying his morning prayers to him; but somehow he could not collect his thoughts, and several horrible apparitions mingled themselves in his prayer, but of which he considered it most prudent to withhold all mention from his wife.

Immersed in thought, his face resting on his hands, in that situation was he found by his wife on her return.

" Rouse yourself, Anshelm; but so it is always with you. You have inherited fear, and the belief in the devil, from your father, who, everybody knows, was not quite right in his head. And what is the meaning of all this? I will explain it to you. You obtained the information yesterday that your uncle, the marshal, was lying dangerously ill, and you then thought of his death and heritage, and thus it was, most likely, the cause of the funeral procession appearing to you in your sleep."

At these words, Anshelm, like one who with the utmost anxiety is attempting to grasp the anchor of hope, directed his look full upon his wife; thought again of his dying uncle and his inheritance; gave a friendly nod, as if he were perfectly satisfied with the exposition of his dream. He then said,—

" On account of my fear I had almost forgotten that I must this day set out on my journey, or perhaps I shall not arrive in time to see my uncle before he dies, and then his property may be swept away by his pretended heirs."

" To be sure," said the wife. " You are perfectly in the right, Anshelm. Ruprerht has provided everything that is necessary; the horse is fed and saddled, and the weather has become fine, or perhaps you would prefer travelling in the chaise; it would be more comfortable and respectable."

" But far more expensive," said Anshelm, in an emphatic manner; " you know not how the rogues of innkeepers treat the travellers. Two horses and the driver will make my purse empty. No, it were better that I should go on horseback, though more fatiguing and unpleasant in the present unsettled state of the weather. I will ride the lean and bony Scheck; he is rather quick in his paces—looks, however, if it had been lent with him, throughout the whole of the year, which, however, will be attended with one advantage, which is, that he is sure not to be stolen. Reach me then my grey saddlebags, they are, indeed, heavy and coarse, but then the thieves will not cast an eye upon them. Reach me also my strong book of ox's leather; my long sword, with the iron handle, and my fur cap. Quick, quick!"

" Why, Anshelm," said dame Elizabeth, " you will look like some poor wretch just come out of the hospital."

" And such is my desire," said Anshelm, " it is now dangerous travelling on the highways. There is scarcely a tree, behind which there is not a lurking robber, and you feel a bullet in your body before you dream of any danger. Let me have a little broth before I depart; my journey is long, and it will save me the expense of stopping at an inn where I am sure to be imposed upon."

Dame Elizabeth repaired to the kitchen to prepare the broth; whilst Anshelm, with his riding-whip in his hand, threatened the children with the application of it, if they did not rise from their beds; which they had no sooner done, than, as their general custom, they began to fight and scratch each others' faces. Having dispatched them into the kitchen to have their morning meal, he took a heavy key, which was hanging round his neck, opened the iron door of a cupboard, and carefully counted the money that was concealed in it, and put a small sum into his pocket wherewith to defray the expences of his journey; he then locked up everything very safely, and from the window made a sign to Ruprerht, his steward, who was standing in the yard talking with the groom. He then cast his eyes upwards to the skies, to take an observation of the state of the weather, and said to himself,—" The ride will drive all the ridiculous fancies out of my head; for broad day and mountain air are excellent medicines, and particularly so as they cost nothing. I cannot comprehend how all that nonsense came into my head; what have I do with the dead? My father rests quietly in his grave, and my mother."

The short, thick, corpulent steward, a striking contrast with the lean and haggard figure of the master of the mansion, and the skeleton figures of the domestics, now hobbled into the room.

" A most blessed morning to you, most gracious sir," he stammered from his bloated throat. " You are most fortunate in the weather; it is now beautifully fine, and everything is ready for your departure; your horse is standing at the door, and I have fastened a small bag, with some bread and cheese, to the front of the saddle, and half a peck of oats I have fastened to the crupper. I know well, most gracious sir, how you like matters to be done."

" You have done well, Ruprerht," said his gracious master; " and now listen to my instructions. The first thing you do is to hasten to the chief constable at Guttenberg, and tell him to keep a strict look out after the vagrant, about whom the simple priest at Owen makes so much noise; then see if the tenant at Bohringen brings his rent to-day. I have given the fellow indulgence enough, and if he does not pay, make no further ceremony with him, but take his cattle and his farm too, and everything that belongs to him, and drive him out of the house."

The little ferret-eyes of the steward sparkled with delight, for there was not a single feature in his countenance which had the expression of compassion. It was the delight of the hard-hearted wretch to take the bed from under the pauper, and drive him pennyless upon the world; but, as it generally happens, there was not a greater rogue in the whole neighbourhood than old Ruprerht, and secretly did he filch the property from his master, who was robbed every day and every hour, although he thought that everything was so well secured that it was impossible to rob him.

" I will now put on my boots and my riding breeches," said Ruprerht, " and I will soon have the fellow out of the house, if he don't pay—he is nothing but a thief; neither corn—nor wood—nor fruit is safe from him."

" I am too good and lenient a master," said Anshelm, " and that you can vouch for, Ruprerht."

" Oh! most certainly," said the steward—" an excellent master!"

" I will now take my broth," said Anshelm; " and then into God's wide world!"

The steward retired, and dame Elizabeth brought in the broth, which her provident husband swallowed with the greatest avidity, but between every spoonful that he took he had some particular instruction to give her for her conduct during his absence. She was to be very economical—to waste nothing—to say her prayers regularly night and morning—and particularly not to forget to pray to God to protect him from every danger on his journey. It was now the time when the women had to bring in their rent in eggs and butter. The former were to be regularly and strictly counted, and the latter weighed most rigorously. The castle gates were to be kept regularly locked and bolted; all beggars were to be driven away, because the corn was then very dear; the mendicant monks were to be told to wait till his return; no hospitality whatever was to be shown to any traveller, because the host was frequently robbed by his guests. Should, however, any old woman come to the castle, some relief was to be given to her, because she might bewitch and enchant the whole house; but still it mattered not how little was given her, for the gift of an apple would put an end to the enchantment as well as a pound of gold.

As soon as the knight had finished his breakfast, and exhausted the list of instructions, he mounted his skeleton of a horse; but it took him some time before he could properly adjust his body between the bag of bread and cheese and the little sack of oats. The rusty stirrups were not exactly right, one being two inches longer than the other; and it took the groom some time to bring them to an equal length; and as the knight was, at length, properly seated in his saddle, such a pair of animals, biped and quadruped, was, perhaps, never seen before. The master was now ready to move—but not so the horse; the former considered spurs to be a very expensive appendage to an equestrian, and, therefore, he always travelled without them. At last he applied his whip to the right ear of the steed, and slowly it bore its unwelcome burden through the gates. It had not, however, proceeded far before it turned suddenly round with an intention to return to its accustomed manger, and the rider took the favourable opportunity of casting his eyes to the narrow windows of his castle, in the corners of which the swallows had built their nests, and he saw also the storks, as they stood on their nests at the top of the tower.

"Shall I ever return to my castle?" said Anshelm to himself, and the thought produced a temporary depression of his spirits; but the recollection of his expiring uncle, and his valuable property, inspired him with fresh courage, so, applying his whip again to his decrepit brute, the castle was soon lost from his view.

Everything was now merry and joyous in the castle, for the absence of the master was always a signal for the commencement of joviality and good living. Ruprerht drank

See page 117.

three times the quantity of wine that he did when his master was at home, and dame Elizabeth, forgetting the instructions of her lord and master, relative to her economy, had her larder now filled with all the good things which the farm or the garden could yield, and sumptuous and luxurious were the feasts which she and her family enjoyed.

There is, undoubtedly, a great deal of happiness connected with ignorance; and, as the miserly Anshelm was wholly ignorant of these proceedings, which were carried on in his house during his absence, he consoled himself with the idea that economy and frugality were the leading principles of his household; and he is not the first husband who, in matters of that sort, have found themselves so egregiously mistaken.

Believing that extravagance was a thing not known in his castle, he travelled gently onwards, and arrived, at length, at the village of Bohringen, and, guiding his horse up a narrow passage, he knocked with his whip at a small window of a dilapidated cottage. It was immediately opened, and a miserable, squalid female countenance projected from it.

"Where is George?" asked the rider. "Is he still snoring in the straw, or is he getting the better of his last night's debauch?"

"Oh! most noble master," exclaimed the woman, "Heaven forbid that he should be guilty of such an act. He is working in the garden behind, and is just about going to his day's labour."

At this moment George appeared at the threshold of the house, and cast upon his creditor a look of defiance, although he was so far gifted with politeness as to uncover his head.

"Now!" exclaimed Anshelm, "you wretched paymaster, you know, I suppose, that your rent is due to-day?"

"The peasant shrugged his shoulders with a piteous and awkward obeisance, and Anshelm continued,—

"If you do not pay it before the setting of the sun, you shall be driven, without any mercy or indulgence, from your house into the wide streets. Remember what I say, and fail not."

Anshelm rode away without waiting for any reply or remark from his tenant, but he saw not the threatening attitude of the tenant as he followed him with his eyes.

"Wait a while," he said: "depend upon it, I will remember you."

The rider pursued his way till he came to the little bridge which crosses the Urach, when he was accosted by a man with a bold and ruffian-like countenance, who was hastening along the road, and, in an insolent manner, asked for charity.

"May God help you," said Anshelm, and he hastened past the pedestrian, looking at times behind him, as if he were looking after a robber; nor did he desist from watching him, until he saw him strike into a wood, and was lost from his sight.

Anshelm had, in the present instance, not formed an erroneous conjecture. The insolent beggar was no other person than Lamparter, the companion of Wildherr; and, not far from the place where Anshelm met him—in the cave of Falkenstein, where the Urach springs from the dark clefts of the rock—lay, reclining, the bold leader of the banditti, with his companions around him, like a bear in his den

Lamparter was on his way from Urach, and his countenance was flushed with the joy that is felt at the misfortunes of others, mingled with the hateful feeling of malice where an enemy has been overcome. He, however, concealed these emotions under a gloomy seriousness, when, after a painful and troublesome climbing over roots, he arrived at the cave, and showed himself in the presence of his leader.

"Well," exclaimed Wildherr, in a tone of sympathy, "what intelligence do you bring of Heinz?"

"What information did you obtain about my family?" asked Martin, with a sly and cunning look.

Lamparter answered,—

"I have only gained so much information, that they are all sitting behind bolts and bars, and depend upon God and us for their liberation."

On hearing this, Wildherr repaired to the old astrologer, bidding his companions not to disturb him.

Lamparter then repaired to the place where Martin was sitting, and whispered with delight in his ear,—

"Rejoice, Father Martin, I have our liberty, and the blood-money, as I may call it, in my pocket. To-night, at ten o'clock, the superintendent of the provost, with a number of armed men, will be at the little bridge in the forest, and I am to be their leader. Our enemies must be overcome, but we shall be as we were before—noblemen, without blame or reproach."

The eyes of Martin sparkled with joy at this unexpected intelligence, and moved to a distance from Lamparter, so that no suspicion might be excited.

In the meantime, he whose life and blood had been so infamously trafficed away, sat in careless tranquillity by the side of the old prophet, and was employed in relating to him his adventures, which he thus continued;—"Thus, as a cast out orphan, I was once more on the path by which I could obtain honour and fortune. But the curse that is upon me would not allow it. We youths at court had frequently some unpleasant and disgraceful services to perform. I was attached to the falconry, and the keeper had confided to me a most untractable bird, which I was to feed and take care of. The owner was absent, and the steward who was left in charge of the establishment had a spite against me. Not a day passed, but for some trivial fault, a punishment was inflicted upon me; at one time, I was obliged to fast; at another I was condemned to kneel on short points of wood; at another I was confined in the tower, where I underwent all kind of suffering. It happened once that I was placed in confinement, and had forgotten to instruct one of my fellow servants to feed the falcon, and when I was released from my confinement, the wild bird had become quite frantic with hunger, and had broken its head against the sides of the cage, in which it was found to be dead. The circumstance was soon well known, and the steward ordered me to receive three hundred lashes, for the bird was of extraordinary beauty, and was the gift of a prince. As the lord was not at home, who certainly would not have allowed me to be flogged, and as I had no mercy to expect from the steward, I took to my heels without my three hundred lashes, and chanced directed me to this very cave, where I concealed myself, and the same night became the prisoner of him, who then made use of the cave as his hiding place. This terrible man was the dreaded robber, Hopp, and I was obliged to serve him, to follow him, to share in all his troubles and perils, and to rejoice when he rejoiced. By degrees I felt so much pleasure in the uncertain, adventurous life, that I became his favourite, his most apt and docile pupil. Since then I have carried on the trade; I have done some good and meritorious actions. I have assisted the poor and the innocent, and I think I can rely upon their intercession, when I go out of the world into purgatory. I have now given you the explanation, why the tears came out of my eyes as we entered the cave."

The old man made an expressive motion with his head, and a tear trickled down his furrowed cheeks. "Well, indeed, may we weep," he said, "when in our later years we come again to the place in which we have stood in the pride and strength of our youth. I was, not less than yourself, a constant guest of the rocky cave, when my hair was yet brown, and my limbs active and supple; often have I come from my pretended home over mountain and over heath, and on the spot have dreamt of wonderful tales and magical things, of the course of the stars, and of the spirits, who, good as well as bad, people this forest, who swim in the floods, and sit in the bowels of the earth guarding their heathenish treasures. I have often been alarmed myself with terrible presentiments, and have wished to open the seal of the mysterious, and to break the ring of Solomon, as the lords of Balderk and Wittlingen have done before me. Ah, they were indeed terrible magicians, and although their castles lay in the forests and the mountains, they stretched forth their magical hand over the country, and no one could withstand them. I have heard with my ears, when at night I have been reclining amongst these rocks, how the two exorcists of the devil rushed out of their castles like flaming meteors, and met high above the tops of the forest, and then shouting, directed their course to the Henberge, where the hellish sabbath is kept."

Wildherr now evidently saw that the imagination of the old man was again carrying him beyond the bounds of reason, and therefore purposely interrupted him in the question, "As I have now been given to understand, you are a native of this part of the country, and that your home was not situated at a great distance hence?"

"You are right," said the old man, after a moment's reflection; "my father's residence is not far distant, and this country is my home, although my language is no more like that of my countrymen; but I have wandered far and wide in the world—have seen the subjects of many kings and potentates—have been nearly half a Saracen, and at the same time a disciple of the stars—and, after all this, to return to my home a grey-headed man, to be obliged to beg, and to eat of the bread of charity from the hand of a robber."

"Did you not find any of your relatives on your return to your family—is your family quite extinct?" asked Wildherr.

The old man burst into tears, and sobbed with childish sorrow,—

"I will confess all to you; for you are also an old man, and, perhaps, you place your hope on the gratitude of a child. Feast yourself no longer with that hope. What the Lord bestows upon us in riches and contentment is destroyed by the wickedness of the wife, or we are robbed of it by our greedy and avaricious sons. I also have sons, and they are alive. They have divided my property amongst them—have themselves become fathers, and I have begged before the door of my eldest son, and his servants have set his dogs upon me; and more cruel and savage than the Turk have branded me with the name of thief, not as the father returning from his chains and his misery, and that I was more deserving the gallows than of the bread of charity."

A frown of the bitterest indignation came over the countenance of Wildherr; but by degrees the old man recovered himself from his sorrow, and spoke again,—

"I was ashamed and wandered away again. I had been long accustomed to a mendicant's life; for during the whole of my travels no one would support me on account of my art, and I was sustained by my fellow-creatures from mere compassion. I then arrived at the convent, and in my spirit I saw the treasure, and if I were but able to obtain ——"

" Would you be able therewith," said Wildherr, interrupting him, " to purchase the sufferings of your long life?"

" No," replied the old man; " but I would build a hospital for starving fathers; and, contiguous to it, I would build a house of correction for bad wives."

" You would give one for ever," said Wildherr, " a disgust for marriage."

" It is well for you," said the old man, " that you are beyond the years of marriage. You have escaped the marriage devil, although the whole of your life may he said to have been lost."

" That is a care," said Wildherr, " that troubles me not. I was obliged to play accordingly as the dice fell. I had not learnt anything and, consequently, I had nothing to hope for. Since a few days I have been wholly abstracted from the world, and the rest of my life shall be devoted to settle my account with those wretches who call themselves noblemen. One of these trampled under his feet the only thing that bound me to the life of honourable people, and his whole family shall, far and wide in the kingdom, pay dearly for his crime; and this I swear, so true as my name is Wildherr."

" Do you know the villain?" asked the old man.

" If I know him," exclaimed Wildherr, " by the blood of the holy Franciseus, but he shall open the ball."

At this moment Scheindenhart came into the cave, and made a sign to Wildherr; behind him, almost concealed by bushes, stood a man, with bold expressive eye, and strongly developed features—it was George, of Bohringen; an old confidant, the assistant—and confederate of Wildherr and his gang.

" A messenger, at last," said Wildherr, with vivacity, and he left the cave to speak in secret with George.

Martin and Lamparter observed what was going forward, and their consciences smote them for their treachery. Anxious to ascertain if their roguish trick had been detected, they listened to the speakers, and it escaped them that Scheindenhart was watching them with a lynx eye, and he whispered to Walzfrieder,—

" There is something very suspicious about those fellows; we will stick as close to them as if we were blisters on their backs."

In the mean time, Wildherr returned, his countenance brightened with joy, and he said to Scheindenhart,—

" The choicest morsel will, it is true, escape us to-day; but it will do for another time. The dog shall, by degrees, be ruined—then despair, and, in the end, fall a sacrifice to our daggers."

Thus saying, he turned to the astrologer and said,—

" Tell me, prophet, is to-day an auspicious one for a bold undertaking?"

" To-day is a very favourable day," said the prophet, with a particular air of consequence; " it is good for blood-letting—good for shaving—good for everything but marriage."

" Psha, about the marriage!" exclaimed Wildherr. " But, in regard to blood-letting and making wounds, that is another business. Make yourselves ready, my brave fellows. Our journey is not a long one; but we must proceed with caution, nor can the old man travel fast. You, my brave Scheindenhart, Lamparter, and George, do you lead the way; we will follow."

Scheindenhart, with a secret pleasure, walked by the side of Lamparter, whose arm he kept hold of as firmly as if it were in a vice. Had he been a prisoner, the grasp of Scheindenhart could not have been stronger. With passion raging in his heart, the traitor saw that his treacherous trick would not on that day be successful.

Walzfreider, according to an agreement entered privately into with Scheibenhart, walked by the side of the discomfited Martin, and slowly the gang took the direction of Bohringen; but striking into many byeways, so that no peasant or traveller should obtain a glimpse of the lawless crew.

After a long rest, and many delays, the robbers, just as darkness had set in, emerged from the forest, and beneath them, on a rocky eminence, stood a castle, with a high projecting tower, and illuminated windows; and from the court sounded the noise of the merry fiddle, and the shouts and laughs of the joyous dancers.

" The mice are enjoying themselves when the cat is away," said George, with an ironical smile, and pointing with his finger to the castle; and Scheindenhart added,—

"Dance away, dance away, ye hungry rats! We will soon be amongst you with our blessing."

Wildherr now gave his orders to his people—commanding them to follow closely their leader, George—to hasten to the castle, and to attack the gates and drawbridge, so that fear and alarm might be spread amongst the dancers. He would himself bring up the rear with Martin and Hunerkogel. Those who were in advance now slid down the eminence, when the astrologer caught hold of the cloak of Wildherr, and said, with a trembling voice,—

"What are you going to do with that castle? I know it well."

"It is the castle of Sperbeneck," said Widherr, in a terrible tone, "and it must burn, that the morning beams may shine on the flames."

"Oh, Jesus!" exclaimed the astrologer, "why should fire be thrown into that house?"

"What does it concern you?" said Wildherr. "There lives the villain who robbed me of my only joy."

"Oh! may all the saints protect me," said the old man, sinking, almost exhausted, to the ground. "It was my father's castle; it was mine; it is now the property of my cruel and hard-hearted son."

Wildherr started; but, with the air and look of an avenging spirit, his arms uplifted over the prostrate sufferer, he exclaimed,—

"It is the finger of God! Our torches shall this day punish a double crime, and the unfortunate father shall be doubly revenged."

Leaving the senseless old man to the care of Nickel, Wildherr rushed to the castle, across the bridge of which his advanced party had already made their way, and had forced their passage through the gate, which was but slightly fastened.

George pulled the bell rather gently, and, in a minute afterwards, the voice of Ruprerht was heard from the court, asking,—

"What is now the matter? Who is without?"

"It is only I, George of Bohringen. I have brought you the rent that is due."

"Go to the devil with you," said Ruprerht; "the time is gone by. I will not take your rent now, and to-morrow I will drive you out of your house."

"No," said George; "you will not be so cruel. The evening bell has not yet sounded. Open the gate, or I will take my rent to the provost of our count."

"You cursed corn stealer," said Ruprerht, "I'll make you remember the provost."

The bolts were gradually withdrawn, the gate was half-opened, and the steward came forth, who gave George a violent blow on the cheek.

"Take that," said he, "for your provost. But where is your rent? Come, pay it me."

"Take it," said George, "and eat thy full of it in eternity!" and, with these words, he stabbed him in the shoulder.

Ruprerht, who was nearly intoxicated, fell heavily on the ground. The robbers rushed over his body into the castle, throwing the dancers on the ground, and, with their swords, cutting and slashing around them as if they were lunatics. The inmates of the castle made the best escape they could.

In less than a quarter of an hour the red flames, pouring from the windows of the castle, told that the work of destruction was completed; and then, calling his men together, Wildherr commenced his retreat to the cave of Falkenstein, glowing with triumph at the vengeance he had taken upon Von Sperbeneck.

"It is a pity," said Scheindenhart, as they made their way quickly through the forest, "that the old rat himself was not in the castle, so that we might have smoked him out."

"Ah!" returned Wildherr, with a savage calmness, "he will live to lament the ruin we have caused, and our daggers can yet do him a service."

Wildherr had not forgotten the old astrologer in his retreat, for he had conceived a great sympathy for him, the more especially as the same person had been the author of both their misfortunes; and he addressed encouraging exclamations to the poor old man, who was so much exhausted by grief that he was obliged to be assisted by both Walzfreeden and Dornhan.

As the band approached the neighbourhood of the cave, Lamparter, who had little anticipated an early termination to their evening's work, contrived to take advantage of a laxity of vigilance on the part of Scheindenhart, and steal away, under cover of the darkness, in the direction of the little bridge, where he had appointed to meet the provost and his men; which place he reached a short time before the hour agreed upon.

On reaching the cave, the absence of Lamparter was remarked by Wildherr himself, who inquired of Scheidenhart what had become of him.

"The vagabond!" returned the robber; "he has caused me suspicion ever since he joined us this evening. This old villain," turning to Martin, who trembled beneath his gaze, " knows where he has gone, and that his purpose towards us is not at all friendly. However, I swear by our Lady that the first appearance of treachery shall be the signal for Martin's death."

" I know nothing," said Martin. " Lamparter does as he pleases; I am not his master."

" You lie, you old wretch," exclaimed Scheidenhart, furiously ; " you know you would both like to save your nest of vipers by selling our chief's head."

Martin returned no answer, but seated himself in a further part of the cave, while Wildherr and his men prepared some refreshment, which they were much in need. of after their excursion.

The bell from a distant convent now tolled forth the hour of ten, and, as the last stroke came with faintness upon the air, the slight clash of swords was heard without the cave, and then silence was resumed. The whole band, with one accord, started to their feet, and looked in alarm towards their leader, who sat motionless and apparently unmoved.

" We are betrayed," exclaimed Scheindenhart, as he turned to Martin; " and the first sword that flashes before us in the hands of a foe, shall bring death to you."

The old man covered his face with his hands, and his whole form trembled with terror.

" Shall I go forth from the cave," asked Huzenkogel, " and reconnoitre ?"

" It is useless, if we are betrayed," said Wildherr, savagely. " Let them come ; we have weapons, and will sell our lives dearly."

Almost before he could finish speaking, twenty or thirty soldiers, well armed, in the midst of whom was the treacherous Lamparter, appeared before the mouth of the cavern, and the leader summoned Wildherr to surrender. The band, however, grouped themselves round the robber chief, and swore to protect him with their lives.

Scheindenhart had seized old Martin by the throat, and, with uplifted dagger, stood over him. The soldiers advanced, and then the old man's death-cry rang through that vault. Lamparter heard it, and his heart grew cold with terror. Though he was surrounded by a force equal to twice the number of the band, he began to wish that he had not played the traitor.

Wildherr now saw that the only hope of escape lay in cutting their way through the unequal force opposed to the band, and he reflected that the despair by which his men would be urged, would counterbalance, in a great measure, the inequality of the combat.

With a loud cry the robber chief led the band upon their foes, and then for a few minutes the cavern rang with angry shouts and painful cries ; and the sparks flew from the clashing blades. The band, however, met with a firmer resistance than Wildherr had expected; they were driven back into the cavern with great determination ; while Lamparter, who was not deficient either in strength or courage, encountered the lieutenant, Scheindenhart, his weapon still red with the blood of old Martin. Hatred sat upon the countenances of both as they faced each other ; the combat was furious, and ended in the death of the lieutenant, whose dying exclamation was a curse upon the wretch who had betrayed them.

Wildherr saw his lieutenant fall ; and, though he was at that moment opposed by three or four of the soldiers, he cut his way to the spot where the traitor stood, and clove his skull in twain.

The conflict was now renewed with redoubled energy. The much feared Wildherr was at length, covered with wounds, stretched dead upon the blood-stained ground, and the rest of the band, either wounded or dead, were strewed about the cavern.

The object of the soldiers being now accomplished, though with loss to themselves, the head of Wildherr was severed from the shoulders, and, being fixed on the end of a pike, was carried in triumph to Urach, much to the comfort and satisfaction of the worthy citizens and nobles. who now considered that for the future their persons and property would be endowed with some small share of security.

The old astrologer had thrown himself into a corner of the cavern, and, overcome by the terrors of the night, he had remained there almost insensible and unnoticed by the soldiery. When he recovered, he found himself in darkness and with the dead. He groped his way to the mouth of the cavern, and, with a strange moaning sound, he disappeared in the woods.

CHAPTER XVI,

Then of itself unfolds the eternal door,
With dreadful sounds the brazen hinges roar ;
You see before the gate what stalking ghost
Commands the guard—what sentries keep the post.—DRYDEN.

WE left the avaricious Anshelm von Sperbeneck on his way towards the castle of his uncle, Herr von Zavelstein, and having given him ample time and opportunity to reach there, which he did without meeting with any mishap, we will now see the result of that journey.

The whole of the distance he had beguiled himself with joyous anticipations of the great access of wealth his uncle's death would bring him, and, if one sorrowful thought did cross his mind, it was because he feared lest his uncle should repent his resolution respecting his nephew, Hurdegen, in which case he felt assured his share of the property would be materially lessened.

Anshelm, too, was in a happy state of ignorance of the destruction of his castle, and entertained a profound belief that the most strict economy would be practised by his careful wife in his absence; so that when he reached the Castle of Zavelstein, his countenance wore a more composed and placid expression than one would expect to find on the face of a man about to visit a dying relation.

The outward appearance of Anshelm, as has already been stated, was far from being prepossessing, and when he rang the bell at the outer gate, and desired the porter to announce to the housekeeper that Herr von Sperbeneck was at the gate, desirous of seeing his uncle, the marshal, the man laughed in his face, and refused to comply. If the words of Anshelm however, made no impression upon the man's mind, the thong of the whip, which was applied most vigorously, certainly made a most decided impression upon his body, and had a really wonderful effect in inducing him to believe that there might be some truth in the assertion of the wretched-looking being before him, that he was the nephew of the marshal.

The porter accordingly complied with his request, though with a very bad grace, and a few minutes afterwards ushered him into the presence of the virtuous Matilda. That lady had seen Herr von Sperbeneck some two or three times, and was well acquainted with his penurious habits: consequently she found but little difficulty in recognizing in the person thus introduced to her, the nephew of the marshal.

She received Anshelm with an austere and demure look, and, in a tone of pretended sorrow, said that Herr Zavelstein, at that moment, was in too weak a state to see anybody, and that, indeed, he had himself given orders that he should not be disturbed.

Anshelm, however, was more than a match for the crafty and arrogant Matilda. He knew her character too well to be deceived by her words. He was acquainted with the ascendancy she possessed over the imbecile old marshal, and he saw that if she was suffered to have her own way, not only would she take good care to see herself well thought of in the marshal's will, but would doubtless do her best to deprive him of what he styled his legal share of his uncle's inheritance.

"I have my uncle's letter here," he said in a firm tone. "He asks me to come and see him in his last hour, and no woman's tongue shall hinder me. I am not such a poor fool as my uncle, Mistress Matilda, and therefore you may as well spare yourself the trouble of attempting to deceive me. I intend to see the Herr von Zavelstein whether you like it or not, and shall go where I like, and do what I like, in this castle, without asking your permission. So now, if you don't choose to shew me the way to my uncle's chamber, I will find it myself."

Matilda bit her lips with rage; she saw that words with such a man would be useless. As Anshelm rose to put his intention into execution, she however came to the resolution that, if she had no influence over the miserly Von Sperbeneck, she still retained a control over the dying Zavelstein, and her presence might in some degree thwart the plans of the former. This was a consolatory thought to a woman of her nature, so she rose from her seat, and said, though with little courtesy in her tone,—

"If the Herr von Sperbeneck insists upon seeing his uncle, howsoever precarious his situation at the present moment may be, I have no alternative but to comply; but, at the same time——"

"Another time will do much better," interrupted Anshelm in a grumbling voice. "Shew me the way to my uncle's chamber."

Matilda obeyed in silence, though she internally vowed to be revenged; and, in a few moments, Anshelm stood by the bedside of Segbold. The invalid turned his face towards them as he entered, and looked inquiringly at Matilda.

"It is Herr von Sperbeneck, your ——"

"Silence, woman," interrupted Anshelm, sternly; "I can speak for myself. Leave the room."

Matilda, however, took no notice of these words more than by a haughty toss of the head, while the marshal, looking tenderly at her, attempted to take her hand, as he said,—

"No, no; let her stop. I have somewhat to say which concerns her much."

"Dotard!" muttered Anshelm.

Matilda saw the vexation of Von Sperbeneck at the words of his brother, and she cast a triumphant look towards him. Anshelm, however, was too busy remarking the ravages disease had made in his uncle's attenuated form to take any notice of what Matilda did, so she felt she might as well have spent her words upon a stone wall.

"Nephew," said the marshal, after a slight pause, "I know that the hand of death is upon me, and I should wish to die in charity with all my relations. Seat yourself by my bedside, for I have a great deal to say to you, if I can find strength to say it."

The countenance of Anshelm shone with eager expectation, and he instantly obeyed his uncle's request; while Matilda, taking her place on the opposite side of the bed, laid the head of the invalid with hypocritical tenderness upon her breast. Anshelm shrugged his shoulders at this, but said nothing.

"Let me ask you one question before I proceed, Anshelm," said the old man—"answer me truly. Reports are going about that your father has returned to his native place, after having been so long thought to be dead. They say, too, he has been to Sperbeneck Castle, and that you denied him, and turned him from your gates like a beggar. Is this true, Anshelm?"

"The old impostor!" returned Anshelm, coolly. "Report speaks false. He is no father of mine. What! ought not I to know my father from a stranger—a vagabond? They are lies that you have heard. Go on."

"I am satisfied," said the old marshal, in a tone of relief. "It were better for your father to be dead than treated like a dog. Now, nephew, I would speak of my will. I feel that I cannot live, and I would therefore wish you to know how I have disposed of my property."

Anshelm's eye glistened as Segbold said these words, and he drew his chair, with an eager movement, closer to the bedside.

"Yourself, Anshelm, I have not forgotten; your portion would have been greater, had I not known that you have much wealth, and had I not forgiven Hurdegen."

"Forgiven Hurdegen!" exclaimed Anshelm in astonishment, and pushing his chair back several inches, while Matilda could not forbear a slight laugh at his emotion.

"Yes; forgiven Hurdegen. His errors are but those of youth, and I have done wrong to harbour animosity against him for so long a time. He shall inherit the greater part of my property; while to Matilda here, who has tended my every want so carefully, who has been my sole comfort—who has declared that she loved me better than anything else in life, and can never love again—I leave twenty thousand crowns ——"

Matilda's eyes sparkled with delight, she imprinted what she intended to be a passionate kiss (how different to those bestowed upon Ulrick!) upon the cheek of the marshal, threw her beautiful arms around his yellow and shrivelled neck, and uttered a broken exclamation of thanks. But Herr Segbold continued,—

"For the purpose of enabling her to enter a convent, so that she may not be tempted to break her vows to me."

"The doting wretch!" shrieked Matilda, in the utmost confusion and disappointment, and rising suddenly she let the head of the marshal fall with a heavy bump against one of the pillars of the bed, and so heavy was the blow that he instantly lapsed into insensibility.

"Mistress Matilda," said Anshelm, with mock courtesy, and without the least concern at the condition of his uncle, "let me congratulate you on your valuable legacy, and on the probability of your availing yourself of it."

"Brute!" exclaimed Matilda, as with flashing eyes she quitted the room, doubtless for the purpose of finding consolation in the arms of the manly Ulrick.

At this moment a heavy ring at the bell came at the gate of the castle, and, before the Herr Anshelm could recover his uncle from the state of insensibility into which he had fallen, young Hurdegen von Sperbeneck entered the room, followed closely by the old astrologer.

"You here, boy!" exclaimed Anshelm, in surprise.

See page 118.

"If it is not my ghost, I am certainly here," returned Hurdegen. "I was recovering from a wound I had received when thrown from my horse, when I received my uncle's letter, containing his forgiveness, and expressing a wish that I should at once hasten to him. Where is he, brother? is he still alive? I have one here with me, whom both you and he ought to be glad to receive."

"Herr Zavelstein is here," returning Anshelm, lifting the curtain, and exposing the form of the insensible Segbold.

"Holy Virgin! surely he is dead!" exclaimed Hurdegen, taking his hand. "No, thank Heaven, he breathes—he lives; and he will yet know that his brother—our father—Anshelm, has returned to us."

"What means the fool?" asked Anshelm, sternly; "and who is this wretched old man?"

"That wretched old man, as you term him, Anshelm, is our father, though denied by you. I met him wandering in the woods as I came hither, and his constant cry was that his children had denied him. I pitied the poor old man, for his reason seemed to be gone, and then I recognized in him our father."

"Foolish boy!" muttered Anshelm, "are you mad? Our father has been dead years since—how then can this old impostor be he?"

"Look, brother," suddenly said Hurdegen, turning and pointing to the bed.

The old astrologer had knelt by the side of Segbold, and was gazing upon the features of the marshal. Suddenly Segbold opened his eyes, and they fell upon the countenance of the astrologer.

"Brother!" he murmured, as a faint smile of recognition played over his features, and then his eyes were closed in death.

"Does not nature speak there?" asked Hurdegen, solemnly. "Is he not our father?"

For a moment Anshelm hesitated. But his avarice supported him, and his only answer was, as he slowly left the room,—

"Our father is dead!"

CHAPTER XVII.

" 'Tis time for thee to quit the wanton stage."

THE first thing the prioress of the immaculate sisters of Gnadenzell did on the morning following the day on which the convent had been visited by the chancellor of the court, was to induct Gisela into her task of soothing the last hours of the fanatic sister Demath. The poor girl undertook the task, painful as it was, with the greatest cheerfulness; and the greater part of the time during which she was not required to take part in the religious ceremonies—for the sisters had thought it prudent to continue for a time the required services of the day—was spent in prayer by the side of the devotee.

Gisela looked forward with impatience to the arrival of the reforming sisters, to whom the prioress had alluded in her conversation with the young girl, immediately after the departure of the chancellor and his suite, and she hoped that their presence would have some effect in producing a change in their conduct, which even Gisela, careful as they were before her, could not help seeing was far from being in accordance with their profession.

About a month passed away, and affairs had assumed the same aspect as they bore on the day of Gisela's arrival at the convent. The prioress had not hinted a word about the reception of Gisela into the church, but the young girl, placing full reliance upon the word of the holy mother, did not doubt for a moment that the promise would be fulfilled. She had found the holy seclusion she had so long wished, and she experienced a tranquillity which had hitherto been a stranger to her breast.

A second unexpected visit of the young Ostertag von Friedingen, however, at length threw the convent into a still greater confusion than on the former occasion. From the account he brought, it appeared that the count, not so easily to be deceived as his envoy, the chancellor, had come to the conclusion that—as there must, at least, be some foundation to the rumours that were afloat respecting the evil practices of the holy sisters of Gnadenzell—the only way to arrive at the truth was to pay the convent a visit personally, and inspect it from top to bottom.

As may be imagined, the greatest consternation prevailed in the breasts of the fair inmates, and in imagination they beheld an end to all the sinful pleasures in which they had indulged. A full conclave sat in deliberation till nearly midnight on the night preceding the expected visit, and the only resolution come to was to adopt the same measures which had been resorted to on the visit of the chancellor; and, in the words of the prioress, "to trust to the mercy of an all-wise Providence for a favourable issue."

But whatever might have been the faith of the holy mother in the all-wise Providence she alluded to, she did not herself seem to place much reliance upon its efficacy in releasing the sisters from the unpleasant situation in which their sinful indulgence had placed them; for, when she reached her chamber, the first thing she did was to divest herself of her veil and gown, and don a suit more adapted for travelling in. Then she brought from its resting-place the heavy casket, the contents of which had so fascinated the eyes and heart of young Ostertag von Friedingen. Having concluded what she thought to be the necessary preparations for her intended flight, she placed herself near the window, and apparently awaited the coming of some other person.

Gisela, of course, had not been called to the council the nuns had held, and consequently she was entirely ignorant of the dangers the coming morrow was charged with. She had prayed late with the sister Demath, and had then retired to her own cell, not so much to obtain repose, as to offer up prayers to Him in whose service only she wished to live and die.

Taking her place by the window, which, it will be recollected, commanded a view of a small portion of the cemetery, she became lost in holy meditation. The moon had risen to its full height, and the dark cypresses which skirted the whole of the burial-ground, threw deep and fitful shadows around them, as they slowly moved their huge limbs under the influence of the night air.

Once or twice Gisela fancied she saw a human form flit rapidly along the path leading to a small portal in the wall of the garden; but she could not be certain that she had not been deceived by the numerous shadows, so she therefore took no particular notice of the circumstance, but relapsed again into meditation.

The chapel-clock sent forth, in solemn tones, the hour of midnight, and, as the strokes, one by one, fell upon the quiet air, there came a shrill, moaning sound from the cemetery, like the voice of some one in extreme agony. Even Gisela felt a thrill of horror creep through her veins as she listened to the fearful sound, now rising in shrill, shrieking accents, now sinking to a low murmur, like some far-off echo.

The last stroke of the heavy-toned bell had sounded—its vibrations had died away, and the sound to which Gisela had been listening also died away. She still stood by the window, her soul chained with horror, and her thoughts, in spite of her wish to raise a prayer to Heaven, turning upon the legend of that burial-ground she had heard from the witless Poppele.

Suddenly the cry came again, and this time it swelled and rose upon the wind, until it seemed as though a hundred fiends had taken up the sound, and prolonged it to a scream of deafening intensity.

"In the name of the holy Virgin! what can it be?" said Gisela, as she leaned from the casement, and gazed in the direction whence it came, almost expecting some sight of terror to meet her eye. But all was solitude without. Nothing with motion, save the waving trees, nodding in the darkness like the plumes over a hearse, was to be seen.

The girl's excitement was now intense. Should she alarm the convent, or should she herself first visit the cemetery, and ascertain, if possible, the cause of that dreadful sound. It might be some poor wretch in the agonies of death, without a friendly hand to close his eye, and from whom intensity of pain had drawn such cries. Gisela at length resolved, herself, to visit the cemetery, and, after offering a prayer to Heaven, she left her chamber to fulfil her intention.

Once a week, it will be remembered, the sister Demath left her cell and walked in the garden. The time she generally chose was that when the sisters had retired to rest, and consequently Gisela had been provided with a key of the outer door of the chapel, which opened into the garden.

Availing herself of this key, Gisela now passed out into the garden, and made her way with cautious footsteps towards the cemetery. An iron railing, with large gates of the same material, separated the garden from the cemetery. One of these gates stood open, and Gisela passed into the burial-ground.

"Ha! ha! ha!" shouted a voice which Gisela recognized as that of the idiot Poppele, and which at once allayed all apprehension on her part, "ha! ha! ha! the virgin has come to see me dig for the treasure. It is mine—it is mine."

The idiot seemed, to the imagination of Gisela, to be occupied in throwing up the earth from a newly-opened grave, and every now and then he gave forth the strange, melancholy sound which at first so alarmed Gisela.

"The black dog has no power over the treasure now," screamed the idiot, as he paused for a moment in his work, and clapped his hands as if for joy; while he looked at Gisela with his dark eyes flashing with an unnatural lustre. "The virgin has come— the virgin has come."

"Poor youh," said Gisela, in a gentle voice, "why are you here at this lonely hour? If the knowledge of what you are doing should reach the ears of the prioress, you will be punished in the morning."

"I seek the hidden treasure," again screamed the idiot; "and shall Poppele not secure it, now that it is within his reach?"

Despite the gentle remonstrances of Gisela, the idiot resumed his task, and the earth was thrown out from the hole in considerable quantities. At length he paused, and appeared to have come to some obstruction. Gisela stood upon the edge of the hole, and looked down upon the idiot. He had a small lamp in the excavation, by the aid of which Gisela, to her great horror, saw that Poppele was deliberately breaking open a coffin.

"Poppele," she said, in a tone of remonstrance, "you know not the fearful sin you are committing. Come forth from the grave, or I will alarm the inmates of the convent."

The idiot did not speak a word in reply, but continued his sacrilegious act. Gisela turned for the purpose of putting her threat into execution, when she beheld, to her great astonishment, the figure of a young and handsome man standing close to her.

"Holy sister," he said, respectfully raising his cap, "may I ask what has brought you into the cemetery at this strange hour?"

Notwithstanding her surprise at the presence of the stranger within the walls of the convent, Gisela, in hurried words, put him in possession of the circumstances of Poppele's sacrilegious search after the hidden treasure.

"I have heard of this youth before," said the stranger, coolly, "and of his madness respecting the hidden treasure. Let him search on. If he finds any, it will make some one all the richer, and the bones of the defunct nun, which he is now so unceremoniously disturbing, will be none the worse for it."

Before Gisela could make any reply to this strange speech, a cry came from the depths of the open grave, and the voice of Poppele was heard exclaiming,—

"It is found—it is found!"

"What is found?" asked the stranger, in surprise, as he leaned over the brink, and looked down.

"The treasure," was the reply; and then the head of Poppele appeared above the surface, the idiot holding in one hand a large casket, while with the other he assisted his ascent.

"Give it to me," said the stranger; "I will assist you."

Poppele involuntarily handed the casket to the stranger, and was preparing to swing himself to the surface, when the latter struck him a heavy blow with the hilt of his sword, and, without a cry, the idiot fell back insensible into the grave. Gisela uttered a cry of horror, and was springing back for the purpose of alarming the convent, when a hand was laid upon her shoulder. Her astonishment was complete when she beheld the form of the prioress, habited in a rich riding dress, standing before her.

"Silence, Gisela," she said; "it is useless to raise any alarm. Before assistance can come we shall be far away. Come, Ostag," she added, "the horses are waiting, and I now long to be miles from these detested walls. Away, Gisela, to your cell, and pray that your superior may not repent the step she's taken. To-morrow, on the arrival of the count, you can tell him I have fled with the man I love, and have freed myself from the trammels of a convent life for ever."

So overcome with astonishment and grief was Gisela, that she could not speak, but was obliged to lean on a grave-stone for support, and to hide the tears that rolled down her pale cheeks. In a few moments the tramp of horses' feet sounded without the convent walls, and Gisela knew that the guilty prioress had commenced her flight.

Then she suddenly recollected the situation of the idiot Poppele, and when she looked into the grave, she found, to her dismay, that the sides had fallen in upon him, and buried him beneath the superincumbent mass.

Shrieking with terror, Gisela flew towards the convent, and in a few moments the loud tones of the alarm-bell aroused every one of the inmates. They flocked round the affrighted Gisela, and endeavoured to extract from her what had occurred. Telling the gardener to bring his spade, she instantly led the way to the grave where Poppele was lying, and then, as the man began to carefully remove the earth, she told the assembled nuns what had occurred. They listened in astonishment, and when Gisela came to that part where she described the flight of the prioress, the greater part, without a thought for the fate of the poor idiot, hurried to the chamber lately inhabited by the superior, to ascertain the truth of what Gisela had stated.

When the earth was at length removed, and the gardener drew forth the body of poor Poppele, it was found that life had fled—the existence of the poor idiot had ceased with the accomplishment of that object for which alone he seemed to live.

When convinced of this sad truth, Gisela returned to the convent with a heavy heart. She found the whole place in great confusion. Several of the nuns had already packed up what few valuables they possessed, not daring to remain and brave the anger of the count, or to endure the rigorous punishment which they were well aware would be inflicted upon them. With the departure of the prioress all control had vanished, and before morning came not one of that unholy sisterhood remained, save the fanatic mother Demath, who, in her lonely cell, was entirely ignorant of what passed in the other part of the convent.

About an hour before noon the count and a numerous suite arrived at the convent, and were admitted by Gisela, who at once informed the former of the occurrence of the previous night, and of the dispersion and flight of the whole sisterhood in evident alarm.

The count listened to the tale in silence, though not in astonishment. He then made a number of inquiries of Gisela respecting herself, and was so struck with her extreme modesty, the beauty of her person, and the sentiments she expressed, that he at once resolved to take her under his own protection, and, if she still persisted in her intentions of taking the veil, to use his influence in getting her admitted into a convent as reputed for the holiness of its inmates, as Gnadenzell was notorious for scandalous behaviour.

During the time that Gisela remained under the protection of the count, Hurdegen von Sperbeneck, whose love for the beautiful votary of Heaven had increased to a pure flame, discovered her residence, and through the count, who respected the young nobleman for his good qualities, though these were somewhat clouded by the follies of youth, he made her offer of his hand. This Gisela firmly declined, and her entreaties to be allowed to enter some convent became so urgent, that the count at once complied, and she entered a religious house at Urach, where she soon afterwards took the veil; and her piety was such, that if the house was famed for sanctity before, it shone with a tenfold lustre through the presence of Gisela.

Now we will see what was the fate of the other characters of our romance. Old Gotz, the father of Gisela, as may be ima ined, never rescued himself from the indigence to which he was reduced, and we may truly say of him that he found death lurking within the bottle.

Hurdegen endeavoured to forget his passion by travel, in which he was successful, and, after several years, he returned, bringing with him a foreign wife, who was as conspicuous for her beauty as for her goodness of disposition. His brother, the avaricious Anshelm, died shortly after the decease of Segbold, as some said, of a broken heart, caused by the destruction of his castle by Wildherr, and the subsequent discovery of the defalcation of his steward to a great amount.

The family of Martin, including Heinz, were all liberated from prison, after a short confinement; and the latter, some short time after, finding means to join the recusant sister Agnes, disappeared altogether—let us hope that they both became better members of society.

As for the prioress, after the lapse of a few months, she was deserted by her lover, Ostag, who carried with him the greater part of the wealth she had taken from the convent; and, joining her sister Matilda, they were afterwards known as two of the most celebrated courtezans in the city of Baden.

The old rogue Saurbein met with a fate which was retributive as it was fearful. His body was found some few miles from the spot where he had deserted Gisela, mangled by wolves.

We had nearly forgotten to mention what became of the frail sister Hailwig, whose unfortunate condition added so materially to the scandal cast upon the convent of Gnadenzell. When the emissaries of the count—who discovered her retreat shortly after the dispersion of the nuns—sought her out, a fine boy was found by her side. She did not attempt to deny its parentage; so, immediately on her recovery, she was removed to a convent at Coln, there to expiate, by the most severe penance, the sin which she had allowed herself to be drawn into the commission of by her passions.

THE END.